The Courage To Love Again

TARA CONRAD

HIS ONE HER ONLY PUBLISHING

Contents

LOVE HEALS

Love Hurts

To all those whose light continues to shine in the darkness.

Note to Readers

A Note to My Readers,

   This book contains dark and, at times, violent themes. Please don't hesitate to put your mental health first and read with caution. For a full list of content please visit my website.

Check Content Warnings Here

Anthony

SEPTEMBER 10, 2001

Excitement courses through me. I feel like a child creeping down the steps on Christmas morning, waiting to see the gifts Santa left under the tree. I know I'm not a child, and what's about to happen—it's the culmination of years of hard work, but the magic is still the same.

Kameron and I exit the subway on West Fourth and walk the last few blocks to Macdougal Street, where we'll sign the lease for my new restaurant. Opening an Italian restaurant has been my dream since I was a little boy. Many of my fondest childhood memories are of being in Nonna's kitchen. She'd stand me on a chair next to her so I could reach the counter. I was happiest with my hands in a dough or figuring out what ingredients our sauce needed.

She instilled in me a love for food. Not the pre-packed stuff, but the kind you pick from the earth and mix together to make a nourishing and delicious meal. Nonna taught me that cooking and serving food is more than a chore. It's a delight and something I learned to take great pride and satisfaction in.

My dream of becoming a chef began all those years ago. Studying, training, saving, and waiting for the right location to become available. Finally, everything's lined up, and my dream's about to come true.

"Have I told you how proud I am of you, Sir?" Kam asks as he squeezes my hand gently.

"You have, *amore mio*." I smile lovingly at the man by my side.

Kameron and I met while I was still in culinary school. I was working as a sous chef at *Flavour*, an upscale restaurant in midtown when he came in one night with a small group of people. It was a stroke of luck or perhaps fate that he and I met. Emmanuel, the Owner and Executive Chef, had a family emergency and reached out at the last minute for my help.

"I'm at the hospital. Beth went into labor with the twins," Chef Emmanuel says when I answer the phone. "She's early. It wasn't supposed to happen like this."

The chef and his wife had been trying to conceive for years. After several rounds of IVF, she finally got pregnant. To say he's been a nervous father-to-be is an understatement.

Emmanuel took a chance on me when I graduated high school and hired me. Arguably, I've learned more in his kitchen than in my two years of culinary school. "What do you need me to do?"

"The FDNY has a reservation tonight. There's a young hotshot in the department. What's his name?" Papers rustle in the background. "Here it is. Kameron Harlow. He's being promoted to Captain of the Midtown Firehouse. It's a big deal because he's only thirty-two and the youngest Captain in the FDNY."

"What do I need to know?" I ask confidently.

Chef takes a few minutes to give me the instructions for the event, which include a personal visit from me to their table to thank them all for their service to the city.

"Fuck, Anthony. I can't put this on you." His voice is strained. "Running the restaurant is my responsibility. I shouldn't be passing this on to—."

"Emmanuel," I say his name loudly, hoping to stop him. "Your wife is in labor. That's exactly where your attention should be." I lower my voice, "Don't worry about the restaurant. I can handle it."

"Are you sure?" he asks.

"I'm positive."

I'll never forget the first time Kameron's eyes met mine. I was standing beside their table holding a bottle of Bollinger La Grand Année when he looked up, and I saw the most beautiful amber eyes. I stood there with my mouth hanging open. It felt like hours, but in reality, it was probably only seconds that I stood there before I found my words.

"On behalf of Flavour, we'd like to extend our sincerest gratitude to the Midtown Firehouse for their service to our city." I turn to face the guest of honor. "I'd also like to personally congratulate Captain Harlow on his recent promotion."

While the men and women at the table applaud, I pop the cork on the bottle of champagne and pour the new Captain's glass first.

"Thank you, Chef," he says, gracing me with a dazzling smile.

"It's my pleasure." His eyes follow me as I make my way around the table, pouring everyone's drinks. "If I can be of any further service, please let me know." With a final glance at the sexy firefighter, I return to the kitchen.

Even though it's a busy night, I struggle to stay focused. My mind keeps returning to the man being celebrated in the dining room.

I'm putting the finishing touches on a dessert plate when one of the servers pops her head into the pastry room. "Hey, Chef," she calls.

"What's up?"

"That hot firefighter is asking to speak to you."

My hand freezes mid-movement. Regaining my composure, I say, "Tell him I'll be out in a minute, please."

"Will do." She starts to go back out into the restaurant but stops. With her hand on the doorway, she turns around. "Do you think you can manage to slip him my number?" I raise my eyebrows disapprovingly. She holds her hands up in surrender and giggles. "Can't blame a girl for trying."

I wash my hands and hurry to the restaurant floor, but he's no longer at the table. I hope he hasn't left already. Looking around, I spot him near the hostess station, leaning against the wall. His arms are crossed over his well-defined chest, making his white button-down dress shirt pull tight around his shoulders.

When he sees me coming, he pushes off the wall. "I'm sorry for taking you away from your job," he says as I get closer.

"It's not a problem. What can I do for you?"

"I just wanted to say—" He stops and bites his bottom lip.

"Was everything to your liking?" I ask, worrying our service didn't live up to his expectations.

"Yes." He laughs softly. "It's nothing like that. I was wondering if you'd like..." He blows out a breath as he runs his fingers through his wavy black hair. "This was a bad idea. Thanks again for everything." Kameron turns to walk away, but I reach out and touch his arm, stopping him.

"Wait." My voice is low. "I'd like to talk to you more, but we don't close for another hour."

"I'll come back," he says quickly.

His promise echoes in my mind for the rest of the evening. Thankfully, there's only one table left—the night's almost over. The back and front of the house get cleaned in record time. After the last employee leaves, I make my way to the front.

I glance outside and am surprised to see Kameron standing by the light post. Part of me was uncertain whether he'd show up or not. My hands tremble as I switch off the lights and step outside. I lock the door before walking over to him. "Hi."

"Hi," he says, and a smile spreads across his face. He kicks at a small pebble on the sidewalk. "Would you like to grab some drinks?"

A bar or club with loud music and people crammed shoulder to shoulder is not my scene. I can't let this opportunity, this man, slip through my fingers, though. So, I take a risk and do something I've never done before. "How about we go back to my place?"

We went home together that night and have been together ever since.

A few months later, I introduced Kameron to the BDSM lifestyle. Although it was something new to him, it came naturally. His job in the FDNY is high-stress and demanding. It often requires split-second, life-altering decisions. Kam's submission allows him to relax. To let someone else take the responsibility for him and make the decisions.

"Mr. Genovese," Charlie, the realtor, says, shaking my hand vigorously. "It's a pleasure to see you again." He turns to Kam. "You as well, Chief Harlow. Congratulations on your recent promotion."

Kam's still with the FDNY and was recently promoted to Chief at the Midtown Firehouse. "Thank you," he responds.

"Let's get down to business." Charlie motions toward what's left of the bar from the previous business. "Let's get these papers signed."

The windows have been covered with heavy-duty butcher paper, blocking any light from outside. That, combined with the dim lighting inside, makes it challenging to read through the document in a timely fashion. Or perhaps it's my anxiousness to get this part over with so we can move forward with the rest of my plans.

When we leave here, we're going to have a romantic dinner at *Flavour*. Then, we're going to stop by the apartment to grab the bags I packed and head to the airport for a late night flight to Bermuda. Tomorrow is our tenth anniversary. It's also when I plan to ask Kameron to wear my collar.

In my pocket is a black leather collar I can't wait to fasten around his neck. Unlike most submissive collars, it won't be locked. Because of his job, it needs to be easily removable. The thought of my sexy firefighter submissive wearing a symbol of my possession makes my dick hard. I'm grateful for the bar in front of me that hides my erection. I have to force my thoughts back to the task at hand —signing my lease.

I'm skimming the last page when Kam's cell rings. "It's the station. I have to take this." He excuses himself while I sign each notated line.

"Congratulations," Charlie says and hands me the keys. "I can't wait to see what you do with the place."

I walk him to the door just as Kam ends his call. "I'll catch a train and be there in about twenty minutes."

My heart sinks. It's not uncommon for Kameron to get called into work on his day off. It's part of the job. In the beginning, it wasn't easy. I worked long hours and late nights, and Kam often got called in at the last minute. It put a lot of stress on us. But we were committed to making our relationship work. Now, it's just par for the course. But tonight, I feel a pang of disappointment. "You have to go in?"

"There's a multi-station emergency," Kam explains as he slides his cell into his pocket.

"Is it something Bailey can handle?" I ask.

"He's out of town." I knew I was taking a chance buying plane tickets for just after midnight when Kam would be on call this evening. "What's wrong?" he asks.

"I planned a romantic evening for us." I don't tell him about the trip. If he's going to a call, he doesn't need to be worried about it. I bought insurance on the trip just in case. "I can reschedule."

"I'll be home as soon as I can. Then we have the rest of the week together."

"That sounds great," I say, trying to mask my disappointment. "Text me when you get there."

"I will." Kam turns to walk away, but I catch his arm and pull him back to me, intending to give him a quick kiss goodbye.

As if my hand has a mind of its own, it grabs him by the back of his neck pulling him to me. Our kiss quickly becomes heated. Kam's erection presses against my stomach. I pull away, leaving both of us breathless. "When your shift is over, you're turning that damn cellphone off so we can have a proper celebration."

"That can be arranged," he says with a grin. "I love you."

"I love you more." I step outside and watch as he walks down the street. Once he's out of sight, I go back inside.

I'm not in a hurry to go home alone. Instead, I peel the paper off the windows, letting the bright lights from the outside stream into the space. Already, it feels more alive. Tomorrow morning, the contractors will arrive to start the renovations. In just a few weeks, this space will go through a complete transformation and become *Italiano Desiderio*.

A crack of thunder reminds me we're expecting some heavy storms. I give Chef Emmanuel a quick call to let him know I have to cancel our reservations and then hurry home before the worst of the storms hit.

Kameron

Tony tried to hide his disappointment from me, but I could still see it. It's been that way since the night we met. Tony wears his heart on his sleeve, and his face is the canvas that reveals every emotion.

Leaving him standing there alone gutted me, but it's part of the job. I'd hoped to be home already, but we had call after call last night. When it finally quieted down, it was closing in on four a.m., and I was exhausted. Instead of trying to stumble home half asleep, I decided to crash at the station and go home today.

The sun is just peeking above the horizon. So far, it's been quiet. I promised the guys a nice breakfast, but right now, they're still asleep. I take advantage of the quiet and go for a run. The early hour means I avoid the congestion on the streets that's certain to come later.

I gaze up at the crystal-clear azure blue sky, marveling at its striking beauty. The storms from yesterday have moved out, blanketing the city in a serene tranquility.

I almost hate to go back inside. Buying myself a few extra minutes, I text Emmanuel.

Me: Is it possible to get a reservation for two for tonight?

Chef E: For you, anything. What time?

"

Me: Can we make it about 8?

Chef E: Done. See you both tonight.

Now, to let Tony know.

Me: I made reservations for us tonight at *Flavour* so we can have a proper celebration.

It might be a bit of topping from the bottom, but I don't think he'll mind.

My World: I have a little something planned for tonight, too. Dinner will be the perfect appetizer.

Me: That sounds intriguing.

My World: When should I expect you home?

Me: I promised the guys a hot breakfast. I'll be home shortly after.

My World: Sounds good. Text me when you're on your way. I love you.

Me: Will do. I love you, too.

When I get inside, the guys are up and around. I was hoping for a quick shower, but that'll have to wait until I get home.

"We thought you ditched us here," Marcus says, elbowing me jokingly.

"And have all of you starve? Not a chance. I don't want my vacation interrupted." Everyone laughs.

I'm thankful they put the coffee on while I was out because I need a caffeine fix. Maybe I'm getting too old for this? Who am I kidding? Fire-fighting is my life. I couldn't see myself being happy doing anything else.

I pull the eggs and bacon out of the fridge and start cooking. Never knowing when we'll get called out ensures we don't waste time getting things done here. Twenty minutes later, the food is done, and we're sitting down to eat when the alarm sounds.

It's just after 8:46 when a call comes in that a plane has crashed into the North Tower of the World Trade Center. I grab a slice of bacon and hurry to my truck, where the chauffeur is already waiting behind the wheel.

While we're en route, my phone rings. I don't check the caller ID before answering.

"FDNY. Harlow speaking."

"Kam, it's me," Tony stammers, his voice trembling. "Are you on your way to the tower?"

"Yeah. We got a call about a plane hitting it. Must've been an inexperienced pilot or engine trouble."

"I have the news on. People are saying it was a commercial jet."

"A jet?" I ask in disbelief. My driver glances at me curiously before returning his focus to the road ahead. "Are you sure?"

"It was impossible not to hear. It echoed through the house." His voice quivers. "It's bad, Kam. There's no way anyone survived."

"We're pulling up now. I have to go." I don't wait for the car to come to a complete stop before I jump out.

"Please be careful, Kam."

"Will do." I disconnect the call and look up, horrified by what I see. There's a massive hole in the tower with flames and black smoke billowing out. I hurry to the makeshift command post across the street to get my orders.

The FDNY chief is already on the scene. "Harlow, I want you in the North Tower helping with the evacuations."

"Yes, sir," I respond and then sprint across the eight-lane highway.

9:03 AM

The roar of the jet engine flying low—too low, is deafening. The ground below my feet shakes from the force. A fireball erupts from the building. I shield my face from the almost unbearable heat and debris. Blinking, I force myself to look up. The plane is gone. It disappeared into the side of the South Tower.

My ears ring, but it doesn't drown out the sound of terrified screams around me. Steel pieces from the building or the decimated jet rain down. Seconds later, a person, I can't tell a man or woman, runs outside. Her body's on fire. She drops to the ground, rolling around to extinguish the flames.

If there was any doubt that the first plane was an accident, it's gone now. This was a deliberate attack.

Anthony

I HAVE AN ALMOST DIRECT VIEW OF THE BURNING TOWER from our Tribeca home. I watch the plumes of smoke rising from the tower in disbelief. In the background, the news anchors speculate about what may or may not have happened. I'm glued to the scene, plagued with a sense of uneasiness.

I'm holding my cellphone when it rings. "Hello?"

"Did you see the news?" Star asks frantically.

"I'm watching it out my window."

"Is Kameron with you?"

"No. He's down there."

"Do you know what happened?"

"Other than the speculation from reporters and what I'm seeing outside, I have no idea."

"When Kam lets you—"

My hand slips from my ear when a second plane flying at my eye level comes into view. "Oh my God." The words come out in a whisper as the jet slams into the South Tower and explodes. The force of the impact shakes my building.

"What was that?" Star screams. "Tony." I don't answer. I can't speak. "Anthony. Are you there? What's going on?"

My hand shakes as I bring the phone back to my ear. "It was another plane," I manage to say, struggling to articulate the gravity of the situation. "Something terrible is going on."

Kameron

9:05AM

Glass shatters. Footsteps pound on the pavement. Sirens fill the air.

The scene looks like something from a horror movie. As far as the eye can see, everything is blanketed in a thick covering of ash and debris. Fire blazes from the top floors of the two towers. Thick smoke fills the air, making it difficult to breathe. I grab the emergency uniform and SCBA gear from the back of my truck and suit up.

Shattered windows line the structures. People lean out frantically, waving anything at their disposal in an attempt to signal rescuers to their location.

Marcus sidles up next to me. "What's the plan, Chief?"

"Get your—" My answer is cut short when two figures, hands clasped together, jump from an upper floor of the tower. "My God," I whisper.

"We can't reach them." Marcus's voice sounds faraway. "How do we get them out?"

"We have to go in. There's no other way."

After I give Marcus the orders for his team, I go against the flow through the crowds of people running out of the buildings. Some are hysterical. Their expressions reflect pure terror as they push their way to safety. Others wander, their eyes wide and faces covered in soot. They're in shock. As much as I want to stop and help them, I can't. These people are out—they're safe. Inside those towers are countless others—they're my target.

Darkness envelopes the space, illuminated only by the beams of flashlights from myself and the other emergency responders. Navigating through the shadows, I head towards the stairwell and climb the steps two at a time. Along the way, I encounter people hurrying down, trying to get to the exit.

"I can't see where to go." A woman cries. "Someone help me, please."

"I'm right here." Grabbing her arm, I put her hand against the wall to help her get oriented. "Keep your hand on the wall," I yell so she can hear me over the commotion. "Don't stop until you're outside."

I wait a second to ensure she follows my command before I continue my trek up.

9:40AM

"Harlow." Miller's staticky voice comes through my walkie. "Do you read me?"

"I can barely hear you," I respond to my boss.

"The Pentagon was hit a few minutes ago. Reports are there's one more hijacked plane unaccounted for."

I stop momentarily to catch my breath. "We're under attack?"

"Unofficially, yes."

9:59AM

Not knowing for sure what's going on outside, I try to concentrate on clearing each floor, pointing the inhabitants toward the stairwell and eventual safety. "Go toward the lights," I yell, knowing those are my brothers and sisters below. "Don't stop moving."

While I climb to the next floor, I listen to the radio calls. Another battalion chief in the South Tower was able to fix a broken service elevator. He and his crew are at the top, evacuating the occupants.

"We have people jumping out here." A call comes across the radio. "How the hell bad is it up there?"

Metal twists and groans. The sound reverberates through the massive structure as if it's crying out in agony. The building shudders with such intensity that I need to cling to the handrail for dear life. Terrified screams join the chaos. Time stretches, creating an illusion that the unsettling tremors persist for an eternity, though in truth, only mere seconds have elapsed.

"What the hell is going on out there?" I yell into my walkie.

The staticky reply comes through. "The South Tower fucking collapsed."

There's no way I heard him correctly. "Can you repeat that?"

"The South Tower is gone."

Collapsed?

Gone?

I can't comprehend what I'm being told. My heart echoes loudly in my chest, a relentless percussion matching the uncertain fate that hangs in the air.

"Get the fuck out of there, Harlow."

I can't leave when there are more people in here. Ignoring the order, I continue on.

"Is anyone there?" A woman's voice calls from the darkness.

I point my flashlight in the direction of the sound and find a visibly pregnant woman huddled in the corner. "I'm right here," I say as I defy every rule ingrained in me and pull off my SCBA apparatus. The air hangs heavy with smoke and debris, triggering immediate coughing on my part. "Put this on. Just breathe normal," I instruct and strap the tank to her back. "It might be heavy." I choke. "But it'll give you clean air until we get you out. Ready to go?" With a nod, she signals her readiness, and I assist her to her feet amidst the challenging conditions.

Guided by the faint glow of my flashlight, we start down the steps. We make it down ten floors before meeting up with a small group accompanied by several other first responders. Their familiar silhouettes materialize in the dim illumination.

"Did you clear the floor?" I yell.

"Yes," an NYPD officer replies.

"Take her." I hand the woman over. "Make sure she gets out. I'm going back up."

10:15AM

Despite the groans emanating from the structure, I persist in my search. My body screams, but I ignore it. I have one purpose, evacuating as many individuals as I can to ensure their safety. The atmosphere is dense, the air carrying a palpable weight that makes breathing increasingly challenging. Unsuccessful in finding anyone on the current floor, I try to go up, but my path is completely blocked by a large steel beam. I'm forced to turn around. On each floor, I test the doors and call out into the darkness, conducting a quick sweep for anyone we might have missed.

10:26AM

I make my way down to the next level. The structural groans reverberate with heightened intensity, creating an ominous soundtrack. I come to a door, but it's jammed. Frustration mounts with each kick and shove, the unyielding door adding an extra layer of difficulty and exacerbating the challenge of breathing.

Gasping for clean air, my lungs cry out in desperation as I slump against the wall. A grim awareness settles over me. I fumble around in my pocket, looking for my cell, desperately hoping for a stroke of mercy that would allow me to make a call.

I try Tony's number over and over and am met with a busy signal each time. I'm ready to give up when it finally rings through.

"Kam, is that you?"

"Yes, Sir." I cough into my arm. "It's me."

"Where are you?"

"I'm in the North Tower." I manage through the smokey air.

"How far up are you?"

"Stairwell B Thirtieth Floor."

"The South Tower collapsed," Tony says through his tears. "You have to get out. Now."

"I don't have my oxygen." My voice is raspy. "I'm not going to make it out."

"Don't say that. I'll call 911 and tell them—"

"Stop." I choke. "I need you to listen to me." I hear the soft sound of his tears. "Do you remember the night we first met?"

"How could I forget?"

"I was so scared when I asked that waitress to get you. I had no clue about your preferences, but I couldn't leave without finding out. It would've haunted me for the rest of my life."

"Kam, please keep trying."

I ignore his pleas and continue, "The way you held me in your protective embrace. I've never felt so cherished. I fell in love that night, and each day for the past ten years, I've only grown to love you more."

"I planned a trip for us. To celebrate."

"Where are we going?"

"Bermuda," Tony says through his tears. "I had a collar made for you. Will you accept it, *amore mio*?"

"I'd love nothing more." Tears slide down my face as I struggle to take each breath. "I'm yours, Sir. I've always have been."

"Then, come home to me. Let me show you how much I love you."

An unsettling groan emanates from the tower, a sound that echoes with the weight of its own existence, sending shivers through the air.

"I'm not going to make it out, Anthony." I cover my head from the falling debris.

An immediate influx of air surrounds me, then another, each conveying an unsettling narrative. The sound bears an eerie resemblance to that ominous moment when the first tower collapsed.

"Never forget how much I love you."

The foreboding sensation intensifies as I am consumed by a visceral awareness of the imminent disaster, a palpable recognition that the tower is collapsing. The phone slips from my grasp.

"Kameron," Anthony screams desperately.

At that moment, an unexpected calmness blankets me. A still, serene acceptance permeates my soul. There's no fear, even as the thunderous crash of eighty floors collapses around me. Enveloped in tranquility, I close my eyes. In that darkness, I see Tony's loving gaze, a comforting sight as I accept the end has come.

Anthony

Hours may have passed, or maybe just moments. Time has become meaningless as I stare vacantly at the space where the Twin Towers stood.

"Tony," Star's voice carries a gentle, soft tone. "Owen and I are here," she reassures, her hand reaching out to touch my arm. "Why don't you come sit down? I'll make some tea." Despite her gentle tug on my arm, I find myself resisting her suggestion.

"Go put some water on," Owen says. "I'll stay with him." He moves closer to me. "They're finding people. We'll hear from him."

"No, we won't," I say absently.

"You have to stay positive." Owen encourages.

"He was on the thirtieth floor. I was on the phone with him when it collapsed." Silent tears make their way down my cheeks. "Kam told me he loves me. I saw it start before I heard it." The sound. I'll never forget the horrible sound. The desperate anguish of the metal, followed by the thunderous roar of the concrete, consuming not just the structure but everything in its way—including Kameron. "Then it was silent, and the line went dead." I shift my focus to Owen. "I can feel it in here. He's gone."

Something shatters inside me, and I fall to my knees, curling in on myself. Owen's arms wrap around me, offering refuge as I lose myself in the dark abyss of grief.

My mind and body are numb as I allow Owen to lead me to the sofa. Outside, the blue sky that was pristine sapphire is now shadowed by an ominous ashen canopy. I struggle to wrap my head around the reality of what I've just witnessed. The two iconic towers that are an integral part of this city have crumbled into nothing more than a pile of smoldering rubble.

Every channel on television has ceased its regular broadcast. Newscasters openly shed tears as they try to cover this monstrous yet historical event. Our country and the world are trying to comprehend what we've witnessed today. Not only did New York City come under attack, but a third plane flew into the Pentagon, killing countless more people.

An ordinary group of people, now hailed as heroes, were on a fourth hijacked plane. As they got phone calls out to family members, they learned their destination was most likely the White House. These passengers made the brave choice to storm the cockpit and take the plane down in a field in Pennsylvania. Their lives weren't spared, but countless others were.

I refuse to accept this is the end. Denial kicks in, and I jump up. "I need to go down there."

"I don't think that's possible," Star says gently.

"Kam's alone," I insist. "I need to be there for him."

"Tony," she says as tears cascade down her cheeks. "It's not safe."

"I don't care. I'm going." I brush past her, but Owen intervenes, blocking my path. "Move out of my way," I persist, frustration evident in my tone.

"That's not happening," he insists, crossing his arms.

"You can either stay here or come with me to find him: your choice, but either way, I'm going."

Owen and I are locked in a battle of wills, but I refuse to back down. When Owen's arms drop to his sides, I know I've won. "Stay here," Owen says to Star.

"You can't go down there." Star's nearly frantic.

"I'll take him as close as possible."

"Owen, please," Star pleads. "What if there's more attacks?"

"If we allow fear to dictate our lives, then we let whoever fucking did this win." Anger, not directed at Star, is evident in his tone. "And that can't happen," he softens his voice. "All flights have been grounded. We're as safe as we can be." He looks at me. "It's something he needs to do."

⸻ 🕯 ⸻

"It's a good thing we brought these," Owen says, pointing to the white rags we're holding over our faces.

Outside resembles scenes from a dystopian movie. A thick blanket of ash cloaks the entirety of lower Manhattan. Papers from the offices within the towers now scatter the streets like apocalyptic confetti. The air is dense with smoke, and sirens wail relentlessly in every direction. However, in a stark departure from the ordinary, the streets are devoid of traffic. Only emergency responders navigate the debris-riddled streets until they're forced to abandon their vehicles to proceed on foot toward the site.

As we draw nearer, the surreal nature of the situation intensifies. It's midday on a Tuesday, and we're walking down the middle of the six-lane West Side Highway. Numerous people, their faces masked in ash, wander aimlessly with vacant stares, undoubtedly mirroring my own.

Approaching the site, the air is pierced by the unsettling chirping of hundreds of PASS devices, a haunting reminder of firefighters in distress. One of those belongs to Kameron. The thought of him trapped somewhere in the rubble, injured and alone, wondering if rescue will come, is agonizing.

"I'm sorry. You can't go any further." An officer stops the small group we've caught up with before turning his back on us to attend to something else.

"I need to get through," I protest and try to push my way through.

He grabs my arm to stop me. "Sir. I can't let you—"

Instantly, I recognize him. "Graham, I have to find Kameron."

"Tony," he says, his voice strained. "I can't let you through."

"He was in the North Tower when it collapsed. Please," I beg, grabbing his hand. "I have to find him."

"Our rescue teams are in there," he tries to assure me. "We'll get them all out."

"I can help," I insist and once again try to push my way past, but Graham puts his hands on my chest, stopping me.

"It's too dangerous." I ignore his directives and continue to struggle. "Anthony," Graham yells my name. "You'll be more of a liability if you go in there. If Kameron survived, he's going to need you in one piece, not injured from being in the middle of that." He stabs his finger in the direction of the fire that burns in the remnants of buildings. "For now, the best thing you can do for Kameron and everyone else is to give them space to do their jobs." He softens his voice and his bottom lip quivers. "My partner was in there, too. I know how much it goddamn hurts to not be over there."

"I can't go home and sit around waiting for a call that he's dead." Pain sears my chest. "I have to do something."

"This is going to be a massive effort," Owen interjects. "These men and women are going to need help to sustain them. Let's go back to your place and use our resources to make that happen. Okay?"

My eyes travel between Owen and Graham, then fixate on the area where the majestic buildings once graced the city's skyline. The gravity of the situation leaves me breathless. They're gone. Reduced to a massive pile of debris—a final resting place for many souls.

Later that evening, as the sun begins to set on what is easily the worst day in the lives of all of us, we watch the continuing news coverage. Lawmakers in Washington D.C. gather on the steps of the Capital Building to address the nation, promising solidarity as we seek justice for the evil committed against us.

In a poignant moment that will not soon be forgotten, the men and women set aside their political affiliations and previous disagreements. Their collective focus shifts to the shared identity that binds us as Americans, uniting their voices in the rendition of "God Bless America."

Anthony

Owen and Star haven't left my house since they arrived Tuesday. Part of me wishes they'd go so I could be alone with my thoughts and sorrow, while the other part is thankful for their constant presence. With every minute that passes, the gaping hole in my heart grows. I'm afraid it will swallow me whole.

When we left the pile the other day, Owen and I devised a plan to try to meet some of the rescuers' needs. I knew I'd need Emmanuel to help make my idea successful.

I tried for hours to get him on the phone, but with the lines down, it was impossible. So, I took a chance and walked to the restaurant. I found him alone, his head in his hands as the television at the bar broadcasted the continued narrative. Together, we made a plan and started putting it in motion. Today, we begin implementing it.

The sky is still dark when Owen, Star, and I arrive at the restaurant. Emmanuel's already there, along with his two adult sons.

"Have you heard anything?" he asks when I walk into the kitchen.

My heart sinks knowing other than a handful of firefighters who were rescued just hours after the collapse, no one else has been found. "No."

"Don't give up," he encourages me.

I offer a faint smile but remain silent, fearing that the fragile threads holding me together will unravel if I speak.

"Where can we help?" Star asks, taking the attention off of me.

"How are you at cooking eggs?" Dylan, Emmanuel's oldest son, asks.

"I think I can manage those."

Star joins him, making dozens of scrambled eggs. Owen and I fry bacon and sausage while Emmanuel and his younger son, Micah, make grits and toast. When we have enough for a small army, we load up the van and head toward lower Manhattan.

I'm not sure how, but the sights around us appear worse today than they did immediately following the disaster. The ash is settling and is thicker than it was. Cars sit abandoned and likely unusable. Every few blocks, we see a twisted metal beam or the remains of office furniture.

What strikes me the most are the photocopied pictures of people—thousands of loved ones frozen in time, that haven't been accounted for. They're hanging from every available surface. A silent plea for a miracle.

The twenty-four-hour mark signaled a grim reality that shifted the mission from rescue to recovery. Because the pile is so unstable, old-fashioned bucket brigades are being utilized to painstakingly sift through the debris for any remains. The work is tedious and dangerous as workers must deal with jagged pieces of metal and scorching fires that continue to burn. In a morbid request, rescue workers have been instructed to write their names and contact information on their arms in case they, too, become victims of this heinous tragedy.

But I, like countless others, have chosen not to give in to despair. The idea of a future without Kameron by my side is unfathomable. Instead, I cling to the hope that despite all odds, Kameron will be found, and we'll emerge from this darkness together.

Our SUV rolls to a stop when we reach a barricade.

An office approaches, and Emmanuel rolls down his window. "I'm sorry. Only emergency vehicles can pass," the officer says.

"We made arrangements with Commissioner to deliver food," Emmanuel explains.

"One minute." He walks away from our car to talk to another officer. They both look back at us before the first officer returns. "There's a spot two blocks down on the right for you to set up."

"That's perfect. Thank you," Emmanuel says.

As we inch through the final few blocks, we find tired rescue workers leaning against their vehicles, seeking a few minutes of rest before they return to the task at hand. Finally, we come to our designated spot, where several pop-up tents and plastic tables wait. We finish setting up just as the sun cuts through the sky, allowing daylight to creep in.

Within minutes, a line forms, and we spend the next two hours diligently filling plates for exhausted men and women. The atmosphere remains somber as they progress through the line. Their eyes reflect the harrowing realities they've confronted.

I'm loading up the empty trays in the van when Star appears in my peripheral.

"Tony," she says, placing a hand on my shoulder. "Someone's asking to speak to you."

I look to where she points and see Bill Miller, the FDNY chief, speaking with Owen. I don't need to hear what they're saying to know. "Please tell him I'll be over in a minute." I take my time finishing my task, doing my best to steel myself for the blow I'm about to be given.

Owen and Bill fall silent when they see me approaching.

"We found him." Bill's words knock the air from my lungs. "They're waiting for you to bring him out." We follow the commissioner to a waiting ambulance near the smoldering pile. Rescuers momentarily pause their work and form two lines reverently flanking the path for their fallen brother.

Silence.

Stillness.

The only movement is the firefighters carrying the flag-adorned stretcher. They stop when they

come to where we stand.

"Anthony, it's my solemn duty to inform you that Battalion Chief Kameron Harlow perished while he was responding to the terrorist attack on September 11. Chief Harlow was heroically involved in the evacuation efforts in the North Tower and unfortunately perished in its collapse," Bill empathetically says. "On behalf of the FDNY, I'd like to express our deepest condolences on your loss."

"Thank you." The words come out in a strained whisper. My hand trembles as I reach out, placing it on the flag. "This can't be real," I murmur. "Please tell me this isn't happening."

"I'm so sorry, Tony," Owen says quietly.

"We need to take him now," Miller says.

"Don't let them do this." Tears blur my vision as I plead with Owen.

"You need to let them put him in the ambulance."

"I can't."

Owen puts his arm around me. "You don't have to do this alone."

"That's where you're wrong. I'm very much alone."

I force my legs to step back and watch as they carefully slide the stretcher into the back of the ambulance and close the doors. The sound echoes in the quiet space.

Motionless, with Star and Owen offering quiet support, I watch as the ambulance drives Kameron away. It isn't until they're out of sight that I silently turn and walk to our waiting SUV.

Anthony

Death—a stark and final reality.

Grief is the unwelcome companion that lingers in its aftermath.

Death doesn't consider readiness. It steals loved ones away, leaving in its aftermath the heavy burden of grief.

The reality is, I knew he was gone the moment the tower fell. When several of his comrades were found in a pocket of safety, my heart naively grasped onto hope. Maybe Kameron was also trapped in a gap of steel and concrete, just waiting for rescue. I tried calling his cell phone over and over, praying he'd answer. But as the hours turned into days, a part of me recognized that wasn't going to be part of our story. Death stole Kameron from me.

Making the call to his twin sister, Kelsey, was one of the hardest things I've ever had to do. They were the only family each other had left. Maeve, their mom, passed away before their first birthday. She found out she had aggressive breast cancer early in her pregnancy. Her doctors gave her the impossible choice of treatment that required her to terminate the pregnancy or take her chances without treatment. She chose the latter. Unfortunately, by the time the babies were born, the cancer had spread and took her away from them a few months later.

Their father, Andy, was a wonderful man. After his wife passed away, he raised Kameron and Kelsey on his own. He never remarried. Andy frequently spoke of Maeve, and though I never had the chance to meet her, it felt as if I knew her through the vivid stories and memories he shared.

Kameron and his father were very close. Even when he came out as gay, Andy's support of his son never wavered. He stood by his son long before it was an acceptable thing to do. Andy lost friends and family members because of his outspoken support. Kelsey, Kameron, and I were by Andy's bedside when he took his final breath. I find comfort in the image of Andy and Maeve, arms wide open, ready to great Kam as he passed from this life to the next.

Kelsey met her husband, Birdie, on a trip to England shortly after Kam and I started dating. They had a whirlwind romance and married three months after they met. Much to Kameron's dismay, she permanently relocated to London. Kelsey and Kam have stayed close. We visit each other several times a year. Kameron and I had our tickets booked for a flight next month, and we were all set to stay with Kelsey and Birdie and eager to meet our first niece. Kam was so excited about becoming an uncle. Sadly, that, too, has been stolen from us.

Kelsey and Birdie have been trying to get to New York since everything happened, but with the flight disruptions, it's taken over a week for them to get here. I expect they'll be arriving any minute. Their flight landed over an hour ago. Birdie called to let me know they got their rental car and were on their way. I could hear their newborn daughter's cry in the background.

The hush of my apartment weighs heavily while I wait alone. I invited Owen and Star to stay, but they declined, wanting to give us privacy.

I'm checking the food in the oven when my doorbell rings, signaling their arrival. I quickly wipe my hands before going to answer the door. With a hesitant breath, I reach for the knob and slowly turn it to let them in.

Kelsey's eyes are red and puffy. When she sees me, a new wave of tears spills from her eyes as she falls into my outstretched arms.

"I'm so sorry, sweetheart," I say and kiss the top of her head. My eyes meet Birdie's worried gaze. "Come on inside." I keep my arm tightly around her shoulder as we walk into the living room.

"Please, say it's a lie," she whispers. "Tell me Kam is here."

"I wish I could." Seeing Kelsey shatter makes my battered heart break even more.

"We were watching it on the news, and I knew he'd be there, but…" Her words hitch with a sob. "I prayed that by some miracle, you two were out of town for your anniversary. Anything so he wouldn't have been there."

It's not the first time I wondered if I'd told him my plans before we left the house, would he have not taken the phone call? We would've been out of the country, and Kam would be here now.

"Kam was at the station when they got the call," I explain as we sit on the sofa. "He was one of the first on the scene."

"What was he thinking?"

"I don't have all the answers, but I can tell you what I know." She nods and wipes her eyes. "The phone lines were jammed, but Kam got a call out." My eyes close remembering the relief I felt when my phone rang, and I saw it was Kam. "He was in the North Tower, evacuating people."

"Did you tell him to get out?"

"I begged him to get out, but he said he couldn't make it." I recount some of our conversation without telling her too many details that would only upset her more.

"Was he scared?"

"I don't think so. He sounded peaceful."

The baby begins to stir in her father's arms. "I think Calliope would like to meet her uncle," Birdie says, trying to lighten the moment.

He passes the tiny newborn swaddled in a pale pink blanket to me, and I set eyes on the most perfect baby I've ever laid eyes on. She steals my breath when she looks up at me, and I see a familiar amber gaze. "She has Kameron's eyes."

"She does." Kelsey rests her head on my shoulder. "I was always jealous of Kam's eyes." She laughs softly.

"Hello, Calliope," I say quietly. "I'm your Uncle Tony." I kiss her forehead and whisper, "Your Uncle Kameron would've just adored you.

"Now, because of those bastards, she'll never meet him," Kelsey says through her tears.

"We'll make sure she knows all about her Uncle Kam."

Kameron planned his funeral years ago. At the time, we'd argued about it, and I tried pulling the Dominant card, but he persisted. He understood the dangers of his job and insisted he make all the arrangements so that if the unthinkable ever happened, it would be something I didn't have to worry about. He didn't want a formal funeral in a church. All Kam ever wanted was a small gathering of his closest friends and family where we could celebrate his life.

Two nights after Kelsey and Birdie's arrival, we gather at *Flavour* for Kameron's memorial service. Both Kelsey and Birdie are well aware of our involvement in the BDSM lifestyle and are acquainted with our friends present tonight. Additionally, two surviving members from Kam's firehouse join us, flanking the side of the table where Kameron's remains rest. They vigilantly keep watch over Kam, positioned next to a photograph of him in full dress uniform and a solitary, flickering candle.

We're sitting down, about to start, when the door to the restaurant opens. Turning in my seat, I see Bill walking in with a very pregnant young woman I don't recognize. I walk over to greet them.

"I'm sorry for interrupting," Bill says quietly.

I look between him and the woman. "I'll get chairs for you and—"

"We can't stay, but I promised Adara I'd escort her here tonight." He touches the woman's elbow. "Adara, this is Anthony, Chief Harlow's partner."

"I'm sorry for interrupting the service," she says quietly. "But I had to speak to you."

"There's no need for an apology." I look down at the familiar item draped over her arm.

"I was at my desk on the eightieth floor in the North Tower when the first plane hit. At first, we were told it was a small accident, nothing to worry about, and that we should keep working. Shawn, my husband, worked in the South Tower. Thankfully, he was out of the office for a meeting, or he wouldn't be..." Her voice falters.

"He heard what happened and called me. Shawn said he didn't have a good feeling and that I should leave." She swipes at her tears. "I thought he was crazy, but I started getting my things together to leave. I wasn't in a hurry until I heard it. The sounds. I keep hearing them, even in my dream. I don't know if I'll ever be able to forget them." My hand extends to touch her arm, and in a tender exchange, she places her small hand over mine.

"The building shook. Pieces of concrete fell through the ceiling. That's when I knew it wasn't *nothing* like we were first told," Adara says with more certainty. Then she continues. "When the power went out, things quickly went from bad to worse. Everyone was screaming and crying. It was chaos, and I was certain we were all going to die." She looks up at me. "But I couldn't let that happen. I had to do whatever was necessary to get us out. So, I put my hand out to try to find the wall. Then I remembered I had a flashlight."

"Shawn works in telecommunications and insisted I have a brand-new fancy cell phone. He was so proud when he brought it home and showed me all the bells and whistles. I thought he was crazy." She laughs softly and shakes her head before becoming serious again. "But at that moment, I was so grateful for that silly little gadget. It lit my path, and I was confident I'd make it to safety."

"But I didn't make it. There was a loud roar." She closes her eyes momentarily as if reliving each detail. "It was so loud, and it wouldn't stop. Everyone started pushing and shoving. I did my best to stay against the wall to protect the baby." She gently caresses her round stomach. "In the commotion, I dropped my phone, and the light went out. I huddled in the corner as the building shook. From what I learned, it was the force of the South Tower collapsing. It still doesn't feel real," she says, her gaze lifting to meet mine.

"The air was filled with smoke, and it was dark, so very dark. All I could think was that I had to find that phone. I needed the light to get out. I searched for so long that suddenly, I realized it was quiet. There were no more voices. I was prepared to die there, alone, until I saw a faint light and heard a voice calling out. I yelled back, and Chief Harlow found me. As soon as he realized I was pregnant, he took off his oxygen and put it over my face. Then, he put his coat on me and strapped the tank on my back."

"We were going down the steps together until we met up with a police officer. Chief Harlow passed me to him and made him promise to get me out safely. Then, he disappeared." Her anguish deepens, and her tears fall faster.

"Thank you for sharing your story with me." I barely get the words out through my own tears.

"I needed you to know I'll never forget what he did for me—for us. And I wanted to be sure to return this to you." She hands me Kam's turnout coat.

The coat carries with it the unmistakable scent of smoke and Kam. "You'll never know how much this means to me." I hold it close to me, savoring the feeling of his presence. "How are you and the baby?"

"I inhaled a lot of smoke, so my doctor insisted I spend a few days in the hospital to monitor me and the baby. They said if Chief Harlow hadn't given me his oxygen, we wouldn't have made it. He saved our lives," she says softly. "But in doing so, he gave up his. I don't know if I'll ever be able to reconcile that."

"Kameron was a helper—a healer. He would get upset if I killed even the smallest insects. One day, I found a spider in our house. He got a sheet of paper and waited for that horrible creature to climb on it. Then he rode the elevator with it to deliver it to safety." I laugh softly at the memory. "Please know that Kameron would be happy to know his sacrifice ensured your survival. He wouldn't want you to question that."

"My baby is a boy," she says in a hushed tone. "With your permission, we'd like to name him Kameron."

The intensity of my tears prevents me from answering. This time, Adara is the one offering a calming touch. After a moment, I find my voice and say, "Kameron would be honored, and I am as well."

"Shawn and I will ensure our child knows the man he was named after," Adara adds. "He'll know that when everyone was running out, Chief Harlow ran back in. He's the true definition of a hero."

Before Bill and Adara leave, I introduce them to Kelsey. The women share a tearful embrace. Then I return to my seat, clutching Kameron's uniform tightly, as we prepare to say goodbye to Kameron.

The man I've loved and shared my life with.

The man who'll always have a part of my heart.

My beloved hero was taken far too soon.

Leopold

TWO YEARS. THAT'S HOW LONG I'VE BEEN LIVING—EXISTING at Walking in Light. Ever since the day my parents caught me with Santiago. We had been best friends since elementary school, but as we matured, so did our feelings for one another.

My parents were supposed to be at church. Usually, I would've had to be there too, but I had a big project due at school, and I was excused from church that night. Ti was here helping me with it, except we got distracted. Neither of us heard their car pull into the driveway.

"We're home, boys," Mom says as she opens the door. "How the—" She freezes when she sees me on my knees with Ti's cock in my mouth.

It was the first time we ever did anything other than kiss.

"Mom." I jump to my feet and cover Ti as he hurries to close his pants.

My father came running to see what all the yelling was about. The only thing that saved Santiago from being physically thrown out of our house was the fact that he was sixteen, too, a minor. My father couldn't risk his perfect image being tarnished by being accused of assault.

Unfortunately, that courtesy didn't extend to me. After Ti left, Dad removed his belt and ensured I would not be able to walk or sit without pain for weeks to come. The following day, I was given a suitcase and told I had fifteen minutes to pack. My parents drove me to the Walking in Light Therapy Center, where I was admitted as a patient.

"This is for your own good," Mom cried as she kissed me goodbye. Dad wouldn't even look at me.

Standing in front of the full-length mirror, I tuck my dark blue button-down shirt and straighten the borrowed tie, ensuring my appearance leaves no room for one of David's punishments. Three days—that's all I have left until I turn eighteen and can sign myself out of the treatment center. I don't know where I'll go or how I'll get there, but I'll be damned if I stay in this hell hole any longer than I have to.

I glance at the clock, noting that I still have thirty minutes—ample time to review my notes. Last time, I missed what they considered *critical details*. The consequences are not something I wish to relive any time soon.

"Leopold," David says as he walks into my room. In this place, there's no such thing as knocking or privacy. "It's good to see you're taking today's assignment seriously."

"I am," I respond, attempting to conceal my intimidation as I lock eyes with his dark stare.

"As long as you don't fail, you will be one step closer to spiritual freedom," he assures. I nod, pretending I buy his line. "Come on, it's time."

I trail behind him, leaving my small room. Our dress shoes click-clack on the black and white checkered linoleum as we walk through the corridors to the meeting room where our daily group therapy sessions occur. He opens the door and motions for me to step inside. The room teems with other boys who are also patients undergoing *treatment*, therapists, and my family. I freeze, and David nearly walks into me.

"What's your problem?"

My eyes are locked on the people sitting in the first row. "You didn't tell me my parents and sisters would be here."

"Your parents and sisters are here." He leans in close and whispers, "If you screw up today, the consequences will be twice as bad as last time."

"Leopold, do you know why I've brought you here?" David, my therapist, asks.

"*I forgot. I mean, I didn't,*" *I stumble over my words.* "*I didn't say the right things.*"

David shakes his head and makes a tsking sound. "*You aren't better yet,*" *he says, lowering his voice.* "*The demon of homosexuality is still in you. But don't worry. I'm here, and I'll fix it,*" *he says as he sticks electrodes to my skin.*

"*Please don't do this.*" *Tears flow over my lower lid.* "*I promise I can do better.*"

"*Why are you crying?*" *he snips.* "*Crying is not what a real man does. Is it, Leopold?*"

I sniffle and try my best to stop the tears but fail. "*No, sir.*" *I know what he's going to do, and I don't think I can survive it again.*

David pulls the screen down and turns the projector on. He passes me the clicker. "*You remember what you have to do?*"

"*Yes.*"

The first image comes onto the screen. It's a heterosexual couple sitting on a park bench. I click, and the picture changes. This time, it's two men holding hands. I click quickly, knowing David will hit the shock button if I'm too slow. I do my best through several more pictures until there's one of a man sucking another man's cock. I hesitate a fraction of a second before hitting the clicker. David is watching my reactions carefully and hits the shock button. My body jerks, and I cry out from the force. The electricity is much higher than it's ever been.

"*Real men are disgusted by those images, Leopold,*" *he says snidely.* "*And they don't complain about pain.*"

In an effort to keep silent, I bite my lower lip and concentrate on not screwing up again. The hour-long session ends with my enduring a total of thirty shocks. At least half of which David gave me just to watch me writhe in pain. The electricity was up so high I had burns that took weeks to heal.

⸺ ♦ ⸺

After Mr. Barry, the director, finishes his speech, I'm called to the front.

"Leopold has been part of our program longer than any other young man in our facility," Mr. Barry explains as I step onto the stage. "At the tender and impressionable age of sixteen, he had fallen deeper into the abomination of homosexuality than most of the other young men we have here." He forces a fake smile, glancing at the families with hopeful expressions. They all wish for this place to cure their sons and return them as perfect heterosexuals. "It's been a challenging journey, but we never give up. Do we, Leopold?"

"No, Mr. Barry," I respond respectfully, needing to get through this without incident.

"This evening, Leopold is taking the next step in his recovery," Mr. Barry announces, motioning for me to approach the podium. "Leopold will reflect on what he's learned during his stay with us." He turns to me. "It's all yours, son."

"Thank you," I say politely, placing my notebook in front of me and adjusting the height of the microphone. "Good evening, everyone." I glance up, but the room remains silent. "I was brought here two years ago after being caught in a homosexual act. Because of the expert treatment I've received at Walking in the Light, I've gained an understanding of the shame I cast on my family by my actions. My education here has taught me how a real man should behave. Today, I'm here to confess my wrongdoing." Looking up, I see my mother dabbing her eyes with a tissue.

"What happened was not a result of my upbringing. I allowed worldly influences to lead me astray. My therapist has helped me to understand how I should talk and behave as a straight man. Homosexuality is something I will not fall prey to again."

David rises from his seat beside my father. "Do you, of your own free will, believe it is unnatural for a man to have sexual relations with another man?"

"Yes," I answer solemnly.

"Do you, of your own free will, agree when you leave this facility, you'll return to the loving care of your parents so they can continue to monitor you?"

I meet the stern stare of my father. "I do."

"Your speech was very well put together," David says, but the tone of his voice is off. My stomach sinks, realizing that things are about to go downhill for me. "However, you neglected to apologize for disgracing your parents."

"I apologized on our last phone call," I plead my case. "And I acknowledged they weren't at fault for my actions."

"I'm afraid that doesn't meet the requirements to graduate from our program," David says and motions to the row of newest arrivals. "You haven't set a very good example for the young men who are at the start of their healing journey."

Dropping my head, I give up trying to convince David of anything. It's pointless. I berate myself for being foolish enough to have hope. To believe that anything I said or did today would be enough to secure my ticket out of here.

"Mr. and Mrs. Wagner." David turns to address my parents and places his hand over his heart. "I wholeheartedly apologize for Leopold's failure tonight. I feel I must take responsibility for his failure. I will rectify this oversight by personally overseeing more intensive therapeutic measures to ensure his future success."

My family remains seated while the assembly is dismissed.

When we're the only remaining people, my father stands and approaches David. "We don't blame you for Leopold's resistance." He doesn't spare a glance at me. "We'll be praying for continued guidance." I resist the urge to roll my eyes, knowing it'll only make whatever David has planned worse.

"I'd like to take him right away. While this experience is still fresh in his mind. Although I understand if you'd like to speak with him in private before we leave."

Mom takes her place beside my father. "I'd like to speak with him."

"Darling," he says, putting his arm around her. "I think it's best to let him go with David."

"Thank you for understanding, Mr. Wagner." David turns to me. "Come over here, Leopold," he demands. "Say goodbye to your parents so we can go get started."

"Goodbye, Mom and Dad." I look to my sisters, who sit quietly on the pew. Arianna refuses to look at me while London watches intently.

"Thank your parents for coming."

"Thank you for coming," I parrot my reply.

"Please listen to what David tries to teach you." Mom reaches out and touches my cheek. "We'll see you soon."

I nod.

Dad takes her hand. "Let's go, girls," he says. My sisters stand and silently follow our parents out of the room.

"You're coming with me." David sneers, sending shivers down my spine. "Tonight's lesson is one you won't forget."

He grabs my wrist and pulls me behind him. David stops suddenly when London bursts back in.

"Can I help you?" David asks her impatiently.

London looks at him, her blue eyes filling with tears as she bats her eyelashes innocently. "May I please speak to Leo for a minute? I have something to give him." She holds up a book about avoiding worldly temptations. "I'd like to point out a chapter I feel could be particularly helpful for my brother," London says piously.

"Such a sweet young girl who clearly understands what we're trying to accomplish here. You'd be wise to listen to her." He smiles at London, and I cringe. David is pure evil. I don't want him anywhere near my little sister. "I'll give you a few minutes. It's imperative I start his session tonight as soon as possible."

"I understand. Thank you," she says sweetly. London waits until David is far enough down the hall to not overhear us. "There's a prepaid card taped inside the bookmark I made. Use it to get yourself as far away from here as possible."

"What?"

"You're going to be eighteen. You can leave," London whispers and looks over her shoulder to be sure we're still alone. "I've been reading about this place online from other guys who were able to get out. They're pure evil." She takes my hand in hers. "I hate knowing you're here. Have they hurt you?"

"No." I squeeze her hand. "I don't know what you've read, but this is a great place." I lie. I can't tell her the truth and have her worrying about me.

She searches my eyes before continuing, "I highlighted some sentences and put a number by them. It's my phone number. When you get a phone, call me so I know you're okay."

London is five years younger than me, so we were never particularly close. She was only eleven when I was ditched here. I feel like she's a stranger to me and hate that I'm about to question her sincerity. But I have to know if this is a trap my father set up. "Did Dad put you up to this?"

"No," she says, taking a step back.

"Why are you doing this?" A tear slips down her cheek. I mentally chastise myself for doubting her.

"You're my brother and I love you." Footsteps get louder, and she leans in close. "Please take care of yourself."

I wrap my arms around her. "I love you, London."

"I love you, too."

"Leopold." David clears his voice. "Let's remember how a man should act."

"I've about had enough of the way you speak to my brother," London says, her hands on her hips, ready to go head-to-head with him.

"London, enough." I tug on her arm. "Thank you for the books. It was very kind. But it's time for you to leave now."

She glares at David for a few seconds before relaxing her posture. "Be sure to read that book. It has a lot of good information for men in your—" Her eyes flicker between David and me. "In your *situation*."

"I will."

"Have a good evening, Ms. Wagner."

As my sister walks out the double glass doors, I silently acknowledge it's the last time I'll ever see her. Staying out of her life is the only way I can protect her. If our father ever found out she helped me, he'd hurt her, and I can't let that happen.

David moves so close I can feel his warm breath on my neck. "Go put your book in your room and be at my office in five minutes."

Leopold

"Strip," David commands from behind his oversized oak desk.

For a brief moment I consider not complying, but quickly course correct. The one time I fought back, I was bent over his desk and received twenty lashes with a whip. I couldn't sit or lie on my back for two weeks. That was all it took to learn that compliance is the only way to survive.

Once I remove my clothes, I go to sit in the usual chair in front of the screen, but David stops me. "We're not staying in here."

"What do you mean? Where are we going?"

He doesn't answer. Instead, he opens the door on the other side of his office. I always thought it led to a private bathroom, but I was wrong—so wrong.

When I don't move, he grabs my arm. "Let's go." He drags me through the door and over to what looks like some sort of torture device. It's meant to position a person on their knees while keeping their arms and legs restrained.

"What the fuck?" I mutter.

"We've tried this the easy way," David says as he pushes my chest against the black leather-like padding. My neck rests in an almost stockade-like device. With my legs spread, he attaches leather straps around them and then repeats the same with my arms. I'm exposed and vulnerable. "But you don't learn Leopold."

I assume I'm going to be whipped again, but why did he bring me in here? Why didn't he do it in his office like last time? Closing my eyes, I refocus my thoughts. Three days, I remind myself. That's all I have to survive.

After double-checking the restraints, David turns his back on me and walks across the room. I strain my neck to see what he's doing. Standing in front of a tall wooden cabinet, he pulls open a set of frosted glass doors. Inside are what look to be medical supplies. Small glass vials with labels on them that I can't read. Syringes. Needles.

"What's going on?" I ask and tug at the restraints.

Paying no attention to me, David picks up a brown-tinted vial and inserts a needle. He pulls back the plunger, fills it, and then flicks it a few times to get the air out. "You've left me no choice, Leopold."

My pulse quickens when he comes back toward me. "What's in there?"

"This?" He holds up the syringe. "It's a little something to make this lesson unforgettable."

"Get the hell away from me," I yell. "I don't consent to whatever you have in there."

David laughs sinisterly. "You don't consent? That's rich, considering you're tied up at the moment." He pierces my skin with the needle.

The liquid is cold as it's injected into my body. "What did you just give me?"

"You'll find out soon enough." David disposes of the used needle, turns off the lights, and walks out of the room.

⚖

Alone in the dark, I lose track of time. But I'm pretty sure, from my raging hard-on, that the injection contained a sexual performance drug.

Sweat beads on my forehead from the fear of whatever evil game David's playing.

The door reveals a crack, allowing the light from his office to seep into the confined space. He walks to the front of me and looks down at the erection jutting out in front of me. "It seems the medication's working."

"You're sick."

"Another thing you seem to have backward, Leopold." He leans down closer to my face. "You're the one here because you don't understand where it's appropriate to stick your dick. But after this therapeutic intervention, I'm certain you won't be looking to put it anywhere for quite some time." He rubs his hands together. "Now, let's get started."

He opens another cupboard and takes out a silicone sleeve. "What's that?"

"This will provide some extra," he pauses. "Stimulation." He reaches out, taking my cock in his hand.

"Don't touch me," I protest. "You can't do this."

"That's where you're wrong. You can either hold still and let me put this on like a good boy, or I'll go back to my medicine cupboard for something to calm you down first. Either way, you lose."

I've never felt so helpless in my entire life. I'm restrained and at the mercy of this psycho. There's nothing else I can do other than watch him lubricate the silicone and slide it over my erection. David walks away and returns with electrodes he attaches to it. Then, he presses a button on the wall, and a screen unfurls from the ceiling. A projector overhead powers on, and an image of two naked men in bed appears.

"We're going to watch a little movie," he says as he sits across the room facing me. "Have you ever had sex with a man, Leopold?" I remain silent. "Tell me. Have you ever had a man's dick inside you?"

"You already know that answer." One of the parts of this so-called therapy has been disclosing not only every fantasy I've ever had but also every sexual experience. He knows I've never had sex.

"You're right," he says, jumping up from his seat. "I almost forgot the best part of tonight's session." David returns to the cupboard and pulls out a flesh-colored dildo. "It's not the real thing, but it should do the trick."

My stomach turns, and I'm thankful I haven't eaten in hours because what's in his hand is enormous. Despite my fear, my cock throbs, and a drop of pre-cum drips from the tip betraying me. David also notices, and that's when I feel what the tight sleeve around my cock does. A jolt of electricity flows through me, eliciting a cry of pain.

He opens the lube and squirts some onto his finger. "Ordinarily, I wouldn't be so kind as to make this comfortable for you," he says as he walks behind me. "But seeing as this is your first time, I'll go easy."

"Don't touch me." But it's too late. His finger is already breaching my opening. "What the hell do you think you're doing?"

"Helping you, Leopold." Another shock. "You'll thank me for this one day."

"That will never happen."

He withdraws his finger and, without warning, pushes the toy inside. My body stretches and

tears from the unwanted invasion. A metallic taste fills my mouth as I bite down on my lip to keep from making a sound. I refuse to give this monster any more ammunition.

"Now, we're ready," David says as he hits play and the screen comes to life.

It's the blond man's first time having sex with another man. David's taken my deepest secrets and is using them against me. Before I can think about it anymore, the dildo in my ass begins vibrating, which intensifies the arousal coursing through my body, courtesy of the drug he injected me with.

Sexual tension builds, both on the screen and in my body. The silicone wrapped around my cock begins massaging my erection. I close my eyes, trying to force my body to cooperate with me. This isn't right. I don't want this. So, why do I feel an orgasm building?

"Open your eyes, Leopold." When I don't listen, he hits the shock button again. But this time, he doesn't let it go, and the electricity continues to flow through the most sensitive area of my body until my eyes fly open. "That's better. You're learning the rules."

The men on the screen are touching. Kissing. Their actions, even though they're only playing to the camera, are consensual. The dark hair man lies on his back, his cock hard and ready, waiting for the blond who carefully lowers himself onto it. They moan in pleasure.

The blond man begins to move slowly as his partner strokes his dick. The dildo in my ass is turned up. My unwanted arousal builds as I'm forced to watch the screen.

"You like this, don't you, Leopold."

"Fuck you," I yell.

"Are you jealous that it's only a toy in you?" David pauses the movie. "Do you want my dick in your ass?"

"Stay the hell away from me, you sick bastard."

"That sounds like an invitation." David stands, and an erection tents his pants. He disappears behind me and pulls the dildo out. It hits the floor. "I'm going to fuck you. To take your virginity and make sure you never crave another man's cock in your ass."

He undoes his belt and zipper. The sound echoes in the small space.

"Get away from me." Although it's useless, I pull at the restraints as if my life depends on it. "Don't touch me."

David's hand digs into my hips as he impales me from behind, making me scream in anguish. He hits play and begins to move. He matches the pace of the men.

David grabs my hair, pulling my head back. "Keep your fucking eyes open, Leopold," he warns.

The blond man throws his head back as his cock spurts wave after wave of cum onto his partner's chest. The dark-haired man grabs the other's hips, taking control and increasing the intensity. David mimics him, digging his fingers into my hips as he pistons in and out of me. The room is filled with the sound of skin slapping against skin.

Despite my disgust, my balls draw up tight as my orgasm builds. Tears pour down my cheeks as I try to hold back, but it's useless. My cock pulses in waves. The electricity starts again, morphing the unwanted pleasure into agonizing pain. David thrusts hard and comes inside me with a deep growl. Everything happening at once is too much. My vision goes black.

Leopold

When I regain consciousness, I'm alone in the room. Somehow my cock is still excruciatingly hard. I try to move my arms and legs but am met with resistance. I'm still restrained—at David's mercy.

"Welcome back." David's voice plays through a speaker in the ceiling. "It's time to continue your lesson."

The words are barely out of his mouth when I feel the familiar vibration in my ass and around my cock. My body tenses at the unwanted sensations. Once again, the screen comes to life as the same movie begins to play from the beginning.

Hours. Days. Weeks. I have no idea how long he has kept me here. David appears every now and then, forcing me to drink, and then he injects me with more chemicals to ensure my body stays primed for more. I've lost track of how many times I orgasm against my will until I'm left trembling and exhausted.

The lights turn on abruptly, forcing me to squint from their brightness.

David enters the room and, without a word, pulls the toy from my ass, discarding it onto the floor, then moves to my front. "I'm impressed," he says as he pulls the silicone off my cock. "You're still reactive. Don't worry. Once the medication is out of your system, this will go away." He moves in closer to whisper in my ear. "If it doesn't, I'll take care of it for you."

This sick bastard masquerades as a therapist. Someone who's vehemently anti-gay. But in reality, he likes men—boys. "You'll pay for this."

"I think you mean I do get paid for this." He disappears behind me. "He's ready. Come in."

Two men dressed in scrubs appear in front of me. I've never seen them before. David stands back as they carefully remove my restraints, and I nearly collapse into their arms. Holding me up by my elbows, I slowly walk back into the office, where a wheelchair waits. They help me sit and then cover me with a scratchy ivory blanket.

Silently, they wheel me to the infirmary unit, where I'm given a sponge bath and a hospital gown. Then I'm placed in a bed. One of the men starts an IV.

"I want to call the police," I say, my voice scratchy. "I need to report a rape."

"You're delirious from dehydration." He continues taping the catheter in place. "Once you get some fluids, you'll feel much better."

"No. I won't. David raped me," I yell, but he doesn't stop. "Do you hear me?"

"If your agitation continues, I'll be forced to give you a sedative." He pins me with his intense stare. "Am I going to need to do that?"

"No," I say quietly.

A short time later a doctor comes in. "You're going to be sore for a few days," he says after examining me. "But there's been no permanent damage done."

That's where he's wrong. David took something that didn't belong to him. He stole an experience that was supposed to be special and tarnished it with his evil.

"Do you have any questions?" the doctor asks, interrupting my thoughts. I shake my head. "Well then, happy birthday, young man."

"Birthday?" I ask, shocked by his statement. "How long was I in there?"

"You're asking how long your therapy session lasted?"

Is everyone in this place insane? "Yes." I correct myself. "How long did my *therapy* session last?"

"Four days," he says matter-of-factly. "You're one of our more severe cases. But I'm certain your therapist's work will serve you well. Our young men always leave here cured of their wicked ways."

"David's methods are very effective."

"I had no doubt you'd see reason." He writes something in my chart. "I'd like to keep you here overnight. Then you can return to your unit to continue your therapeutic recovery."

"Thank you. I look forward to it." I offer him a fake smile, knowing I have to be smart right now. I'm eighteen and can walk out of this place at any time. But I fear if they think I'm a flight risk, I'll be given that sedative. They need to believe I'm returning to treatment. "Is it possible for someone to bring the book my sister brought for me? I want to read it while I'm here. You know, continue my progress."

"I'll let the orderlies know."

My book arrives a short time later, and I mindlessly flip through the pages, pretending I'm taking in the information. What I'm really doing is plotting my escape.

The overnight staff is in, which means David is gone. I've been allowed to change into my sweatpants and a T-shirt. I'm given socks, but, per the rules, I'm not permitted shoes. Now, I have to wait and hope for the right opportunity.

Shortly after midnight, it does. A boy is brought in, screaming and completely freaking out. My heart aches for him, but right now, I have to focus on getting myself out. Once I make a police report, they'll come and shut this place down.

Taking a deep breath, I pull the IV from my arm. Blood spurts from my arm. I use the sheet to put pressure on it. As soon as it stops, I climb out of bed, slip the pre-paid card into my pocket, and stick the book in the waistband of my pants. I don't intend to contact London, but I won't leave evidence that she helped me.

Cracking open the door to my room, I check to be sure the walkway is empty and then quickly walk to the infirmary's exit leading to the residential unit. The halls are monitored, but with the smaller overnight staff busy with the behavioral incident, I don't meet any resistance.

There's one hurdle between me and the free world outside the main doors—the front desk staff. This is a locked unit. There's always someone stationed there. I have to hope they're reasonable and don't try to force me to stay or call for backup.

"Shouldn't you be in your room?" the woman asks when I approach. "It's past curfew."

"I'm signing myself out."

"I don't think—"

"I'm eighteen. You can't keep me here." I stand taller, hoping to show more confidence than I'm feeling. "The police know I'm coming. If you try to stop me, I'll make sure your name"—I look closer at her badge—"Cindy, is on the police report."

"Um. Of course." She starts typing. "What's your name so I can call your therapist. He has to do the discharge paperwork."

"That's not happening. Either give me something to sign or open the door," I say forcefully. "I'm leaving now."

"If I don't follow protocol, I'll lose my job."

"If you know what's good for you, you'll quit before it's too late." I glance from her to the door, my last obstacle before freedom. "Open the door."

She hesitates for a few long seconds before I see her hand move and hear the lock click. I don't hesitate. I push through and inhale my first breath of fresh air in two years.

I'm finally free.

Anthony

Ninety-nine days. That's how long rescue and construction workers grappled with persistent hotspots flaring up and emitting plumes of smoke into the sky above Manhattan. Presently, Ground Zero resembles more of a construction site rather than the epicenter of a terrorist attack.

Work continues around the clock, removing the remaining piles of concrete and rubble. Earlier this week, they opened a viewing platform for anyone wishing to pay their respects. Several of my friends have gone and describe it as a moving and somber experience. I don't need to visit the site to relive the destruction and loss of that day.

Throughout Manhattan, weathered pictures of loved ones still dangle, torn and frayed. They're the constant reminder of the families whose loved ones' remains haven't been recovered. The unspoken hope of a miraculous reunion. Their prayers are a silent plea to discover their missing family member in a shelter or a hospital—a bewildered or injured survivor of this mass tragedy.

Yet, with each passing minute, that glimmer of hope fades. The harsh reality sets in, forcing more families to confront the same truth I've already come to terms with—their beloved is gone. Their lives were snuffed out in a senseless act by a terrorist organization. It's the stark new reality we're all learning to live with.

Kelsey and Birdie stayed for two weeks after Kameron's memorial service. It was an honor to spend that time with them and Calliope. In the quiet stillness of the night, the newborn and I spent many hours together. Caring for Kameron's niece brought me comfort—a sense that he was near. I knew their time here was finite, but that didn't stop the tears I shed when we said goodbye.

The house has been too quiet since they left. This is the first time since that fateful day that I've been alone. I've heard the saying that silence is deafening, but I never fully understood it until now. Working in the food industry means I'm constantly bombarded with people and noise. Coming home at the end of a busy night was my sanctuary. The quiet was something I craved. Then, Kameron moved in. His presence filled each tiny crevice in both my home and my heart. The once comforting silence in my home has turned unwelcome, echoing the loss that now permeates every corner.

Although we weren't legally married, we were married in spirit and commitment. Our bond extended past the romantic into our unique lifestyle, where Kameron was my devoted submissive. The closeness we shared was unparalleled. His absence has left a gaping hole in my life. My home is once again quiet, but it's unwelcome.

In the days following the attack, I lived in a constant state of denial. It was unfathomable that my Kameron died—a mistake. A nightmare I'd soon wake from. Then, they pulled Kam's body from the rubble. After the initial shock, I was angry. How dare Kameron leave me? We were supposed to spend forever together. We didn't have enough time.

More than one night was spent bargaining with God or any other higher power who would listen to somehow bring Kameron back to me. When that didn't happen, I felt myself sinking into an abyss. Kam's memorial service was a poignant mix of profound grief and the brightness of hope. I was forced to say goodbyes to the man I loved beyond words, but I also met Adara.

Listening to her recount how Kameron selflessly gave her his lifeline, his oxygen, didn't surprise me. Kameron's instinct to prioritize others went beyond his professional duty—it was intrinsic to his character and the reason behind his chosen career. As angry as I might've been at him for going against all his training and giving up his source of oxygen, it all melted away as I witnessed Adara caressing her stomach.

At that moment, I realized that Kam saved not only Adara's life but also the life growing inside her. The knowledge that this unborn child would bear Kameron's name brought a deep sense of peace, offering the reassurance needed to begin the process of moving forward.

It's been four months since I've stepped foot in the empty space that should be my restaurant—the last place I saw *amore mio. Italiano Desiderio* started as my dream but quickly became a shared dream. Kameron had a hand in every decision, from the interior design to the menu. Which is why I have to continue on. The loss of Kameron and many others on that tragic day has cast a shadow of grief over everyone in my circle. The impact of the tragedy was felt far and wide, leaving no corner of the world untouched.

My loss is not greater than that of anyone else's. I've spent too much time at home wallowing in self-pity. Whether I fully embrace it or not, the time has come to put a smile on and get back to work. I arrive early at my soon-to-be restaurant and take a few moments to myself.

I'm lost in a daydream when the door opens unexpectedly. "I didn't mean to startle you."

"It's all good."

"You must be Mr. Genovese," he says.

I smile and extend my hand. "Please, call me Tony."

"I'm Al. It's a pleasure to meet you." I was tied up at the club when he first came out to take measurements. I'd sent Margot, my childhood friend and interior designer, to oversee that day. So this is our first official meeting. "Please accept my condolences on your loss."

"Thank you. Shall we sit and discuss how we proceed?" I ask, motioning to a table and chairs left over from the previous business.

Over the next hour, Al details all of the permits that have been pulled, a start date for the demolition, and a timeline for completing the construction part of this project.

"Barring any unforeseen complications, we should have everything on our end completed in ten weeks," Al explains.

"This has been so long in the making I can hardly believe it's finally happening," I murmur, part of me still not wanting to do this alone.

My hand trembles as I put pen to paper. The absence of a line for Kameron's signature isn't lost on me. It pains me to move forward without him, but I can almost hear him telling me to keep going.

"My crew and I will be here at seven am," Al says as he gathers his papers.

I reach into my pocket. "For you." I hand him my extra key.

"Thank you, mister—Tony."

After we finalize a few details, I see Al out and lock up.

The afternoon wanes, and the sun casts a low glow in the January sky. Despite the cool air, I choose to cover the mile to Fire and Ice on foot. I've been carrying Kameron's collar with me since the night I was supposed to give it to him. Tonight, surrounded by the love and support of my chosen family, I'll pay tribute to the commitment Kam and I once shared.

Anthony

It's still quiet in the club when I arrive. I avoid the area set up for us and instead make a beeline for the café.

"How's everything coming in here?" I ask the small kitchen staff who are hard at work. Lawrence, the sous chef, is at the stove working on what looks like the pasta.

"The food will be ready in twenty minutes." Marcy, our very talented chef, assures me.

"Did the champagne arrive?" On one of our visits to see Kam's sister, we attended an exclusive wine tasting. Kam fell in love with Armand de Brignac Rosè. We toasted with that champagne after we exchanged vows.

"Yes, Chef. It's chilling as we speak."

"Where is the—"

"Tony." Marcy puts her tiny hand on my arm. "Your guests are arriving." I glance out of the kitchen window. Brandon and Alex are just arriving. "Go out and greet them. I have everything under control," she reassures me.

"Okay," I finally concede.

Star and Owen closed Fire and Ice to everyone other than the small group of my close friends so we could pay a special tribute to Kameron.

A large round table sits on the main floor of the club. It's already been set for dinner. In the center is a glass box that will hold Kameron's collar.

For the past few months, I've carried it with me, afraid that if I let it go, I'd lose my final connection to him.

"I'm glad you could make it tonight." I shake Alex's hand.

"I wouldn't be anywhere else."

"Thank you for coming." I turn to Brandon and extend my hand, but he pulls me in for a hug instead.

"Anything for you," he says, and I hear the emotion in his voice.

While everyone chats, I step off to the side.

Owen comes over to where I'm standing. "How are you holding up?"

"I'm fine." I offer him the smile I've gotten good at showing others. "Is Scarlett here?" I ask, hoping to distract him.

"She's in the back with Star. They'll be right out."

"Great. I'm going to go check on Marcy."

I attempt to make an escape, but Star stops me on the way. "I believe everyone's here. Are you ready to get started?"

"I was going to check on the food."

"Marcy's on top of it," she says reassuringly.

"Right." I nod and walk with her to the table. "Tonight, we're gathering to honor Kameron's devotion to our Dominant/submissive relationship. The night before Kameron passed away, I'd made plans to not only celebrate our anniversary but also to ask him to accept my collar. Unfortunately, he was called in to work. When he called me and told me he wasn't going to make it out, I asked him to wear it, and he accepted." A sharp pain stabs my chest, and I momentarily can't take a breath. "I've carried it with me since that day. I couldn't let it go."

"When Owen and I had lunch last week, we discussed my dilemma. He asked if I'd be willing to display the collar at the club to honor Kam. I immediately said yes." I take a deep breath, composing myself. "Tonight isn't meant to be another tearful sendoff, but rather an evening to remember the man we all knew and loved. And to honor Kameron's devotion to our Dominant/submissive relationship. Kameron loved this place, and he loved each of you." I look around the table at my chosen family and silently chastise myself as I blink back the tears that are threatening to fall.

There are several chuckles as plates of mozzarella sticks are brought out. Kameron's preferences in food ranged from sophisticated five-star dining to simple microwave meals.

"It didn't matter where we went," Brandon says. "Kam always searched the menu for cheese sticks. If they weren't on there, he'd offer to pay the kitchen extra to make them."

"Do you remember when we surprised him at the fire station?" Scarlett asks.

"How could I forget?" Owen laughs.

Two years ago, Owen made a mozzarella stick cake for Kam's birthday. It looked incredibly realistic.

"Poor Kam was almost in tears when he picked one up and took a bite." She laughs. "I felt so bad that after we left, I baked a whole tray full and brought them back to the fire station."

After our Caesar salads, Marcy and Lawrence serve the penne alla vodka.

"I'll never forget the first night you brought Kameron here," Alex says. "You sat front and center with him for the knife play scene Kam was obviously not expecting."

"I had looked at the wrong date and thought there was supposed to be a Shibari demonstration," I recall, a smile tugging at my lips.

"That explains why his jaw dropped when the scene started. I was waiting for him to sprint out the door," Brandon adds.

"To be honest, so was I," I say, and we all share a laugh. "Yet somehow that night, after we left, he lowered to his knees and asked to submit to me."

Over the course of the next two hours, everyone takes turns sharing their favorite and often comical memories of Kameron.

The conversation turns more serious when Star says, "Witnessing Kameron's submission was breathtaking. Too often a man's submission is viewed as a sign of weakness, but that's rarely the case," she explains and glances to the man at her side. "It takes a strong person, regardless of gender, to gift another something so precious."

"The connection we shared was indescribable." I reach out and stroke the leather collar.

Each of us at the table falls into a heavy silence, the air thick with unexpressed emotions.

"Are you ready?" Owens asks quietly.

"I am." His firm grip on my arm conveys a silent message of support.

"It's clear from all the stories tonight that Kameron has left an indelible mark on everyone's lives and our community as a whole." I rise from my seat and lift the collar from the table. Owen stands beside me.

"Star and I are honored that Tony has agreed to allow us to display Kameron's collar," he says, clearing his throat. "It will forever symbolize the commitment Anthony and Kameron shared. The love we were all privileged to watch blossom." Owen lifts the lid, opening the box.

"Thank you for your gift of submission and your love," I whisper as I set the leather band onto its silver velvet resting place, then carefully close the box.

"We." Owen motions between Star and himself. "Had this lock made. There's no key signifying a bond that can never be broken."

Despite my resolve not to cry all evening, I lose the internal struggle. Quiet tears stream down my face as I hold the silver lock, bearing the engraved words, *Kameron Harlow—Forever in our hearts.* With trembling hands, I secure the lock.

After inhaling deeply, I lift my face and address my friends, "Please join me for a toast," I request, raising my glass. Everyone gets to their feet. "To the man who filled my life with excitement, joy, unwavering support, and, most importantly, unconditional love. My heart will forever be yours. Until we meet again, *amore mio.*"

Leopold

I FIND MYSELF IN SAN DIEGO, A CITY ENTIRELY NEW TO ME. The soles of my socked feet are throbbing as I wander the dimly lit streets, mentally marking locations of stores that might have reasonably priced shoes and an affordable spot for breakfast come morning.

Exhausted, I walk until my legs can no longer carry me. Collapsing onto a park bench, I curl up, drawing my limbs close in a protective cocoon. As my eyes shut, the world blurs, and I slip into a restless sleep, shadows dancing on the periphery of my consciousness. Grateful, I welcome the rising sun for bringing its warmth to my body and opening a new chapter in my life.

The streets look different in the daylight, and it takes me a little while to find my bearings and remember where the secondhand store is. People sharing the sidewalk with me shoot disgusted looks my way as they give me a wide berth. Stopping, I look at my reflection in a store window.

My hair is mussed, poking in all directions. I pick a stray leaf out of it. The T-shirt I was given is too big for my frame and hangs loosely off my shoulder. My baggy sweatpants have torn knees, and I'm wandering shoeless. With tears blurring my vision, I look around and am relieved when I spot the secondhand store at the end of the block. When I step inside, I almost expect to be thrown out. I'm thankful the woman working the checkout is busy with another customer, allowing me to sneak past.

Making my way to the back of the store where the shoes are set up, I search the racks for something that's my size. Several minutes later, I find a used pair of Nike sneakers. They're well-worn, and the laces are tattered, but beggars can't be choosers. Passing on the offered bag, I hurry outside and slide my feet into my new-to-me shoes.

My next stop is a fast-food place a few doors down, where I grab a bacon, egg, and cheese bagel, a hashbrown, and an orange juice. Finding a cozy corner booth, I slide into it. It's been two years since I've tasted anything besides cafeteria food. My eyes close as I savor the taste of the processed sandwich.

Stepping back into the warmth of the day, my nerves shift into overdrive as I contemplate where I need to go now. I've been waiting since shortly after I arrived at Walking in the Light for today—my opportunity to make a police report against David and get that hall of horrors shut down.

The day has barely begun, and I'm already exhausted. Thankfully, the police station is only a few blocks away. I walk through the sliding glass doors into the air-conditioned lobby and make my way to the desk where a uniformed officer is stationed. "Can I help you?" he asks as he looks up.

"I'd like to file a police report," I say, my voice cracking, betraying my nervousness.

"Have a seat." He points to a small sitting area behind me. "Someone will be right with you."

My slightly too big shoes scuff on the linoleum floor, making a loud squeak. I look over my shoulder, expecting to be scolded for the noise, but the officer hasn't looked up from whatever he's writing. Carefully, so as not to press my luck, I continue the short walk to the outdated upholstered chairs and sit. My leg bounces nervously while I wait to be called back.

After a brief wait, an older man emerges. "Are you the one looking to file a report?"

"Yes, sir." I stand and cross the room.

"This way." He motions for me to go through the door ahead of him. "We're going to interrogation room three. It's on your left." My heart races as we walk down the narrow hallway and into the room. "Have a seat." The officer opens a brown metal filing cabinet and searches through the hanging folders.

The room is sparsely furnished, with only a small rectangular table surrounded by four plastic folding chairs. I walk around, sit facing the door, and wait for the officer to join me.

"I'm Lieutenant Pierce," he says as he sits across from me and clicks his pen. "Let's start with your name."

"Leopold Wagner."

"Address?"

"I don't have one," I mumble under my breath, the confession delivered in a low tone.

"Pardon me?"

"I don't have an address." Embarrassment floods through me, and I glance over the officer's shoulder at the door, debating if I should leave.

"Are you homeless, young man?" Lieutenant Pierce's tone is compassionate.

Beneath the table, I wring my fingers nervously in my lap. "Yes, sir," I affirm quietly.

Setting his pen down, he folds his hands. "Do you have any family in the area I can help you get in touch with?"

"My family and I are no longer in contact."

"I see," he says and flips to the next page. "What's the nature of the crime you wish to report?"

"I was raped." I discreetly fold my hands on the table, attempting to conceal the tremors.

"Would you mind if I brought in one of my colleagues to assist with this report?"

"Um." I bite my lip and shrug. "I guess not."

Lieutenant Pierce stands, his chair squeaks loudly on the floor. "Can I get you anything to eat or drink?"

"May I have a water?"

He smiles kindly, saying, "Sure. I'll be right back." Then he steps out and leaves me alone.

My foot taps nervously beneath the table while I silently review the story I practiced while I was in the infirmary. Several minutes later, Lieutenant Pierce returns with a female officer.

"This is Detective Ridley," he says and motions to the woman beside him before passing me a plastic bottle of water. "She's specially trained to help with reports of sexual violence."

"Thank you." I take the offered drink, unscrew the cap, and take a drink. The ice-cold water soothes my dry throat.

"First, please call me Julie," the detective says as she sits in the chair next to the Lieutenant. "Do you prefer to be called Leopold or Leo?"

"Leo, please."

"Okay, Leo," she responds, her smile radiating warmth. "We have a lot of questions to get through," Julie explains. "I know this process can be difficult, so if you need a break at any point, just say the word. Okay?" I nod. "Where would you like to start?"

"I'm not exactly sure where to begin."

"Are you able to tell me when or where the assault occurred?" she asks patiently.

"It all happened at the Walking in the Light Therapy Center," I say a little louder, finding my voice. "The abuse has gone on for two years. I was raped four days ago."

"What are you able to tell me about what happened?"

Over the next few hours, I tell the officers everything I remember, starting with the very first *therapy session*, where I was repeatedly held under water as they tried to cleanse me of my *sins*.

At one point, Lieutenant Pierce excuses himself. When he returns, he has a tray of pizza. "We've been at this a long time," he says, passing out paper plates and napkins. "I thought we could all use something to eat." My mouth waters looking at the delicious round pie on the table, but I don't dare make a move.

"It's okay, Leo," Julie says, pushing the box toward me. "Help yourself."

I hesitate for another second before tentatively reaching out. Jule nods, encouraging me to keep going.

They try to keep the conversation light while we eat, but I'm anxious to tell the rest of my story. I want this over as soon as possible.

They listen carefully and ask several questions, trying to get as many details as I can give.

"When were you discharged?" Lieutenant Pierce asks.

"I wasn't discharged," I say and explain how I was able to get out while the nightshift was busy.

"When did you turn eighteen?" Julie asks.

"Yesterday."

She sits up and asks, "So, this happened when you were still a minor?"

"Yes, ma'am."

"At the risk of sounding callous," Lieutenant Pierce says, "I do want to wish you a Happy Birthday."

"Thank you."

"I think we have enough information," he says, tapping the papers on the table.

"Leo," Julie says, a serious tone in her voice. "I'd like to ask if you'd consent to having an exam and rape kit done."

"Even though it happened days ago?"

"Ideally, the exam would be done sooner," she admits. "There's still the chance we could get some DNA evidence to support your claim."

"Um." I chew on my bottom lip. "If you think it would help."

"It's a long shot, but I think it's worth doing."

"Okay, then."

She offers me an empathetic smile. "Leo," she says, reaching out to touch my hand. "What you've done here is very brave."

"I guess." I shrug and look down at my lap.

"Before you leave, I'd like to discuss your living arrangements," she continues. "Lieutenant Pierce explained that you're homeless." I nod, embarrassed by my current situation.

"We can help with that."

"You can?" I ask, my head popping up.

"There's a local program, Safe Haven, that offers transitional housing to young adults in the LGBTQ+ community," she explains. "While you're with them, they'll help you with finding a job and a permanent place to live as well as provide you with the mental health services you'll need as you recover from this trauma. Does that sound like something you'd be willing to try?"

The past two years, confined in a supposedly safe place, have left me wary of diving straight into another one.

"I understand your hesitation," Julie says. "I can personally vouch for Ramiro and the Safe Haven program. The rest of the Special Victim's Unit and I personally oversaw the organization of this program. Ramiro works closely with us." She pauses, searching my face for a reaction. "The doors are not locked there."

"I can leave if I don't like it?" I ask.

"Yes," she says. "I can take you there and wait while you have the exam done."

My hand instinctively covers my mouth to stifle a yawn. Despite the lack of physical exertion, mentally reliving the events takes its toll. Add to that a night spent on a park bench, and I'm ready to sleep for a week. "Okay," I concede.

Leopold

I'VE BEEN AT SAFE HAVEN FOR THE PAST MONTH AND FINALLY feel like I'm letting my guard down and settling in. Julie checked in on me multiple times during my early days here to make sure I was settling in okay. It was a reassuring experience to spot a familiar face amid so many strangers. Safe Haven's been a sanctuary while I work towards getting on my feet and figuring out my next steps.

Within a few days, Ramiro, the program's leader, helped me find a job at a small bodega. It's not glamorous, but it's a steady paycheck.

Today, I have the day off and have spent it in my room, diligently studying for my GED test scheduled for next month. Despite the claims of Walking in the Light having a high-quality educational program for its residents, the reality is starkly different. Two hours each day were designated for *school,* and I use that word very loosely. It was more important to the powers that be that we attended their brainwashing sessions. It ensured we all remained dependent on them—stuck.

"Hey, Leo." Ramiro pops his head into my doorway. "Julie is here."

"I didn't realize she was coming today." There's a rush of both nervous energy and excitement within me.

"I'm assuming she has an update," he says with a hopeful smile. "She's in my office waiting for you."

"Thanks. I'll be right out."

"I'll let her know." He raps his knuckles on my doorframe before disappearing down the hall.

Closing my book, I neatly put it away before scrutinizing my appearance in the mirror. My heart thuds with anticipation as I walk towards Ramiro's office. Julie stands when she sees me round the corner.

"I hope I didn't come at a bad time," she says.

I crack my knuckles nervously. "Not at all."

"Do you have a few minutes to talk?"

"Sure."

"It's a beautiful day. Are you up for a walk?" she suggests.

I follow her outside and across the street to the park. We walk in companionable silence, listening to birds chirping in the trees. Deciding I can't take the suspense any longer, I ask, "Has there been any progress on my case?"

"That's what I came to talk about. A few things have transpired," she says, motioning to a nearby bench overlooking a fountain, and we both sit. "David Lewis and his attorney came in last week for questioning. We also had one of our detectives visit the treatment center. Everything we collected was sent to the prosecutor's office." She takes a deep breath before continuing. "There wasn't enough evidence, so they closed the case."

I'm taken aback. "What do you mean, closed the case?"

"The charges you made against Mr. Lewis have been dropped."

"Dropped?" I face her squarely. "So, he gets off the hook for what he did to me?" I question, raising my voice. "What about the rape exam? They saw the tears."

"We talked about the difficulty with the exam since so much time had passed," she says calmly. "There was no DNA evidence to substantiate your claim. After interviewing Mr.—"

"Stop." I hold up my hands, interrupting her. "Let me guess. David convinced you he's an upstanding therapist doing everything possible to help the troubled gay kid."

"I can't divulge what was said during his questioning."

"Of course. We need to protect *David's* rights," I say sarcastically.

"I know you're upset," she says.

"Upset? That's an understatement. David raped me." My voice resonates loudly enough to draw the attention of passersby. "He raped me," I add, lowering my tone. "And he's going to get away with it."

"I'm very sorry, Leo. There's nothing more we can do right now."

"I guess that's it, then." I stand.

"Leo, sit down, please. Let's talk about what happens next," Julie encourages me. "I have the name of a good trauma therapist. She specializes in cases like yours." She reaches into the pocket of her slacks.

"No thanks. I've had enough of *helpful* therapists." I rock on my heels, needing to get away. "Thanks for trying." I shrug and start walking.

"Leopold, please," she calls after me, but I wave her off and hurry away.

⚭

Hours pass as I walk, and it's only after sunset that I come to a standstill outside *Prism*, an all-ages club for the LGBTQ+ community. Some of the guys from Safe Haven like to hang out here. Several times, they invited me along, but I didn't feel ready.

Other than the short-lived relationship I had with Santiago, I've never been in a relationship, and it's only been a little over a month since I was raped by my therapist. My life has been on hold, waiting to see David on the witness stand and hearing the hammering of the judge's gavel pronouncing his prison sentence. It was supposed to fix the pain—chase away the nightmares. But now there's nothing to heal what's broken inside me.

I swing the club's door open, only to be stopped at a security check point.

"ID," the burly bouncer demands.

Reaching into my back pocket, I pull out my wallet and hand the guy my picture identification. Eventually, I'll get my driver's license, but this is a start.

A bright yellow band is affixed to my wrist, identifying me as under twenty-one and unable to drink. Something I don't really care about. My goal is to get lost in a sea of faces. To pretend, even if just for one night, that I'm not some screwed-up gay kid who everyone thinks needs to be fixed.

I grab a seat at a table in a dimly lit back corner. The thump of the bass is hypnotic and distracts me from the jumbled thoughts in my head.

"Is this your first time at *Prism*?" a server asks.

"It's that obvious?"

"I've worked here for a long time and am familiar with most of the regulars," he says, a friendly smile accompanying his words. "I'm Nick."

"It's nice to meet you, Nick. My name's Leo."

"Here's our menu." Nick hands me a cardstock menu. "Take a few minutes to look it over. You can't go wrong with anything on it."

Nick leaves me to decide what to order when I spot *him*. He's tall and broad-shouldered, with jet-black hair that hangs past his shoulders. His emerald-green eyes meet mine, and something within me stirs to life. I quickly avert my gaze, not wanting to be the wierdo staring with his mouth hanging open. But even without looking up, I feel his presence getting closer.

"How is it a man who looks like you is here by himself?" he asks in a deep, gravelly voice.

"I'm um," I stumble over my words. "Just getting a quick bite to eat."

"Mind if I join you?" He motions to the empty chair across from me.

"Sure," I answer shyly.

"I've never seen you here before. Do you go to the university?"

"Me? No." I'm feeling all kinds of flustered by this man. "I was just in the neighborhood. Looking for…"

He raises an eyebrow. "Looking for?"

I'm at a loss for how to respond. I don't know what I started out looking for, but I know what I found.

Him.

An unfamiliar electricity courses through my body. The sexy stranger studies me while I search for the right words.

"This place is too loud," he says, leaning closer. "How about we get out of here and go someplace we can talk."

Setting the menu on the table, I meet his penetrating stare. "Go somewhere? I don't know you." As soon as the words are out of my mouth, I realize how juvenile they sound and want to hide under the table.

He chuckles. "That's something easy to fix. I'm Krew."

"Leo."

"Now, we know each other." His tongue wets his lower lip. "I have an apartment a few blocks away. We can—"

Nick returns, interrupting us. "Are you ready to order?"

"He isn't going to be ordering," Krew says, his eyes never leaving mine. "I'll take care of him at my place.

My dick springs to life at his innuendo.

"I wasn't asking you." Nick turns to me. "Leo?"

"Thanks for the menu." With my eyes locked onto Krew's, I pass the menu back to my server. "But I won't be needing it."

Nick narrows his eyes at Krew before addressing me, "I don't think that'd be a good idea."

"I think you need to mind your own business, Nicky," Krew says as he sits back and crosses his arms over his broad chest.

"Leave him alone, Krew." Nick turns his attention back to me. "You seem like a good kid, Leo. You don't need to get mixed up with someone you don't know."

Krew and Nick watch me expectantly. I'm at a pivotal moment—a crossroads. Should I play it safe, acknowledging the unspoken warning in Nick's tone, or embrace the instant attraction I feel towards Krew?

"I appreciate your concern," I say to Nick. "Krew and I were supposed to get together earlier, but he was running late." I glance at Krew, who curls his lip in a smile. "I was going to order while I waited for him, but plans are changed now."

Krew pushes out his chair and stands. "Let's go, Leo." He offers me his outstretched hand.

Standing, I place my hand into the handsome stranger's and allow him to lead me away.

Leopold

Krew tightens his grip on my hand as he guides me away from Prism. Though not well-acquainted with the city, I remember Ramiro's caution about staying out of the East Village, particularly after dark. My heart races as we turn down a dimly lit side street. We stop in front of a three-story brown brick building, its first-floor windows secured with bars.

"This is where you live?" I ask hesitantly.

"It is." He pulls the solid steel door open and steps aside. "Unless you've changed your mind," he says, raising an eyebrow.

Summoning courage, I pull my shoulders back and respond, "I haven't."

"Good," he says, his voice tinged with desire. "Up the steps, first door on the left."

"How long have you lived here?" I ask, attempting to make conversation.

"About four years." He stops at another steel door that has a peep-hole. Unlike the exterior door that had a lock and key, this one has a black box where Krew punches in a code. A locking mechanism clicks, and Krew opens the door. He enters first, and I follow suit. As soon as I step across the threshold, Krew turns around, closing the door behind me and trapping me against it with his arms.

Leaning into me, his lips meet mine, and his tongue seeks entrance. Instead of relaxing into the kiss, I flinch and resist.

Krew pulls back and studies my face. "Did I get this wrong?"

"No. It's. I—"

"You're not into men?" he asks.

"I am," I answer quickly.

"Are you with someone?" He takes a step back. "I'm into a hell of a lot, but I'm not about to be someone's side piece."

"There's no one else," I admit, looking up to meet his intense gaze. "This is unfamiliar territory for me. I've never just gone home with someone."

"Well then," Krew says, pressing himself against me. "I'm more than happy to be the first."

This time, when his lips meet mine, I welcome him. His kiss is demanding and rough. His hard cock presses against my stomach. I was afraid, after what David did to me, that my body wouldn't respond, but that's not the case. My dick is hard and strains against the zipper of my jeans.

In a bold move, I reach down and grab his cock through his pants.

"I want you to suck it," he says, and although I'm surprised by his command, my hands move to his zipper. I push his pants down and lower to my knees. Taking his cock in my hand, I stroke it gently. It's much bigger than I anticipated. My experience with blow jobs is limited to that one night with Santiago, and that didn't end well.

Hoping not to embarrass myself, I open my mouth and wrap my lips around the tip. I try to take all of him in but gag on his length. My movements are erratic and sloppy as I repeat the motion. Krew threads his hand in my shaggy blond hair. With a firm grip, he pushes me all the way down so his cock is deep in my throat and holds me there. My eyes water, and my vision blurs. Grasping at his thighs, I struggle to get free.

He pulls me back and watches as I cough and struggle to catch my breath. "Have you ever sucked a man off before?" he asks, and I shake my head. One side of his mouth cracks up in a smile. "Are you ready to learn how to please me, Leo?"

"Yes."

"Good boy," he praises me. "Now, open your mouth and relax." He thrusts his dick into my mouth, and I suck. "Take it all," he commands, grabbing my hair and pushing me down until my face is against his groin. I gag, and he laughs.

Over and over, he guides my head up and down his length until I start to relax under his control.

"That's my boy," he says, looking down at me with lust-filled eyes, and I feel my face flush. "Take it out and show me how much you like it."

I pull his cock out of my mouth, stroking him with one hand while the other massages his balls.

"Mmm. Just like that." He closes his eyes.

Seeing him enjoy my ministrations makes me feel powerful. I run my tongue along his slit, tasting his salty pre-cum then circle his velvety tip before taking him in all the way down my throat. He groans as I suck him.

"You're a natural," he says. "Are you ready for me to fuck your face for real now?" I nod. Krew grabs me by the back of my neck, holding me tightly as his cock slams against the back of my throat with each thrust. Saliva runs down my chin as he pumps in and out.

I gag and choke on his cock, but he keeps going. "Take it," he says through gritted teeth. My eyes water as fucks my face. "You like this, don't you?" My hand moves between my legs and rubs my hard cock through my pants. "Do not touch yourself," he commands.

I grab his thighs to steady myself as he thrusts harder and faster. "I want you to look at me while you suck my dick," he says, and my eyes shoot up to his. "I'm going to cum." Thrust. "You're going to swallow everything I give you," he roars as he slams to the back of my throat and empties himself. He pulls out halfway and strokes his cock a few more times, ensuring I take every last drop.

"Now, lick me clean." I do as I'm told, licking his salty and musky cum off his dick and balls. "You're a good little cocksucker," he says as he tucks himself back into his pants. "I'm going to put a frozen pizza in the oven."

Krew walks away, leaving me on the floor. I sit back on my heels and wipe a mix of spit and cum from my chin. Once I've caught my breath and am confident I can stand, I make my way across his apartment and ask, "Can I use your bathroom?"

"Down the hall," he says without turning around. "It's the only door on the right."

Silently, I walk away from him down a dimly lit hallway. There's an open door on each side. I peek my head into the room on the left. It's a cramped bedroom with white walls. There's a full-sized bed with no headboard. The blankets are in a sloppy pile. Across from it is a dresser with clothes hanging out of several drawers. I don't want to linger too long, so I back out and go into the bathroom right across the hall.

Like the bedroom, it's not well kept. The old tub is yellowing and has chips broken off it. The frosted shower doors are half off their track. I rinse off my hands and face in the lavatory-style sink. I look around for a towel to dry my face but don't find any.

Gripping the edge of the sink, I stare at my reflection in the cracked vanity mirror. That was my first consensual sexual act. I always imagined it would be different, more romantic. Maybe my expectations for a relationship with another man are unreasonable?

Krew is the epitome of drop-dead gorgeous with a side of danger. He's a man who knows what he wants and isn't afraid to go after it. That kind of confidence is sexy as hell. How he took charge and showed me exactly how to please him made me feel powerful. It was after that things were different than I'd imagined. I guess this is where I need to man up and stop romanticizing things. I want a relationship with a man —a real man, not some fictional version who's all hearts and flowers. I won't let unrealistic and childish expectations sabotage a chance with this guy.

Gathering my composure, I step out of the bathroom, heading back to the kitchen to join Krew. "Do you need help with anything?"

"Grab two beers from the fridge. The pizza's almost done."

"Where's your glasses?"

"I don't need a glass. The bottle works just fine." Glasses?"

"I'm not legal." I pull up the sleeve of my hoodie.

Krew's head snaps up. "You're not eighteen?"

"I'm eighteen, but I'm not legal to drink."

"I don't care how old you are," Krew says coolly. "No one's going to be checking IDs here." He pulls the pizza out of the oven and sets the hot tray on the stovetop. "Now get the beers, and let's eat."

Four beers and a frozen pizza later, my head is feeling all kinds of fuzzy. Krew watches me from across the table. Struggling to maintain eye contact, I grapple with uncertainty about what to say or do next.

"I guess I should probably get going," I say awkwardly.

Krew takes a long pull from his bottle before replying, "I wasn't finished with you yet." He leans forward, resting his elbows on the table.

"Oh?" I ask, surprised.

"I want you in my bedroom." Slowly, I get to my feet. "Now." He follows close behind me as we enter his room. "Take your clothes off," he orders.

I turn to face him. My heart pounds and my palms are sweaty. I look at Krew's dark eyes and swallow hard. I don't know what to do.

"I said take off your clothes."

His gaze tracks the path of my hands as they reach for the hem of my shirt and slowly pull it over my head. I remove the rest of my clothes and stand naked before him. Krew looks me up and down. My cock is swollen and hard. Pre-cum beads on the tip, and I hope I don't embarrass myself and come too fast.

Krew removes his black biker jacket, tossing it casually onto the dresser. Following that, he peels off his white T-shirt. "Holy shit," I murmur.

Krew smirks.

I itch to reach out and run my hand along the well-defined muscles of his chest and stomach. To drag my tongue over his tattoos.

He kicks off his black leather boots and then lowers his pants. His cock is erect, and I swear, even bigger than it was earlier. My cock twitches in response to the incredible site standing in front of me.

"Do you like what you see?"

"Very much," I say and take a step toward him. I can't help myself. I reach out to touch him, but he catches my wrist.

"Turn around. I want you on your hands and knees." I walk to the bed and do as he instructs. "Spread your legs." I spread them wide apart and look over my shoulder. "You like being told what to do, don't you?" he asks as he strokes his cock.

"Yes."

"As long as you're in my bed, I'm in charge, and you'll call me master."

His demanding tone intensifies my arousal even further. "Yes, master."

"That's a good boy." He smacks my ass.

"Put your head down and spread your ass wide open for me."

I lower my head onto the bed and spread my cheeks wide. Krew drags his finger around my entrance. "I'm going to fuck this tight hole." His breathing becomes heavier as he leans over my back. His mouth is close to my ear. "I'm going to fuck you hard and make you beg for me to come inside you."

"Please be gentle," I say quietly.

"I don't do gentle, Leo." He spits on his hand and rubs it on his cock. Positioning himself behind me, he pushes his thick cock into my ass. Red searing pain blurs my vision. I bite down on my lip to keep from crying out as every muscle in my body tenses.

"You're resisting," he says with a strained tone as he continues to force my body to take him. "Let me in." I close my eyes and try to relax. "That's it," he says as he pushes in deeper. My body burns as it stretches to accommodate him. "I want you to beg me to fuck you."

"Please, fuck me," I say.

His hand makes contact with my ass. "What did I tell you?"

"Please fuck me, master, I beg.

Krew grabs my hips and pushes the rest of the way in. His dick is so big it feels as though I'm being split open, and I cry out.

"You like my cock in your ass, don't you?"

It hurts, but at the same time, it feels so good. "Yes," I say quietly.

He strikes me painfully hard. "Yes, what?"

"Yes, master."

"Say it," he demands as he pulls almost all the way out.

"I like your cock in my ass, master."

He slams into me. "That's a good boy." Krew grabs my hair, pulling my head back. "Do you want to come too?" I nod. "Beg."

"Please, master." My tone is desperate. "Please, can I come too?'""

He reaches around and grabs my balls. "Come for me, boy."

That small amount of contact is all I need. "Oh my God," I scream as my cock explodes. My body convulses as I shoot waves of cum onto the bed. I've never come so hard.

"Good boy," he whispers.

His grip on my hips tightens. Krew holds me in place as he pounds into me.

"You're mine, boy."

"Yes, master."

His thrusts become faster and harder.

"Do you like my dick in your ass?" I nod. "Tell me."

"I love your dick in my ass, master."

Krew growls as he slams into me over and over. He's getting close.

"Come in my ass."

His balls slap against me as he fucks me wildly. "Fuck," he roars as he pulls out and spurts cum all over my back. A moment later, the bed dips as he gets up, leaving me alone.

"I asked you to come inside me," I say, hating the needy tone in my voice.

"You didn't call me master," he says as he pulls his jeans up. "You won't make that mistake again, will you boy?"

"No, master." Between the alcohol and the sex, I'm exhausted and can't keep my eyes open.

"You're going to make a good little play toy," he says and walks out of the room, leaving me alone.

Anthony

ADJUSTING TO A NEW NORMAL IS A SLOW BUT ONGOING process. New York City has forever changed since September 11th. Yet, each sunrise, each new day bears the promise of healing and the growth of newfound resilience.

With my coffee in hand, I walk the final few blocks to what will be my restaurant. Al and his crew have made significant progress over the past several weeks, and he needs me to sign off on a few things. Margot, my childhood friend and interior designer, will also be there. When I open the door, I'm hit with a gust of warm air, a nice change from the ice-cold winter air outside.

"Tony," Margot says coming over. "It's good to see you."

"You too." I kiss her cheek.

"Al and his team have been hard at work." She motions around the room. "What do you think?"

Stepping back to take it all in, I see the changes around me. New walls have been raised in once-empty areas. A crew of men is hard at work placing the quartz countertop, a focal point in the room. Its blues, greens, and white veining resemble the whitecaps on the sea.

"It's all falling into place." A familiar ache grips my chest as I realize

Kameron should be here. This wasn't solely my dream. It was ours—a shared vision.

"Anthony?" Margot uses my full name. Something she only ever does when she's frustrated.

"I'm sorry. Can you repeat that?"

"I was saying before we delve into design decisions, Al needs your approval for the installation of the French Doors."

"I didn't know they were done."

The pocket doors in the archway open. "We're about a week ahead of schedule," Al informs as he walks into the room.

"I'm truly impressed with everything." I shake his hand, conveying my admiration. "The progress you've made since my last visit is nothing short of remarkable."

With a pleased nod, he replies, "I'm happy you like it."

Peeking over his shoulder into the back room, my eyes land on the doors. Leading the duo through the future main dining area, we step into the private back room. "They're breathtaking," I express as I swing open the oak doors to gauge the atmosphere. Glancing back at Margot, I acknowledge, "Your suggestion for the solid glass panes was spot on. Once summer comes and the gardens are in full bloom, they'll provide a spectacular view."

"If you're good with the installation, I'll grab your signature and get out of your way." Al passes me an electronic tablet, and I sign the screen with my finger.

After bidding farewell to Al, Margot and I dive into the tasks at hand. After settling on ivory walls and mid-tone grey travertine tile for the floor, Margot pulls up the digital blueprints for the grand archway—the focal piece for the restaurant. The wall around it will become a living wall with ivy growing and trailing along a manufactured branch.

"The lanterns suspended from the branches will create a warm and inviting ambiance," she describes. "What do you think?"

"It's absolutely breathtaking," I reply, leaning back. "I can't believe that my dream of owning a restaurant is finally materializing after all this time."

"It's the only thing you ever talked about as kids," she laughs softly.

Margot and I shared the same neighborhood growing up—she was the girl next door. Fostering my love for cooking and my entrepreneurial aspirations, my parents set up a play restaurant on the lower level of our house. On weekends, our friends would come over and be the diners. I'd whip up small snacks while Margot played the role of my waitress. "You were always such a good sport."

"You made it easy," she says, a warm smile gracing her lips. "Did you ever wonder what would happen if we got together?" Margot asks and places her delicate hand on my arm. For years, my parents had subtly hoped I'd date Margot, and that hope was one reason I chose to come out to them when I did. Fortunately, they were nothing but supportive. "It's not too late, Tony," she says softly. "I'm willing to share you with a man. I'd be happy just having a small piece of your heart."

"I'll always love you—as a friend. But you deserve more than to have a piece of someone's heart." Placing my hand over hers, I give it a tender squeeze. "There's a man out there ready to give you the moon and stars. He'll pick you above everyone else. And you deserve nothing less."

Margot rests her head on my shoulder. "Can't blame a girl for trying."

"You should come to the club. My friend Alex is single, and I think you'd hit it off."

"As if," she laughs. "The kink scene isn't my cup of tea." Motioning towards the samples we've selected, she asks, "Are you happy with what we've chosen?"

Contemplating the assembled mix of textures and colors, I confidently answer, "I think they'll work perfectly."

"I'll order everything tomorrow," she says as she closes her laptop. "Between the high-end décor and the five-star food, this will be New York's hottest restaurant."

Now it's my turn to laugh. "I think you're dreaming a little too big."

"What's that saying about dreaming big and reaching the stars?"

Once upon a time, I had big dreams for this place. Then, my world fell apart. Now, those dreams are overshadowed by tragedy. "Would you care to join me for a bite to eat before you go home?"

"I'd love that." She pulls her bag onto her shoulder and then links her arm with mine as we step out into the brisk evening air.

Piercing the evening sky, two beams of sapphire light stand tall. "I completely forgot they were illuminating the Tribute in Light tonight," I whisper, stirred by the view.

A heavy silence envelops Margot and me as we stand motionless for several minutes, each of us offering a silent tribute to the six-monthanniversary of the tragedy that shook the world.

It's just after eleven pm when Margot and I finish our dinner. The memorial lights have been extinguished, plunging the sky into darkness. With the late hour, the air has gotten significantly colder. I pull on my hat and wrap my scarf around my face to shield me from the wintery chill. After walking Margot to the subway station, I turn around to go back to the restaurant. Somehow, I forgot my phone there and need to grab it before going home.

Macdougal St. is an eclectic mix of shops and restaurants. During the day, it's a bustling street full of tourists and locals alike. At this hour, however, the street is eerily deserted, with businesses closed until dawn.

Turning the key to unlock the door, I step into the shadows of my restaurant. Choosing a subdued ambiance, I illuminate only half the space. Even though I was here earlier, I can't resist the urge to linger and admire the extensive work that has transformed this place. Wandering through the main room, I imagine a backdrop of soft music accompanying diners relishing the delectable offerings before them.

The allure of the French Doors beckons me. Despite the bitter cold, I swing them open and step outside. Adding to the charm of this property is the expansive green space. Securing it was a stroke of luck. My vision for this space is to transform it into a flourishing garden, with one section designated for al fresco dining and the rest dedicated to cultivating an array of fresh ingredients.

A sharp, unexpected shattering of glass disrupts the quiet, and I go back inside to investigate the noise.

"We don't want any fucking terrorists in this neighborhood." Another of my front windows explodes as something is thrown through it. "Towel heads are not welcome. Go back where you came from," a male voice yells.

"What the hell?" I hurry toward the front of my restaurant.

"There's someone inside," one of them yells. "Let's get out of here."

Grabbing my phone off the table, I fumble with the screen to open my camera app as one of the people stops and yells, "Take your raghead and get the fuck out of our country." I take several pictures before they turn and run after their cohorts.

My attempt to vocalize something, anything, proves futile as my voice fails me. In their eyes, I'm one of *them*—the terrorists who changed our city, hell, our entire country on September 11th. Why? Is it because my skin isn't as white as theirs? Or because my hair and eyes are darker than they deem appropriate?

For the first time since the towers collapsed, stealing Kam from me, I feel soul-consuming hatred.

"Fuck," I shout as I turn and drive my fist through the glass door, shattering it just like the adjacent windows. Blood oozes from my knuckles, but I ignore it. Storming through the restaurant, I overturn the only table that's there.

Tears cascade down my cheeks, the agony of being labeled a terrorist and likened to the darkness that stole Kameron engulfing me. I stagger through the room, grappling to draw my next breath. A piercing pain slices through my chest, and I'm convinced I'm having a heart attack. Crossing the threshold into my office, I slump against the wall, embracing the thought of death—a welcome reunion with Kameron.

Anthony

"Tony," a familiar voice cuts through the black fog surrounding me. I push the hand off my shoulder, reluctant to leave the dream realm. In that world, Kameron and I exist together. When I open my eyes, Kameron will disappear, and I'll be alone again. "Tony. Wake up."

Grudgingly, my eyelids blink open and slowly begin to focus. "What are you doing here?"

"I got a call from the NYPD that they were looking for you," Owen explains. "They went to your apartment building, but you weren't there either. The super gave the police your emergency contact information."

"Why are they looking for me?" I rub my eyes.

"The guy who owns the business next door saw the mess when he went to open his shop this morning and called the police." He looks down at my hand, that's covered in dried blood. "What the hell happened here?"

I push up off the floor and get to my feet as I recount the events of last night. "They think I'm one of *them*," I yell and grab my chest as another pain slices through my chest.

"What's wrong?" Owen asks as he grabs my arm.

"Nothing." I attempt to take a step and nearly fall over as blackness creeps into my vision.

"Sit down." Owen helps me to my desk chair. "I'm calling an ambulance."

"I don't want an ambulance."

"Is this Mr. Genovese?" an NYPD officer steps into the doorway of my office.

Owen holds up a finger while he relays information to the 911 operator on the phone. "He's having chest pain and nearly lost consciousness." A pause. "Okay, thank you." He disconnects the call. "Sorry." He turns to face the officer. "I think he's having a heart attack. There's an ambulance on the way."

The officer approaches, stooping to my eye level. "Mr. Genovese, are you having trouble breathing?" he asks.

"Unfortunately, no," I mutter. "And call me Tony."

"Tony, I'm Officer Lucero," he says, standing. "Are you able to tell me anything that happened here?"

Owen steps between the police officer and me. "Do we really have to do this right now? Can't it wait until after he receives medical attention?"

"I'm fine," I interrupt Owen. "I was here last night to grab my phone when three men started yelling racial slurs and smashed my windows." I stop to catch my breath.

Officer Lucero nods sympathetically, responding, "Unfortunately, since the attack on the towers, we've seen an increase in hate crimes."

"I'm Italian, not Muslim!" I shout, the pain returning with such intensity that I find myself reaching for the chair.

"We're done here until after he sees a doctor," Owen insists. There's a flurry of activity outside of the office as two EMTs arrive on the scene.

Officer Lucero steps aside, allowing the EMTs to initiate their assessment. They bombard me with medical questions,

"We're going to do a quick EKG," the female EMT says as she puts stickers on my chest and hooks them up to some wires while simultaneously hooking me up to machines for blood pressure, oxygen, and heart rate measurements.

"This is all really unnecessary," I protest, rolling my eyes.

"That's okay if it is," she says, offering me a reassuring smile. "It gives us some extra practice."

After they're done with their initial assessment, they get me settled on a stretcher and load me into the back of an ambulance. Memories of Kameron's body being put into the back of a similar ambulance flood to the surface. My heart rate skyrockets, causing everyone to descend on me.

Once they're certain death is imminent, they allow Owen to climb in.

"You really don't have to come. I'm sure you have better things to do."

"There's nowhere else I need to be," Owen says as he sits on a bench off to the side.

With lights flashing and sirens wailing, the ambulance maneuvers through the city streets.

Anthony

My arrival at the ER was met with a line of doctors and nurses ready to save a man suspected of dying from a heart attack. Vials of blood were drawn, and I was hooked up to more machines. Once they determined I was stable, a physician's assistant cleaned up my bleeding hand. He told me I was lucky to only have minor cuts and scratches.

We've been here for hours. The constant beep from the monitor tracking the rhythm of my heart is starting to drive me crazy.

"Clearly, I'm fine. Can you get a nurse so I can sign myself out?" I ask, annoyed.

"No," Owen says without looking up from his phone. "We're waiting until you see a doctor."

We revert to tense silence, waiting for a physician. A knock on the door breaks the stillness.

"Hi. I'm Dr. Patel," the man in the white coat says as he approaches the bed. "I apologize for the long wait."

When I don't respond, Owen takes charge. "It's not a problem."

"I've reviewed your test results," he explains. "Everything looks okay."

"He didn't have a heart attack?" Owen asks, surprised.

"It doesn't appear that way. His cardiac enzymes, troponin, and CPK are within normal range." The doctor rattles off his medical jargon. "His EKG showed tachycardia, but no ST elevations, indicating what Mr. Genovese experienced was most likely stress related." He takes his stethoscope from around his neck. "Do you mind if I do a quick exam?"

"If it gets me out of here sooner, go right ahead."

"Have you been experiencing any other symptoms?" Dr. Patel asks.

"Sometimes my heart feels like it's beating too fast. But it goes away quickly." I shrug.

"How long has this been going on?" He types something into his laptop.

"I don't know," I respond, holding onto the unspoken truth that it's happened since a part of my heart died.

Leaning against the counter opposite my bed, the doctor explains, "I suspect you may have had an anxiety attack."

"I knew I didn't need to come to the hospital." I shoot Owen an annoyed glare.

"The symptoms often mimic those of a heart attack. It's a good thing you decided to come in for a check-up," he adds quickly. "Are you still experiencing shortness of breath or chest pain?"

I hesitate, looking between Owen and the doctor, who are both watching me expectantly. "A bit."

"There's a medication we often prescribe for anxiety. Would you be open to trying it to see if it helps?"

"If I try it, how much longer do I need to stay?"

"Once you take it, you should start to feel better in fifteen to twenty minutes," he says patiently. "Then, as long as you're okay, I'll get your discharge papers and let you go home."

"Fine." I rest my head back and look at the ceiling.

"I'll go put the order in. A nurse will bring it to you shortly," the doctor states as he walks toward the door.

"Thanks, doctor," Owen says appreciatively.

When the door clicks closed, I sit up and say, "I told you there was nothing wrong with me."

"That's not exactly what the doctor said," Owen states.

"Whatever." I know my annoyance with him is misplaced, but I can't help myself.

The room feels saturated with an unspoken heaviness, an all-encompassing force that seeps into every nook and cranny. Neither of us utters a word, and right now, silence is a blessing. Conversation is the last thing on my mind.

The nurse takes an agonizingly long time to deliver the medication. The nurse finally arrives with the medication, but her explanation becomes background noise. I tune her out, watching her lips move without absorbing any of the words.

"You might get a little drowsy," she explains after I dissolve the little white pill under my tongue. "Don't hesitate to use your call button if you need anything."

"Can you take this out?" I point to the IV in my arm.

"Not yet," she says apologetically. "I'll be back to check on you in a little bit."

With spread legs, Owen leans forward, burying his head in his hands. I mirror his action, dropping my head back and closing my eyes. I never take pills, so I feel the effects quickly.

"Tony," Owen says, looking up at me. "I think you need to talk to someone."

"What?"

"About Kam's death." He sits up straight. "I don't think you've dealt with the loss."

"I'm fine."

"That's what I mean. Your concern is always focused on being strong for everyone else. So much so that I don't think you've allowed yourself to grieve your loss. And this, today, brought it all to a head." I open my mouth to speak, but he shakes his head. "You didn't have a heart attack—this time. But if you don't deal with everything simmering below the surface, you might not be so lucky next time."

Though I recognize the truth in his words, admitting it feels like an admission of defeat. "I've tried so hard," my voice falters, catching on the lump in my throat. "I thought I was doing okay. But they compared me to the terrorists. The ones whose actions led to Kam's death. I snapped." I meet Owen's gaze. "At that moment, I didn't care if I lived or died.

Actually." I correct myself. "That's not true. I welcomed death. How could they do that?" Tears stream down my cheeks. "Why would anyone say something so hurtful?"

"There's no excuse for what they said and did." Owen gets to his feet and sits on the edge of my bed. "They'll get what's coming to them. But right now, I'm more concerned about you. Are you ready to let someone help you heal?"

It's as though a dam has burst, and I find myself unable to contain the torrent of emotions. A feeble nod escapes me just before I feel Owen's strong arms enveloping me in a supportive embrace.

"I'm sorry to interrupt," the nurse steps into the room. "I can come back."

"You good?" Owen asks quietly.

"Yeah." I wipe my face with the back of my hands. "Come in."

She looks between us curiously as Owen returns to his seat. "I was just checking to see how you're feeling."

"Much better," I convey with a small, appreciative smile.

"Good." She hesitates. "There are two NYPD officers in the hall. They said they need to speak with you."

"I told them they were going to need to wait," Owen says, getting to his feet. "I'll get rid of them."

"It's okay," I say, stopping him. "Tell them to come in so I can give my statement."

"Are you sure?" he asks.

"The sooner I tell them what happened, the sooner they can find out who did this."

"I'll let them know they can come in," the nurse says.

I spend the next half hour giving my statement to Officer Lucero and his partner, including giving him the pictures from my cell phone.

"Thank you for your cooperation, Tony," he says as he finishes writing in his notebook. "We'll do everything to be sure these people are brought to justice."

Leopold

"I HAVE TO GO OUT," KREW YELLS INTO THE BEDROOM where I'm getting dressed. "Make sure this kitchen is cleaned up before I get back."

"I will," I call as I hear the door slam.

I'm in the middle of doing the dishes when my phone rings. Glancing at the caller ID, I see it's Ramiro. I've been dodging his calls for the past week, but I'm unsure what to say. I know I can't avoid him forever. Now seems as good a time as any. "Hello?"

"I've been trying to get in touch with you for days," Ramiro says when the call connects.

"I'm sorry about that. I've been a little busy." I wipe my hands on the dish rag.

"You haven't been back to the center. Where are you?" he asks, concern evident in his voice. "I've been staying with a friend."

"Frank called earlier," Ramiro informs me. "He said you've missed three of your shifts. That's not like you. What's going on?"

"Um." I sink onto the couch. "My friend wasn't feeling well, and I've been taking care of them."

"Try again, Leo." Ramiro isn't convinced. "I know when I'm being lied to."

There's a long pause while I try to come up with something. Fumbling with my words, I mutter. "I'll be at work tomorrow."

"I hate to do this, Leo, but you'll need to come pick up your things."

"What?"

"We discussed the rules when you moved in," he clarifies, emphasizing the importance. "If you're gone for longer than forty-eight hours without prior approval, you automatically forfeit your room at Safe Haven."

"I'm sorry," I say quickly as panic surges through me. "I'll be back tonight."

"I wish I could bend the rules for you, I really do, but there's a mandatory six-month wait period before you'll be eligible for a room again."

"Shit," I mumble.

"When you come to get your things, I'll give you a list of local shelters," Ramiro offers, compassion in his voice.

"Thanks."

We disconnect the call, and after I take a few seconds to calm down, I get back to the dishes. Krew and I haven't talked about my living arrangements. I've been staying at his apartment since the night we met. He seems to enjoy having me in his bed, but we haven't broached the topic of how long I'll be staying.

As I clean up the house, I rehearse how I'll bring up the subject when Krew gets home. The last thing I want is to stumble over my words like a bumbling fool. But how do you ask a guy you met just a week ago if there's potential for more than a passing fling?

I'm still working out the correct phrasing when I hear the apartment door open and Krew's heavy footsteps echo in the other room. "Where are you?"

"Right here." I step out of the bedroom. "I was just making the bed."

"The place looks good. I'll have to give you a reward later," he says, lowering his voice in that sexy way that makes my stomach get butterflies. Krew isn't the romantic, touchy-feely, kinda man I always imagined falling for, but not much in life has turned out the way I'd hoped. But what he lacks in affection, he makes up for in so many other ways.

"I have to go back out," he says as he pulls his T-shirt over his head and tosses it onto the bedroom floor. Opening a drawer, he grabs a clean black shirt and walks out of the room.

"Do you have to go right now?" I ask, following him.

"Why? Do you have plans I don't know about?" he asks, slightly annoyed.

"Kind of." I exhale slowly. "There's something I need to talk to you about."

Krew leans against the edge of the kitchen counter and crosses his arms over his chest. "Go on."

Everything I'd practiced seems to have vanished. "I don't have an actual apartment. The place I live." I stumble over my words. "It's called Safe Haven. It's a program—" I realize he's starting to tune me out, so I fast forward some. "I'm not supposed to be gone for more than 48 hours without checking in with them. I didn't do that, and I lost my room. They called while you were out and told me I have to pick up my things." I search Krew's face, but he doesn't give away his thoughts. "This past week has been great, but I don't want you to feel like you have to let me move in."

"Put your shoes on so we can go grab your shit." He pushes off the counter and grabs his black leather jacket.

"I can stay here?" I ask, surprised.

"That depends," he says with a seductive smile. I don't have time to contemplate what he means before he points. "Get on your knees."

I lower to the floor and open my mouth as he pulls out his hard cock. Without warning, he grabs a handful of hair as he thrusts deep. I've become adept at relaxing my throat, a skill acquired through intensive practice over the last few days. My dick strains against my zipper, but I know the rules and don't touch myself. Any pleasure I get comes only with Krew's expressed consent.

He fucks my face hard and fast before letting out a loud groan as he comes down my throat. After I lick him clean, he tucks himself into his pants.

"Let's go." He walks toward the door, and I scramble to get to my feet. "We need to be back before my friends get here."

†

"Are you coming in?" I ask when we get to the building.

Krew lights a cigarette. "I'll wait out here. Don't be long."

When I get inside, I stop at reception and wait to be let into the back offices. Ramiro's sitting behind his desk, taking a phone call. He motions for me to come in. Quietly, I sit and wring my hands in my lap while I wait for him to finish his call.

"It's good to see you," he says when he hangs up.

"You too." I look around the room. "Do you have my things? I'm kind of in a hurry."

"I'll get them in a minute. There're a few papers you need to sign first."

"Okay."

"This one outlines the reasons why you—" He stops talking when I grab a pen and scribble my name. "You shouldn't sign anything before you know what it is."

"Like I said, I don't have much time. Krew's waiting for me."

"Krew? As in Krew Ramos?"

"Yeah, I guess." I give a casual shrug, a touch of embarrassment creeping in. His last name wasn't on my mind the night we crossed paths, and I haven't thought to inquire about it since then.

"Please tell me you're not mixed up with him." There's a pleading tone in Ramiro's voice. "He's not a good guy."

"He treats me well," I argue.

"Listen to me, Leo." Ramiro leans forward, resting his elbows on his desk. "There's only one Krew around here, and he's not someone you should be hanging around with."

"I'm certain you're talking about the wrong person." I stand up. "Like I said, I'm in a hurry."

93

"There's a six-month waiting period before you can reapply for a room with Safe Haven." Ramiro slides a packet of papers across his desk. "Here's a list of shelters. Please call one of them and find somewhere to stay."

"Can I get my things?" I ask impatiently. "I really need to go."

Ramiro pushes to his feet and walks to his office closet. He reaches in and grabs a black duffle bag. Turning back to me, he says, "Please promise me you won't go home with him. I don't want to see you get hurt."

"I assure you everything's good." I reach out and take my bag. "Thanks again for everything." I ignore Ramiro's warning and walk away.

When I get back outside, Krew is pacing while talking on the phone. "He's here now. We're on our way." He disconnects his call and slides the phone into his front pocket. "It took you long enough."

"Leo, wait," Ramiro's urgent voice reaches me as he hurries through the glass doors to catch up. "It breaks every rule, and I could lose my job for doing this. Come and stay at my place. Just don't go with him." Time seems to freeze as I glance between the two men.

"Are you fucking this loser, too?" Krew asks, grabbing my arm.

"Back off, Krew," Ramiro warns.

"Or what?"

"I'm only with you," I say, putting my hand on Krew's chest, hoping to back him down. "I've told you that."

Krew directs his gaze over my shoulder toward Ramiro. The stark differences between them are impossible to miss. Krew's jet-black hair falls untamed, accentuated by the worn black leather jacket that hugs his broad shoulders. His hours at the gym are evident, even if the hottest part of him—his tattooed back—is currently concealed.

On the flip side, there's Ramiro. Considerably shorter than Krew, his brown hair is always meticulously groomed. Clad in the usual khaki pants and a polo shirt, he exudes the aura of the stereotypical preppy guy—the good guy everyone would advise me to listen to. Instead, I find myself clinging to Krew.

"Tell him who you belong to," Krew whispers so only I can hear.

I turn to face Ramiro. "I'm with Krew. I'm his now," I say, keeping my voice steady.

"You have my number," Ramiro says, his shoulders falling in defeat. "Call me anytime."

"Fuck off, Vega." Krew takes my hand. "Let's go."

"My offer's always open," Ramiro calls after us.

Leopold

KREW WAS QUIET ON THE WAY HOME. HE SPENT MOST OF IT texting back and forth with someone. It isn't until we get home that I find the courage to ask, "Is everything okay?"

"No." He slides his phone into the pocket of his jeans. "I have to go out for a while."

"Are you going to be late?" I hate that I sound so needy.

Krew pins me with his stare. "You move in, and now I have a curfew?"

"Of course not," I say quickly. "It's just if you're going to be late, I might be asleep already."

"Why?"

"I have to work in the morning."

"You didn't tell me you had a job."

"It hasn't come up in conversation." I shrug. "I work part-time at North Park Bodega."

"I know the place." Krew grabs the keys to his motorcycle. "Blow off work tomorrow."

"If I *blow off* work again, I'll lose my job."

"That's fine with me," he says as he heads for the door.

"I need my job." I follow him, hoping to get him to see reason. "I can't go without money."

Krew turns to face me. "You live in my house now, and I don't want you working for them." I drop my head and sigh. "Don't you trust me to take care of you?" he asks, lifting my chin with his finger.

Do I trust him? I've only known him for a short time, but he's been good to me, and now he's extended an invitation to live with him. That must mean he feels something more. Right?

If that's true, why do Ramiro's warnings echo in the recesses of my mind? The initial belief that Ramiro was referring to someone else was shattered when they confronted each other. It's evident—they not only recognized each other but also shared a mutual dislike. That shouldn't surprise me. Ramiro tends to be more conservative with his choice of associates.

Krew watches me closely, waiting for my answer.

"Yes," I respond, silently wrestling with the doubts swirling within me, hoping they don't overshadow my words. "I trust you."

"Good. Text them and quit."

"But—"

"If it means that much to you," Krew drawls. "You can work for me."

"I'd really appreciate that."

"Good." He leans in and kisses me. "We'll talk more about it tomorrow."

After Krew leaves, I settle on the sofa next to my black duffel. All of my worldly possessions fit into this one bag, a thought that weighs heavily on me. Yet, in the same breath, I find a glimmer of hope. I'm no longer confined to a nondescript shelter room—a castaway from society. Now, I have an apartment with my boyfriend. It's a step up.

Even though I'm uneasy about leaving my job and relying on Krew, he did mention discussing how I could earn a living working for him. I'm unsure about his line of work, but hopefully, it's something I'll be good at.

With trembling hands, I reach for my cell and open a new text.

Leo: Do you have a minute?

Frank: I have a line right now. I'll check the messages when I can.

I take my time to decide what to say next.

Leo: Unfortunately, I won't be able to continue working. I'm grateful for the opportunity, but my circumstances have changed.

Pressing send, I wait for a reply. When none arrives, I grab my bag and head to the bedroom to organize my belongings. Krew has graciously allowed me to use his clothes this past week, but with him being taller and more solidly built, they don't fit quite right. It'll be nice to have my own clothes to wear.

Compared to Krew, I don't have much. I make space in one of his drawers for my pants and hang my handful of T-shirts in the closet. Since there's no toothbrush holder, I place mine next to his on the bathroom sink.

Returning to the living room, I check my phone, but there's still no response. With the house in order, there's nothing to do until Krew gets home. I switch on the television, hoping to find something to watch. While flipping through the channels, my phone dings.

Frank: I don't understand what's going on. When I hired you, we discussed that you'd give notice if you were going to leave your job. You've been a no-show three shifts in a row, and now you just up and quit?

I hate doing this to Frank. He hired me based on Ramiro's recommendation. Because of this, I'll stain not only Ramiro's word but also my own name. But I'm helpless to stop myself because of my desperation to please Krew.

It's in the way he gazes at me, his eyes filled with lust, just before he fills me. The way his hand tangles in my hair or wraps around my throat moments before he closes his eyes and releases inside me—it's a potent mix, one I crave. The empowerment I feel, knowing it's my body providing him pleasure, is intoxicating. I've wanted a man to look at me the way Krew does for so long, I'm not willing to give it up.

Leo: Like I said, things have changed for me. I no longer live at the shelter, and my commute would be too long.

Frank: I was speaking with Ramiro earlier today. He didn't tell me you left the program.

I don't like being dishonest, but I feel like there's no other choice.

Leo: I asked him not to say anything.

Frank: This feels very out of character. Like there's more to this story.

Krew's very private, and knowing he doesn't like Frank means I must be extra cautious about what I say.

Leo: The truth is, I met someone. I hadn't said anything to Ramiro about it until earlier today. We decided to move in together, and he lives on the other side of the city. Unfortunately, working for you isn't going to be practical.

Frank: At the risk of sounding too much like your parents, I think you're moving too fast.

Leo: I appreciate your concern.

Frank: You understand because you didn't keep your end of the agreement up to give notice before quitting, I won't be able to provide you with a reference for your next job.

Leo: I understand. I'm sorry it had to be this way.

Frank: Good luck, Leo.

Dropping the phone into my lap, I let my head fall back onto the sofa. Burning bridges has never been my style—it's not a wise move. However, even in the short time we've been together, I have to trust that Krew cares about me as much as I've grown to care about him. People like Frank, observing from the outside, might think I'm moving too fast, but when you realize you're falling in love, there's no reason to wait.

For the first time in my life, I'm actually looking forward to the future.

Anthony

I CAUTIOUSLY ENTER THE STREAM OF LIFE CHURCH through its side door, uncertain about what awaits me inside. Their online bulletin board ad painted a picture of a dynamic and inclusive community that embraces individuals from diverse backgrounds. Curiosity gets the better of me, prompting me to give it a shot.

After the intervention from Owen and experiencing a miniature emotional breakdown, I've come to the realization that maybe I need to address my emotions. Kameron's absence is a harsh reality—I can no longer avoid the truth that he won't be coming back. The dreams we once shared for our future now linger as bittersweet memories. For the past six months, I've been navigating life without a clear sense of purpose.

Owen's advice rings true. I can't continue in this state of emotional limbo. It's time to lay Kameron and our shared dreams to rest and embark on a journey to discover a new path in life.

"Welcome to Loving Arms," a petite brunette woman with an edgy undercut says. "I'm Pastor Andrea." Her appearance defies the traditional pastor stereotype, instantly putting my mind at ease."I'm Tony," I introduce myself, shaking her hand. "Pleasure to meet you."

"We're just about to get started. Grab a coffee and a seat." She smiles warmly.

A large metal coffee maker, reminiscent of the one my parents used for holiday parties, sits on a rectangular folding table. I grab a Styrofoam cup and fill it almost to the brim, leaving no room for cream. Taking a cautious sip, I navigate my way to find a seat.

The room is filled with white plastic folding chairs arranged in a spacious circle, with only two left unoccupied.

"Hi," the woman in the adjacent seat greets me.

"Hi," I reply, reciprocating the friendly gesture as we settle into the circle.

"Good evening," Pastor Andrea gathers the group. "It's wonderful to see everyone here tonight. First, let me apologize—I ran out of nametags and forgot to order more." She chuckles. "So, we're going to do this the old-fashioned way. We'll go around the circle, say our names, and if you're comfortable, share a bit about why you're here. It'll help facilitate our conversations and hopefully support you in your grieving process."

I listen attentively as each person makes their introductions. Some keep it concise, while others speak openly. I learn that the woman seated beside me goes by the name Jennifer. Her loss also occurred on September 11th, and it becomes evident that she's a regular attendee.

When it's my turn, I muster the strength to speak. "Hi, my name's Tony," I begin. "My partner, Kameron, was a Fire Chief in the FDNY. He was in the North Tower when it collapsed." Emotions overpower me, and my voice falters.

"We're glad to have you with us," Pastor Andrea says warmly.

"Now that we're all friends, we can move on," Kelly chimes in with a grin, "We often discuss the process of grieving and what to expect. Tonight, I'd like to explore something a little different. As you know, no two individuals experience grief exactly the same way." She pauses for a sip of her coffee. "Even though there are steps we can expect to move through in processing our loss, unexpected things often occur. Would anyone be willing to share something they've found surprising, frustrating—anything other than," Kelly air quotes, "by the book?"

Several people shift nervously in their seats before Jennifer slowly raises her hand. "I'd like to share something."

Kelly motions with her hand. "The group is all yours."

"Most of you are aware that my three-year-old has been struggling since Jeff passed." Several heads nod. "Last week was Jeff's birthday. I didn't know what to do—should I let it pass quietly or honor him? Anna's therapist suggested we go ahead and have his favorite birthday dinner. We also decided to release balloons to Daddy in heaven," she says, shifting nervously in her seat. "It was a hard day. The girls were fighting all day. Anna was super clingy. Dinner ended up burning. It was a disaster. I was so mad at Jeff. He was supposed to be here raising the girls with me. I wasn't supposed to be alone." She looks up, her brown eyes glistening with tears.

"I'd given up and ordered takeout. When I sat on the couch, Chloe, my eighteen-month-old, started pulling at my leg. I tried to pick her up, but she wriggled out of my hold, telling me no. I was at my breaking point, but then she started pointing toward the kitchen, yelling *Daddy*. She was smiling and giggling. I know you'll all think I'm crazy, but I could feel him." Chills run down my body. "Even though I didn't see him, it helped me feel less alone. Reminded me that he's still here watching over me and the girls."

"That's beautiful," Kelly says, swiping at her eyes. "It's been said that those we love never really leave. They walk beside us every day."

"I'm a believer now," Jennifer says, laughing softly.

As the meeting progresses, a few group members share their unexpected experiences—some positive, others negative—each falling outside the realm of what's anticipated.

Pastor Andrea brings the official part of the meeting to a close. Some members hurriedly exit, while others linger, conversing in smaller groups. I dispose of my cup, check my phone for missed messages, and casually make my way toward the exit.

"The first few meetings can be overwhelming," Pastor Andrea notes as I approach the door. "But I hope you'll join us again."

"Yes, I plan to," I say, expressing my commitment.

"I'm glad to hear that," she says with a smile, offering me her card. "If you need anything during the week, don't hesitate to reach out."

Despite the cold, I choose to walk instead of taking the subway, allowing myself time for quiet reflection on tonight's group session.

Initially, I went into it with the belief that I didn't truly need to be there, attributing my panic attack solely to the stress of the hate crime. However, as I sat there listening to others share their stories of loss, a profound realization struck me. I've never allowed myself to truly feel anything after Kameron's death.

Subconsciously, I've been avoiding the harsh reality, unwilling to accept the permanence of Kam's absence. I've been living in a state of denial, pretending he's away for work as he's done in the past. Like when he traveled to battle wildfires in California last year, spending weeks away. Despite the memorial service we had, I've never embraced the fact that he's really gone. Never allowed myself to feel the profound loss and grieve for the man I loved. Tonight's support group was a stark wake-up call. I've lost someone I love, and Kameron is truly gone—he's not coming back.

When I finally get home, I'm physically and mentally exhausted. I look out the floor-to-ceiling windows in my kitchen. Eight months later, the bright lights still shine at Ground Zero as work continues around the clock clearing the area. Construction workers and firefighters have painstakingly been clearing through the debris, hoping to find anything that'll give closure to the families whose loved ones have not been recovered. That hope dwindles a little more with each day that passes.

I still volunteer at the site a few times a month. The day after the attacks, we hastily organized a makeshift restaurant to provide sustenance for the weary rescue workers. Our operations have since moved to Trinity Church, located just across the street. Astonishingly, the building remained untouched and now serves as a twenty-four-seven place of respite.

Volunteers and emergency personnel put in days of relentless work without going home. Trinity becomes their refuge, providing not only a place to tend to their physical needs—offering showers, meals, and rest

—but also a sanctuary for emotional and spiritual comfort amidst the challenging work they undertake.

Too tired to cook, I prepare a quick sandwich before showering and settling into bed. Tomorrow, I'll be at my restaurant, overseeing the installation of new windows and the sign I ordered. Once completed, there should be no doubt that I'm opening an Italian eatery with no connection to the terrorists.

Anthony

W{\small ITH MANY TRADES SCHEDULED AT THE RESTAURANT TODAY} and the kitchen still unusable, I make a stop at a local deli to pick up lunch meat and buns for everyone. A well-fed crew is a happy and productive crew. Although I'm just picking up a pre-order, there's a line. While waiting my turn, I check my email and find the confirmation for the class I signed up for at the local community center that starts later this afternoon.

I've always been the creative type. Back in high school, many years ago, I took art classes. During culinary school, I channeled my creativity into the plates I crafted. It wasn't until I met Kam and used his body as my canvas that I felt truly fulfilled. Now, with that outlet gone, a part of me feels empty.

I'm not ready to play with another sub. I don't know if I'll ever be ready. For now, I'm opting for a canvas and easel. Who knows, maybe I'll be the next Bob Ross. The notion prompts a spontaneous laugh, drawing curious glances from those around me. I quickly look down at my phone, pretending I'm watching a video and not laughing at my internal monologue.

When I get to my restaurant, the wood barricading the spaces where windows were missing has been taken down. One side has a newly installed window, and workers are currently getting the other side ready for replacement.

"Hello, Mr. Genovese," Abe, the foreman, says when he sees me. "What do you think?"

"It looks great." I inspect the side that's completed. "This has the force resistance glazing, right?"

"It does." He knocks on the glass. "Nothing is getting through these."

"Good." I nod. "I brought food for everyone. How about you all come in to eat?"

"That would be terrific." Abe turns to his workers. "You heard the man. It's lunchtime."

"Once the kitchen is finished, I'll invite everyone for a proper meal," I say as we enter the building. Setting the tray on the bar, I grab the paper plates and napkins I keep here for our working lunches. "There's bottled water in there," I point to the mini fridge on the bar.

While the men enjoy their meal, I head to the back of the restaurant, where the drywallers are on stilts mudding the tops of the walls. There's been significant progress since my last visit. I snap a few pictures and send them to Margot to keep her in the loop.

While waiting for the sign company to arrive, I sit down and pull out my sketch pad to work on the design for the back garden.

On the right side, accessible through the back door of the kitchen, a vegetable and herb garden will be surrounded by a privacy fence. *Italiano Desiderio's* appeal will include fresh, handmade food. I plan to grow as many ingredients as possible, supplemented by sourcing from some of the best markets in Chelsea.

Outside the French doors will be a flower garden. Currently, the space features several mature trees. I plan to add a few more evergreens for year-round beauty. In spring, landscapers will plant this area with lush flowers that will bloom throughout the summer and into the fall.

There's another parcel of land for sale behind my current property that I'm in the process of purchasing. The plan for that space is to create an exclusive outdoor wedding venue—a dream Kam and I shared for our wedding if gay marriage ever became legalized. Since his death, I've struggled with whether I should continue with purchasing the space or if I should give up on it. Despite the heavy emotional weight, I've decided to continue pursuing the property.

As I sketch out plans for the flagstone path with deep purple creeping thyme growing between the stones, I envision the sides adorned with layers of pure white flowers that, under the moonlight, will appear to glow. At the end of the path, tall, wrought iron gates will open to an intimate venue area.

My concentration is interrupted when squeaky brakes outside catch my attention. I look up and see a bright yellow box truck with *Signs-R-Us* painted on the side. My heart picks up a beat as I stand and go outside to meet the installation crew. They inform me it'll take a few hours to get the sign in place. With the window crew finished, the sign installers can get right to work.

Not wanting to be in their way, I return inside and keep busy cleaning up the leftovers from lunch before sitting back down with my sketches. Just as I'm getting back into my creative stride, my phone rings. The name on the caller ID makes my pulse spike. Considering whether to send the call to voicemail, I decide at the last second to swipe the green button and answer.

"Hello?"

A familiar voice asks, "May I speak to Mr. Genovese?"

"This is him."

"It's Officer Lucero. I hope I didn't catch you at a bad time."

Is there ever a good time for the NYPD to call?

"No, you didn't," I reply. "How can I help you, Officer?"

"There's been a development in your case," he shares with me. "All three individuals linked to the incident at your restaurant have been apprehended."

My breath catches, and I quietly respond, "Oh."

"The trio is currently in police custody," he discloses, delivering the awaited news. "They face multiple charges, including criminal mischief and terroristic threats."

"What happens from here?"

"They're being held for arraignment. Two of the men have prior records. One was wanted on an outstanding warrant," he explains. "The third is a minor who already has quite an impressive record. Because of that, the district attorney is pushing for them to be held without bail."

"Is that something that can happen?" Shaken by the report, I close my sketchpad.

"Yes," Officer Lucero states matter-of-factly. "You'll probably be called to testify."

I slide my things into my brown leather messenger back. "Do I need a lawyer or something?"

"No," he chuckles and tries to cover it up with a cough. "The district attorney will be working on your behalf."

"Is there anything else I need to be aware of at this point?"

"Once a trial date is set, the DA's office will be in touch," Officer Lucero explains. "In the meantime, you have my number if you have any questions."

After we hang up, I take a few minutes to gather my thoughts. I really didn't think any arrests would be made. All I was able to give the officer was a blurry photo, not even a description. It wasn't until after everything happened that I had a discrete, high-quality security camera system put in place inside and outside the restaurant.

I've waited as long as I can to see the sign installed. However, the ticking clock reminds me of my impending art class. Stepping outside, I navigate carefully under the temporary scaffolding and shift my gaze upward. The sign, still being secured, proudly takes its place in the designated spot.

The hand-painted design exudes elegance with a touch of minimalism. *Italiano Desiderio* graces the façade in dark charcoal lettering. Below it, the phrase *Entri Come Amini, Vada Come Famiglia* extends a warm invitation. At night, soft backlighting will highlight the graceful script.

Witnessing my restaurant name on the building adds a tangible reality to my venture. However, the circumstances leading to this prompt installation tempers my excitement. Initially, I planned to unveil the sign once the interior was complete. Yet, in the aftermath of the hateful act that transpired here, I felt compelled to assert my identity and showcase the business so no one would be able to confuse me or my establishment again.

Leopold

Krew and I have been living together for almost a month now. Things between us are good. Actually, they're better than good. He's a sexy, alpha man who likes to take charge in and out of the bedroom. After living in such a restrictive environment at Walking in the Light, I didn't think I'd want to be in a relationship where I handed that much power to someone else, but surprisingly, this feels so right.

We've fallen into a comfortable rhythm, and despite enjoying my new domestic role, I still want to earn my own money. I'm not entirely comfortable with our current arrangement, where he covers all the expenses. Whenever I bring it up, Krew insists caring for me brings him joy. Then, the conversation is put to rest by him fucking me senseless.

Despite thoroughly enjoying every second with Krew, I've made up my mind to have a serious discussion with him when he returns home today. I need him to understand how important it is for me to have a job and earn a paycheck. My brief stint working for Frank left me with a deep sense of pride each time I received my wages—a sentiment I genuinely miss.

My phone is in my hand, and I'm scrolling down job listings when Krew gets home.

"We're having company tonight," he says in lieu of hello.

"Who's coming over?" I ask excitedly, setting my phone down.

"Some friends."

"Are they coming for dinner?"

"I'm sure we'll eat." He glances at me. "Call that Chinese restaurant and order a bunch of stuff." He opens his wallet and hands me a credit card. "I'm going to shower."

"Can we talk first?"

"About what?" he asks, his tone carries frustration.

"About my having a job."

"I thought we went over this already," he says as he kicks off his shoes.

"We did, sort of." I shrug. "You said we'd talk about me working for you, but we haven't actually—"

"Have I not been caring for you and ensuring you have everything you need?"

"Yes, but it's not the same as me paying my own way."

"Fine," he says as he walks down the hall toward his bedroom. "Order the food and make sure there's cold beer in the fridge." He slams his bedroom door shut, ending the conversation.

I drop my head on the couch. Upsetting him wasn't my intention. I guess it's all part of learning how to communicate with each other better —something I'm clearly not good at. The last thing I wanted to do was sound ungrateful for his generosity. Hopefully, he'll see reason when he thinks about it for a few minutes.

Krew's showers are usually pretty quick, so I don't waste any more time before calling the restaurant to order takeout. I'm cleaning off the cluttered counter when Krew returns to the kitchen. His dark hair hangs wet, and a few droplets of water drip onto his naked chest.

"Wow," I say and lick my lower lip.

"Is the food ordered?" he asks, ignoring me.

"It is. I don't know how many people are coming, so I ordered a lot."

"Two."

"Another couple?"

"Something like that," he says, not looking up from whoever he's texting.

"I'm sorry for upsetting you." I walk over to him and rub his shoulders.

He shrugs my hands away. "It's fine."

I may not have a lot of experience in relationships, but I know when the other person says *it's fine,* nothing is ever really fine. Not wanting to push him on this right now, I change the subject. "I'm excited to meet your friends." This will be my first time meeting anyone in Krew's social group.

"They're going to like you." He looks up from his phone and trails his eyes up and down my body. "A lot. And I'm going to like you with them." I tilt my head to the side, confused by his statement. "You wanted to earn money, right?"

"Yes," I say hesitantly.

"You'll have your first chance to do that tonight."

⚶

The food arrives just minutes before his friends do. I'm setting the containers on the table when the door opens, and a man and woman walk in.

"You're late," Krew says when he sees the couple.

"Talk to this one." The man points to the woman. "She took forever getting ready."

"It seems to be worth it. Get your ass over here." She walks over to where Krew sits on the couch and straddles his lap. He pulls her to him, kissing her deeply. I stare, shocked, and don't even realize I dropped a glass. It shatters at my feet. Krew pulls away from the woman and gives me a look.

"I'm sorry. I'll clean it up." I hurry to get the broom and dustpan, ensuring every sliver is up off the floor.

"What's his problem?" the man asks as he pulls out a wobbly kitchen chair and sits. The woman leaves Krew's lap to join him at the table.

"I might've forgotten to mention a few details about tonight." They both laugh and start serving their plates.

Uncertain about my role, I turn to the man, extending my hand. "I'm Leo. Nice to meet you." He makes no move to return the gesture, leaving me slightly embarrassed as I drop my arm.

"This one has pristine manners." He motions with his fork.

Turning to Krew for an explanation, I silently hope he clarifies the situation. "Sit down and eat, Leo," he instructs. I obery, lowering into my chair. "That's Dion, and this is Fawn." She glances at Krew and bites her lower lip. "What do you think of my new friend, Fawn?"

"He's cute," she says, her eyes not leaving Krew's.

"You're going to have fun with him tonight, aren't you?" She nods. "See, Leo, I told you they'd like you."

I look between the three of them, feeling like an outsider. The way Krew kissed her tells me they've been together before. He didn't tell me he was bi or that he was involved with anyone else. "I don't understand. You told me you don't share."

"I don't." He takes a bite of his sweet and sour chicken.

"Then what was that?"

"What did it look like?" I'm speechless, so he continues, "Fawn came to play tonight."

"Play?" My voice cracks, and Krew rolls his eyes.

"Fuck." He pins me with his stare. "You said you wanted to work for me. To earn your own money, right?"

"I. Uh." I have no idea what's going on or why the rules suddenly seem to have changed.

"You need to loosen up. Go grab us some beers." Silently, I walk across the kitchen, my head spinning, and open the fridge to grab four cold brown bottles. "Now sit and eat before it's time for you to work," Krew says before turning his attention to Dion.

The men have a cryptic conversation while I pick at the food on my plate, wondering what's going on and what Krew will have me do tonight. It doesn't take long before the answer to my question becomes apparent.

Krew motions to Fawn. She stands and saunters around the table, swaying her hips before she settles on her knees between his spread legs.

I watch as she undoes Krew's pants and wraps her red lips around his dick.

"Jealous?" Dion leans over and asks me quietly.

The roiling in the pit of my stomach tells me that, yes, I'm very jealous. "I thought she was here with you." My voice is quiet. "That she was your girlfriend."

"Unlike my good friend here," Dion chuckles as he motions to Krew. "I like to share my things."

"Take care of my friend," Krew says.

"What?" I ask, shocked.

"You wanted to work for me. Get on your damn knees and let him fuck your mouth."

Dion opens his pants and pulls out his cock. I look over my shoulder at Krew, whose hand is wrapped in Fawn's long red hair while she bobs her head up and down on his length.

My body moves without my consent until I realize I'm on my knees between Dion's long legs.

Dion leans over and says quietly, "If you're a good boy, maybe I'll let you sample her too."

"I don't. I'm not." The words are barely out of my mouth before Dion grabs my head. "Open," he says a second before pushing me down on his cock. Krew's taught me how to relax my throat so I don't gag.

Everything happens in a blur as Dion lifts his hips, keeping a fast and almost frantic pace. On the other side of the table, I hear Krew groan, and my heart breaks knowing he's orgasming in Fawn's mouth. I suck harder, not out of pleasure, but to get this over with faster. Dion slams my face down over and over. His movements become erratic as he grunts. His cock spasms shooting cum down my throat.

He pulls out, and I sit back on my heels to catch my breath.

"You taught this one well," Dion says as he tucks himself back into his pants.

"Come here, Leo," Krew calls me. I stand on shaky legs and go to him. "I want to watch you with Fawn." I open my mouth to protest, but he holds his finger up. "You don't want to disappoint me, do you?"

I should feel angry, but instead, I crave his approval even more. "No."

"Take your clothes off. Let them see you." He points to Fawn, who slides her short, tight dress over her head. She's not wearing anything underneath. I quickly turn my head away. "She's fucking hot, and she's willing to pleasure you. The least you can do is be grateful." Krew points to the couch. "Take him over and undress him."

Wordlessly, Fawn takes my hand and leads me to the sofa. She turns me to face her and stands on her tiptoes to kiss me. She traces the seam of my lips with her tongue, but when I don't open, she moves away and begins taking my clothes off.

I take in her delicate form. Her breasts are small, and her nipples are tight. My eyes travel lower over her flat stomach and curvy hips to her waxed pussy. She sees me looking at her and smiles seductively. When she has my pants off, she puts her hand on my chest and gently pushes me back so I'm lying on the couch.

Despite her obvious physical beauty, her kisses and touches do nothing to arouse me. She takes my flaccid cock into her mouth, trying her best to make me hard, but my body isn't responding.

"Does he need some help?" Krew asks as he comes over. I see something shiny in his hand.

A surge of memories flashes in my mind, sending my heart rate skyrocketing. "No, Krew, please," I beg.

"This will make you feel good," Krew croons.

"I'll get hard. Just give me—" The needle pricks my arm, and a cold liquid shoots into my vein.

Fawn crawls up my legs and straddles my body. She brings her hands to her breasts, rolling her nipples between her fingers as she rubs her pussy over me. It doesn't take long before I feel my cock get hard. She moans seductively as she wraps her hand around me and lowers herself down. With my cock inside her, she leans forward, her breasts flattening against my chest. Her lips meet mine, coaxing my mouth open.

I've never been turned on by a woman, but whatever Krew gave me has lust running through my veins, and my hips move of their own accord. I no longer have control of myself. I exist for one reason—to seek relief inside Fawn's tight, wet body.

"Fuck her, Leo," Krew says. "I want to see you enjoy her."

Any doubts or inhibitions I had before are gone, and I'm left only feeling what's happening at this moment. I grab her hips and move her body up and down faster, harder, chasing my release. Fawn reaches between her legs and plays with her clit while I continue to fuck her. Feral noises fill the room, and I realize they're coming from me. My release comes out of nowhere, taking me by surprise as it explodes through me. I squeeze my eyes shut from the intensity. Fawn cries out as her body squeezes my cock, drawing out my own pleasure.

When I open my eyes, I see Krew and Dion have their phones out. "What are you doing?" I attempt to shield Fawn's body with my own.

"You insisted on wanting to work for me." Krew narrows his eyes. "This video will make us a pretty penny."

Fawn climbs off me and looks between the men. "You did good, sweetheart," Dion compliments her. "You can have your pick who you want next."

"Both of you," she says sweetly.

"That can be arranged."

"Get this place cleaned up," Krew orders as he lifts Fawn over his shoulder. She laughs as he smacks her ass. "You can come join us when you're done."

Leopold

"GET UP," KREW SAYS, STARTLING ME AWAKE.

After cleaning up last night, I settled on the couch, grappling with what to do next. Ramiro's contact was pulled up, but uncertainty gripped me. I must've fallen asleep because now the sun is shining brightly. Pushing myself into a sitting position, I search for my phone, my hands moving between the cushions.

"Looking for this?" Krew holds up my phone.

"Yes." I stand up, my body cracking and popping from the odd sleeping position. "I don't think this is working out between us. I'm going to call Ra—"

Krew drops my phone on the floor in front of him and steps on it with his black leather biker boots. The plastic and glass crush under the weight. My stomach sinks.

"I was content to care for you and keep you for myself," Krew says, running his knuckles down my cheek. Instead of it being comforting, it sends chills down my spine. "But you insisted on wanting to work for and earn your own money."

"I was wrong."

"You should've listened to me when I said you didn't have to." He points to the broken phone. "Clean this up. I have guests coming shortly." When I don't move, he yells, "Now."

I hurry to sweep up the remnants of my phone. Fear courses through my body at the realization that this now useless device was my only connection to anyone outside of this apartment. I should've called Ramiro last night. I was stupid to let my guard down and fall asleep. Now, I'm on my own.

I was so deep in my thoughts that I didn't see Krew make us a plate of leftovers from last night's takeout. He's sitting at the table eating when I go over to him. "I'm going to get my things and go."

"Look, Leo," Krew says, lowering his voice. "I should've told you what I hoped for last night. I like to have a good time with Dion and Fawn. You can't blame a guy for that, right?"

"Of course not," I say, trying to appease him. "It's just not my thing."

He raises his hands. "Fair enough. Sit down and eat."

"I don't think that's a good idea."

"You barely touched your food last night. You must be starving." He kicks my chair out with his foot. "Have a bite to eat while we talk. If you still want to go after that, we'll figure it out from there." I don't move. "I'm not a bad guy, Leo. You know that. And we're good together. I don't want what happened last night to come between us."

"What about my phone?"

"That was a stupid move on my part. I'll buy you a new one. Now, have some lunch with me." Even though I still feel uneasy, I am hungry, so I sit. "That's my boy." Krew's praise still causes my stomach to flutter.

"What are you going to do with that video from last night?"

"Dion and I run a website," he says between bites. "We make a killing from videos like that. You and Fawn looked fucking hot together. It'll get a ton of views and bring in a lot of money." I don't look up while I chew. "It's nothing to be ashamed of, Leo."

"I'm not," I say quickly. "I just don't think I'm comfortable doing that sort of thing."

"I sell sex, Leo." He shrugs. "You didn't have to be a part of it. I was content to keep you for myself, but that wasn't good enough for you."

I see his mouth moving, but his words are beginning to slur. "What's happening?"

"I put a little something in your food," he says as if it's nothing. "It'll make you feel lighter and much more agreeable." I grab my head, trying to stop the feeling. Krew stands up and comes over to me. "You like to please me, don't you, baby?"

"Yes." Tears drip down my cheeks

"That's my good boy." He wraps me in his arms, and I rest my head against his chest. "This is how you please me." I feel a familiar stick in my arm.

"No," I cry.

"Shh," he whispers as he strokes my hair.

"I don't want this."

"Give it a few minutes, and you'll feel much different."

"What did you give—? I can't form words.

Time seems to stretch as everything moves in slow motion. Krew's voice reaches my ears, but the words are a blur.

Pain. Splitting. Burning. I try to fight to get away, but strong hands hold onto my waist. That's when I realize someone's inside me, thrusting hard. I cry out. Krew's hand grab's my hair and pulls my head up as a cock slides into my mouth. "Be a good boy and show them how well I've trained you, and maybe I'll even let you come."

I gag on the dick hitting the back of my throat. I don't want this. I don't want any of this. The man behind me thrusts furiously. He grunts as a warm sensation spurts all over my back. Seconds after, the man fucking my face releases down my throat. Krew pushes me off to the side, and my head hits the floor. I don't move while I try to catch my breath.

My entire body throbs with pain, and I notice a trickle of blood running down my leg.

"What's wrong?" A fat man with brown curly hair stoops in front of me. I'm so tired I can barely lift my head. "Are you jealous that you're not being fucked right now?" His cackling fills the air, and the stench of his rancid breath hits me square in the face.

In a shaky voice, I utter, "No." My head feels clouded, and the surroundings are unrecognizable, leaving me utterly clueless about what's happening.

"No? Your dick doesn't seem to agree with you. Billy, get your ass over here," He calls over his shoulder. "Our boy here wants to fuck it. He's earned a little reward." The guy grabs my arm in an attempt to pull me to my feet.

"Let me go," I plead, attempting to pull away, but weakness and lack of coordination hinder my efforts.

"It looks like he might need some more *encouragement*," Krew says, coming into my view.

I grab onto his leg. "Please, help me."

"Hearing you beg turns me on." Krew strokes my dick, and despite not wanting any part of this, his strong hand wrapped around me, pumping up and down, feels so good. I can't help the moan that slips from my lips. "That's right. Tell me how much you like this."

When I don't answer, he stops.

"If you don't tell me, I won't let you come. And you want to come, don't you, Leo?"

Whatever drugs Krew's giving me keeps my body desperate for more. Despite the disgust I feel inside, my physical body can't resist. "I like it," I mumble.

"Louder. Tell the camera how much you like this."

"I like it," I say louder.

Gripping me tightly, Krew starts moving his hand again. My body tenses as my orgasm builds.

"That's right, Leo," Krew whispers. "This is what we've been waiting for. You're doing so good."

I look up and see two of the guys with their dicks in their hands. They're jerking off watching this sick show. I know it's disgusting, but somehow, seeing it turns me on even more, and I groan loudly.

"Come for me," he orders.

My body trembles as I shoot wave after wave of cum over Krew's hand.

"Such a good boy," he croons.

Movement catches my eye. "What's that?"

"A reward." My skin pricks as he pushes a needle in. "Something to keep you feeling good."

It's only seconds before I feel my body falling. The all-too-familiar fog begins to creep back in.

No, not again. When will this hell stop?

Anthony

EXCITEMENT FILLS ME AS I HEAD BACK TO ART CLASS TODAY. In just three weeks, I've found a sense of calm through this creative outlet, as if I've reclaimed a part of myself.

I arrive at the community center early, anticipating setting up my easel and getting started. On my way to the classroom, I stop in the snack room and purchase a bottle of water from the vending machine.

"Tony?" a woman asks from behind me.

I spin around. "Jennifer?"

"What are you doing here?" she asks while balancing a little girl on her hip.

"I'm taking an art class." I step off to the side so I'm not blocking the machine. "I'm surprised to see you here."

"The girls take a tumbling class. They've been out sick for a few weeks, and I guess I'm out of practice. I forgot their water bottles, so I wanted to grab them a drink for during class." I wait while she takes her turn. "How long have you been taking art classes?"

"Come on, Mommy. We're going to be late." The older of the girls tug on her arm.

"Be patient, Anna. We have more than enough time."

"Who's 'dat?" the younger of the girls asks, pointing her chubby finger at me.

"This is Mommy's friend, Tony," she says as she gently lowers her daughter to the floor and takes her hand. "And these are my girls. This is Anna." She pats her older daughter's head. "And this is Chloe Bear."

"I'm not a bear." She giggles.

"It's very nice to meet you both," I say as we step into the hall. "It was nice bumping into you."

"You, too." We start walking and laugh when we go in the same direction. "The girls are in the preschool gym in the back hall."

"I'm going that way, too. If you don't mind, I'll walk with you."

Anna eyes me warily as she clings to her mother's hand. "Do you promise you won't leave?"

"I'll be outside like always."

"Promise?" She looks up, her big blue eyes filling with tears.

"I promise."

"This is my stop," I say when we get to the door of my classroom, which is next door to the preschool gym. "Have fun tumbling."

"It was nice seeing you again," Jennifer says.

"Same to you." Though I know I should head inside and get set up, I can't help but watch as Jennifer tries to drop the girls off. Chloe runs right in, but Anna cries and clings to her mom.

"We come here every week," Jennifer says patiently, getting down to her daughter's eye level. "You love Miss Bry."

"I don't want you to leave," Anna sobs.

"I'll be out here with all the other Mommies."

"Anna," a young gym teacher says, trying to intervene. "Would you like to be the line leader today?"

Big fat tears drip down her cheeks as the little girl takes her teacher's hand and walks into the gym. Jennifer stands up, taking a deep breath, revealing the stress and exhaustion etched on her face.

"Jennifer," I call as I hurry toward her.

She quickly composes herself when she sees me coming. "I'm sorry you had to see that."

"There's no reason to apologize."

"She's had a hard time adjusting to any changes since her father died."

"That's understandable." I know how difficult it was for me to figure out how to navigate life without Kameron. I can't fathom how hard it must've been for Jennifer to explain to two young children why their Daddy wasn't coming home. That's when I get an idea. "How long is the girls' class?"

"An hour, why?" she asks warily.

"Art class is only forty-five minutes. Why don't you come join us?"

"Oh no," she laughs. "I am not an artist."

"There are people of all different skill levels in there. You can let the gym teacher know you'll be in the room next door if they need you."

Jennifer looks between the gym and me. "I don't know."

"There are no naked models in there, I promise," I say with a grin, and she laughs. "Try it once,' I suggest a compromise. "If you hate it, you never have to go back."

"I might regret this, but okay." I wait while she lets the tumbling teacher know she'll be next door. Then she rejoins me.

"Ready?" I ask with a smile.

"As I'll ever be."

Our class consists of ten people, making it the perfect-sized group—large enough not to be overwhelming and small enough not to feel singled out. Jennifer and I choose easels next to each other. Today's lesson is drawing what we see, concentrating on composition and shading. I've never drawn with charcoal on a canvas. It feels good to try something new.

"Have you always lived in the city?" I ask Jen while we work on our sketches.

"It's been about six years. I moved into Jeff's apartment when we got married," she explains. "What about you?"

"I was born and raised here. Wouldn't trade it for anything."

"I grew up in Clearfield. It's a small farming town in Pennsylvania. While Jeff and I were dating, I fell in love with it here." She turns to look at me. "But since September, things haven't been the same."

"Do you have any family close by?"

"No. Jeff's parents passed away a few years ago. I tried to get my mom to come live with us, but she refused to leave her home. We try to visit her as much as possible."

We draw in silence for a few minutes until Jennifer leans over. "Holy shit, Tony," she says a bit too loud, and several heads turn. "Were you an artist in a former life?"

"Something like that." I chuckle. "Let's see yours." I lean over and take a look at her canvas.

"I told you I can't draw," she says as she waves her hand at the smudged drawing in front of her.

"It's not that bad." I walk over to her canvas. "May I?"

"Please."

"If we get rid of this spot." I use my eraser to clean up the reflections in the water. "And add a little shadowing here." I touch up the buildings that line the water's edge. "Then all you need to do is add the trees." I take a step back. "What do you think?"

"I think you're magic." She giggles.

"Nah. I just touched up a few areas. You did the rest on your own."

Before we know it, class is wrapping up for the day. "Thank you so much for inviting me to come with you. It's the most fun I've had in a long time."

"I'm glad you enjoyed it. Maybe you'll consider coming back next week?"

"I really enjoyed myself. I think I will," she says as we walk into the hallway and turns to me. "The girls and I usually go out for an early dinner. Would you like to join us?"

Aside from work and therapy activities, I haven't been out in a long time. "I'd love to."

Anthony

KAMERON'S DEATH LEFT A HOLE IN MY LIFE IN MORE WAYS than I realized for many months. The incident at my restaurant seemed to be the catalyst I needed to admit I was struggling. I've been regularly attending the grief support group, which has given me a place to safely explore the emotions associated with the loss I experienced. Successfully managing the stages of grief hasn't been easy. Being surrounded by others walking a similar path has made it manageable.

A big part of that healing has been my friendship with Jennifer. We've talked daily since I had dinner with her and the girls a few weeks ago. In a way most others might not understand, some might even call morbid, the fact that we both lost our significant other in the North Tower is comforting. It has allowed us to develop a fast friendship.

We're at Loving Arms when she gets a text. After she reads it, she leans over to me. "It's my sitter. Anna's having a tough time. I'm going to have to leave early."

"I can go with you if you think it might help."

"It certainly won't hurt."

The group knows that Jen's daughter has been struggling, so when she tells them we have to leave, it's met with well wishes.

Jennifer's quiet on the subway ride from the church to her neigh-

"

borhood in the Village. We walk the last few blocks in silence until we're outside of her building.

"Jeff and I bought this house early last summer. We were so excited to move from our cramped apartment to a three-bedroom home close to the school we wanted the girls to attend." She sighs. "This neighborhood was ideal. Everything was supposed to be perfect."

"I understand having to change the vision for the future."

"I still get angry with Jeff for leaving me alone," she admits, looking up at me. "I didn't want to be a single mother. Jeff was supposed to be here with me."

"I wish I could bring him back," I say, feeling the discomfort of helplessness.

"Nothing is okay right now, Tony. Anna's getting worse," she adds, her hand moving to her chest. "I'm barely holding it together. I'm so tired of being alone."

I wrap my arms around her. "I'll never be a replacement, but I'm more than willing to help however I can."

"I feel like I'm failing them," she cries.

"Don't say that. The girls know you're here for them and love them," I encourage her. "Eventually, it'll get easier," I echo the advice I've often received.

"Did you and Kameron want to have children?" she asks, wiping away the tears.

"We talked about someday, but obviously, that wasn't meant to be." I shrug. "But now I get to spoil your girls," I say, smiling.

"I believe people are put into one another's lives for a reason." She opens the door to her ground-floor apartment.

"Mama," Chloe, wearing her princess pajamas, yells as she races around the corner. "Uncle Tony," she shrieks when she sees me and comes barreling at me.

"It might not be how you originally planned, but there are two little girls here who've adopted you," Jennifer says softly.

Her words warm my heart. "I missed you, Chloe bear," I say as I lift the little girl and give her a hug.

"I'm sorry I had to text you," Rachel, the babysitter, says as we enter the living room, where a sobbing Anna sits on her lap.

"It's okay," Jennifer says, sitting next to her. "You did the right thing."

Anna climbs onto her mom's lap, tears streaming down her face.

"What's wrong, sweetheart?"

"It got dark. You didn't come back."

"We talked about this. I would be gone until after dark, but I'd come back," she explains patiently. "Did you try cuddling your special stuffie?"

"I did, but it didn't help." Anna continues crying. "I was scared."

"Mommy's here now." She holds her little girl tight, trying to console her. "Thank you for keeping them, Rachel. I hope they behaved."

"They're always angels," the young girl says as she stands.

"Are you leaving?" Anna sits up suddenly.

"I have to go home."

"Please don't go," Anna begs, holding onto her babysitter's leg.

She smiles at her young charge. "I'll come back."

"Promise?" She asks, her bottom lip quivering.

Rachel exchanges a worried look with Jennifer, who nods.

"Do you remember what we talked about?" Rachel asks as she crouches down to Anna's level. "I will always do my very best to come back to your house, but I can't make that a promise."

"It's something our family therapist is helping us with," Jennifer whispers. "To not make promises we might not be able to keep."

"That makes a lot of sense." I watch the scene unfolding before me. Anna's crying and rubbing her puffy red eyes.

Looking around, I see the girl's art supplies on a shelf in the corner of the room. "Can I try something?"

"Please."

I walk over to the shelf and grab some paper and a box of crayons. "Do you like to draw?" Anna nods. "So do I." I smile as I sit on the couch next to the girl. "Would you like to draw with me and then, when Rachel comes back next time, you can show her all your pictures?

"What if she doesn't come back?" Anna asks quietly, her voice catching on a sob. "Like my daddy."

"I know how scary that is. I had someone I loved very much not come back, too."

"Were they in the tall building, too?"

"They were."

"That's sad." She swipes at her face.

"It is. But I'm learning how to not be so sad or scared anymore."

"You are?" she asks, releasing Rachel's leg.

"Yep. Do you want to know how?" I ask and set the paper and crayons on the coffee table in front of me.

"Mhm."

"I started drawing pictures. My favorite pictures are of the happy memories I have with the person I loved. When I get sad or scared, I look at them to remind me how to be happy."

"That's such a good idea," Rachel agrees.

I get on my knees next to the table and open the crayon box. "Would you like to draw one with me?"

Anna walks over to me. "Okay."

I put a blank sheet of white paper in front of her and move the crayons between us. Anna takes a blue crayon and starts drawing.

"When I come back next time, will you show me your drawings?"

"Yep," Anna says without looking up.

"I can't wait." Rachel kisses the top of Anna's head. "I'll see you in two days, kiddo."

"Me draw, too," Chloe says as she climbs onto my lap.

I look over my shoulder, and Jennifer mouths *thank you* before she walks Rachel out.

When Jennifer returns, the girls make her sit and draw pictures with us. Time flies, and before I know it, it's almost ten pm.

"It's getting pretty late. I should really get going," I say and get to my feet.

"I didn't realize what time it was," Jennifer adds. "It's way past both of your bedtime."

"Please don't go, Uncle Tony," Anna wraps her arms around my neck.

"It's past my bedtime, too," I say as I squeeze her back.

She releases me and studies my face carefully before saying, "You can sleep here."

"That's very kind." I grin. "But I didn't bring my clothes or my toothbrush."

Anna chews on her lower lip. "Can you come back tomorrow?"

"I have to work tomorrow. But if your mommy says it's okay, I'll come back another day, and we can draw some more."

"Is that okay, Mommy?"

"It's absolutely okay."

"Yay." Anna claps and bounces on her toes.

The girls are happily drawing when we walk out of the room.

"This is the first time since Jeff left us that she hasn't had a melt-down when someone was leaving," Jennifer says as we walk toward her front door.

"I'm glad I was able to help."

"Mommy," Anna yells. "Chloe's eating my crayons."

"Sounds like you're needed in the other room. Thank you for having me over." I hug her goodnight. "I'll call you tomorrow."

Leopold

Stepping out of *Walking in the Light* brought overwhelming relief. I believed the worst was behind me. I trusted the legal system to punish David and the rest of the staff in that horrible place. To make sure all of the boys that were being held hostage there were set free and would be safe. Looking back, that was a naïve thought. Of course, they'd have a story to cover up their crimes. And who'd believe the kid who was placed there by their loving family because of their delinquent behaviors?

But at least I was out and was okay. Safe Haven was the first place I'd ever lived where I was accepted for who I was—no question. Ramiro was the father I'd always longed for. He accepted all of us just as we were. He worked tirelessly, helping us get our education, find jobs, and eventually a place of our own. I lost my chance at a promising future the day I refused to heed Ramiro's warning and chose Krew over him.

Now, I've been reduced to nothing more than a whore to be fucked by whoever walks through Krew's door. There's a constant stream of men and women who show up at all hours of the day and night. Clothes? I haven't worn them in weeks. I suspect that's part of Krew's plan. He keeps me naked and strung out so I can't run. I have no choice but to stay here and be subjected to his sick plans.

Whatever poison Krew's pumping through me ensures I don't ever fully lose consciousness. At least when the drugs are at their height, the almost non-stop sex is a relief. It's when they begin to wear off that I realize I'm trapped—a slave to my treacherous body. Thankfully, whenever that happens, Krew is there with his needle in my vein. The clear liquid is a relief. It silences my thoughts once again.

"He won't get hard," a stick-thin woman with rotting teeth says. "How is he supposed to fuck me if he's like this." She motions to my deflated dick.

"Maybe he's not into you," Krew snickers.

I know he's been making me take Viagara. I've swallowed so many little blue pills I lost count. At some points, he gave me so much that no matter how many times I orgasmed, my dick stayed painfully hard. I'm not into women, especially this one, but that's never stopped my body's physical reaction before. As long as he feeds me the drug, my dick stands at attention for whoever's here, but even though I took them a few hours ago, nothing's happening.

"He's fucked me before," she whines. "Can't you give him something else?"

"I already gave him shit that should work." He walks away.

She marches over to Krew, not caring that she's fully naked. "I paid good money for this."

"You paid for time with him. I can't guarantee results," he snickers.

"I'll take you then." She reaches out to undo Krew's pants, but he grabs her wrist.

"Don't touch me," he warns, his voice lethally dark.

She crosses her arms across her nearly flat chest. "I want my money back."

"I don't give refunds, sweetheart," Krew lights a joint. "Put your clothes on and get the fuck out."

"What?"

"You heard me." He picks up her clothes and tosses them at her. "You've overstayed your welcome. Get out."

She pulls her dingy T-shirt over her head and slides her stretched-out yoga pants up her bony legs before giving Krew the finger and slamming the door behind her.

"You're lucky that wasn't one of my important clients," Krew snarls. "What the hell is wrong with you?"

I pull my knees against my chest, trying to preserve some warmth, but don't answer him. I've learned to stay quiet when he's in this kind of mood.

"I have to do a quick run to restock." He stabs the joint out on the cracked Formica counter and kicks some trash out of the way. "This place is a dump. When I get back, it better be cleaned up and ready for tonight." He squats down to make eye contact with me. "You have a very important guest coming this evening." I make the mistake of lifting my head to meet his eyes. "That got your attention. Do you want to know who it is?"

"No," I say quietly.

I don't care who's coming. One body is the same as the next. All of them are unwanted. I begin to tremble as the drugs start to wear off.

Krew stands back up, and I assume he's going to get a needle, but instead, he walks toward the door.

"Can I have a shot before you go?" I ask, desperate for relief.

"No." Krew stops with his hand on the doorknob. "This client has requested you to be present. He prefers you to fight him."

He prefers me to fight him? I've never resisted any of Krew's so-called clients.

I watch as he reaches out and turns the handle. "David can't wait to see you again." The door slams behind him.

Silence.

My brain struggles to digest Krew's words.

David?

When I finally comprehend his words, fear sets in. I don't know how long I've been here or how many people have used my body. Their names and faces mean nothing to me as long as Krew keeps my mind numb. But I won't survive being raped by David again.

I don't know what to do. How to get out of my current situation.

When I woke up after the first time Krew drugged me, I wasn't in his apartment anymore. I'm pretty sure we're in the same building, just one of the other empty apartments. This one has a solid steel door like Krew's place, but there's no lock on the inside. The times Krew leaves, the door is locked from the outside. There are windows, but they have bars trapping me inside.

I grab the cushion of the couch and struggle to get on my feet. Even though it's futile, I stumble to the door and shake it. I'm not surprised when it doesn't budge. I search the mostly empty space, frantically looking for anything I can use to help me escape.

"Dammit," I yell when I find nothing.

My body shakes so hard that my teeth rattle. My escape efforts are now combined with desperation for more drugs. I've watched where Krew gets the vials from, but the cupboard has a padlock on it. I punch the wood so hard that my knuckles bust open, and blood drips down my arm.

I try the doors to the two other rooms but find them all locked. The only one that opens leads to the bathroom. Lying on the floor, I see one of Krew's black T-shirts. Sliding it over my head, I'm thankful for the little bit of clothing offering warmth to my body.

Tearing open the medicine cabinet on the wall, I'm disappointed to find it empty. My heart pounds against my ribs as if it's trying to get out of my body. I grab the sides of my head and scream, hoping it stops my torment. That's when I look up and notice the small window without bars.

It's a fixed window, so I know my only hope of getting out is to break the glass. There's a worn towel lying in the bottom of the stand-up shower. I grab it and wrap it around my fist, hoping it provides some protection. It takes several tries before the glass finally shatters. Using the towel, I wipe away the shards as best as I can. Slivers of glass are embedded in my bare feet as I try to hoist myself up, but I'm weak from the lack of nutrition and the drugs.

My vision blurs in and out as I stumble back through the dark hallway to the kitchen and grab one of the metal folding chairs. It takes my remaining strength to drag it back to the bathroom. I climb onto the chair and am close enough to slide one leg through the small opening. As I fold my body to fit through, shards of glass I miss slice my skin, but I don't care. Freedom is just on the other side.

It's dark as my foot searches for something, anything, to steady me. But there's nothing there. My grasp on what's left of the windowsill slips, and I fall from the second floor. The dead remnants of a bush slow my body's fall to the ground. Even still, I land on my left arm.

Slowly, I push up, keeping my injured arm cradled against me as I catch my breath. I remain still, listening for any hint that people are outside the building, but there's nothing. Knowing I need to get out of here before Krew returns, I drag myself to my feet and walk as fast as my weary body will take me. I don't know exactly where I'm going other than away from this neighborhood.

Leopold

Silently moving through the shadows, I cover what feels like miles until the lights of a corner store become visible. I contemplate if it's too close to Krew's building to gamble on whoever might be inside, but there's no other option. I won't last much longer. If I collapse on the street, the odds of being saved are slimmer than the risk I take going inside.

Clad in a T-shirt that provides minimal coverage, I cautiously watch for a few minutes, waiting until the parking lot is empty. I hope to make it inside without causing too much of a scene. Once I'm relatively sure the store is empty, I step out from behind the corner of the building, which provides me shelter. I hurry across the street and slip inside the store.

The door beeps, and the girl behind the counter looks up. "Oh my God," she yells.

"Please," I stumble and grasp onto the counter to keep me upright. "I need help."

She steps back but doesn't take her eyes off me. "What do you want?"

"Could you make a call for me?" I cast a worried glance over my shoulder, afraid Krew or one of his friends would have realized I was gone or followed me and are ready to drag me back.

"Um." She chews on her lower lip. "Is it your dealer or something?"

"No. I'm not..." I look down at myself and see what she's seeing. "His name is Ramiro Vega."

Cautiously, she pulls her cell phone out from under the counter. For a second, I'm afraid she's calling the police, and I consider running. Then, she says, "What's his number?"

"I don't know." My head falls.

"I'll try searching his name," she says.

A car pulls into the parking lot, and my pulse kicks into overdrive. "I can't let them find me. Would you hide me?" I steal another glance when the car door closes. "Please?"

She looks from me to whoever's outside the door. "I might end up regretting this, but come on." She motions for me to go behind the counter.

I move as fast as possible and drop to the ground, curling up as small as possible. The door beeps. She briefly looks up but then resumes scrolling on her cell phone, a move that doesn't attract any attention.

The back-and-forth of two male voices catches my attention. One unmistakably belongs to Krew. I lower my head, pulling my legs closer, silently pleading with the universe to be on my side.

The girl discreetly slides her phone under the counter as they come nearer, and items are placed on the counter. "Are you ready to say yes to my offer, sweetheart?"

"Fuck off, Krew," she says as she punches numbers into the cash register.

The door beeps again.

"I'd like to fuck you," Krew says crudely, and both men laugh.

"Is that so?" A third man joins the conversation. "What are you doing in my neighborhood?"

"We were just passing through and got thirsty." More snickering.

"Lindsay told me you've been sniffing around." His voice grows louder as his feet come into view. He casts a downward glance, his dark stare briefly locking onto mine. Without showing any reaction, he looks back up. "You know you don't belong here, Krew. This is the only warning you're going to get. The next time I find out you're on my streets, you won't be leaving alive."

"The offer stands, sweetheart," Krew says.

Click.

My glance shifts upward, and I see the man holding a small black handgun.

"Come on, Krew. We don't need any trouble."

"You should listen to your friend," the man with the gun says.

The door opens. "Let's go."

The man doesn't replace the gun's safety until tires squeal and the sound of a car fades. Then he slides the gun into the holster on his waistband. "You okay, Linz?"

"Yeah," she says. "I don't think he is, though." She points in my direction.

"Who the hell is this?"

"I don't know," she says softly. "He stumbled in a few minutes before they did."

"What's your name?"

"Leopold," I stammer.

"Are you high?"

"Maybe?"

"Get up." He grabs my shirt by the collar, dragging me to my feet.

"He's hurt and needs help," the girl pleads, grabbing his arm.

"I don't want any drug-addicted losers in here—"

"No. Please," I beg. "I can't go back to Krew."

The guy freezes but doesn't let go of the T-shirt. "What are you talking about?"

"He asked me to call someone named Ramiro Vega," she adds.

"Vega? From Safe Haven?" he asks, pinning me with his stare.

I nod.

"Get him into the back room," he instructs the girl. "I have a call to make."

Anthony

Tonight's the grand opening for *Italiano Desiderio.* Owen's outside and has texted me that the line extends down the block and around the corner. We're opening in less than five minutes. I've gathered my staff for a final pep talk before we open the doors.

"It's going to get busy in a few minutes. I've been in your shoes and know the nerves you're experiencing right now," I say as I look at the eager faces of my employees. "I have faith in every one of you. We're going to continue working as a team and show this city what authentic Italian cuisine is all about. Are you ready?" A resounding chorus of yeses and applause fills the room. "Let's do this."

The group disperses to their stations, and I walk to the front doors, opening them wide. "Thank you all for your patience," I address the waiting crowd. "I'd like to welcome you to *Italiano Desiderio.*" I step inside and watch the first of my patrons enter.

I'm thankful for all the familiar faces in the sea of people.

"Congratulations, Tony," Alex shakes my hand. "This place is gorgeous."

"Thank you for coming." I turn to Raina. "Please seat Alex in the back room with my other personal guests."

"Right this way," she says, batting her eyes at him.

"Uncle Tony," Anna calls as she wraps her tiny arms around my waist.

"There's one of my favorite little girls." I swoop her into my arms, making her giggle.

"I can't believe all the people out there," Jennifer says as she kisses my cheek.

"It's unreal." I set Anna down. "I can't believe it's finally happening," I confess.

"I'm so proud of you." Jennifer beams.

Anna tugs on my pant leg. "Mommy says we're on an all-girls date tonight."

"She did, did she?" I chuckle.

"Mhm."

"Where's Chloe?"

"Rachel offered to keep her," Jennifer explains.

"I'll make sure you get an extra scoop of ice cream with your dessert," I whisper, winking at Anna.

"Yay," she cheers and claps her hands.

"Raina," I say when my hostess returns. "Please escort this little princess and her Mom to the back room."

The topic of my involvement in the BDSM lifestyle wasn't on the agenda to discuss with Jennifer. However, I had to spill the beans when Star texted during our afternoon at Chelsea Market, asking for help with the club's food delivery. Reluctantly, I shared everything with Jennifer on our way to the club. To my surprise, she was unfazed by my revelation.

Since then, Jen's gotten to know my closest friends from the club. While she's not interested in the lifestyle, she's open and accepting of all of them—especially Alex. Although he's made it clear, he's not interested in a woman in or out of the lifestyle.

Several hours pass before the line outside dissipates, and the number of diners inside starts to decrease. My team has been troopers. They're exhausted, but they keep pushing and are giving our customers an excellent experience. Owen has also worked tirelessly. He's dedicated the entire night to managing the crowd and engaging with guests waiting for their tables.

"I'd say tonight was an overwhelming success," he says, giving my shoulder a reassuring squeeze.

"I was afraid no one would come out. I'm absolutely stunned," I confess. I'm hit with a familiar sadness. "I just wish Kam were here to see this."

"I have no doubt he is," Owen says with certainty. He gestures to the framed drawing on the wall of the Twin Towers, standing majestically with an angel in an FDNY uniform above them with outstretched arms. "That's a beautiful picture. Who's the artist?"

No one knows that I draw. It's been a secret of mine. I pause for a second before responding. "I am.'"

Owen's eyes grow wide. "I knew you were a master with wax. I had no idea you were a bona fide artist."

A laugh escapes me at his words. "I'm not sure I'd use the term *artist* for myself." I open up to Owen about the art class I'm taking and how it has become a grounding force for me. "I've missed being able to express myself with wax."

"I know things haven't been easy for you since Kam passed," Owen says.

"I have to thank you for the come-to-Jesus talk in the ER. If it wasn't for you, I would've fallen deeper into the black hole I was in."

"I'd like to take all the credit," he smiles, a hint of modesty in his expression. "But all I did was make a suggestion. You've done the rest."

I've been blessed with friends who courageously share the difficult truths. Individuals who supported and loved me through my darkest days. Because of them, I'm standing here tonight as a man who's no longer afraid of what tomorrow may bring.

Anthony

Time was once divided into B.C. and A.D. Now, we distinguish between pre-9/11 and post-9/11. The era of visiting historical monuments without walking through metal detectors is long gone. Boarding a plane is no longer as straightforward as rushing to the gate at the last minute. Passengers must now arrive early at security checkpoints, where they go through the process of removing shoes, emptying pockets, and having bags scanned by high-powered X-ray machines. The world as we once knew it has been irrevocably changed.

September 11, 2002. It's exactly one year since that fateful day when the world lost 2,801 innocent lives. The day I lost Kameron. I've experienced so many emotions in the days leading up to today as I've reminisced about the last days Kam and I spent together and how happy we were.

Last night was one of the hardest nights I've endured. President Bush and his wife, Laura, laid a wreath at Ground Zero. Many of the gathered family members and I had the opportunity to speak with the President and First Lady. It was an emotional night for everyone in attendance.

When I arrived back home, I had a panic attack. I couldn't remember what Kameron's voice sounded like. I feared losing the saved voice messages from him and never being able to hear him speaking to me. What if I forget what he looks like? How his amber eyes sparkled when we were together. It was the first time I called Pastor Andrea and Kelly outside of a group meeting. They spent several hours on the phone helping me feel the feelings but not letting them rule me. Being afraid or sad is okay, but I don't have to stay there.

This morning, Jennifer and I, along with Owen and Star, arrived at Ground Zero with thousands of others to pay tribute to the lives lost as a result of the senseless tragedy. Amidst arriving family and friends of the victims, we reverently place photographs and flowers at the site where the World Trade Center once stood. The haunting notes of Amazing Grace, played by bagpipers, wafts on the breeze, adding a poignant touch to the atmosphere.

Mayor Bloomberg opens the solemn ceremony, pausing for a moment of silence at 8:46 am, the exact time the first plane hit the North Tower. Former Mayor Giuliani begins reading the names of the victims. At 9:03, silence once again falls over the gathered crowd, and bells chime, marking the time the second hijacked plane struck the south tower.

Fifty-six minutes later, bells chime, marking the South Tower's collapse. Finally, at 10:29 am, the moment I've been dreading, we silently memorialize the collapse of the North Tower.

Jennifer grabs my hand for support. Despite my efforts, my heart splits open, and tears flow uncontrollably as Owen and Star wrap us in their protective embrace. The pain is just as visceral today as it was when I stood in my kitchen, Kameron and I expressing our love to one another in his final moments of life.

The reading of the names lasts for almost three hours. As the soul-stirring melody of Taps played on the trumpet drifts through the air, I close my eyes and allow memories to wash over me.

The tingling rush of excitement when I spotted him leaning against the wall, biting his bottom lip, waiting for me the night I met him.

His laughter was an infectious melody that held the power to brighten even the gloomiest of days.

The profound moment when he lowered to his knees, offering me the most precious gift—his submission.

His lips, soft and tender, caressing mine in a whisper of shared intimacy.

An unspoken commitment, a love that saw beyond imperfections, painting a portrait where each perceived flaw was a stroke contributing to the masterpiece of our relationship.

Our promises of forever—cruelly snatched away by a heartless twist of fate.

Until we are reunited again, amore mio.

Leopold

THE DOOR OPENS, AND THE MAN WHO CHASED KREW AWAY returns. In his hands are a hot coffee and a wrapped sandwich

"You look like you could use something to eat," he says as he sets the food on the desk. I eye it warily. "It's sealed. I didn't tamper with it."

Greedily, I grab it, examining it from all angles, before ripping off the wrapper and taking a big bite. My mouth is dry, and I choke when I attempt to swallow.

"The coffee's safe, too," he encourages. When I don't reach for it, he opens the door. "Linz, grab a bottle of water from the cooler, would ya?"

"Sure."

A moment later, she opens the door and passes him the water. "Let me know when Vega gets here," he says and closes the door softly. "Here." He passes me the cold bottle.

"Thank you." I turn the cap, relieved to hear the crack of the plastic seal, and drink half of it in one gulp.

"So, Leopold," he says as he leans against the desk, watching me carefully. "Judging by your reaction to Krew, I take it he's involved in what's going on with you."

I take the last bite of the cold-cut sandwich and lick my fingers so I don't waste even the tiniest crumb.

"With all those marks," he says, pointing to my arms. "I'm going to assume you're a client of his, and he cut you off."

"No. Krew was my boyfriend, or so I thought," I say quietly and then finish the water bottle, hoping it soothes my dry, scratchy throat. "Then something happened. He changed."

"Did he happen to pick you up at *Prism?*" the guy inquires, and I nod. "That's his usual MO."

I try to wrap my head around this new information. "He's done this before?" I ask.

"He has," the man says. "Most of the boys he brings back disappear. How did you get away?"

"I broke the bathroom window. It was the only one without bars," I add.

"You're lucky."

I glance at the door. "Can I have another water?"

"Sure," he says, one side of his mouth lifting in a smile. "I'll be right back."

After the man disappears from the office, I bring my legs onto the chair and wrap the T-shirt around them, trying to generate warmth. My head drops onto my knees, and my eyelids gently droop shut.

The door opening causes me to jump, and I nearly fall off the chair.

"Hey there," the man says, grabbing my arm. "No one's going to hurt you here."

"Where is here, and who are you?" I ask and then slap my hand over my mouth at my brazenness.

"You're fine." He passes me the plastic bottle. "My name's Donnie. This is my store."

Before I can ask any more questions, there's a soft knock on the door. "Who is it?"

"It's me," the female voice says. "Mr. Vega's here."

Donnie opens the office door. "Come on in."

"Leo," Ramiro says, brushing past Donnie and hurrying over to me. "What happened to you?"

"I'll give you two a few minutes. I'm going to lock up the front," Donnie says, then disappears.

"I didn't think you'd come," I whisper, tears streaming down my face.

"Absolutely, I wouldn't hesitate to come," he says, placing neatly folded clothes on the desk. He then envelops me in a protective embrace. "I'm thankful you had them call me." Ramiro let's go and studies my condition. Opening the door, he calls, "Donnie?"

"What do you need?"

"Can I buy some first aid supplies? I want to try to clean him up some."

"You're not buying anything," Donnie says, returning to the office. Opening a cabinet, he pulls out a first aid kit and passes it to Ramiro. "Some of those cuts look deep. He might need stitches."

"No hospital or doctors. I'm fine." I go to stand up, and the room spins. Ramiro catches me and lowers me back onto the chair.

"Take it easy, Leo." He opens the kit and takes out some alcohol pads. "These are going to sting." My hand jerks from his when the cleaner hits my busted knuckles.

Lindsay appears in the doorway. "I can help with that," she offers.

"Thanks, but I've got it."

"Are you still hungry? I can get you something else to eat." She looks at me expectantly.

I nod appreciatively, "Yes, please."

"When's the last time he fed you?" Donnie asks, and I shrug. "This is the last time that bastard is going to do this. I'm going to kill him."

Ramiro finishes putting a bandaid over one of the more minor cuts before addressing Donnie. "I hate the guy as much as you, but killing him is only going to land you in prison. Leo's free. Once I get him cleaned up, I'll call the police and let—"

"For fuck's sake, Vega. The police won't do shit, and you know it."

Ramiro shakes his head and returns his focus to me. "You're shivering. Let's get you dressed, and then you can drink the coffee to warm up." He holds my arm, steadying me as I slide on the soft sweatpants. "Sit down, and I'll help you change your shirt."

"He's not cold," Donnie says, leaning against the wall. "He's going through withdrawal."

"Leo is not an addict," Ramiro says, coming to my defense.

He motions with his chin. "His arms tell a different story."

"Donnie's right," I say, my voice small.

Ramiro's head shoots over to me. "You started using?" he asks in a hushed tone.

"It wasn't by choice," I say, and a fresh wave of tears falls. "Krew kept me drugged, but I haven't had anything all day."

"What else did he do to you?" Ramiro asks.

I look between him and Lindsay, who's standing in the doorway holding a cup of microwave macaroni and cheese.

"Thanks," Donnie says and takes the food. "Can you wait in the store, please?"

"Sure." She looks at me with tears in her eyes. "Let me know if you need anything." Lindsay leaves the room, closing the door softly behind her.

With my head feeling fuzzy and my thoughts challenging to piece together, I do my best to tell them even a little of what happened. While attempting to recall details, my eyes start to close.

"That's enough, Leo. You're exhausted," Ramiro interrupts gently. "Let's get you home."

"Vega, can we talk for a minute?"

I put my head down on the desk as they move to the back corner of the room. Despite my closed eyes, I can hear their hushed conversation.

"Are you bringing him to Safe Haven?"

"He lost his room there, so I can't," Ramiro says quietly. "I'm going to bring him to my house."

"Withdrawal's going to be a bitch. You don't want your wife and kids to see that."

"What else am I going to do?"

"I'll bring him to my place," Donnie offers. "It's not the first time I've seen someone go through withdrawal."

"This kid's been through a lot. Everyone in his life has betrayed him," he explains. "I don't know if he'll go with you."

"In his current condition, he doesn't have much choice."

There's a long pause before Ramiro says, "I'll call my wife and let her know I'm going to be staying at your place for a few nights."

"You sure about that?"

"Positive."

Leopold

Donnie and Lindsay flank my sides as Lindsay holds
the door to the apartment open with her foot. Movement is excruciat-
ing. My muscles are already cramping from the lack of drugs.

"Can you give me something?" I grab Donnie's arm, desperate for
relief. "Anything?"

"The next few days are going to be fucking hell," he says. "If I give
you drugs, it's only going to prolong it."

Sweat drips from my forehead as I shuffle up the concrete steps.

"Where's Ramiro?" I strain to look over my shoulder for the only
person I know I can trust.

"Vega went back to his house to grab a few things," Donnie explains
patiently as he helps me sit on his grey leather sofa." Linsday's getting
the guest room made up for you. I want you to be as comfortable as
possible while you're here."

"Is comfort even going to be possible?" I ask, already knowing the
answer.

"Not at first," he answers frankly. "It'll get better, though."

"Why are you helping me? What do you want?" Skepticism clouds
my judgment. "I hope I didn't offend you."

"No offense taken." He offers me a kind smile. "Make no mistake,

I'm not a good guy. I allow drugs and weapons to be bought and sold on my streets. Some people say I'm worse than Krew. Who knows. Maybe they're right." He shrugs. "But one thing I'll never condone is taking unsuspecting people and using them to further his prostitution and trafficking rings."

"Trafficking?"

"Krew lures in young girls or guys, making them believe he's interested in a relationship," Donnie explains, pausing as I absorb his words. ""Then, he blindsides them and keeps them drugged. Usually, they vanish. You're the exception. I'm hoping you can shed some light on what else happens."

It takes me a few seconds to find the right words. "He said he was inviting friends over. I thought it was for dinner or something, but it was for sex." My body starts trembling again as a wave of nausea washes over me. "Everything happened so fast. I didn't see the needle coming. You have to believe me," I beg as the pain in my temples threatens to split my skull into two. I grab the sides of my head as tears blur my vision.

"How about we pick this up when you're feeling better?" Donnie suggests.

"Okay," I mumble.

"Come on." He helps me to my feet. "Let's get you to your room so you can lie down and try to get some sleep."

※

Sitting up quickly, a moment of disorientation washes over me. The room is filled with screams, and it takes a minute to comprehend that the agonized sounds are coming from me.

"Make it stop," I yell and dig at my arms and legs. "There's so many. Oh my God. Please make them go away."

"It's okay, Leo," Ramiro says gently, attempting to still my fingers that dig into my skin. "There's nothing there."

"Yes, there is," I argue, fighting his hold on me.

"It's just drugs coming out of your system."

"I can feel them." I continue to struggle.

"Your mind is a powerful thing." He tightens his grasp, remaining patient when he says, "But you're stronger than the drugs, Leo. I need you to take some slow, deep breaths and try to relax. Okay?"

⸎

One second, I'm freezing and shivering uncontrollably. The next, I'm trying to rip my clothes off because I'm burning up from the inside out. My body is entirely out of control. Currently, I'm sitting on the bathroom floor, my head hanging over the toilet as I empty what little I've swallowed over the past few days.

"It hurts so badly," I sob.

"I know it does," Donnie says, rubbing small circles on my back.

He and Ramiro have taken turns in my room, ensuring I'm never alone. Lindsay is never far, either. She makes sure they have food, and I have soup and smoothies.

"I can't do this anymore," I say as I slump over on the floor, breathless.

"You can and you will." His tone leaves no room for argument, not that I have the energy to do so. "You have no choice, Leo. Do you hear me? I won't let you give up."

I push my weary body off the floor as my body starts dry-heaving again.

⸎

The notion of a peaceful night's sleep feels like a distant fantasy. Each time I lay down and close my eyes, a restless dance ensues. My muscles protest with painful cramps. Beads of sweat cascade down my body, leaving me shivering once again.

"Lean on me," Lindsay urges as she threads her arm under mine and around my back, helping me from the bed. "You need a dry T-shirt. This one is soaked." Gently, she helped me lift my arms and remove the drenched shirt. "Are you okay with sitting here while I put clean sheets on the bed?"

"You don't have to do this," I confess, my embarrassment evident in my voice as I struggle with my basic needs.

"I know," she says reassuringly, her actions speaking volumes as she wipes my face with a warm washcloth. "I want to help."

"I'd rather you didn't see me like this."

She lets out an amused huff. "Now you sound like Donnie."

"He wants to protect you from the evil in the world."

"I'm not a child," Lindsay protests as she drags the washcloth over my chest. "My boyfriend is the president of a motorcycle gang." She sticks her tongue out at me, trying to lighten the mood.

I try to laugh but end up doubled over with stomach cramps. "I'm sorry," she says, rubbing my back. "Take slow, deep breaths and relax your muscles."

It takes a few minutes for the cramping to subside. Slowly, I slacken my arms and sit back up. "How do you know what to do?"

"I'm a nurse," she admits as she helps me pull a soft T-shirt over my head.

"But you work at a convenience store?"

"I used to work at the ER at Rady Children's Hospital, but the stress got to be too much," she sighs. "Right now, I'm taking a break from it," she explains while she strips the bed. "Donnie owns the store. I'm working there a few days a week while I figure out the direction I want to take next."

"Yet you're here taking care of me while I go through withdrawal. You're an angel."

"Leo," Ramiro says my name as he shakes my shoulder gently. "You need to get up and try to eat."

"How long have I been sleeping?" I ask as I stretch my arms above my head.

"Twelve hours. Give or take a few." He turns the bedside lamp on, illuminating the room in soft lighting.

I throw my legs over the side of the bed. "Why does it feel like it was only an hour or two?"

"The past few weeks have been hard on you," he explains. "Your body's still recovering."

When Donnie said the next few days of my life would be hell, he wasn't exaggerating. Over the past two weeks, my mind and body suffered in ways I never dreamed imaginable. Sweats. Chills. Muscle cramps. Itching. The feeling of bugs crawling over every centimeter of my skin. Nausea. Vomiting.

There were countless instances when the desperation brought me to my knees, begging for more drugs. In those dark moments, the allure of staying addicted seemed preferable to enduring another agonizing second of withdrawal. In those gut-wrenching moments, Donnie's stern talks became my lifeline. He insisted I was stronger than the torment I was enduring.

"I need to ask you something." I look Ramiro in the eye, finally having the courage to ask the question that's been on my mind since the night I was rescued. "Why did Donnie step in to help me? He doesn't know me."

"That's Donnie's story to tell, not mine."

"Are you two coming?" Lindsay pops her head into my room. "The food's going to be cold."

At this precise instant, my stomach makes itself known with a growl. "What's for dinner? I'm starving."

"I'm so happy to hear that." Her face lights up. "Donnie's grilling steaks and I made baked potatoes and fresh broccoli."

"That sounds delicious." I stand and start walking toward the door. "What are we waiting for?"

Anthony

It's a busy night at Fire and Ice tonight. I look out at the club's main room from the door to the kitchen. I've been here all day putting together a new menu and ensuring the new ordering system is all in place and working correctly. Now that everything's in order, I need to find Owen and let him know I'm going home. Between all the hours I'm putting in at *Italiano Desiderio* and the hours I put in at the club's restaurant, I'm ready for an early night.

I wander through the club, stopping to say hi to a few friends before I spot him. "I'm heading out. I wanted to say goodbye before I left."

"Why don't you stick around?" Owen slides the print off of the subs who are looking to play toward me.

"I don't know." It's been over a year since Kam died. I've thought about trying to play with a new sub but haven't taken any steps to do so. In my head, I worry about what people will think. Is it too soon? Has it been too long?

"I'm not suggesting you make a lifelong commitment. Between here and your place, all you do is work. It's okay to take some time to relax and have fun," he encourages. "There are several good-looking men who haven't stopped watching you since you got here."

"Is that so?" Owen has me intrigued, and I skim the list again, paying attention only to names that are looking for a non-sexual scene. Where I'm willing to play, I'm not ready to get *that* involved. "What about this one?" I point to a name on the list. "What do you know about him?"

Owen quickly types the name into his system. "Trevor's been a submissive for ten years and is not interested in being collared. He's bi and is open to playing with one or more partners. Is looking for a sexual or non-sexual scene." He looks up at me. "And he hasn't taken his eyes off you the entire time you've been talking to me." He motions behind me with his chin.

I look over my shoulder to find a man, Trevor, I presume, watching us. My initial thought is he's incredibly handsome. Tall and well-built, not in the chiseled gym workout kind of way, but rather a man who stays fit through physical labor. He's standing with a small group of people, but he's not listening to them. Instead, his eyes are locked with mine.

"Wax play is on his green list," Owen adds, knowing I won't be able to resist.

"Can I reserve a room?" I can't believe the words that just came out of my mouth.

"Room Four is all yours." Owen grins like the Chesire Cat. "Happy playing."

It's been over a decade since I've had a first meeting with a man. My stomach is in knots as I approach the group. "Excuse me, folks." They fall silent, and all heads turn toward me. "Trevor, may I have a word with you?"

"Yes," he answers, and we step off to the side.

"Your name was on the list of submissives looking to scene tonight. Are you still open to that?"

"Yes, sir." His voice is deep and smooth.

I extend my hand to shake his. "I'm Tony."

"You obviously already know I'm Trevor," he remarks, a smile accompanying the handshake.

"Do you have experience with wax?"

"I've participated in a few scenes."

"I'd like to do a wax scene. In a private room," I hesitate before continuing, "There will be no sex. Are you good with that?"

"I'd be honored."

He follows me down the hall. With each step, the music and voices from the main room become quieter. When we reach room four, I swipe my membership card and step inside. I wait until the door clicks closed before continuing the conversation.

"You'll remain partially clothed. I prefer to keep you blindfolded during the scene," I continue in a matter-of-fact tone, ensuring there are enough barriers to prevent any emotions or feelings from creeping in. "Are you in agreement with all of that?"

"I am, Sir."

"I'd prefer you to call me Tony." Trevor's eyebrows raise slightly in confusion. "I don't want any of the labels or power dynamics. Tonight, we're just two men, equals, enjoying a relaxing scene."

"I understand, Tony." He offers me a kind smile that makes his beautiful brown eyes light up.

"Undress down to your underwear. I'll get the candles ready." This room has been designed explicitly for scenes involving wax. Owen and Star keep it stocked with all the necessary supplies. I go to the black lacquered chest of drawers and take out a new set of colored soy candles. They're not the ones I usually use, but I have experience and am comfortable using them.

"What do you do for a living? I ask and watch out of the corner of my eye as Trevor removes his dark green T-shirt, pulling it over his head and folding it neatly before setting it on the table.

"I'm an ironworker," he says as he removes his sneakers before undoing his dark denim jeans and adding them to the pile.

I set the candles on a small table next to the bed. "Do you work in the city?"

"I travel quite a bit with my job," he explains. "I've been in Manhattan the past few weeks, working at Grou—." He abruptly stops.

"You're working at Ground Zero?" I ask and notice the look of apprehension on Trevor's face, so I attempt to clear the air. "I'm sure you know I lost my partner on September 11th."

"I do, and I'm very sorry for your loss."

"Thank you." The familiar ache I feel in my heart when I talk about Kam returns. "You don't have to walk on eggshells, though. I'm okay to talk about it."

"If it's all the same, *I'd* rather not talk about it." A dark shadow crosses his face. "Being there every day is difficult. I need a break from the stress and heavy emotions."

"I can respect that. Lie down on your back." I gesture to the bed. "Let's get started on that relaxation."

While Trevor gets comfortable, I dim the lights and pull up my meditation playlist before returning to the table. "Lift your head." I slide the blindfold in place and then light the first candle.

Slowly, I allow the black wax to drip low on his abdomen, right where his muscles form a v, and dive below the waistband of his boxers. Next, I add grey, drizzling it through the black, creating a dark base.

Even though we're not going to be having sex of any kind, the scene wouldn't be complete without exploring the sensual aspects of hot wax. Taking a dark blue candle, I move higher and allow it to drip over Trevor's nipples. He inhales sharply.

I continue covering his muscular chest, creating a dark and stormy sky.

Creating art on a person is something I love to do. It's an extension of who I am, and it's been missing this past year. Although it feels good to be back in my element, something about this feels off. Kameron and I shared a special connection. We were in love. Words weren't necessary between us. His breaths naturally synched with my movements. Even blindfolded, he could sense my every step. This, tonight, feels stilted— wrong.

I struggle to not let my internal conflict affect Trevor's experience. He communicated the stress he's trying to escape, and I want to be able to give him that. I pause briefly and refocus my thoughts before continuing to work on my living canvas.

Going into this scene, I didn't have a plan for the design. I allowed the music and the mood to dictate my art. The product is a striking scene. The sky is a tumultuous mix of blues as if it's angry. Below it, blacks and greys resemble a pile of rubble—twisted steel. I'm taken back by the darkness.

"I'm going to set a candle on your chest. I need you to stay very still."

"Okay."

The candle adds the necessary light and hope to an otherwise bleak picture.

"Do you mind if I take a few pictures before I remove the wax?"

"I don't mind at all."

Grabbing my phone, I snap photos from several angles, being sure to capture every aspect of the design. "Are you ready?"

"To be honest, no," Trevor laughs softly.

After extinguishing the candle, I start lifting the wax from his torso. My hands skate across his skin, and although I notice the erection tenting his boxers, I choose to ignore it. "I think I got everything," I say as I finish wiping his chest.

"Would I be able to have a copy of the pictures?"

"Of course. What's your number? I'll text them to you." Trevor tells me his number, and I attach the photos to a message and hit send.

An awkward silence fills the room as Trevor gets dressed. This isn't like any scene I've ever done. I've broken many rules by not having a more in-depth conversation about experience and limits.

What do I do now? Typically, I'd give aftercare, but since I dismissed our roles as a Dominant and submissive, I don't think that's the proper next step. Shaking hands and parting ways doesn't seem right either.

"These are incredible," Trevor says as he scrolls through the pictures. "Thank you again, Tony. This was exactly what I needed."

"I'm glad you had a good time." I continue cleaning up the candles, still debating what my next move should be.

Trevor steps up next to me. "Can I help you with this?"

"I've got it."

"Tony." Trevor places his hand on my arm. "Please let me clean up. It's the least I can do."

I take a deep breath before stepping out of his way. "I appreciate it."

I watch as he collects the remaining candles and strips the waterproof sheet off the bed.

After he finishes sweeping up, he comes over to where I'm sitting. "I think I got it all," he says and pauses. He looks around nervously before continuing, "If that's everything, I'll just head out."

"Have a good evening." I nod and watch as he walks toward the door. An internal battle rages within me, debating whether to muster the courage to stop him. I don't want to lead him on, but I also know I shouldn't let him leave like this. I jump up just as he reaches for the handle. "Wait." He pulls his hand back and turns to face me. "Do you want to grab something to eat?"

"I'd like that a lot."

Anthony

down the busy New York City street to a small but busy restaurant a few blocks away. I debated staying at Fire and Ice but knew everyone would be watching and wondering if something was developing between us. I didn't want to put Trevor or myself under that much pressure.

We're sat in a cozy booth. Our server comes over right away and we order our drinks. I'm perusing the menu when Trevor abruptly sets his down and admits hurriedly, "I apologize for my body's reaction at the end of the scene. I know you said nothing sexual, and I went and did that."

I set my menu down. "Please don't apologize."

His shoulders drop as he speaks. "My lack of self-control made things uncomfortable."

"I didn't see it as a lack of anything. Wax scenes are inherently sensual." I stop talking when I see the server approaching. We give our orders. I wait until we're alone before continuing, "Your arousal was natural. I wish I could've offered you more."

"I wasn't expecting more. I knew exactly—"

I hold up my hand, interrupting him. "Please let me apologize." Trevor's eyebrows draw together in confusion. "I'm an experienced

Dominant, and I handled tonight entirely wrong. You deserved more—better than what I gave you."

"May I say something?" he asks, waiting for my approval. "You stated the expectations clearly, and I accepted your offer with the understanding that it wouldn't be a typical scene."

"You're being too gracious." Our food is brought to the table, pausing our conversation once again. We begin eating in silence. I don't want the rest of the evening to continue as awkward as it feels right now. Trying to lighten the mood, I say, "Tell me about yourself."

"I'm originally from upstate New York," he says, then explains that he enlisted in the Army right after high school graduation. "My plan was to be career military, but life had other ideas in mind for me, and I retired two years ago."

"May I ask why?"

"My sister, Lisa, was in the wrong place at the wrong time," he says, his voice cracking from emotion. "She was shot in a drive-by."

"I'm so sorry."

"She left behind a six-month-old baby girl, Paisley." He closes his eyes for a moment. "I was stationed in South Korea when I got the call."

Before losing Kameron, I never paid attention to or considered just how many people have suffered significant losses and are walking around with pieces of their hearts missing.

"That must've been awful."

"I've never felt so helpless." He blinks back tears. "Knowing Paisley was here alone, and I was halfway across the world." Trevor must sense my confusion because he explains further. "Paisley's father walked when he found out Lisa was pregnant. It took ten days for me to get back here. Thankfully, my SO was able to pull some strings, and Paisley was able to stay with his wife back on base until I got home."

"I'm sure that was a small relief for you."

"It was. Even though Paisley didn't know them, at least I knew she was being cared for until I could get to her."

I smile. "So, now you're raising a little girl."

"I am." Trevor beams as he grabs his phone and turns the screen toward me. "She's two and a half now."

I look at the picture of a beautiful blonde-haired, green-eyed little girl smiling at the camera, hugging a stuffed animal. "She gorgeous."

"She's become my whole world."

The longing to be a parent tugs at my heart. "I can imagine."

"It's been a huge adjustment. My job requires a lot of travel, so I had to hire a nanny I could trust to move around with us. That's who's with her tonight." He sets his phone down. "I don't go out much these days. But Andrea, Paisley's nanny, insisted I take a night to myself."

"I haven't gone out much since Kameron passed." I look up at Trevor. "But I'm glad I went to the club tonight."

We enjoy more pleasant conversation while we finish dinner. By the end of the evening, I find myself hating to see it end.

After settling our check, we go back outside. It's late, and the heavier crowds have dispersed, leaving only a few people walking about. "I had a great time tonight."

"So did I." Trevor pauses, looking uncertain. "I'm leaving to go back home in the morning. But I'll be back in the city after Christmas. I'm wondering if you'd be open to seeing each other again?" I felt nothing toward him when we were doing the scene and find I'm at a loss for a reply. "I'm sorry," he apologizes quickly. "I shouldn't have asked that. You made it clear this was a one-time thing." He tries to wave me off.

"It's okay," I assure him, placing my hand on his arm. "I have to be honest. I don't know if I'm ready for another relationship, but I'm open to keeping in touch," I respond, wondering if putting more effort into this might spark attraction. Perhaps I'm just out of practice.

"I'd like that very much." He offers me a dazzling smile.

We part ways as Trevor heads back to his hotel, and I return to my apartment. Alone.

Leopold

DINNER WAS FANTASTIC. IT MARKED THE FIRST TIME I COULD eat without the constant fear of vomiting. Despite not wanting to ruin the positive vibes, there's a pressing question that's been on my mind. "What happens next? I know I can't go back to Safe Haven. Donnie and Lindsay have been generous in opening their home to me," I convey my gratitude. "But I know I can't stay here forever."

"You're welcome to stay with us as long as you need," Donnie adds.

"Leo's right," Ramiro interjects, setting his fork down. "We need to have a serious conversation about where he goes from here. I tried appealing to the board at Safe Haven, but they were resistant to making an exception and letting you back before the six months are up."

"I thought that program was yours," Donnie adds, annoyed.

"It is. But we have a board of directors who oversees policies and decision-making," Ramiro explains.

"He can't go back out there alone," Lindsay says panicked.

"We're not letting him go anywhere on his own." Donnie takes her hand, placing a gentle kiss on it.

"My biggest concern is that Safe Haven's in Krew's territory. Even if he came back..." Ramiro's voice trails off.

"There's room in our building. He can stay with my guys." Donnie leans forward, resting his elbows on the table. "They'll make sure he's safe, but he'll have to stay confined to my neighborhood."

"Having your movement restricted and always feeling the need to look over your shoulder is no way to live." Ramiro sits back in his chair and sighs loudly.

"Hello." I wave my hand. "You two are talking about me like I'm not here."

"Sorry about that," Donnie apologizes with a slight shrug.

I look between the two men who are trying to decide my future right in front of me. "Don't I get a say in where I go?"

"For once, Vega's right," Donnie admits, tapping on the table.

"Can you say that again?" Ramiro holds his hand to his ear and laughs.

The banter between Ramiro and Donnie suggests they've known each other longer than the past few weeks. A subtle undercurrent suggests they might not be exactly friends.

Donnie narrows his eyes at Ramiro. "Don't push it, Vega."

"You're not going to like my suggestion, Leo." Ramiro shifts his attention to me. "I think it would be best for you to relocate."

"Leave San Diego?" My stomach sinks.

"Leave California," Ramiro says cautiously.

For a moment, I'm too stunned to speak. "And go where?"

"I reached out to some contacts I have in Manhattan," he says cautiously.

I nearly choke on a mouthful of water. "As in, New York City?"

Ramiro explains this couple runs a program similar to Safe Haven and that he's already contacted them to see if they'd be able to help. "They have an opening in one of their group apartments," he finally says.

"Group apartments?" I question, a noticeable hesitation creeping into my voice. "What does that mean?"

"Instead of having one building where you get a room, they own several properties around the city. You'll share an apartment with a few roommates who are also in the program," Ramiro explains, with a measured tone indicating thoughtful consideration. "They offer significantly discounted rent to the young people in their program."

I listen carefully to what he's saying. "There are four people in an apartment, and there are no co-ed living spaces," he adds. "They also have connections with employers in the city who prioritize giving people in their program a first chance at any job openings."

I was born and raised in Rolling Hills. It was all I knew until my parents dumped me at Walking in the Light. San Diego took a lot of getting used to, but at least I was in California. I was starting to put roots down for myself.

Now, because of the mess I made getting involved with Krew, I'm faced with leaving everyone and everything I know to start over on the East Coast. I want to be mad. To scream and fight. Heck, I'll even beg. How dare they tell me I have to leave? I sigh in resignation, knowing there's nothing I can do. There's no one to blame for this. No one other than myself.

"Oh," I say quietly.

Donnie eyes me carefully before saying, "You don't have to decide anything tonight. Let's get you back on your feet before you make any major life plans."

Ramiro's phone chimes. He checks it before saying, "It's my wife. I promised her I'd be home tonight." He shifts his focus to me. "As long as you're comfortable here without me."

"Of course," I smile, hoping to hide the tumultuousness churning just below the surface. Ramiro's already given up enough for me. I can't ask him to do anything more.

"Can I talk to you about something before you leave?" Lindsay asks Ramiro.

"Sure," He gets to his feet. Giving me a final glance, he says, "I'll give you a call tomorrow."

I nod and watch as Linsday walks outside with him, leaving Donnie and me alone in the house.

"You okay?" he asks, running his hand over his face. "That was a shit ton of information to swallow."

Am I okay? I'm numb. It's like I'm watching a movie about someone else's life. Except it's not a movie. It's real life, and I'm the star. "I guess." I shrug. "It's not like I have any choice."

"I'll admit, your options are limited, but you always have a choice."

He motions toward the door. "If you don't like what Vega's suggesting, we'll figure out something better."

I gather the dinner plates and bring them to the sink. "His offer is very generous." I turn around and force a smile. "It's a chance to start over." Donnie crosses his arms over his. "Have you ever been to New York?" I ask him.

"Me? No." He shakes his head.

"I'll be sure to let you know what it's like there."

Leopold

I HAD HOPED FOR MORE TIME, BUT ONCE RAMIRO MADE THE call, I was given no more than two weeks to get to New York and complete the intake into the program before I'd lose my place. Getting me ready for my cross-country move has been the top priority.

None of Krew's *clients* used protection, so one of the many things on my to-do list was blood work to make sure I was clean. Donnie and Lindsay brought me earlier this week. The results came back yesterday. I got lucky, and I'm okay.

Ramiro has been more than generous, ensuring that not only do I have a safe place to go but that I have clothes to go with. He and his wife purchased me a small wardrobe of clothes to get me started. They also included a winter coat and boots—clothing items I've never owned or considered needing. They also purchased me a bus ticket, which was the last thing I needed to leave for New York later tonight.

I'm stuffing my clothes into my new black duffel bag when Donnie appears in my doorway. "Do you mind if I come in?" he asks.

"Of course not."

He enters the room and takes a seat on the chair, the same one that he and Ramiro occupied for countless hours while the effects of the drugs leaving my body attempted to overwhelm me.

I stop what I'm doing and turn to him. "There's something I've been wondering about."

"Okay," he says and sits back, his legs spread.

"How do you and Ramiro know each other?"

His eyes take on a far-away look before he says, "I didn't come from upstanding people. The sperm donor, whoever he was, didn't stick around. The woman who gave birth to me, well, that's the only credit I can give her. Hell, most days, I wished she'd aborted me. In many ways, it would've been kinder." I pull my legs onto the bed while I listen to his story.

"My mother was a drug-addicted whore who had a revolving door of men in her bed. Anything to get her next fix," he adds. "It was a wonder I survived my early childhood years. By the time I was thirteen, she was rarely around anymore," he says. "Child Welfare Services showed up one day and took me away. They relocated me to an upscale neighborhood with a two-parent family and a new *brother* that was my age."

"Ramiro," I say quietly, and Donnie nods.

"Within an hour of my arrival, his parents brought me for a haircut and purchased a new wardrobe so I'd fit in with their fancy friends. Couldn't have the foster child from the city making them look bad," he says with a touch of sarcasm." Before I knew it, we were in front of a judge, and they were adopting me." I try hard not to react to his bomb-shell. Donnie crosses his legs before continuing. "I didn't harbor any notions about going back to my biological mother, but I also didn't want to be adopted—not that anyone asked my opinion. I hated them," he states matter-of-factly. "I made it my life's mission to make their lives hell. A punishment for adopting me."

Donnie continues, "I'd sneak out at night looking for trouble. The funny thing is when you're looking for it, you'll always find it. I started stealing and running drugs. I was sloppy, though, and ended up in juvie." He chuckles. "They were there to bail me out and brought me back home to love me through it. I didn't want to be loved, though. So, I scaled up my behaviors at home and school—when I bothered to show up. Things went downhill fast when they found a gun in my room."

"Why did you have a gun?" I ask, my chin resting on my hands.

"I joined a gang," he says matter-of-factly. "Alfonso, Ramiro's father, lost his shit on me. He'd brought in the wooden paddle, but before he could use it, Ramiro started screaming in the other room. Ella, his mother, had collapsed. They brought her to the emergency room and found out she had a heart attack. The doctors denied that stress had anything to do with it, but I knew." He runs his fingers through his hair. "Alfonso didn't leave her side while she was recovering in the hospital. That's when Vega and I had a fight."

"A physical fight?" I ask, unable to picture Ramiro being violent with anyone.

"Yes. It wasn't much of one, though. Vega's strong suit is not fighting," He grins. "I landed a few hits and broke his nose. He was lying on the floor, curled in a ball. I thought it was over and stepped over him to walk away. Then, I heard the safety of my gun click off. I spun around and found him pointing it at my head."

I'm invested in his story and inquire, "How did he get your gun?"

"Like I said, I was sloppy. I left it out in my room. Vega was extremely protective of his mother, and he became desperate. He grabbed the gun and threatened to kill me if I didn't agree to leave and never come back." My mouth hangs open in shock, unable to picture Ramiro doing something so extreme. "He didn't have to ask me twice. Not because I was afraid of him, but because I didn't want to be there anyway."

"How old were you?"

"It was my sixteenth birthday. But with everything going on, no one remembered," Donnie admits. For the briefest of seconds, I see the look of disappointment on his face, but he quickly schools his features. "I grabbed my bag and a few pieces of my shit and never looked back."

"I can't believe he was that cruel," I mumbled, disappointed in the man I look up to as a mentor—a father figure.

"Vega wasn't cruel. He did what he had to do to protect his parents," he says without hesitation. "I didn't see or hear from him again for many years. Not until Ella was dying. Vega came looking for me because her last wish was to have her two boys back together again."

"How did he know where to find you?"

"Vega was here in San Diego. He opened Safe Haven a few months prior, and I was making a name for myself in other circles. One afternoon, he showed up on my corner and told me I had to go with him." He laughs at the memory. "You had to see his face with more than one weapon pointed at him."

I can't help the quiet chuckle that escapes, picturing Ramiro trying to force Donnie to do anything. "Did you go with him?"

"It was the least I could do for all the shit I put them through. They were good people who really cared about me, and I was a fucking punk who tried to derail their lives." He shifts uncomfortably in his seat. "We got to the hospice with enough time to promise her that Vega and I would make amends and would take care of each other. Alfonso passed away a year before, and Vega had no other family. I couldn't say no to a dying woman, so I agreed," he says softly.

"Even though we don't have the best relationship, I understand he's a good guy who's trying to make a difference." He shrugs. "Maybe that was part of the problem all along. I knew he was a much better person than I'd ever be."

"I don't think that's true," I interrupt. "Anyone who takes in a stranger and nurses them through withdrawal can't possibly be a bad person."

"We're going to have to agree to disagree, kid." Donnie smiles. "Anyway, I came in here to give you this." He reaches into his pocket and pulls out a wad of folded cash.

My eyes grow wide. "I can't take that."

"I might not have ever visited the place, but I can tell you that New York's expensive. You'll need some cash until you get on your feet." He pushes the money into my hand.

"I don't know how I can ever repay you for everything you've done for me." I'm beginning to get emotional, and my voice cracks.

Donnie stands, and I swear I see him quickly wipe under his eye. "You're a good kid, Leo. Go to New York and do something great with your life. Make a difference."

He doesn't wait for my reply before walking out of the room. I sit stunned not only at the history between Donnie and Ramiro but also at the two thousand dollars in cash he left me with.

Before I know it, Ramiro arrives to bring me to the bus station.

Lindsay sobs as I hug her goodbye. Donnie stands off to the side, his arms tightly crossed over his chest. Catching his eye, he nods subtly, prompting me to respond with a warm, understanding smile, conveying my gratitude for everything he's done for me.

"Ready to go?"

I can't hold back my tears any longer, and I fear if I don't leave now, I'll change my mind, so I hurry out the door without looking back.

With a heavy heart, I am closing the book on the only life I've ever known. A surge of fear accompanies a small but tangible excitement as I set my sights on the uncertain path that lies ahead for me in the bustling landscape of the Big Apple.

Anthony

ITALIANO DESIDERIO HAS QUICKLY BECOME *THE* PLACE TO eat in lower Manhattan. Since our opening, we've hosted more stars than I can count. Our reservations are booked out for the next six months. I never imagined my restaurant would reach this level of success ever, let alone in its first year.

The reality of owning a restaurant is far from glamorous. It's a continuous effort. Managing staff to meet a standard I can be proud of requires long hours and dedication. Tonight was exceptionally busy, so I joined my kitchen staff to stay on top of orders. The experience was both invigorating and exhausting, capturing the essence of the demanding yet fulfilling nature of the job.

The employees left over an hour ago. I stayed to catch up on some paperwork. No longer able to focus, I decide to call it a night. After doing a final walk-through, I switch off the lights and am about to lock up when my phone rings. I glance down, a smile coming to my face when I see it's Jennifer.

"Hello."

A sob-filled voice responds, "It's me."

My pulse shoots up instantly. "What's wrong?"

"I just got a call. My mom fell again," she says and stops to blow her nose. "Her neighbor hadn't seen her in a few days and tried to call her. When Mom's answering machine kept picking up, she decided to go over. She knocked, but Mom didn't come to the door."

Jennifer's mom lives alone in a two-story home entirely too big and dangerous for an eighty-three-year-old woman. She's had several falls in the past six months. Jenn's begged her to either move to the city with her or into an assisted living facility, but her mother refused. As a compromise, Jennifer hired home health aides, but her mother is challenging to deal with, and they all quit after a few weeks. She's been at her wit's end as to what to do.

"Is she okay?"

"I don't know." She starts crying again. "Apparently, she called 911. The police and fire department came and had to break a window to get into the house. They're on the way to the emergency room now."

"What can I do?"

"I know it's late, but can you come here?" she asks.

"I'm getting on the train now. I'll be there as soon as I can."

I arrive at her house about twenty minutes later. When I walk in, she's on the phone with the hospital.

"How long will she be in the hospital?" She asks. "Yes, I understand. Thank you, doctor."

Jen sets the phone on her kitchen counter and drops her head into her hands.

"What did they say?" I ask, putting my arm around her for support.

"Mom fell down the stairs. From the looks of it, she was there for a few days. They have her on fluids for dehydration. She had five stitches for a gash on her forehead, and she fractured her ankle. Thankfully, there are no internal injuries." She drops onto a stool at the island in her kitchen. "I can't keep doing this, Tony. Without being there full-time, I can't keep her safe."

Jenn and I have become close friends over the past few years. We've been there for one another as we've healed from our losses. I've been privileged to be a part of her girls' lives and have watched them grow. I've also had a front-row seat as Jennifer struggled with how to deal with her ailing mother's health.

Over the past year, she's traveled back and forth as much as possible.

The girls and she spent the summer in Pennsylvania. But now that Anna's starting kindergarten, she can't pick up and go whenever her mom needs something. It's added a significant amount of stress to her already burdened shoulders.

"After Mom's last accident, I met with a realtor," she admits, crestfallen. "I'm sorry. I should've told you sooner."

I try to mask my surprise. "You don't owe me any explanations."

"I know, but we're friends," she says, wiping her eyes. "Selling this house breaks my heart. Jeff and I started our family here. It's the only place I feel close to him. At the same time, my mother needs me."

"You'll take Jeff with you wherever you go," I say and take her hands. "As much as I'll hate your leaving, you need to do what's best for you and the girls."

"There's been a lot of interest in the property already. It won't take long for it to sell," she adds, and again, I'm shocked at how much effort she's already put into moving. Jennifer looks down at where our hands are joined before continuing, "It's going to be so hard on the girls. Everything they know is here."

"It'll be an adjustment, but kids are resilient." I offer her a reassuring smile. "They'll be okay."

She picks up her phone and opens a web browser. "I have to find plane tickets. The doctor said she'll be in the hospital for a few days, but I want to get there as soon as possible."

Knowing Jennifer and the girls are leaving for good is an emotional blow I wasn't expecting. But I can't wallow in self-pity. She's struggling and needs me to be strong for her. "What can I do to help?"

"Can you stay the night and help me explain everything to the girls in the morning?"

"Of course."

Anna and Chloe are up with the sun and excited to go on an airplane to visit their Nana. Jennifer tries to explain that they'll be moving to Pennsylvania. However, the girls are still young, and I don't think they completely grasped the concept.

Jenn and I spent the better part of the day packing suitcases they'll take on their flight and packing a few boxes filled with things she and the girls will need right away that I'll take to the shipping center.

The adults are exhausted when we're finally piling into our Uber on the way to JFK. Jenn stares out the window, swiping at her eyes. I attempt to keep the girls distracted, giving her some time to sit with her emotions. It also keeps my mind off the fact that I'll miss them all terribly.

"The realtor said we can handle everything online," Jenn says, pulling herself together as the airport comes into view. "I'll have to hire a moving company to pack the house and get our stuff to Clearfield."

"You know I'll be here to help with whatever I can," I say as I grab the suitcases out of the trunk.

"You have enough on your plate with the restaurant." She clicks the handle into the up position on a Disney princess suitcase. "Anna, I need you to take this."

"Are you coming too?" Chloe asks, looking up at me with her big blue eyes.

And I thought my heart couldn't break anymore. "No, Chloe Bear." I scoop her into my arms. "Uncle Tony has to stay here."

"Will you come visit us?" Anna asks, pushing out her bottom lip.

"Of course I will." I grab Chloe's bag with my free hand. "Come on. If we don't get moving, you'll miss your flight."

We keep Anna between us as she wheels her pink princess suitcase through the busy airport. Jennifer talks about everything and nothing, something she does when she's nervous, until we stop at the security checkpoint. Jennifer takes Chloe's hand when I set her down.

"I guess this is where we say goodbye," Jennifer says with tears in her eyes.

"How about we say see you later instead?" I suggest, unable to say goodbye.

"I like that better." She manages to force a smile. "Give Uncle Tony hugs."

Getting down to Anna's level, she wraps her tiny arms around my neck. "Will you come to see us soon?" she asks, her bottom lip quivering.

"As soon as I can," I say and kiss her forehead.

I move to Chloe, who gives me a big kiss on my cheek. "I love you, Uncle Tony," she says, looking back at me and waving from the other side of the checkpoint.

I wait until they're out of sight before returning to the waiting Uber.

Loneliness overwhelms me as I sit in the back of the much quieter car. I drop my head onto the seat behind me. I'm tired of saying goodbye.

When will the universe bring someone into my life and, this time, allow them to become a permanent part of my story?

Anthony

I'M AWAITING MY MIDWEEK FOOD DELIVERY AT *Italiano Desiderio*. Unfortunately, winter limits my ability to cultivate more than a few herbs inside the restaurant. Thankfully, one of the perks of living in Manhattan is the availability of high-quality fresh groceries.

A gust of cold air blows through the restaurant when the front door opens. The delivery guy is precariously balancing several boxes.

"Let me give you a hand with those." I hurry over and grab the top box.

"Thanks," he says from buried beneath his scarf. "It's freezing out there."

"It's certainly a chilly one today." I set the box down and follow him outside to grab another one. It's only mid-November, and we're already getting a taste of what winter will bring. "You're not Joey," I remark. "Are you new?"

"Yes and no," he says, setting the last box on the stainless-steel kitchen counter. After peeling his scarf open, he says while removing his gloves, "I usually work in the stock room, but Joey quit without notice, so I'm doing the deliveries today."

"I'm Tony." I extend my hand, the warmth of the room contrasting with the cool touch of my skin.

"Leopold." He smiles, the corners of his lips curving with an inviting charm as he shakes my hand.

At that moment, an instant attraction sparks within me, a magnetic pull that lingers in the air, though I'm unsure if he senses it, too.

With a tactful retreat of my hand, I offer, "It's nice to meet you, Leopold." I test the feel of his name on my lips. "Do you have time for a quick coffee? It'll warm you up before you have to go back out," I say, glancing outside at the gentle snow that's begun falling.

A moment of hesitation flickers across his face as he bites his lower lip before answering, "Sure. That'd be great."

"Grab a seat while I go get it."

While I busy myself making two cups of espresso, I can't help watching as Leopold unzips his dark green puffy jacket, draping it over the back of the chair. Then, he removes his beanie and shakes out his shoulder-length wavy blond hair. He's an attractive young man. Note the *young* Anthony and quit staring at the guy. I mentally chastise myself.

However, I can't shake the overwhelming desire to do something nice for him—to care for him. Looking around, I spot the cannoli I just finished filling. With the dessert in one hand and the espresso in the other, I bring them to where he's sitting.

When he spots the sweet treat, his ice-blue eyes light up. "Thanks," he says and doesn't waste a second picking up the pastry and taking a bite. His eyes close as he moans, and God help me. The sound stirs something in me that hasn't felt alive in a very long time. "Mmm. This tastes like heaven."

A smile plays on my lips as I say, "I'm glad you like it."

"Like it?" He meets my gaze. "I love it." His tongue licks at some stray powdered sugar from his lower lip, and I force myself to look away. "Are you the manager here?" he asks.

"I'm a little of everything," I laugh softly. "This is my place."

"Oh wow. That's really awesome." His voice is filled with awe. "I can't imagine being able to own my own business," he says as he continues eating.

Some days, I still can't believe that not only is this place mine, but it's also hugely successful. "I did my fair share of working for other people. This was a long time in the making," I say as I grab my cup off the bar and return to the table. "If having your own business is your dream, I have no doubt you'll achieve it."

"I'll have to take your word on that." He wipes his mouth and pushes the chair back to stand. "I should be getting back. Where can I put these?"

"Leave them there. I'll take care of it."

"Thanks for the snack," he says as he hurries to grab his coat.

I can't help but chuckle watching this kid bundle up like we're in the Arctic. "Not a fan of the cold?"

"I wasn't made for winter," he says as he tucks his blond locks back into his hat. "I much prefer the heat and sun."

"Where are you from, Leopold?"

"You can call me Leo," he says, gracing me with a smile. "I'm from California."

"You're a long way from home."

"Tell me about it," he mumbles.

Something about Leo has me scrambling to find a way to keep him here longer. "What brought you to the East Coast?"

He wraps his scarf over his face before responding, "Looking to try something new. I guess." He shrugs. "Can you sign this for me?"

"Sure." I grab a pen from the hostess station and scribble my name on the bottom.

He pulls them apart and hands me the top copy. "Thanks again for the coffee and snack."

"Anytime."

Leo walks out of my restaurant, looking like the weight of the world is on his shoulders, and I'm left with a longing to fix it all for him.

Leopold

Getting out of the stockroom to make each day's deliveries is the most exciting thing that's happened in my otherwise dull and lonely life since I've been in New York City.

Ramiro's friends claimed their program was similar to Safe Haven, but that couldn't be further from the truth. Safe Haven offered so much more than just a roof over my head. Ramiro and the rest of the staff were invested in helping us make something more of ourselves. We were assigned the responsibility of earning our GEDs and were then encouraged to apply for post-secondary education. Job training and assistance securing employment were provided so we could each experience the pride and satisfaction of earning a paycheck.

The residential side of the program offered support by teaching us things like how to cook and do laundry—skills most people take for granted but that many of us were never taught. I didn't realize how good things were there until it was too late.

This program, and I use the word program loosely, is no more than subsidized housing and a packet of papers with a list of places to apply for a job. The vast majority of the businesses listed were no longer operating, which made finding a job challenging.

The apartment is a barely habitable space I share with three other men. We're crammed into one bathroom and two bedrooms. I'm lighter than my roommate, so I got lucky and was assigned the top bunk.

My roommates had lived together for several months before I arrived and were already tight with each other. They have little interest in doing anything other than playing video games or trading stories of the women they're sleeping with. Once they found out I was gay, something that only took about thirty seconds, they'd made up their minds to not include me in anything. When the weather's nice, I try to spend as little time there as possible.

I'm exceedingly thankful for the extra cash Donnie gave me before I left San Diego. He wasn't kidding when he said things were expensive here. The job at the market only pays minimum wage. It's about the best a kid with no high school diploma or GED can expect. My paycheck, combined with the money from Donnie, barely covers my share of the rent and utilities, leaving little extra to buy my own groceries—which the other guys always manage to eat. I'd love to move out, but I'm barely affording this dump with three roommates. There's no way I'd be able to afford anything else.

It's just my luck that my promotion comes during winter when the sun teases from the sky, giving the allure of warmth, but it's actually frigid. The cold air whips off the harbor as I load the boxes into the back of the taxi. Since Joey, the regular delivery guy, left my boss in a lurch, he's desperate today and is paying my taxi fare.

"Are you in there, Leopold?" Jerry, my boss, asks, looking closer at me.

"It's freezing out here." I pull my hat down further.

Jerry laughs. "It's only November. What are you going to do when it really gets cold?"

"I might not come back out until Spring." I grin, although he can't see it beneath my heavy scarf.

Although my job doesn't pay much, my boss is terrific. Jerry's had his market for over forty years. He and his late wife have been very good to me since I came here. They never had children, so they kinda took me under their wing. Now that Esther's gone, Jerry's my only friend in this otherwise lonely and unfamiliar city.

"Here's your inventory slip." Jerry hands me a handwritten invoice.

Even though most of the other employees keep telling him he needs to upgrade to a computer system, he refuses. They poke fun at him for being a dinosaur, but I find it endearing. "Be sure to give this to whoever receives the order. They need to sign here." He shows me with a shaky hand. "Give them the white paper and bring the pink one back to the store."

"That's easy enough."

"You're a good kid, Leopold." He squeezes my shoulder.

Jerry watches while I continue loading boxes into the trunk of the car. "Go on back inside," I say, but he waves me off. "You're going to get sick out here with no coat." I shake my head at his sheer stubbornness. It isn't until I'm sliding into the back seat of the yellow cab that Jerry finally goes back inside.

Twenty minutes later, the cabby is screeching to a stop outside *Italiano Desiderio.*

"Here goes nothing," I say, earning a curious glance from the driver. "As soon as I unload, you can go." It might be cold, but I don't want Jerry to have to pay for my ride back to the shop. It's only a little over a mile. I can walk.

Grabbing two boxes from the opened trunk, I balance them on one arm and reach to open the door.

"Let me give you a hand with those." I hear the voice but don't see a face until he takes the top box.

"Thanks," I say, thankful my face is hidden beneath the scarf. Otherwise, he might've noticed my mouth hanging open. This man is older, but he's seriously gorgeous. He stands shorter than me by about five or six inches. But it's his eyes that strike me most—they're dark and incredibly kind. I try not to stare but fail miserably.

"Thanks. It's freezing out there," I add, a chill running through me, but I'm unsure if it's from the cold air or the man standing next to me.

"It's certainly a chilly one today," he says before following me back outside to grab the rest of the boxes.

What's with these New Yorkers going out in this weather without a coat on? They're all crazy.

"You're not Joey," he says while I'm reaching into the trunk. "Are you new?"

"Yes and no," I reply, hastily placing the last and heaviest box on one of the counters in the restaurant's kitchen. I remove my gloves, tucking them into my coat pocket, and loosen my scarf. "I usually work in the stock room, but Joey quit without notice, so I'm doing the deliveries today."

"I'm Tony," he introduces himself, extending a hand.

"Leopold," I breathe, feeling a magnetic pull as our hands connect, a subtle yet electric current passing between us.

"It's nice to meet you, Leopold." The look on his face does funny things to my insides. "Do you have time for a quick coffee? It'll warm you up before you have to go back out there."

I start to open my mouth to respond but quickly close it. I promised myself not to be as naive or foolish as I've been in the past. To be more cautious with those who show kindness. Then, I stop myself. This guy isn't asking me to marry him. He's simply being friendly and offering me coffee because it's cold out. I take a deep breath and try to relax. "Sure. That'd be great."

"Grab a seat while I go get it," he says, disappearing into the kitchen.

I remove my jacket and put it over the back of the dark wood chair. Then, I pull off my hat and gently shake out my hair before sitting down. While I wait, I look around and take in the restaurant. It looks like a scene straight out of Italy.

A few minutes later, Tony comes out of the kitchen with a plate in one hand and a small glass mug in the other. He sets the dish in front of me, and my mouth waters. Although I've been careful to live as frugally as possible, going without many creature comforts, the money Donnie gave me is almost gone. I had a leftover slice of pizza for breakfast but haven't eaten since, so this is a welcome surprise. "Thanks," I say and sink my teeth into the cannoli. I'm not an expert, but I'm confident this is freshly made. My eyes close. "Mmm. This tastes like heaven."

"I'm glad you like it." he smiles.

"Like it." My eyes meet his. "I love it." I take another bite and lick the powdered sugar off my bottom lip. "Are you the manager here?"

"I'm a little of everything." He laughs softly. "This is my place."

"Oh wow. That's really awesome. I can't imagine being able to own my own business." I'm closing in on twenty years old, and I don't even have a high school diploma. I was lucky Jerry took a chance and hired me. Otherwise, I don't know where I'd be right now. Something like being a business owner is out of the question for a loser like me.

"I did my fair share of working for other people. This was a long time in the making." My eyes are drawn to the way his muscles flex as he walks across the room to get his coffee cup. I look away quickly when he turns back around. He takes a drink of his coffee. "If having your own business is your dream, I have no doubt you'll achieve it."

"I'll have to take your word on that." I finish my coffee and get to my feet. "Where can I put these?"

"Leave them there. I'll take care of it."

"Thanks for the snack." I slide my arms back into my coat, not relishing the thought of going back out into the snow.

"Not a fan of the cold?" Tony asks with a smile on his face.

"I wasn't made for winter," I say as I gather my hair and put it inside my hat. "I much prefer the heat and sun."

"Where are you from, Leopold?"

The sound of my name coming from his lips has the power to make me melt. I have to put a stop to any of those thoughts. "You can call me Leo," I say and smile, not wanting to sound rude. "I'm from California."

"You're a long way from home."

Home. Do I even know what that word means anymore? I can't remember the last time I felt as if I was home. "Tell me about it," I mutter.

"What brought you to the East Coast?"

Although his question sounds like he's genuinely curious, I'm not sure how to answer it. He's a complete stranger, just trying to be friendly and make small talk. He doesn't want to hear about what a screw up I am and that I had to come here to seek safety. I buy myself a few seconds by wrapping my scarf around my neck. "Looking to try something new. I guess." I reach into my pocket to get my gloves and feel the invoice. I can't believe I almost forgot it. "Can you sign this for me?" I hold out the papers.

"Sure." He steps over to the hosting station and grabs a pen. He signs his name and hands the paper back to me.

Pulling them apart, I hand him the white copy and put the pink one in my pocket. "Thanks again for the coffee and snack," I say as I put my gloves on.

"Anytime."

With that, I pull open the door and step back into the cold.

Leopold

WHEN I LEFT THE SHOP TO DO A DELIVERY, I WAS NOT expecting to find myself face-to-face with Tony—the most beautiful, soft-spoken man I'd ever laid eyes on. Hurrying to the end of the block and rounding the corner, I press my back against the brick building, feeling the cold permeate my coat. My unexpected reaction to Tony catches me off guard. His presence filled the room, yet he was soft-spoken. Despite my jaded perspective on life, he radiated not only positivity but also encouragement.

I've learned the hard way to be wary of strangers, yet I felt an inexplicable sense of safety in his presence. I didn't want to leave, yet a part of me wanted to run. I'm left grappling with conflicting emotions, unsure what to make of the puzzling encounter.

"It doesn't matter," I say, pushing off the wall. "It's not like I'll ever see him again." There's no way Jerry will keep paying my taxi fare when he owns a delivery truck and can hire someone who can drive it, and I can't afford to eat in a place like that.

My walk is brisk because of the temperature and my desire to return to the shop. Jerry didn't give me a timeframe to be back. However, I'm still on the clock and feel a sense of responsibility to get right back to work.

"How did that go?" Jerry asks as soon as I walk through the door.

"I think it went well." I reach into my pocket. "Here's your invoice."

Jerry inspects the document. "The in-house orders are packed and ready for you."

"Really?" I ask, surprised.

He looks at me curiously. "I told you that you were promoted to delivery."

"Yes, but I didn't think you meant permanently." I shift uncomfortably. "I don't drive."

"That's easily remedied." He walks behind the counter and pulls out a booklet. "Here."

I take the offered item and look at it. It's a study guide for the driver's exam. I look around to make sure no one is listening and then say quietly, "Even if I pass, I can't afford a car."

"You will pass," he says confidently. "And I have a car. It's old, but you can learn with it. I'll pay for driving instruction lessons."

"That's a very generous offer," I say, trying to give him the booklet back. "But I can't let you do that."

"Let me?" Jerry chuckles and shakes his head. "As your boss, it's my responsibility to provide you with training to do your job, and deliveries are now part of that job. You need to learn to drive to do it. So, as your employer, I'll ensure you get the training to do so."

"Thank you." His generosity nearly overwhelms me. "You're amazing, Jerry."

"Don't say that too loudly. I don't want anyone around here thinking I've gone soft." He gives me his signature wink. "The boxes are loaded on the dolly in the back. You missed your lunch, so I left a sandwich and drink back there for you, too."

"Actually, I had a bite to eat at the restaurant."

"Then you met Tony." He grins.

"I did," I admit, my stomach doing excited flips as the image of the attractive man crosses my mind.

"I've known him for years. He's a good man."

Needing to change the subject, I ask, "Is it okay if I bring the sandwich home for dinner?"

"Of course, it's yours, son."

Son. When I first walked in here, I was a stranger to this man. Yet Jerry's always treated me like family. On more than one occasion, he told me he felt like I was the son he never had. He would've made a wonderful father.

I'm thankful for his presence in my life, but at the same time, it hurts. Why doesn't my father care about me? Once he realized I wasn't his idea of the *perfect son*, it was so easy for him to get rid of me.

I'll never forget the look on his face when he left me at Walking in the Light. It was the first time I experienced pure hatred. What made it cut especially deep was that it was from one of the people who was supposed to love me unconditionally.

Then there's Jerry. He's older than my own father. He could probably be my grandfather. His generation wasn't raised knowing what it meant to be gay. If someone had a sexual orientation outside of the societal norms, they had to keep it hidden. Yet somehow, he recognized I was gay and accepted me—no questions asked.

I beam with pride at being called this man's son. "I'll get right on those deliveries."

⚊ 🕯 ⚊

Making today's deliveries was so much fun. I loved every second of meeting and talking to so many people. But it's left me exhausted. After a quick shower, I eat the ham and cheese sandwich from Jerry and collapse into bed.

Restlessness consumes me throughout the night as I dream about a strikingly handsome man. His olive skin glows with an inviting warmth, and his eyes, a kind and gentle chocolate brown, linger in my thoughts.

Anthony

SLEEP WAS ELUSIVE AS I TOSSED AND TURNED ALL NIGHT, consumed by worry about the upcoming court appearance in the morning. Finishing my shower, the sound of my phone ringing echoes from the bed. With a towel hastily wrapped around my waist, I rush to answer it, half-expecting the district attorney on the line. To my surprise, Jennifer's name illuminates the screen. I'm sure she's calling to offer me her support.

"Good morning." My effort to sound cheery falls short.

"I'm sorry to call so early," she says, her voice hoarse.

"Are you sick?"

"It's my mom," she says, barely above a whisper. "She's gone, Tony."

My heart shatters. "Oh my God, Jennifer. What happened?"

"I don't know. I came downstairs to start breakfast before I had to wake the girls up for school. Mom usually gets up as soon as she smells the coffee," Jenn pauses to catch her breath. "She's been slowing down lately, and I assumed she slept in. I was glad because I've been telling her she doesn't need to get up and help me."

"I knew. I don't know how I knew. I just did." She cries softly on the other end. "I waited until the bus came for the girls before I went in. She looked so peaceful." Her voice carries a haunted tone. "Sweetheart, I'm so sorry." I wipe the tears from my own face. My instincts urge me to pack a bag and get on the next flight to Pennsylvania, but I can't. "I have to be in court," I murmur.

"I know. I wish you didn't have to be," she says quietly. "I had at least talk to you."

Putting her on speaker, I dry off and dress in my suit and tie. The past few weeks leading up to the trial have involved extensive conversations with the district attorney. While she isn't certain I'll be called to the stand, I must be present in court, just in case.

Two of the men involved opted for plea deals, avoiding a trial. The current trial pertains to the third person involved, the minor—the one I captured in a picture, the one who threw a brick upon seeing me. Considering his past encounters with the law and the nature of his actions, the district attorney's office refrained from offering him a deal.

"My phone will be silenced, but if you need me, text or leave a voicemail. I'll check it as often as I can."

"I don't know how to tell the girls."

"Will Brian be there with you?"

Jennifer was apprehensive about moving back home. It had been a long time since she'd lived in a rural area, and other than visits, the girls only knew city life. Fortunately, Jenn reconnected with her childhood friends, who loved on her and the girls and helped them adjust to their new lives.

Despite being a full-time caregiver for her mother, Jennifer has found time to volunteer for the PTA and establish herself within the small community. Anna and Chloe are also thriving. Both girls are developing friendships, engaging in playdates, and excelling in school this year. They tell me all about it on our weekly video calls. Shortly after Christmas last year, Jennifer unexpectedly crossed paths

with her high school boyfriend, Brian. Brian, who never married, remained in Clearfield and took over the family farm. Unaware of her return, they began talking, and just like a Hallmark movie, the feelings they shared in their youth resurfaced. I met him the last time I went out to visit Jennifer. I was feeling skeptical and overprotective, but it only took minutes to see how much he adored her and the girls.

Anna has formed a strong bond with him, which was beautiful to witness, especially after how much she struggled with losing her father. Clad in her overalls, plaid shirt, and boots to match Brian's, she helps him feed the animals and get the eggs from the chickens. As much as I miss them, there's comfort in seeing all three of them so happy.

"Yes. Brian came over as soon as I called him," she explains. "He just ran out to grab a few groceries while I get the house ready. Some of my extended family is on their way. They'll be here tonight."

"I'm sure he'll help you when it's time to talk to them."

"What if this sets Anna back? I don't think I can stand to see her scared and crying all the time again. Not after how far she's come," Jenn says, her words hurried.

"She's older and can understand things better now." I do my best to reassure her, but this is uncharted territory for me. "She's going to be sad, but Anna's strong. I have no doubt she'll be okay."

We continue our conversation for a few more minutes before I reluctantly have to hang up. I'm late leaving the house and will have to hustle to get to the courthouse on time.

Who would've thought sitting all day listening to lawyers questioning experts and witnesses would be so exhausting? The prosecution wrapped up their case yesterday. Today, the defense gave their closing arguments. Thankfully, it was a short day.

I'm taking advantage of having the afternoon free and decide to stop by Fire and Ice. The club isn't open to the public right now, but I'm sure Owen or Star will be there, and right now, I could use some company.

The lights are on inside, but I don't immediately see anyone.

"I thought I heard someone come in," Owen says as he walks out of the café.

"Court let out early, and I wasn't ready to go home."

"I'm glad you came here," he says, motioning toward the kitchen. "I was just getting ready to make myself something to eat. Can I make you a plate too?"

"I can do it."

Owen holds up his hand. "Nope. Today, I'm doing the cooking."

"That would be great."

After Owen disappears in the kitchen, I check out the setups on the stages. This weekend, Fire and Ice is hosting three Dominants, Kiernan, Briar, and Charlie, from a club in the Hamptons, who will be teaching some classes and conducting demonstrations for our members.

The first stage is set up to look like a tiny apartment. There's a loveseat, a part of a kitchen countertop, and a door. Laid out on a table is a mix of spanking and sensory implements. There's a hairbrush, a feather duster, a wooden spoon, a silicone basting brush, and a silk scarf. Kiernan is known for his out-of-the-box demonstrations that show how easily BDSM can be practiced using household things rather than pricey kink-specific items.

On the middle stage is a more clinical-looking setting, complete with a violet wand, butt plugs, cock rings, nipple clamps, and an electro-Wartenberg Wheel. Charlie's clearly teaching a class on electro-play. I've sat in on their classes in the past and know they are a very experienced Dominant and a fascinating instructor. I'm sure their class will be a huge hit.

The last stage is set up for Briar to do a presentation on Disabilities and Kink. She's not only an experienced Domme, but she also holds a Doctorate in Human Sexuality. Briar's a beautiful soul who's passionate about ensuring everyone who wishes to live the BDSM lifestyle is able to find a way that works for them and their partner. I'm skimming through her class notes when I hear footsteps behind me.

"Excuse me. Are you Owen Keller?"

I spin around and am pleasantly shocked at who I'm looking at. "Hello again, Leopold."

"Tony. I didn't expect to see you," he says as he looks around nervously. "What is this place?"

"This is Fire and Ice."

He takes a few more cautious steps into the room. "Is this like a dance club or something?" he asks hesitantly.

"It's a BDSM club."

"Oh. I've heard of that before." He looks at me, his ocean-blue eyes widening, drawing me in deeper. "Do you work *here*, too?"

"If you're interested, we always have informational sessions," Owen interrupts us as he steps out of the kitchen and wipes his hands on a rag.

A tiny spark of hope ignites inside me. Maybe he'd be interested, but it's quickly extinguished when he ignores Owen's offer.

"I'm not here for... I'm Leopold," he stumbles over his words. "I have a delivery."

"My apologies," Owen chuckles."It's a pleasure to meet you. I'm Owen. This is—"

"Tony," Leo interrupts, smiling when he meets my gaze.

"You two know each other already?" Owen asks, surprised.

"We met a few weeks ago," I reply without breaking eye contact. I'm content to drown in their depths.

"I deliver to his restaurant, too," Leo says quickly. "Nice place you have here."

Leo's made several deliveries to *Italiano Desiderio.* Since our first meeting, I've planned ahead for his arrival and always have espresso and a plate ready for him when he arrives. Witnessing the pleasure Leopold experiences from such a small act has become something I look forward to—crave more of.

I wish I knew he was coming here. I would've made sure to have something for him to eat.

"I see," Owen says, giving me a questioning glance. "If you want to bring the hand cart this way, we can unload it in the kitchen."

"Sure." Leo follows, pulling the squeaky cart behind him.

"I'll give you two a hand," I offer, knowing it'll give me a chance to see what Owen's been cooking. Hopefully, there's extra so I can to invite Leo to join us.

Owen's whipped-up chicken stir fry and noodles. Thankfully, there's enough for an army.

"Owen and I were just about to have a late lunch. Would you care to join us?" I ask as casually as possible.

"I don't want to intrude," Leo says, uncertainty clouding his features. And something else. Is it fear?

"I made plenty. You're more than welcome to stay." Owen pins me with a curious glance.

"Are you sure?" Leo bites his lip.

"Of course." This time, it's me who answers too quickly. I wasn't expecting to see Leo today. But now that he's here, I don't want him to leave.

He hesitates, and I think he'll say no until he asks, "Do you have a phone I can use to let Jerry know I'll be longer than expected?"

"There's a phone at the front desk," I say. My eyes track Leo as he walks across the room and out to the club's entrance, where the phone is located.

"You're awfully eager to not let him leave," Owen says quietly.

"Me?" I try to make light of my reaction, a light-hearted chuckle escaping me. "He's been delivering to my place, too. Leo's new to the city, and I get the feeling he doesn't have many friends here. He's always kinda down on himself," I explain. "I try to have something for him to eat and drink so he doesn't rush right out. Just trying to show him some kindness."

"Mhm." Owen clicks his tongue.

"The food looks ready." I attempt to divert his attention away from me. "I'll make our plates while you put that stuff away."

Leaving the dishes under the warmer, I bring out the cutlery. Leo doesn't hear me, so I have the chance to watch him. He walks past the stages, pausing to look at each one. For a moment, I allow myself to imagine Leo on one of them while I drizzle hot wax over his naked body.

I shake my head, knowing that train of thought is a slippery slope, and bring the silverware to the table. When I look up again, Leo's attention is fixed on Kameron's memorial. I walk over and stand near him.

"I'm so sorry," Leo says quietly.

"Kam was a good man," I murmur, my gaze fixed on the picture of him and me side by side.

"You two looked very happy together."

"We were."

"So, I guess you don't just work here." Leo turns his attention to me. "You're a part of all this."

"I am," I say and nod slightly. Something about this younger man makes me feel alive inside, and it's on the tip of my tongue to ask if it's something he's into as well.

"Soda or sparkling water," Owen interrupts as he calls from the kitchen doorway."

"Water," Leo and I answer in unison.

The moment slipping away, I say, "Come on and have a seat. I'm going to help Owen get the food."

Taking our seats at the table, the three of us start to eat. I pay close attention as Leo takes his first bite. He consistently savors whatever food is on his plate, and I take pleasure in watching his reactions.

"Are you a chef too?" he asks Owen.

"No," he chuckles. "I just enjoy getting in the kitchen every now and then."

"Well, this is delicious," Leo says as he savors another bite. "Thank you again for inviting me."

"Tony told me you're new to Manhattan. Where are you from?"

"California."

"Whereabouts? I have family in San Jose."

"I'm originally from Rolling Hills," Leo says between bites.

"What brings you all the way out here?"

I don't miss the almost imperceptible way Leo tenses before he mumbles, "I was looking for a change of scenery, I guess." And just like every time I ask too many questions about him, Leo changes the subject. "You said you aren't a chef, but I assume you work here."

"I'm co-owner of Fire and Ice."

"Oh," Leo says, surprised. "Does everyone in this city own their own business?"

Owen laughs. "Not the question I was anticipating."

A blush creeps up Leo's cheeks. There's something about his innocence that's arousing.

"I wasn't sure what's proper to ask." He shrugs.

"This is a safe space to ask any questions you have," Owen says, his tone serious.

Sex clubs of any kind are still viewed as taboo by much of society. Leo's reaction is not uncommon for us to hear. It's the hope of all of the more senior members of Fire and Ice to educate interested people and provide a safe environment to practice the BDSM lifestyle on a community level.

Leo looks at his watch, and not for the first time I realize I've never seen him with a cell phone. That's curious in a day and age when practically everyone has one. "Thanks, that's a very nice offer." He wipes his mouth and sets the napkin next to his plate. "But I have to get back to the store."

"Give me a minute," I say and get up quickly. "I'll get you something to bring the rest of your lunch with you."

"Thanks." Leo smiles.

Another thing I've noticed about Leo is how grateful he is when I package his leftovers. It makes me wonder about his situation, but I don't want to spook him with such personal questions. Grabbing a take-home container, I put the rest of the stir fry into it before returning to the table.

"Owen made enough for an army," I say. "I hope you don't mind that I put some extra in here."

"Not at all. I appreciate it very much, Tony," he says, gracing me with a smile that makes his eyes sparkle.

"I'll walk you to the door," Owen says. "I have a list of things we forgot to put on this week's order."

Leo gives me a small wave before following Owen out front. I'm envious. I wish it was me getting those extra few minutes with Leo.

Anthony

I've been in court every day for the past two weeks for Levi Young's trial. Although he's a minor, given his history and the fact he was involved in a hate crime, the state was able to try him as an adult. Thankfully, I wasn't called to testify. Levi didn't plead guilty, but the evidence against the seventeen-year-old was damning, allowing the state to wrap up their case reasonably quickly. His counsel did their best to mitigate the damage, but it didn't do much good. The jury only deliberated for two hours before returning with a guilty verdict on all counts.

Today is his sentencing. I've grappled with my emotions every day while sitting in the courtroom, watching this young man, his head hung low, as the evidence against him was presented. But it wasn't the crimes he was accused of that struck me most.

"Mr. Genovese," Judge O'Malley says my name, interrupting my internal thoughts. "I'm told you wish to address the court before Mr. Young's sentence is delivered."

"Yes, Your Honor." I get to my feet and am ushered to a podium with a microphone.

"Like yourself, Your Honor, I've been present in your courtroom each day listening to the case made against Mr. Young and the defense counsel's statements about his role in the crime. I don't possess your knowledge and understanding of the law," I say respectfully. "However, I do have the experience of being there during the crime itself."

I turn so I'm facing Levi, intending to address him directly. "We haven't been formally introduced. I'm Tony Genovese. You know now that the place of business you vandalized is my restaurant. I don't know how much your attorney has told you about me. I want to tell you a little bit, if it's okay with you, Your Honor?" I look to the judge, who nods.

"I'm a second-generation Italian-American. My grandparents married while young—Nonna was sixteen, and Nonoo was seventeen. With the dream of finding prosperity in the United States, they left everything behind. They immigrated from Sicily shortly after their marriage. They were proud of their Italian heritage, but in many ways, they were even prouder to call themselves Americans." I flip to my next page of notes.

"My parents fostered my love of cooking the meals I learned to prepare as a little boy with my Nonna. They also encouraged my dream of having my own restaurant—which should've been open a long time before that night, but September 11th happened."

"My partner, Kameron, was a fire chief in the FDNY. Kameron was one of the first rescue workers to respond after the first plane hit. While most people were running away, he looked fear in the face, and he ran toward the burning buildings. He was inside the North Tower when it collapsed. Kam didn't make it out." Levi's head pops up, and his wide eyes meet mine. "Opening that restaurant was a dream he and I shared together, but it was one I was forced to see come true alone."

"I've lost a lot of people in my thirty-eight years, but losing Kameron was the single most difficult thing I've ever endured. I learned what it's like to feel truly alone. The night you and your buddies paid my establishment a visit, I found myself at a crossroads. After hearing the hateful things you yelled about me—to me, I considered ending my life. I prayed for death." A hush descends upon the courtroom as I speak. "I ended up in the emergency room because they thought I had a heart attack. God, it hurt. It hurt so bad."

I take a second to compose myself before continuing, "Hate has always been part of the world, but on September 11th, hate took center stage. The men who hijacked those planes and altered the course of the entire world were pure evil. Being compared to the terrorists felt like the final blow for me." Images of the plane slamming into the side of the building sweep through my mind.

"There's been a lot of focus on the property damage incurred during your crime. But you know what? I don't care that the windows were smashed. That's fixable. Anyone who sees it now will never know they were at one time broken. But the words, the hateful words that were spoken. The names I was called—"

"Once upon a time, I was like this paper." I hold up a clean, white sheet. "As I've gone through life, especially after I came out as a gay man, I've been on the receiving end of ridicule and hate more times than I'd like to recall. My heart, like this paper, became damaged." I crumble it until it's in a ball. Then, I work to open it back up as I continue, "Each time I heal, but like this paper, I will never be unwrinkled. No matter how much you smooth it, there will always be wrinkles. You see, that's the problem with words and why they must be spoken with great care." Tears slide down Levi's cheeks. "Words can never be unspoken. No amount of punishment or apologies can erase the pain they inflict."

"Your right to have those thoughts and opinions isn't why you're on trial today. The founding principles of our country protect your right to voice your opinions. You could've made signs and even marched through this city blasting your beliefs, and no one would've been able to stop you. But I'd like to ask you to think about what I will say next. Our country is at war with the ideals of terrorism—one of the crimes you've been convicted of. Men and women, boys not much older than you are right now, are overseas, putting their lives in harm's way to protect each of us. To protect you and ensure you continue living in a country where you're free to voice your opinions," I pause.

"Depending on your sentence, you may go to jail, still being kept safe, while our soldiers fight on the front line. Many will lose their lives to ensure you continue to live in a land where you have a voice. How will you choose to use your voice moving forward?"

I flip to the last of my notes. "The crimes you've been convicted of are grave. Because this isn't your first offense, the state is asking for the maximum penalty. You're facing the potential of spending the next decade or so behind bars." Just saying that out loud makes my heart pound. "It's been suggested to me that I stand here and petition the court to impose the strictest punishment on you. I've been told that I should *want* to see you in prison. That you deserve it and the streets would be safer with you behind bars. I'm told that's how I'll get closure and heal from the trauma your actions inflicted on me," I say, taking a moment to let the gravity of my statement sink in. "But that's not what I'm here to do."

A murmur fills the courtroom.

Judge O'Malley bangs her gavel. "Order in the court," she calls. She waits until the people have settled before saying, "Please continue, Mr. Genovese."

"Your Honor, I'm asking you today to look at Levi Young, not the troubled young man convicted of these crimes, but try to see him like I've seen him. Levi is a seventeen-year-old boy—not much more than a child, yet somehow, he was involved in a very adult crime. How did that happen? Who was looking out for him? I've been in the courtroom every day for the past two weeks and noticed that with the exception of the free counsel he was afforded by the provisions of the law, no one has been here to support him." I glance at Levi, whose head is lowered as tears continue to fall. "I don't know his story. I don't know where his family is or why he doesn't have anyone supporting him and showing him unconditional love and support. I don't have to have those answers to know that sending an impressionable young man to prison when he's on the cusp of adulthood won't benefit him. It's not going to fix anything."

The judge studies me curiously before she speaks. "What are you suggesting?"

"In the days following September 11th, I spent countless hours volunteering to feed the rescue workers. I was able to witness firsthand how those efforts affected them. I also experienced healing within myself that I believe only comes through the giving of one's time." I turn so I can look at both Judge O'Malley and Levi. "Despite the nature of the crime and Mr. Young's participation in it, when I look at this young man, I don't see a hardened criminal the likes of which time in prison is the only answer. I do believe time in prison will only harden his heart and ensure when he's released, there will be no hope for him."

"The criminal justice system's goal is not only to punish criminals but also rehabilitate them and reintegrate them into society. I'm asking the court to forgo the maximum penalties and instead choose community service and education."

Once again, the courtroom erupts in shocked chatter. "Please continue," Judge O'Malley says after again silencing the audience.

"Our city is filled with opportunities for Mr. Young to give of his time to help others. To perhaps meet a caring adult willing to take him under their wing and to learn imperative life lessons that will serve him better than time spent in a jail cell. Levi," I say, waiting for him to lift his head. He watches me intently. "You've listened to everything I've said. You know how deeply wounded I was that night. I want you to know that I understand the anger and fear you felt after September 11th. It's an anger and fear I shared with you, but it's one we chose to express in very different ways. When you were questioned about that night, you asked for forgiveness. I want you to know—to hear from me, that I forgive you." My voice cracks with emotion.

"What happened is over. It's part of your past. Do not allow it to shadow your future." Levi blinks through his tears but doesn't break eye contact. "I don't know what's going to happen now—what sentence the court will impose. Whatever it is, whatever happens from here, I ask that you move forward and make a positive impact on the world. If each of us chooses to be the light, we'll extinguish the darkness, and the world will change. I believe in you."

I step away from the podium and return to my seat.

"I hope everyone in my courtroom never forgets what occurred here today. Mr. Genovese," the judge addresses me. "Every day, but especially in the wake of the tragedy that occurred on September 11th, the kindness you've just shown is an example of the kind of person we all should strive to be. You had every reason to hate, yet you chose compassion and forgiveness. I, for one, will never forget what I witnessed today." She clears her throat. "The court calls a one-hour recess, at which time we'll reconvene, and I'll hand out the sentencing."

"All rise," the bailiff calls out. Everyone gets to their feet and waits for the judge to exit before they file out of the courtroom.

"Thank you for everything," I shake the district attorney's hand.

"Do you want to grab a quick lunch before we return to hear the outcome?"

"No, thank you. I've said my peace. I won't be returning to see what the judge decides."

I walk out of the courtroom, filled with a sense of peace. I hope my actions have a positive impact, even in some small way. It's all a person can hope to do.

Leopold

I'VE LOOKED THROUGH MY ROOM AT LEAST TEN TIMES AND can't find it. It's gone. The last of the money Donnie gave me, three hundred dollars—my rent money, is gone. One of my roommates must've been in my room, and there's nothing I can do about it. I can't prove that I had it or that it's gone. Again, my stupidity rears its ugly head.

What am I going to do now? The rent is five hundred dollars, and I only have two hundred in my bank account. I haven't squandered anything, either. After taxes and all the other deductions, my paycheck is only a little over six hundred dollars. I bought groceries and paid my share of the utilities two weeks ago. The cash I had here, along with the money I saved from last week's paycheck, would've covered it. I was going to stop by their office on the way to work.

Now, what am I going to do? I pace back and forth, trying to come up with a plan.

Phil and Maureen, the couple who run the program, always tell us to call if we need anything. I've never taken them up on their offer, but I have no other options. I'm glad the other guys are all at work right now because I don't want them eavesdropping on my conversation.

I make my way to the kitchen, where the house phone is located.

We're required to have a landline. My roommates think it's old-fashioned to have one. That's easy for them to say. They all have cell phones. It's essential for me because I don't have one.

"Hello?"

"May I speak to Phil?"

"Speaking."

"Hi. It's Leo Wagner." I try to keep my voice calm and even.

"Hello, Leo. How are you?"

"I'm doing okay."

"What can I do for you?" Phil asks.

"I'm a bit short on my rent money," I say. "I was wondering if I could pay you what I have today and get you the rest after I get paid."

"When do you get paid?"

"Next Friday?" My words come out more like a question than a statement.

"Unfortunately, that's not going to work. The program agreement only allows a forty-eight-hour grace period."

"I've never been short or late. I have two hundred today. I promise I'll get you the rest the minute I get paid," I beg.

"There's no exceptions to our policy," Phil says. "If we let you do that, we'd have to let everyone, and that won't work."

I thread my fingers through my hair and grab it tight. "What can I do?"

"You can try borrowing money from a friend."

"Yeah, maybe." I can't tell him I have no friends here. "If I can't get the funds. What happens?"

"Like I said, you have a forty-eight-hour grace period. If at the end of that you don't have it, you'll be asked to leave the program and the apartment immediately."

"Where will I go?"

"That's up to you." There's a pause. "Why don't you come and drop off what you have. Maybe you can ask your boss to give you an advance for the rest?"

I don't want to have to ask Jerry for a loan, but there's not much else I can do. But at least it'll buy me a little time. "I'll be there shortly."

When I walk into the shop, I look around but don't see Jerry in any of his typical spots.

"Zeke, have you seen Jerry?" I ask my co-worker.

He doesn't look up from whatever he's doing on his cell phone when he mumbles, "He's in the hospital."

"The hospital?" My anxiety level spikes. "What's wrong?"

"How should I know? Someone's in his office. Go ask them."

I hurry down the back hall and find the door open. A woman is sitting at his desk, her back is to me. "Excuse me," I say without entering.

She spins the chair. "Hi."

"Zeke told me Jerry's in the hospital. What happened? Is he okay?"

"And you are?" she asks.

"I'm Leo. I work here. Is Jerry okay?" I ask, my words hurried.

"I've heard Uncle Jerry talk about you," she says. "We're not ready to discuss what's happening with his employees."

"Oh."

She grabs a stack of papers off the desk. "What time are you scheduled to work until? I can't find anything in this mess of papers." She makes a big deal of flipping through the ones in her hand. "I've told him he needed to switch to a computer system for years. This is a mess," she mutters.

"I work until close," I say. "I usually do the deliveries first and then return and take care of the stock."

"We already sent someone out with today's deliveries. Here it is." She pulls out a paper with the handwritten schedule. "We didn't get any new stock today. Do you know how to run the register?"

"No." Jerry never trained me on any of that. "I do all the back-room stuff."

"It's your lucky day then."

"What do you mean?"

She looks up at me. "There's nothing for you to do, so you get some extra time off."

"No new stock doesn't mean there's no work. The stock room still needs to be swept. I have to tally the—"

The woman holds up her hand. "I'm not worried about any of that right now. You're free to go." She spins her chair back to the desk, dismissing me.

Quietly, I walk a few aisles over to avoid Zeke. I don't feel like talking to anyone. Jerry's more than my boss. He's also my friend. And I have no idea what's happening with him. Selfishly, I didn't get a chance to ask about an advance on my paycheck, and even worse, they sent me home, so I'm not earning anything tonight.

This cannot be happening. "What the hell am I going to do?"

Leopold

It's Christmastime in the city. Everyone says it is the most wonderful time of the year. I question their logic. This is my second year here, and I'm still shocked by the sheer number of people descending upon this island for the Christmas shopping season. Busy and congested are understatements.

Last Christmas, Ramiro and his family flew out to spend the holiday with me. I stayed at the Plaza Hotel with them, where they ensured I had the whole holiday experience. Unfortunately, they can't make it this year. Ramiro and his wife, Jacinta, are expecting their third baby any day, so they aren't able to travel.

Every day, I watch couples walking hand-in-hand, their love for one another evident. Families smile and laugh as they take selfies in front of the many iconic decorations throughout the city. Everyone seems to have someone except me. I'm alone, and unless I get a miracle, I'm about to become homeless.

I've just gotten out of the shower and am getting dressed when there's a knock on the bathroom door.

"There's a phone call for you," my roommate calls through the door.

"Okay. I'll be right out." It has to be Ramiro. I've been waiting for his call to tell me the baby's here. I didn't want it to come to this. To tell him I screwed up and that I needed his help, but I'm desperate. It's the middle of the winter, and I'm facing being homeless. It's humiliating, but I'll work hard at repaying him. Someone in this city has to be willing to hire me. Even without a GED, I'll find a second job.

Quickly, so I don't keep him waiting, I pull on my jeans and throw my sweatshirt over my head. With my socks in hand, I hurry to the shared kitchen where the phone is. "Congratulations."

"What? Uh. Leo?"

"Who's this?"

"It's Billy. From work."

"Hi," I say hesitantly. "What's up?"

"I know you're scheduled to come in today, but... I don't know how to say this, man." My stomach sinks. "Jerry's dead."

I grab the counter for support. "Dead?"

"You know they brought him to the emergency room yesterday," he says. "I guess he had a stroke or something and never woke back up." I can't believe what I'm hearing. "You still there, Leo?"

"Yeah. I'm here. Are you at the store?"

"Not anymore. I got there this morning to start my shift, and his niece was there again," he explains. "She was putting a sign on the door that the store is closed indefinitely."

"Closed?" I ask, my voice barely above a whisper.

"She said when they figure out his estate, they'll be in touch to get us our final paychecks." This can't be happening. I pinch myself, half-expecting to wake up from a cruel dream. "I figured I'd save you a trip."

"Thanks," I mumble.

"No problem. Merry Christmas."

I can't answer him. I'm left speechless, the weight of the moment silencing me, and I hang up without saying goodbye.

The news of Jerry's passing has cast a heavy shadow over my world. In the wake of this loss, I find myself not only unemployed but also on the brink of homelessness. The ground I stood on has collapsed, and once again, I face an uncertain future.

Sensing the walls closing in, I have to escape before I suffocate. Quickly grabbing my coat, I hurry out the front door.

⚓

I've been walking the streets of New York City for hours, attempting to wrap my head around everything that's happened today. But try as hard as I might, none of it makes sense.

My stomach growls, and I realize I haven't eaten all day. I reach into my back pocket for my wallet, but it's empty.

"Shit." In my hurry to leave the house, I must've forgotten to grab it. I have no choice but to walk back across town to get it.

I'm not even halfway there when the sky unleashes a torrent of ice-cold rain. I arrive back at the building thoroughly soaked and shivering. I enter my code, but the lock doesn't open.

I must have pressed the wrong button. Removing my bulky gloves, I give it another try, but the lock remains unresponsive. Growing frustrated and sensing an issue with the lock system, I press the buzzer. I wait anxiously, but no one answers. I try my code several more times. That's when the harsh reality slams into my chest.

I yank the elastic of my coat sleeve over my wrist to check my watch. It's seven pm. "No. No. No." The deadline for delivering the rest of my rent to Phil was five pm. After Billy's call, I lost all train of thought. In my hurry to get away, I completely forgot about calling Ramiro.

Sitting on the wet concrete stoop, I drop my head into my hands. How did everything fall apart so fast?

Ignoring the doorbell is a common occurrence with my roommates. I resign myself to waiting out here and catching them before they go out tonight. Hopefully, they don't act like their typical asshole selves and take pity on me just one time. Then, they never have to see me again.

The hours pass. The rain turns into snow. I'm soaked and freezing. Before I know it, it's midnight. The guys must've left early. Once they're gone, they won't be back until Sunday evening.

What am I going to do now? Where do I go?

Once again, I find myself wandering with no destination in mind. I don't realize where I'm at until I stop outside of the market. Is it too much to hope that Billy was playing a horrible joke on me? Yet, even from a distance, I notice the bright yellow paper taped to the door. As I approach, I read the handwritten note, "Closed Indefinitely."

This isn't a nightmare, and I'm not waking up from it.

"There's no loitering," a security guard calls.

"Sorry. I'm leaving."

I walk the few blocks to Hudson River Park. In the daylight, it's a bustling spot for locals and tourists to stroll along the river's edge. However, at nearly midnight, there's no one around. I stand by the metal rail, gazing out into the darkness. My heavy breaths are visible in the cold air.

I thought I was doing good this time. I meticulously followed every rule, crossing every T and dotting every I. I had a steady job that I loved and was studying for my GED and learner's permit. Jerry told me once I had my driver's license and could drive the delivery truck, I'd be getting a raise.

Jerry.

The pain cuts like a knife.

Jerry's dead. Just like that, I lost a father figure. The only person in this city who cared about me. I've held back tears all day, but now, in the darkness, I allow them to spill over and slide down my cheeks.

In a matter of hours, my life has fallen apart. I have nothing.

My hands are freezing, I stick them in my pockets, but they're not there. Instead, my hand touches something cold and hard. My boxcutter.

It's a sign. A small voice in my head whispers. *You're a screw-up. You have been since you were sixteen.*

"That's not true," I whisper into the night air.

Nothing's ever going to change. The voice grows louder. *You're just not good enough.*

Pushing the shiny silver blade out, I acknowledge that maybe that voice is right.

Just do it. No one's going to miss a worthless loser like you. Get it over with.

I *am* worthless, just like my father and David always told me. I've tried my hardest to make something of myself. To prove they were wrong, and look where it's gotten me. Nowhere.

I no longer feel the cold or the pain. The noise and lights of the city behind me fade as I push the blade against my wrist.

Epilogue

ANTHONY

The club is still packed with people for our annual Christmas Eve Eve party. I must be getting old. It's not even midnight, and I'm ready to leave.

"I'm going to head out," I say to Owen, who's talking with a small group of people.

"Already?"

"I had a long day at the restaurant. I'm beat."

"No problem." He smiles. "What time's dinner?"

For as long as I can recall, my house has been the gathering place for all my friends without family on Christmas dinner. It's become a tradition we look forward to. "Six, but I'll be there all day. You're welcome to come over whenever."

"Okay. I'll text you tomorrow."

Several people stop me on my way out to exchange Christmas greetings. I stop for only as long as is necessary to be polite before excusing myself. Then, I continue toward the door.

The rain has finally switched to lightly falling snow. It's the perfect backdrop for the holiday. I'd intended to go directly home, but a stirring in my soul urges me to walk along the pier. Kameron and I used to love walking this path, but I've avoided the area since he died. I try to again tonight, not wanting to face those painful memories, but an irresistible force compels me.

A serene tranquility envelopes the area. The only sound is the gentle water lapping against the concrete wall.

A flicker of movement up ahead captures my attention. With each step forward, the silhouette by the river's edge slowly becomes clearer.

"Leopold?"

When I say his name, he startles and spins around. As he does, something falls from his hand and bounces off the metal lamp post with a ping before landing on the concrete.

It's a razor.

"Tony?" he asks, his voice trembling.

"What are you doing out here?"

"I was... Um..." He brushes his face, leaving a streak of blood on his cheek.

A razor.

Blood.

My body tenses with the realization of what he was about to do.

"I don't have anywhere to go," he confesses, his voice choked up with tears.

"Tell me what's going on," I say softly.

"Where do I start?"

"Wherever you're comfortable." I approach him cautiously, taking a tentative step to avoid startling him. "I want to understand."

"My roommates stole my money, leaving me short on cash. While I was trying to figure that out, I got a call that Jerry died, and I no longer have a job." He runs his hands through his hair. "I'm a hot mess. A loser with nowhere to go and no one who gives a shit if I live or die."

I open my arms, and he collapses into them, his body trembling as he cries.

The realization of why I had to come this way is clear. I'm certain Kameron had something to do with this. Silent tears escape from my eyes as I hold Leo in my protective embrace.

"I'd care," I whisper.

Their story isn't over yet. In *Love Heals*, experience the redemptive power of love as they face their deepest fears and fight for the future they deserve. Don't miss the heartwarming conclusion to their emotional and unforgettable journey—start reading today!

Become one of Tara's VIP readers. Sign up for her newsletter today! https://subscribepage.io/FireandIceBooks

Love Heals

This book is dedicated to those who have been made to feel like less than, marginalized, or rejected because of who they love. Know that your love is valid, your identity is worthy, and your presence makes the world a better place.
May this book serve as a reminder that you are not alone and that your story matters.

Leopold

"I'M A HOT MESS. A LOSER WITH NOWHERE TO GO AND NO one who gives a shit if I live or die," I say through the tears that are pouring down my face.

Tony opens his arms, and I collapse into them. Shamelessly, I bury my head against his chest as he closes me in the safety of his embrace.

"I'd care," he says softly.

Snowflakes float through the air while I fall apart in Tony's arms. He holds me against him, rocking me gently, providing me a safe place to cry until numbness finally washes over me, and I lift my head.

"I'm sorry," I say, wiping my face with the back of my hand. "You caught me at a bad time. I'll be okay." I look around for my box cutter. When Tony leaves, I intend to finish what I started.

My vision's blurry from all the crying I've done, and I don't spot it fast enough. Tony bends over, reaching for the metal glinting from the streetlamp's light.

"Are you looking for this?" He holds the blade up.

"Can I have it back?" I reach out for it, but Tony pulls his hand back. "That's mine for work."

"Didn't you just tell me you no longer have a job?" he asks, grabbing my wrist. Blood trickles down my arm, staining the pure white snow a crimson hue.

"Yeah," I say and attempt to pull my arm back.

Tony tightens his grip while he examines my arm. "It doesn't look too deep, but you'll need a bandage."

Pulling the elastic of my coat sleeve over my wrist, I say, "It'll be fine."

"You're right. That wound will heal." He slides my box cutter into his pocket. "I'm more concerned about the wounds on the inside." I turn my head, ashamed to look at him. "Leopold," Tony says my name softly. "Please look at me." When I don't respond, he takes his finger and gently turns my face toward him. "Come home with me—"

"No way." I hold my hands up, cutting him off, and take a step back. "The last guy who said that to me... Let's just say I almost paid with my life. I'm not about to make that mistake twice."

"There's no way I'm leaving you out here," Tony says. "Do you have anywhere else to go?"

"No," he whispers. "I'll take my chances on the street."

"I can't leave you out here. Do you have anyone you can call? You can let them know where you're going," I propose. "I'll give them all my contact info. That way, someone you trust knows where you are."

"I don't have any way to call them." Tony reaches into his pocket, pulls out his phone, and hands it to me. "What do I say?"

"Whatever you're comfortable with. I'll give you some privacy." Tony motions off to the side. "When you're ready for me, let me know."

"Wait," I call, stopping him. "Why are you doing this?"

Tony studies me thoughtfully before answering, "The first day you walked into my restaurant, I was drawn to you. I looked forward to seeing you and was sad when you left." His tone sounds sincere, but clearly, I'm a poor judge of character. "Kameron and I used to walk this path all the time. I've avoided coming here since he died, but I couldn't tonight. Something in here." He places his hand over his heart. "Told me I had to come here." Tony points to the phone. "Call whoever you want," he says and steps away.

I type in Ramiro's phone number and wait while it rings. Part of me hopes he doesn't answer because I don't know what to tell him. How do I say I screwed up again? Do I tell him I tried to end my life?

"Hello?"

"Ramiro? It's me, Leo."

"I didn't recognize the number and almost didn't pick up," he says, chuckling. "Did you finally get a cell phone?"

"I'm borrowing one from a friend." A fresh wave of tears begins to fall.

"Is everything okay?" he asks, but I don't answer. "Leo, what's wrong?"

"I don't even know where to start." I hiccup. "I'm such a screw-up."

"What happened?" Ramiro asks calmly.

"I've been trying so hard, but I lost everything." I turn away from the phone as my body tries to expel the contents of my empty stomach. Between my sobs and dry heaving, I can't take a deep breath and fall to my knees.

"Leopold," Tony calls as he rushes to my side. "It's okay. I've got you." He helps me to my feet and walks me to a nearby bench, lowering me to sit. Then, he puts the phone on speaker. "Hello?"

"Who are you?" Ramiro asks defensively.

"Tony. I'm a friend of Leo's."

When I got the job promotion, I told Ramiro all about him. So, thankfully, he's familiar with Tony's name. Although it doesn't seem to help right now. "What's going on? Is Leo okay?"

Tony looks at me, and I nod, giving my unspoken permission for him to tell Ramiro what happened.

"Leopold's received a lot of bad news," Tony explains. "His boss passed away, causing him to lose his job."

"I'm so sorry," Ramiro says.

"It gets worse," I say quietly. "I don't have a place to live anymore."

"What do you mean?"

"I couldn't make rent, and I got evicted." A tear slides down my face and plops onto the screen of Tony's phone.

"Why didn't you call me?"

"Everything happened all at once. They locked me out, so I—"

"What do you mean they locked you out? They didn't give you any notice?" Ramiro asks, raising his voice. "This is my fault. I haven't been there for you like I should. Let me get you a hotel room for the next few nights until we figure something else out."

"I've invited Leo to stay with me," Tony interjects. "I understand he's had some bad experiences, so if he agrees, I'll give you all my contact information so you know where he is. You can check on him whenever you'd like."

"A bad experience is an understatement," Ramiro says. "I'd feel more comfortable if he was in a hotel."

"I'd rather he not be alone," Tony insists, and I'm sure this is where he'll tell Ramiro what I did. Instead, he says, "Christmas is tomorrow. Leo shouldn't be alone in a sterile hotel room for the holiday." Tony takes my hand in his and gives it a reassuring squeeze.

"What are your thoughts, Leo?"

I chew on my lower lip as I struggle with indecision. My thoughts are so jumbled right now I can't decipher one from the next. I'm cold and exhausted. Resigned to whatever happens, I mumble, "I'll go with him." My eyelids droop closed.

"You have my number on your caller ID," Tony says.

"Yes. Give me a second to get a pen so I can write down your address." There's a quiet pause before Ramiro comes back. "I'm ready." Tony gives him the address as well as the number of the front desk. "Keep your phone on you all at times," Ramiro instructs. "I expect you to call me when you get to his house so I know you got there safely."

"I don't have a phone," I interrupt.

"Shit. I forgot."

"He can use mine," Tony offers.

"I don't like that Leo's dependent on you for his ability to make a phone call. No offense," Ramiro adds.

"There's a twenty-four-hour mart a few blocks from my house. We'll stop, and I'll buy him a pre-paid phone."

"No," I say quickly. "I have no way to pay you back." My body shivers, and my teeth chatter.

"I'll send him the money," Ramiro offers.

"We can figure that out later," Tony says. "It's snowing, and Leo's freezing. I want to get him home before he gets hypothermic."

"Are you sure about this, Leo?"

"Yeah. I'm sure."

Reluctantly, Ramiro hangs up, and I pass the phone back to Tony.

"No," he says. "I told your friend you'd keep my phone until you have one of your own."

"You don't have to do that." I try again to give it back.

"I gave both of you my word, and I intend to keep it," Tony says. "Let's get moving before you freeze out here."

After we emerge from the subway, we stop at a small, well-lit bodega where Tony purchases me a pre-paid iPhone. With the bag in hand, we walk the last few blocks to Tony's Park Place building in silence.

When the doorman sees us coming, he pulls the glass door open. "Happy Christmas Eve, Anthony."

"Same to you, Wendell." He motions to me. "This is my friend, Leo. He'll be staying with me for a while."

"Pleasure to meet you, Leo," Wendell says, offering me a friendly smile.

"You too," I respond, being sure to keep my hands inside my pockets so he doesn't see the blood.

After we pass through the door, Tony leads me to the front desk, where he introduces me to Joe. He takes my personal information and Ramiro's for my emergency contact.

"Would you like a keycard, sir?" Joe asks.

"No th—"

"Yes, he would," Anthony interrupts.

A few minutes later, Joe holds out a black and silver card. I hesitate to accept it until he says, "This is for you."

I look to Tony, who nods. Pulling my hand from my pocket, I tentatively reach for the card. When Joe sees my bloody hand, he gasps. "Do you need medical attention?"

"This? Um..."

"He had a small accident at work." Tony glances at me, and I smile at him with a small but appreciative smile. "Nothing serious."

"I'm glad to hear that."

I take the offered card and slip my hand back into my pocket, hoping not to draw any more attention to myself.

"Thanks, Joe," Anthony says. "Merry Christmas."

The elevator dings, signaling its arrival, and we step inside. As soon as the doors close, I turn to face him. "You didn't have to give me a key to your apartment."

"I didn't have to, but I wanted to." After a quick ride up, the doors open. "There's only two apartments on this floor," Tony says as I follow him down the ornate hallway. He swipes his card and the door lock clicks.

Tony's apartment has a minimalist, modern design. Pocket doors that are currently open connect the spacious living room to a modest-sized kitchen with a wall of floor-to-ceiling windows overlooking lower Manhattan.

"It's late, but I'm starving. Would you like something to eat?" he asks.

"I don't want to be a bother."

"You could never be a bother," Tony says. "You can get cleaned up while I cook if you want."

Shivers travel down my spine as memories of Krew saying eerily similar words push to the surface. "I'm okay. There's no need to go through any trouble," I mumble.

Tony changes the subject. "Come on, I'll show you to your room."

The walls of the guest room are creamy white, and the curtains are light grey. The room isn't overly big, but the high ceilings and the corner windows give it an airy feel. The furniture is minimal, a king-sized bed with a crisp white bedspread and a chest of drawers.

"I'm sorry it's a bit bare," Tony says. "It was recently renovated, but I haven't gotten to decorate it yet."

"It's beautiful," I reply.

Tony smiles. "You can help me pick out the décor and bedding you'd like after the holiday."

"That's not necessary. I'm not staying—"

Tony holds his hand up, stopping me. "Let's not put a timeframe on it tonight, okay?"

"Okay."

"We do need to talk about what happened." I look down. "Do you want to do that now or after you get cleaned up?"

"Can I shower first?" I ask, hoping to buy myself some time.

"Of course. Wait here. I'll get you something to change into." Tony leaves for a minute. When he returns, he has a pair of sweatpants and one of his T-shirts. "I'll be in the kitchen if you need anything," he says, then leaves me to shower.

I sit on the edge of the king-size bed and bring his clothes to my face. They smell of lavender, lemon, and a woodsy cedar—of Tony.

The room has two doors. One is closed, and the other is cracked open, so I go there first, finding an attached bathroom that rivals the size of the bedroom. The walls and floor are adorned in luxurious grey and white marble, making the room feel elegant. Fluffy light grey towels hang meticulously from a wall-mounted bar. Stripping off my damp, dirty clothes, I carefully adjust the water before stepping beneath the soothing cascade.

A stream of red flows down the drain, a stark reminder of my suicide attempt. Holding up my arm, I look at the cut. It's deep, but hopefully not enough to warrant stitches. I'm pretty sure it's going to leave a scar.

Tony already reminded me that we're going to have a conversation about what happened. He's going to want answers about why I was trying to end my life. Up until now, I've been able to dodge most of his questions about my past, but I'm afraid that time is up.

Not wanting to use too much water, I shower quickly and pull on Tony's clothes. Despite their loose fit, wearing his things brings a rush of desire, igniting an unmistakable attraction to him. Before I go back out to the kitchen, I set my new phone up and call Ramiro.

"Hello?" he answers on the first ring.

"It's me."

"I was beginning to get worried."

"I took a shower and got into some dry clothes," I murmur.

"I'm sorry I wasn't there for you." Regret laces his voice. "I should've been more present—"

"You're not responsible for the messes I make. I'm an adult. What happened is all on me."

Once a loser, always a loser. You'll never be good enough.

"Do you feel safe with Tony? At least until after the holiday."

"Yeah, I do." I relay the building information to him and explain he can also contact them to check on me.

"I've already called Phil and left a voicemail. There're a few things I want to say to him," Ramiro says, an angry tone in his voice.

"You don't need to do that."

"I very much do," Ramiro responds. "Evicting someone in their program without trying to help. Hell, without warning is wrong."

There's a knock on my door.

"Come in," I call.

Tony opens the door but makes no move to enter. "The food's ready whenever you are."

"Ramiro, I have to go. Tell Jacinta and the girls Merry Christmas."

"Hang in there, Leo. We'll get you back on your feet."

He might get you on your feet, but you'll screw up again. You always do.

Anthony

On the counter is a charcuterie board, laid out with cheeses, meats, and a variety of other goodies that I threw together quickly. "Wow," Leo says quietly. "You didn't have to do all this."

I glance up and catch sight of Leopold wearing my clothes. His blond hair is damp and tousled. Attraction, mixed with a profound desire to care for him, completely floods my senses. The urge to envelop him in my arms and provide for him in every way consumes me entirely.

"It's the Italian in me. I can't cook just a little bit," I chuckle, trying to lighten the mood. "Before we eat, let me take care of your wrist."

I lead him to the table where the open First Aid kit waits. Leo sits on the upholstered dining chair.

"May I see your arm?" He tentatively extends it. Blood slowly seeps from the slice on his wrist. "This is going to sting," I say a second before I wipe it with an alcohol prep pad. Leo hisses and bounces his leg. "I'm sorry." I blow on it like my mom did for me when I was a child. "The boxcutter was pretty rusty. Is your tetanus shot up to date?"

"It is. Before I left California, Ramiro made sure I was able to see a doctor," he explains.

"We need to talk about this."

"I know," he says without looking up.

Working in the culinary field, I have plenty of first-aid experience. I put two butterfly strips on the wound to keep it closed and then cover it with gauze. "Let's make our plates," I suggest, closing the plastic case and sliding it back into the cupboard. "Would you like a drink?"

"No," Leo says too quickly.

I pull two cold plastic bottles out of the fridge. "It's only water."

"I'm sorry." He wrings his fingers.

"You don't need to apologize." We make our plates and sit across from one another at the table.

We begin eating in an awkward silence. I'm unsure what questions to ask and don't want to pressure him, but we do need to have an honest conversation.

"I guess you want to know why I did this?" Leo asks.

"I'd like to understand," I say softly, my gaze steady as I lock eyes with him, silently urging him to open up.

"My life has been one fuck up after another," Leo says and forces a laugh tinged with heaviness. "Do you want the long version or the cliff notes?"

"Whatever you're willing to tell me," I answer, trying to convey patience.

Leo's voice falters as he describes the day his parents caught him with another boy, the anguish of that experience palpable in his words. The next day, they packed him up and sent him off to conversion therapy. My jaw clenches as he recounts the abuse he suffered at the hands of his therapist—not that the piece of shit deserves that title.

"When the police told me they couldn't prosecute, I couldn't handle it and took off. That's when I met Krew," he explains.

As Leo bares his soul, I realize his story is far more devastating than I ever imagined. Tears spill from his eyes as he reveals the torment inflicted upon him by the man he thought he loved. Suddenly, his apprehension about coming home with me becomes painfully clear.

"New York was supposed to be my fresh start. I tried so hard to make things work, and I did everything right," he sobs. "And then, in a matter of a few hours, it was all gone. I had nothing. I was alone." Leo presses the heels of his hands under his eyes, trying to stop the tears.

"The voices in my head. Everything everyone's ever said about me. It got so loud, you know? When I reached into my pocket and felt the boxcutter, it was like a promise of the pain finally ending. I just cut." He looks up at me, his blue eyes shimmering with tears. "And then you showed up."

It takes me a few seconds to get my thoughts and emotions under control. Part of me wants to gather up everyone who ever hurt him and do worse to them. The more rational part of me realizes it wouldn't change anything. The only thing that matters now is ensuring Leopold's okay from today on. "And how do you feel now?"

"Numb." He shrugs. "Part of me wishes you didn't stop me. That I'm better off dead."

My heart sinks. "I know what it's like to feel hopeless. After Kam died, my world was black. We were on the phone when the tower collapsed on him. Just like that, he was gone. I didn't see a reason to keep living for a long time," I explain. "If it wasn't for my friends and their tough love, I don't know if I'd be here today. They helped me realize my life wasn't over. I had a purpose to be alive even if I couldn't see it at the time."

"There's one of the many differences between you and me," Leo says. "You had people around you who cared. I have no one."

"You have me." Leo's beautiful blue eyes meet mine. "I'm not a therapist. I don't know all the right things to say or do, but I'm going to ask you to do something for me. Will you hear me out?"

"Okay," he says hesitantly.

"I want you to give me thirty days."

"What do you mean?"

"I need your word that you won't do anything to harm yourself for the next thirty days. I'll find you a therapist, someone trustworthy," I add. "Who can guide you through this darkness. We'll get you a job, and I'll introduce you to all my friends." I reach out and touch his hand, feeling that undeniable spark of attraction, the same magnetic pull I felt the first time we met. "Let me be the one to show you that your story isn't over. That there's so much love waiting for you on the other side of this pain."

Leo bites his bottom lip as he considers what I've proposed. "I don't want to bring all my shit to your doorstep. You don't deserve to have to deal with it."

"You didn't *bring* anything. I asked you to be here." I give his hand a gentle squeeze. "Please, Leo. I know thirty days seems like a long time right now. We'll take it one day at a time. I promise you won't be alone."

He closes his eyes for a brief minute and sighs. "Okay. I promise."

"Thank you." I release the breath I was holding. "First things first. Do you know the number for your landlords?"

"I do." Leo relays it to me.

"What they did is illegal. Star, one of the owners of Fire and Ice, is also an attorney. I'll text her. We'll get your things back and the money they took."

"You don't—"

"I know," I interrupt. "I don't have to. Anything I do is because I want to."

"Thank you," Leo says quietly.

I'm in so far over my head right now, but there's no way I can walk away from Leopold. I'll fight with everything in me to make sure he comes out of this. He has to. I refuse to accept anything less.

Anthony

When I finally get Leopold settled in his room, it's after four am. It takes all my willpower not to stay and watch over him while he sleeps. Instead, I settle for leaving my door open in case he needs me. Although I'm mentally exhausted, my body is wired. My eyes refuse to close. Instead of fighting an unwilling body, I put my time to good use.

First, I text Star.

Me: I'm sure you're still sleeping. When you get up, please text me.

Several minutes later my phone vibrates with an incoming call.

"Hello?"

"Is everything alright?" Star asks.

"No." With the knowledge that she's one of two people I know I can confide in, I tell her what's happened with Leopold over the past twenty-four hours. Starting with the theft of cash from his room and the death of his boss. "The landlords took the last of his money and locked him out of the apartment without warning. He only had the clothes on his back."

"What's their number? I don't care that it's Christmas Eve. Come morning, they'll be getting a call from his attorney."

"Thank you," I say, grateful to have such good friends.

"At the risk of overstepping," Star adds. "Leo's going to need a therapist. You know that, right?"

Star's co-owned Fire and Ice for close to twenty years. During that time, she's encountered all kinds of situations. Over the years, she's compiled a list with numerous resources.

"Can you point me in the right direction?"

"I'll text you a few names."

After we hang up, I text Owen.

Me: Dinner is at six tomorrow.

Owen: You're up early.

Me: I haven't gone to sleep.

Owen: What's wrong?

Me: After I left the party, I ran into Leo.

Owen: Oh? That sounds exciting.

Once I realized Leopold was doing the food deliveries for Fire and Ice, I made it a point to be there every week. The three of us would sit down and have lunch together. I was desperate to spend whatever time I could with him. At first, I played it off as a coincidence, but Owen quickly saw through my story. I haven't said anything, but I'm sure he knows I'm interested in Leopold.

Me: It's not like that. I found him at the park—cutting his wrist.

Owen: What the fuck? How bad is it?

Me: A few minutes later and he wouldn't be here. Thankfully, it isn't too deep. I was able to take care of it. He's here with me.

Owen: What do you need? What can I do?

Me: Help me give him a reason to live.

Owen: I'll do everything I can. Leo has all of us by his side now.

Me: Thank you.

For the next few hours, I scour the internet for every resource I can find on helping someone suffering from depression or who's suicidal. Most of what I read suggests he should be inpatient, where professionals can counsel him and administer medication, but I'll be damned if I'm going to trust a stranger to care for him. Leopold's scared and vulnerable. He needs to be with someone who cares about him.

While I'm engrossed in reading, a text from Star arrives, containing a list of therapists for Leo. Before sharing the names with him, I take a moment to check each one's reviews. I'm oblivious to the time passing until sunlight streams into my room, breaking my concentration.

It's only when I reluctantly tear myself away from my reading that I notice the time glaring back at me – 8 am. I've completely lost track of the hours. I take a quick shower and pull the blankets up on my bed. On my way to the kitchen, I pause outside Leo's room. He appears serene and at peace, curled on his side, his hands cradling his cheek as he sleeps. With a soft smile, I leave him to rest while I go to the kitchen and start cooking.

The last two pieces of French Toast sizzle on the griddle as footsteps approach from behind. Glancing over my shoulder, I find Leopold rubbing his eyes. His blond hair tousled from sleep.

I feel an overwhelming urge to close the gap between us and press a soft kiss on his lips. Suppressing the impulse, I opt for a friendly greeting. "Good morning. How did you sleep?"

"Better than I have in a long time," he says with a yawn.

I flip the toast before it burns. "I'm glad to hear that."

"That smells delicious," he says as he steps closer. "Can I help with anything?"

"Would you mind getting plates and silverware?"

"Sure thing," he replies, and I guide him to the appropriate cupboards and drawers. Leo takes charge of setting the table while I pull the bacon out of the oven.

"Star called Phil and Maureen bright and early this morning."

"She did?" he asks, his forehead wrinkled in worry.

"After she identified herself as your attorney, they informed her about the mistaken lockout," I remark with a roll of my eyes. "They provided her with a code so you can access the apartment to gather your belongings," I explain as I place the food in the center of the table and take a seat.

"You're kidding?"

"We can go over after breakfast if you want."

"It's Christmas Eve." Leo pushes his food around on his plate. "I'm sure you have better things to do."

"I wouldn't be anywhere else but by your side," I assert warmly.

"They'll be returning your two-hundred and fifty dollars as well," I add. "You can pick it up after the holiday."

"She didn't have to do this. I don't deserve any of it," Leo says, his eyes filling with tears.

"That's where you're wrong. You deserve this and so much more," I say tenderly. "You're not alone anymore."

"I don't know what to say."

Tears spill over his lower lids, and I ache to wipe them away.

"You don't need to say anything."

The expressions of disbelief etched on Leo's ex-roommates' faces as he and I entered the room are unforgettable. I'm grateful Leo remained unaware of the whispered snide comments they made while he retrieved his personal belongings.

While I wait, I make a pre-planned phone call to Star.

"It's me."

"You got into the apartment without issue?" she asks.

"We did." It's showtime. "Have the authorities been contacted?"

"They most certainly have," she says. "I spoke to someone I know in the department."

"Yes, I understand."

"There's not much they can do, but he's going to send someone out to question the roommates."

"The NYPD will be coming to the apartment to look for evidence of a robbery?" I repeat what she told me.

"If we get lucky, they'll just confess, and Leo will get his money back. At the very least, he'll put the fear of God into them for the next person," she chuckles.

"Yes, ma'am." I glance at the three young men. Their previous chatter is now silent. All attention is on me. "I have faith that they'll uncover evidence of whoever stole Leopold's money."

"You two good there?" she asks.

"Thank you for representing Leopold on such short notice, Ms. Winslow."

"I'll see you tomorrow."

The room has gone deadly silent. When Leo reenters, he casts a quizzical glance between the guys and me. Hurrying over, I take one of the bags from him. "Your attorney called while you were in there."

"She did?"

"A report has been filed," I say, turning my attention to the stunned boys. "An officer will be stopping by to question you about who may have had access to the apartment," I continue firmly. "I trust you'll fully cooperate with the NYPD's investigation."

"Investigation into what?" the dark-haired one asks.

"The stolen money from Leopold's room."

"What would we know about it?" he asks with a cocky attitude.

"That's for the NYPD to figure out." I turn my attention back to Leopold. "Are you ready to go?" He nods. I open the door, allowing Leo to exit first. "Merry Christmas, gentlemen."

It's mid-afternoon when we arrive back to my apartment. While Leopold finishes putting the few items of clothing he owns into the dresser, I sit on the edge of his bed. "I know you lost your job." He stops and eyes me warily. "Don't feel obligated to say yes if you don't want to work in a restaurant, but I'd like to offer you employment as a busser."

He returns to folding a pair of pants before he replies nervously, "I didn't graduate high school."

How did he slip through so many cracks? My heart aches for this man. "Do you have a GED?"

"No."

"Do you want to get your GED?"

"Yes," he says without hesitation. "I started studying for it when I was at Safe Haven. When I moved here, I wanted to but didn't know where to start." He turns to face me. "Phil and Maureen weren't anything like Ramiro, and without a computer or cellphone, I was at a bit of a disadvantage."

"The community center where I take art classes offers GED prep courses on weeknights. We can get you signed up after the new year if you'd like," I offer.

"I'd like that very much."

"If you're interested, you can start work this week. If not, we'll find a job you'd prefer."

"I don't know much about working in a restaurant, but I'd like to give it a try," he says, the corner of his mouth turning up with a small smile.

"It can get pretty fast-paced on a busy night, but overall, it's not a difficult job. I'm sure you'll do just fine."

"I don't know why you're taking a chance on me," Leo says, his blue eyes that hold so much innocence for someone who's lived through hell lock on mine.

Every fiber of my being yearns to hold him tightly and confess that my heart was his from the moment he stepped over the threshold at *Italiano Desiderio*. I want to tell him that he's mine now, and I'll never allow anyone to hurt him again. Just as I'm on the brink of confessing feelings I have no right to have, my cell rings, sparing us both from a conversation Leopold may not be ready for.

"Hello?"

"Where's Leo?" Ramiro asks, his tone almost frantic.

"He's right here. Why?"

"I've been trying to call him for the past two hours. When he didn't pick up." He pauses. "Let me talk to him?"

I hold the phone out. "It's Ramiro."

Leo brings it to his ear. "Hello?"

"You had me worried sick." Ramiro's voice rises, anxiety evident in his tone. "Where have you been?"

"We went to my old apartment to get my things," Leo explains.

Standing up, I make my way to the window, offering them a semblance of privacy.

"I'm not used to having one. I didn't even think about bringing it." Leo goes quiet. "Why are you on the phone with me when your wife is in labor?" He pauses again. "Please don't worry about me. I'm in a safe place." Leo stops again. "I'll keep my phone on me, I promise. Let me know when the baby's here."

Leopold

With everything that's gone on today, I almost forgot it was Christmas Eve. Tony lets me know he's hosting his annual Christmas dinner party tomorrow.

"I don't know much about cooking," I admit.

"I'll teach you everything you need to know," he says, and my stomach gets butterflies.

We spend the rest of the afternoon and evening baking cookies and prepping all kinds of fancy foods for tomorrow's dinner. Being beside Tony in his kitchen feels natural. Somehow, we don't get in each other's way. Instead, our movements are in sync as if we've done this every day for years.

Several times, his arm brushes against mine. The contact sends electricity coursing through my body. It's exciting and alarming. This man stumbled upon me last night while I was trying to take my own life. He not only saved me but opened his home to me. I don't know what my future, let alone tomorrow, holds. I'm safe with Tony, but I can't be stupid and screw this up.

"Have you heard anything from Ramiro?" Tony asks as he loads the last of the dishes into the dishwasher.

"Nothing yet." I pick up my iPhone triple checking that my ringer is turned up. I don't want to miss any texts or calls. "Is it normal for it to take this long?"

"Kam's sister was in labor for three days before Calliope was born," he says.

"My mother's labors were fast. A few hours at most." I feel a pang of loss thinking about my family, especially today.

"How many siblings do you have?" Tony asks as he wipes his hands on a dish towel.

"I have two younger sisters. Arianna's twenty and London will be turning eighteen on New Year's Day."

"Do you keep in touch with them?"

"Arianna and I never got along," I explain. "London and I were always close. She gave me her cell phone number and a gift card to help me get out of Walking in the Light, but I haven't ever reached out to her."

"Why not?" he asks with genuine curiosity.

"My father. I don't trust him. I didn't want to risk him turning on London."

"Despite everything you've been through, you're always thinking about others," Tony says. "You're a good man, Leopold."

I shrug. "I don't think so."

"Look at me," he says with a quiet authority, and I lift my eyes to meet his. "Negativity is often louder than positivity. I understand that. But don't you go believing any of that. You, Leopold," Tony says, taking a step closer to me. "Are a good man."

For the briefest of moments, we stand close, our gazes locked with each other. I almost think he's going to lean in and kiss me, but then he takes a step back, and I realize what a ridiculous thought that is.

Why would a man like him be interested in a loser like you? He's just pitying you.

I force a yawn. "I'm pretty tired. Do you mind if I turn in?"

"You don't have to ask."

"I didn't want to ditch you if you still needed me."

"You were a huge help today," Tony says with a smile.

"I had a good time. Thank you for being so patient with me," I say quietly. "Goodnight, Tony." I turn and start walking out of the kitchen.

"Leopold." I stop and turn around. "Merry Christmas."

"Merry Christmas," I smile.

I reach into my wallet and pull out the piece of paper with my sister's phone number on it. I haven't allowed myself to think about London in a long time. Even though five years separated us, she and I were always close. She could always brighten any day. I swore I'd never reach out to her, but my resolve wavers. I pull out my phone and start typing in her number until I come to my senses.

"Don't be selfish, Leo," I say aloud. "You can't risk London getting hurt because you're feeling sorry for yourself."

I tear up the paper and flush it down the toilet, ensuring I won't do anything stupid in the midst of another weak moment.

Last night, Tony left my bedroom door open. I was grateful for that. It made me feel less trapped and alone. Tonight, I do the same thing. Then, I crawl beneath the covers and fall into a dream-filled sleep of a man with soft brown eyes that hold a quiet strength.

The sounds of Christmas music playing in the other room wake me. I stretch my arms above my head before sitting up. Swinging my legs over the side of the bed, I stand and pull up the blankets.

When I get out to the living room, I find a Christmas tree with twinkling lights and wrapped gifts under it. Tony's in the kitchen, standing over a large pot on the stove. I watch him move around the kitchen with practiced ease, enjoying the way his muscles flex as he reaches into his upper cabinets.

"Good morning," I say when he turns around and sees me watching him.

"Merry Christmas." He smiles brightly.

"You should've woke me up so I could've been out here helping you." I make a note to set an alarm to ensure I don't oversleep every day.

"I don't mind," he says. "Have a seat. We'll eat and then open gifts."

I freeze. "I didn't get you anything."

"It's nothing big," he says as he sets several plates in the center of the table. "The espresso will be ready in a minute."

"Did you stay up all night decorating?" I ask, motioning to the tree that wasn't there yesterday.

"I haven't put up a tree in a few years." He sets a small cup of coffee in front of me and another by his plate. "I decided it was time to take it out."

"I'm glad you did."

"Help yourself."

"It looks so pretty. I hate to mess it up."

"Don't be silly," Tony says, sliding the plate with the halved pears over to me. "Food is made to be enjoyed."

I've gone hungry more often than not over the past two years. Once I started deliveries, Tony always had something ready for me to eat at his restaurant and at Fire and Ice. I began to look forward to those days partially for the food but more so because I got to spend time with Tony.

"You're going to spoil me," I say, only half-joking.

"I fully intend on doing just that."

Anthony

LEOPOLD'S ALWAYS GENUINELY HAPPY WITH ANY FOOD I make him. It's the kind of joy that only someone who's been deprived of food, something I consider a human right, can exhibit.

"How do I eat this?"

"May I?" Leo nods and passes me his plate. He watches as I make a bed of ricotta and lay two pieces of the poached pears on top. "I didn't know if you were allergic to nuts, so I kept them separate."

"I'm not."

"Good. The candied walnuts are my favorite part," I sprinkle some over the pears and top it with a drizzle of honey. "I hope you like it," I say as I set his plate in front of him.

Watching Leo carefully load his fork with a bit of everything, I can't help but be captivated by the fluid motion of his lips as he savors the flavors. His tongue darts out to capture a stray drop of honey from his lip. For a fleeting moment, my thoughts veer into more sensual territory, imagining his lips wrapped around my cock. Thankfully, the table obstructs the view, and Leo doesn't notice. I avert my eyes, forcing myself to focus on my own plate.

"This is incredible, Tony," he gushes. "I've never tasted anything like it."

"It's not very hard to make. I can teach you if you'd like."

"I'd like that very much." Leo's smile lights up his face.

While we enjoy a leisurely meal, Leo begins to inquire about this evening's party. Apprehension is palpable in his tone. I offer reassurance, promising to stay by his side throughout the evening and suggesting we can slip away to take a break if it gets too much.

After we finish eating, Leo insists on loading the dishwasher. That frees me up to get started on the tomato sauce for tonight's meal.

With the sauce simmering lightly, I ask, "Are you ready for your present?"

"I wish you didn't get me anything. I have nothing to give you."

"I didn't do it to make you feel bad or because I expect something in return," I explain. "It's something small that I thought about yesterday."

"You didn't leave the house, though."

"I asked Owen to grab it for me," I say as I walk into the living room. Leo sits on the sofa with his legs pulled up under him while I get his gift from under the tree. I pass him the package wrapped in shiny silver paper and topped with a red bow, and then I sit beside him.

Leo bites his lower lip as he carefully unwraps the gift. He folds the paper and sets it on the sofa beside him with meticulous care. With a sense of awe, he lifts the lid of the white box, revealing the soft brown leather journal resting inside.

"Embrace the storm, for within its fury lies the promise of a rainbow," Leo reads the inscription, his voice carrying a mix of contemplation and hope.

"I wasn't sure if you preferred to draw or write, so I made sure it had both unlined and lined paper," I explain. "I wanted to give you a safe place to express your thoughts and feelings."

Leo's voice trembles as he confesses, "I don't know what to say." He meets my gaze with wide baby-blue eyes that mirror the wonder in his voice.

"I hope you like it."

"It's the most thoughtful gift anyone's ever given me. I love it." Leo surprises me by wrapping his arms around me and resting his head against my chest. Without hesitating, I return the embrace, feeling a sense of warmth and connection. "I'm sorry," he whispers, pulling away and flushing pink. "I shouldn't have done that."

"Don't apologize." I smile warmly. "I liked that you did."

My words hang in the air until his phone rings, breaking the spell we're under.

It's Ramiro," he murmurs.

"You should answer it."

With a look of regret, he swipes the screen, connects the call, and puts it on speaker. "Is she here?"

"The baby was born early this morning. But it's not a she," Ramiro says.

"What do you mean?"

"The ultrasound was wrong. It's a boy," he says excitedly. "I have a son."

"Oh my gosh." Leo brings his hand to his mouth. "You and Jacinta must be so happy."

"It's the best Christmas surprise we could've ever asked for."

"Congratulations. How's your wife feeling?" I ask.

"She's tired but doing well. Thank you for asking."

"Tell me everything," Leo says excitedly.

"He's tiny. Five pounds and sixteen inches with a head full of dark curly hair," Ramiro gushes.

"What's his name?"

"We'd planned to name our daughter after our mothers. Instead, we decided to name our son after our fathers, Tiburan Alfonso Vega."

I leave Leo to talk with Ramiro while I return to the kitchen to assemble the lasagna. Yesterday, Leo and I made homemade noodles, which have sat out to dry all night. I have a few layers put together when Leo comes to stand beside me.

"I'm sorry I took so long. Ramiro couldn't stop talking about the baby."

"You don't need to keep apologizing," I say patiently. "This is your home to come and go as you please."

Leo studies me before asking, "Can I help?"

"Sure."

While he washes up, I stir the sauce.

"Here's what you do," I explain, showing him the order for the noodles, sauce, and cheese, then stepping aside to let him take over. As he works, he occasionally shakes his head, struggling to keep his hair out of his eyes. "Do you have anything to tie your hair back?"

"No." He blows out a frustrated breath.

"I'm sure I have something around here."

Opening a large drawer filled with miscellaneous odds and ends that have no other home, I rummage around until I find what I need. Approaching Leo from behind, I comb my fingers through his silky, soft hair. Leo tenses from the unexpected touch, and I realize my mistake. Leaning in, I murmur softly, "I'm just pulling your hair back." His tension melts away instantly, and I gather his hair and tie it back with a rubber band. "It's a bit messy, but it should keep it out of your face."

"Am I doing this right?" he asks, his brow furrowed in uncertainty.

"You're doing great," I reassure him, offering him an approving smile that he reciprocates with one of his own.

When he finishes, I cover the tray with aluminum and slide it into the oven.

"That's the last of the big things. We can take a little bit to relax before Owen and Astrid get here," I say as I wipe down the counter. "He always comes early."

Broaching the subject of therapy with Leo is daunting, to say the least. While I'm cognizant of the trauma he's endured at the hands of his previous therapist, I have to believe there are trustworthy individuals who could provide him with the support he deserves. Despite my apprehension, I'm acutely aware that delaying seeking help from a trained professional will only prolong his suffering.

"There's something I want to talk to you about."

Leo wrings his fingers, a nervous habit I've noticed. "That sounds serious."

I join him where he's sitting at the kitchen island. "First, I need to be completely transparent with you," I say, my voice steady. "Star and Owen are aware of the situation," I continue, choosing my words carefully. "You have my word that your confidence will be respected. It won't go any further than them."

"I'm sure they think I'm a huge screw-up," Leo says, looking at his hands in his lap.

"No, they don't." Leo knows how I lost Kam, but we've never talked about my own struggles with suicidal thoughts. If I'm going to be able to connect with him, I need to be transparent and tell him everything. "After Kam died, I put up walls to keep everyone at arm's length. I tried to convince everyone I was fine. All the while, I was slowly withering away inside." I shift in my seat. Talking about the night of the attack on my restaurant still affects me—I'm a work in progress. "My carefully constructed façade fell apart when I was the victim of a hate crime."

"A hate crime?" Leo asks, shocked.

I recount the details of that awful night. The names I was called. "Being compared to one of the terrorists whose actions stole the person I loved broke me. I ignored what I thought was a heart attack."

"Why would you do that? What if it had been something serious?"

"I couldn't see a way out of the suffocating grief I'd been struggling to hide. I wanted to die."

"What happened?" Leo asks quietly.

"Owen found me and practically dragged my ass to the emergency room. After a battery of tests, they decided I was having anxiety attacks," I say, motioning with my hands for dramatic effect. "He pinned me down and had a serious heart-to-heart talk with me, pointing out the fact that I hadn't processed my loss and suggesting I go to therapy," I continue. "As upset as I was that night, I'm thankful for his persistence despite my difficult demeanor that night."

"I refuse to go to a treatment center," Leo says and stands. "I need to get out of here."

I place my hand on his arm, a silent plea in my touch, "Please stay and hear me out," I implore softly. He hesitates for another moment before sinking back into his seat. "I want to make something clear—I would *never* suggest you go inpatient," I assure him. "This is your home for as long as you want it to be. But I do believe seeing a therapist is crucial to your recovery," I pause, choosing my next words carefully.

"You've had experiences that no one should ever have to bear. A compassionate and trustworthy therapist will help you find the peace and healing you deserve," I pause again, letting my words sink in. "I need you to know you're not alone in this. I'll be with you every step of the way."

"How do you know if they're safe?" he asks.

"Star gave me the names of therapists she knows personally. I trust her judgment implicitly."

"I don't have insurance," he replies quickly. "I can't afford a therapist."

"I give my employees insurance on day one." My part-timers don't usually get insurance, but Leopold doesn't need to know that he's the exception.

"I don't know," he hesitates.

"You promised me thirty days," I remind him firmly. "While I won't use that to control you, attending *outpatient* therapy is nonnegotiable. I hope you'll come to realize it's in your best interest. That this world is a brighter, better place because you're in it."

Leopold

"You've done so much for me already. You can't keep doing—"

"I can and will," Tony interrupts. "We'll get all the paperwork taken care of tomorrow. Will you agree to go to therapy?"

The answer to his question should be easy. In today's society, going to therapy is more normalized than ever, but for me, it's synonymous with abuse—trauma.

You're being set up again. He only wants to use you. Hurt you.

The doorbell rings, startling me.

"It's okay." Anthony reaches out and touches my arm. "It's just Owen and Astrid." He walks away to answer the door. "Merry Christmas."

"Merry Christmas." Owen, who's wearing a Santa hat, chirps. "You put up a tree?" he asks, shocked.

"Don't act so surprised. It is Christmas, isn't it?" Tony turns his attention to the dark-haired woman and kisses her cheek, "Merry Christmas." Then, motioning toward me says, "Astrid, this is my friend, Leo."

"It's a pleasure to meet you," she says.

"You as well."

"It's good to see you again," Owen greets me, giving me a hug. "I'm not sure what you did to get that Scrooge to decorate, but thank you."

"I don't think it had anything to do with me."

"It had everything to do with you," he says quietly.

Tony's the epitome of the perfect host. Within minutes of his guests' arrival, he's already serving coffee and an extravagant lunch spread, including a wreath-shaped antipasto salad, clam and mozzarella dip, mouthwatering stuffed mushrooms, and arancini.

"Everything's perfect as always," Astrid compliments him.

"I can't take all the credit. Leopold was a huge help," he humbly remarks, a smile playing on his lips when he looks at me.

Tony's gaze is filled with warmth and kindness, sending a gentle flutter through my heart as our eyes meet.

"I really didn't do much," I say, averting my eyes.

"Do you like to cook?" Owen asks.

"I think so," I respond with a shrug. "But I can't make very many things."

These people are accomplished and confident. I can't help feeling inadequate in their presence.

"You're already better than me," Astrid says kindly. "Sir has been trying to teach me how to cook since we met, but all I can manage to make without burning are scrambled eggs and grilled cheese."

"Tony's a pro. He'll have you cooking like a five-star chef in no time," Owen reassures, offering a supporting smile.

While Tony and Owen discuss the club, Astrid shifts her attention to me. "How did you and Tony meet?"

"At his restaurant. I was delivering food," I reply nervously.

"He's quite taken with you," she says quietly. "I haven't seen him look at anyone like he does you in a long time."

"Oh no. We're not." My words come out rushed. "I'm just staying here for a little while."

"I'm sorry. I didn't mean to assume," Astrid apologizes.

"It's okay," I say, eager to shift the conversation away from me. "How long have you and Owen been together?"

"I've been his submissive for four years. It's only the past few months that we've started exploring our feelings outside of our dynamic," she says dreamily.

"I don't know what all of that means, but it sounds good," I admit with a chuckle.

"It is." She looks at Owen admiringly before saying, "You should come to the club sometime. I bet you'd love it."

Sensing my unease, Tony gracefully shifts the conversation to Astrid's job as a high school science teacher. Her enthusiasm for teaching shines through as she animatedly discusses her students.

With him deep in conversation, I didn't realize he was paying attention to our discussion, but I'm grateful and offer a relieved smile. It's not the first time he's come to my rescue, and I'm starting to realize it's one of his many talents.

As the afternoon shifts into evening, the house fills with a small gathering of Tony's friends. We indulge in yet another exquisite meal, surrounded by friendly and easy-to-talk-to individuals. Despite the knowledge that Owen and Star know my situation, they treat me with the same warmth and kindness. I find myself relaxing and enjoying the party.

Tony's sitting on his sofa talking with Star's submissive, Corbin, and a few others. Uncertain if it's appropriate for me to join, I approach hesitantly. Tony catches my eye and motions for me to join him.

"Are you enjoying yourself?" Tony speaks softly to me.

"I am," I reply, finding comfort in our private exchange.

"I'm pleased to hear that." His voice carries a hint of something more profound.

With the laughter and chatter of the gathering swirl around us, Tony's question affords us a moment of intimacy, allowing our connection to deepen amidst the whirlwind of activity.

As the night winds down and the last guest departs, I feel a twinge of regret. Despite my initial hesitations, I found myself relaxing and enjoying their company.

"You look exhausted," Tony remarks. "Why don't you turn in."

"But there are still dishes."

"I'll take care of them."

"Are you sure?" I ask, not wanting to ditch him with a mess.

"I'm positive," he reassures me. "Sleep well."

"You too." He responds before turning to load the dishwasher.

"Tony?" I call, and he pauses, turning to face me. "Would you stay with me? At least for the first session?" I ask nervously, feeling the weight of my request hanging in the air.

"Of course," he replies without hesitation.

As I make my way down the hall to my bedroom, an unfamiliar emotion begins to stir within me—a feeling I haven't experienced in a very long time—hope.

Leopold

WORKING IN A RESTAURANT ISN'T ANYTHING LIKE I'D imagined. When Tony warned me that things could get busy, I thought I understood, but I hadn't fully grasped the reality until now. It's a constant battle keeping up with clearing tables, fetching drinks, and doing whatever else is necessary to help the other team members.

Surprisingly, though, I find myself enjoying the challenge. There's a certain thrill in the hustle and bustle of the dining area, a satisfaction in knowing that I'm contributing to the smooth operation of Tony's business. I never would've guessed that I'd enjoy working in a restaurant. Still, there's a sense of accomplishment that comes with each successfully cleared table and satisfied customer.

In addition to supporting me at work, Tony also followed through on getting me set up with health insurance and a therapist. Now, as we sit in the luxurious waiting room, awaiting my first therapy appointment, I can't help but feel overwhelmed with gratitude. It's a new chapter in my life, one that wouldn't have been possible without Tony's unwavering support. As I glance at him, a sense of peace washes over me, knowing I'm not alone in this journey toward healing and self-discovery.

Don't get used to it. He's not going to stick around. He'll leave you like everyone has.

"Leopold?" a red-headed woman snaps me out of my thoughts when she steps out of her office and calls my name.

"That's me," I say as I stand.

"I'm Sarah," she introduces herself. "Come on in."

I look back at Tony, who rises to his feet, a determined expression on his face.

"You can wait out here," she says kindly.

"No." My feet freeze in place. "He needs to come with me."

"Okay. We can do that," Sarah assures me, her kind smile easing my nerves a little bit.

When I don't move, Tony places his hand on my lower back, a silent show of his unwavering support. "I'm right here with you."

I step inside the office, Tony and Sarah following close behind. When Sarah moves to close the door, a surge of panic washes over me. "Is it possible to leave the door open?" I ask nervously. "I don't mean to be a pain."

"Asking a question is never a problem," she reassures me with a comforting smile. "I'll always do my best to accommodate your requests."

Tony and I sit on a beige microsuede sofa, our legs brushing against each other. Looking around her office, I mentally note the differences between Sarah's office and David's.

This office is bright and welcoming. Sunlight shines through the large window behind Sarah's desk. One side of the room contains bookshelves. The other, where we are, is a sitting area with a couch and two chairs. There are no other doors, something that puts me at ease.

"Do you prefer Leopold or Leo," Sarah asks as she picks up a notebook and pen from her desk.

"You can call me Leo."

Sarah sits in one of the chairs across from us. "May I ask who you've brought with you today, Leo?"

"This is my friend, Tony."

"It's a pleasure to meet you," she greets him.

"You as well," he replies politely.

"Can you tell me a little about you, Leo?"

"What do you want to know?" I shrug, uncertain what to say.

"Let's start with why you've come today?"

"Right before Christmas, I tried to kill myself," I confess.

"How did you do it?"

"I tried to slit my wrist." I look down at my arm and run my finger over the lightly colored scar. "Tony was the one who stopped me."

"Before we continue, I have to ask. Are you still thinking about hurting yourself?"

"Sometimes I wish I'd been successful," I say, refusing to look at Tony. I don't want to see what I know will be a hurt expression. "I still hear the same thoughts I did that night."

Sarah jots something down on the paper before asking, "Are you willing to share any of those thoughts with me?"

"Things like I'm a screw-up. I'm not good enough. That I'm better off dead." I look up. "Stuff the people in my past told me all the time."

"I'm sorry you were subject to that kind of cruelty," she responds empathetically.

You deserved everything you got. She probably thinks the same thing. Because it's true. You're a loser.

"Thank you," I whisper, feeling a lump form in my throat.

Sarah nods, her expression filled with compassion. "Understandably, those words would linger, but they don't define you."

"I want to move past them," I say quietly.

"We'll work on that together," Sarah's voice is steady and reassuring. "You're not alone in this journey."

Sarah begins by asking about my family history, a topic that's full of tangled emotions and buried memories. A knot tightens in my stomach as I reluctantly talk about my upbringing, tiptoeing around certain painful truths. With each question, I find myself grappling with conflicting emotions, torn between the desire to be honest and the fear of exposing too much.

When the conversation shifts towards my history with therapy, a wave of nausea washes over me. Sarah notices right away and changes the direction of our conversation.

"You're doing great," She encourages with a kind smile. "Before we finish up, I'd like us to develop a safety plan."

"What's it for?" I ask.

"It's a personalized tool you can rely on if your anxiety becomes overwhelming. It'll help empower you by offering support and strategies to help you maneuver rough patches and hopefully prevent another crisis."

"Okay," I answer hesitantly.

"Who do you consider your support system?"

I look at the man sitting next to me. "Tony."

She writes his name down. "Who else?"

"That's everyone."

Sarah looks up at me. "There's no one else?" I shake my head.

"What about Ramiro?" Tony asks.

"I guess so, but he's in California."

"He can still be a support," She adds.

Tony also suggests I add Star and Owen.

We discuss potential triggers, but other than closed doors, I don't know any. Sarah lets me know there are blank lines that Tony and I can fill in if something comes up. Next, we make a list of coping strategies including listening to music, meditation, and writing in my new journal. The last section contains Sarah's office number and an after-hours emergency number where I can reach her.

"Don't hesitate to call or text me during the week," she offers.

Despite my apprehensions, I sense that Sarah is genuinely invested in helping me unravel the complexities of my story and guiding me toward a path of healing.

Leopold

JANUARY 23

I've had three sessions with Sarah. She's very nice, and she lets Tony come into my sessions with me. When I told her I had a rough past, I don't think she was anticipating how rough—and we only got through my first few weeks at Walking in the Light. She did her best to school her features, but I saw the subtle way she crossed and uncrossed her legs and how, at times, she struggled to maintain eye contact. That's when I decided to be more cautious with what I tell her. I don't want to scar her for life, or worse, she asks me to not make my next appointment.

It'll be fine. I can get by without confessing my darkest secrets.

And then there's Tony. Occasionally, I think I've seen him watching me, only to look away quickly. Several times, he's brushed up against me, and I've gotten hard. Thankfully, Tony didn't notice. I don't want to embarrass myself in front of him.

That man is everything. Every dream I never dared to dream. Every wish I never dared to wish.

If only I could be deserving of him.

Anthony

Owen: Why don't you come down to the club tonight? It's been too long since we've seen you. I am.

Owen: Then get your ass down here.

Me: I'm home with Leo. I can't.

Owen: You can't stop living your life. At some point, he's going to have to be alone.

Me: Not yet.

Owen: This is getting to be unhealthy for you.

Me: I have to go.

I turn my ringer off and slide my phone into my pocket. Owen means well, but he doesn't understand. He has no idea what I went through during those first few weeks. I'm the one who was with Leopold when he'd wake terrified from nightmares. It was me who held him and rocked him until he settled. I saw each time he startled at a loud noise or stiffened when I reached out and touched him.

I've seen him smile more. I fall for him a little more each time I see his lips turn up and his eyes sparkle. But even though everything appears to be going well, I'm still terrified to leave him alone. Leopold promised me thirty days, but we're past that, and I feel as though we're living on borrowed time. I refuse to let my guard down. I cannot lose him.

When I opened *Italiano Desiderio* and stressed the importance of teamwork and precision with my staff, I didn't realize how much I'd come to rely on it one day. Since Leopold came to live with me, I've been putting in fewer hours at the restaurant to be with him. Knowing my restaurant is being run properly in my absence is one less thing I have to worry about.

Leopold has kept his word and attends therapy every week. I still go with him, but now I'm able to stay in the waiting room as long as Sarah leaves the door open. I'm not an expert, but I think he's making progress. He's also enrolled in GED prep classes at the community center. While I go to art class, he goes to study. He's an intelligent man, and I have no doubt he'll excel and pass the exam without issues.

"Dinner's almost ready," I say when Leo walks into the kitchen.

"What did you make tonight?"

"It's only a frozen pizza."

Leo's eyes open wide, and he takes a step back.

"What's wrong?"

"I—"

I reach out to take his hand, but he jerks it away. "Leo, talk to me."

Without warning, he turns and runs down the hall, slamming his bedroom door.

"Leo," I call and knock on the door. "What's going on?" There's no reply, so I knock again. "Please talk to me."

I don't know what happened, but this doesn't feel right. I try the handle, but it's locked. The hairs on the back of my neck stand on end. Hurrying into my room, I grab the master key.

"Leopold. Please open the door," I call one last time. He still doesn't respond. Ordinarily, I'd never unlock the door and enter his private space, but this is different. What if he's harming himself? "I'm coming in," I warn. My hands shake as I slide the key into the lock. Not knowing what I'll find, my hand trembles as I open the door.

I find Leo sitting on the floor on the far side of the room. His legs are pulled up to his chest, his arms wrapped tight around them. Silent tears are streaming down his face.

"Hey," I say quietly as I lower to my knees. "What's wrong?" I reach out, placing my hand on his knee. He flinches from my touch, pulling his legs in tighter. His eyes are open, but he looks far away. "I'm not going to hurt you." I use my thumbs to wipe away his tears. "Please talk to me."

A few long seconds pass before his eyes focus, and I know he finally sees me.

"Tony?"

"I'm right here." Reaching out, I tuck some loose hairs behind his ear. Leo leans into my hand, and I cup his face. "I won't let anything happen. You're safe." He closes his eyes as I stroke his cheek with my thumb.

"I'm sorry," he says, lifting his head.

"What happened?"

"The pizza. You never make frozen pizza," he says, his voice cracking.

"It's not something I do often, but every now and then, I give in to the desire for something not homemade." I shift from my knees to sit against the wall beside him.

"The night Krew brought me home, he made a frozen pizza," Leo confesses.

My stomach sinks as the weight of Leopold's anguish settles over me. "I had no idea," I admit, my voice laced with remorse. Opening my arms, I silently offer him the shelter of my embrace. Leo accepts without hesitation, settling onto my lap as though seeking refuge from the storm raging within.

Holding him tightly against me, I offer silent reassurance through the warmth of my touch. "I'm so sorry," I murmur quietly, my lips brushing against the soft strands of his hair in a tender kiss. It's a move that feels natural, a gesture born from a deep-seated need to provide him with comfort and reassurance.

"But you like it," he says quietly.

"I like you more." He shifts on my lap to meet my gaze. "It's something that bothers you, so I'll never buy it again."

"You like me?" he questions, his eyes searching mine for confirmation.

"Yes, Leo," I say, my voice low. "I like you very much."

He lifts his face, and our lips meet tentatively as if testing the waters of forbidden desire. The kiss is soft, almost innocent, but with each passing moment, it deepens into something more profound. As our tongues entwine, a surge of longing courses through me, setting every nerve ablaze with desire. Unable to resist the magnetic pull between us, my hand instinctively finds its way to his hair, fingers tangling in the soft strands as I deepen the kiss. Leo responds eagerly, a soft groan escaping his lips.

But as quickly as the passion ignites, a wave of reality crashes over me, dousing the flames of desire with a harsh dose of truth. With a sharp intake of breath, I pull away, my chest heaving with the weight of realization. "We can't do this," I whisper, my words heavy with regret.

Leo's expression crumbles, his eyes filled with hurt as he pulls away, putting distance between us as if to shield himself from the pain of rejection. "I get it," he mumbles.

"I don't think you do."

"You're letting me stay here, and you're being nice because you feel bad for me." His voice trembles with raw vulnerability, and I can see the pain etched in the depths of his cerulean eyes. "When you said you liked me, you didn't mean like *that*."

"I'm attracted to you," I confess, my voice faltering under the weight of his accusation. "I have been since the first day you walked into my restaurant all bundled up." A fond smile tugs at my lips as I recall the memory of that moment.

"Then, why did you stop?" His question hangs heavy in the air, laden with uncertainty and longing, echoing the ache in my own heart.

"You just had a panic attack and locked yourself in your room," I clarify gently, hoping to convey the sincerity of my words. "As much as I wanted to keep going, it wouldn't be right." Despite my explanation, I can see the doubt lingering in his eyes, his uncertainty palpable. "If... No, when—" I correct myself, realizing the weight of my words. "When we take our relationship to the next level, I want to be sure it's for the right reasons."

"You want to be with me?" His voice trembles with a mixture of hope and disbelief, uncertainty coloring his every word.

The tension between us crackles in the air. The unspoken attraction that I've been trying so hard to conceal is now laid bare before us.

"Yes, Leo," I answer, my voice steady despite the tumult of emotions swirling within me. "I very much want to be with you."

Leopold

I kissed him. I had a meltdown over a frozen pizza, and then I kissed him. What was I thinking? Sure, he's gorgeous, and he's always kind to me, but why did I assume it was because he felt anything other than pity for me? I mean, why would a man like Anthony want to be with someone like me? I was devastated when he pushed me away, certain I just ruined everything. But then he said it. At first, I wasn't sure if I heard correctly. But then he said 'when' not 'if' we take our relationship to the next level, and I felt the evidence of his attraction between his legs.

What happens now? I'm not exactly an authority on healthy relationships.

I wish I could talk to Ramiro about this. But after what happened with Krew and then Phil and Maureen, he's become even more protective —almost suffocating. He's begged me to come back to California despite any threats Krew may or may not still pose. But my answer is always no.

Ramiro was already familiar with Tony's name. I told him I met him when I was doing deliveries and that we'd sometimes talk and have lunch. I left out that it was every time and that some of those times were at Fire and Ice. I also left out that I'm attracted to Tony. Ramiro was already distrusting of everyone. I didn't want Tony to become an argument between us.

Tony's unlike any man I've ever met. He's genuine and kind. Over the past month, he's proven that he has no ulterior motives for opening his home to me. When I told him I never graduated high school, he helped me enroll in GED prep courses. In a few weeks, I'll be taking my test. He's also given me employment. Unlike Krew's 'job' offer, this one is legitimate. I get paid more than a fair wage with health insurance benefits that have made it possible to see Sarah regularly.

Therapy. I have a love-hate relationship with it. Sarah, my therapist, is very nice. She allowed me to bring Tony into my sessions until I felt comfortable being in the room alone with her. Then, we took baby steps until I could be in her office with the door shut and Tony in the waiting room.

Talking about my memories and feelings isn't comfortable, though. As nice as Sarah is, I don't trust her enough to open up fully. To tell her the darkest, most depraved things that I lived through. No one knows the worst of what happened, and no one ever will.

Leopold

"Leopold," Tony calls from the hallway as he walks into the house from work.

Tony's gradually grown more comfortable with the idea of leaving me alone. I'm glad to have earned his trust, but I can't deny how much I miss him when he's not with me.

"What is it?" I ask as I hurry from my room. "Is everything okay?"

He holds up a large white envelope, waving it slowly. "Your scores came."

My GED exam was several weeks ago. I knew the results would come in the mail, and until now, I couldn't wait for them. Now that they're here, I'm hesitant to open them. "What if I failed?" I wrap my hands around my waist, trying to calm the queasiness in my stomach. "I don't think I can open it."

"You've been waiting for them for weeks," Tony encourages, holding the envelope to me.

"I can't." I shake my head. "Will you open it?"

"Are you sure?" he asks, and I nod.

Carefully, Tony slides his finger under the seam, opening the envelope. He pulls out a sheet of white paper, studying it intently. Slowly, a subtle shift in his demeanor hints at his disappointment as he reads.

"It's bad, isn't it?" I mumble, a knot of dread forming in my stomach. "I failed. I knew it."

Tony's laughter fills the room. "You didn't fail, not even close."

"I didn't?" I ask in disbelief.

"You scored 175 on Reading through Language Arts. 150 on Mathematical Reasoning. That was your lowest score, by the way," Tony adds. "190 on Social Studies and 165 on Science for a cumulative score of 675." He reaches into the envelope and pulls out another paper. "Congratulations, Leopold. You've earned your New York State High School Equivalency Diploma."

My hands tremble as I take the diploma and read aloud, "Be it known that Leopold Wagner, having satisfactorily completed the requirements prescribed by the Commonwealth of Education, is thereby entitled to this High School Equivalency Diploma." I turn to Tony, whose eyes gleam with pride. "Is this even real?"

"Yes, it is," he murmurs, his voice low and velvety, sending shivers down my spine.

"I did it. I finally have my diploma," I say proudly. The sheer satisfaction I experience while clutching this piece of paper is beyond words.

"I'm incredibly proud of you, Leopold," Tony says warmly, opening his arms. I step into his embrace. "Let's go out and celebrate tonight."

"I'd like that," I whisper, resting my head against his chest as he holds me tight. Since that first kiss, we've become more accustomed to these tender gestures. "I wouldn't have been able to do any of this without you." I lift my head to meet his gaze.

"That's not true." He gently runs his knuckles down my face. "You did this all on your own." He leans down, pressing his lips to mine.

Tony's touch is both tender and insistent as he trails his tongue along my lower lip. Yielding to his advances, I grant him access, and our mouths merge in a heated exchange. With one hand firmly grasping the back of my neck, he guides me closer while the other traces down my spine to my ass, melding our bodies together. I feel the heat of his desire pressing against me, matching my own arousal, and I can't help but moan into his mouth.

His cell rings, but Tony makes no move to answer it. Instead, his mouth descends to my neck, where he expertly nips and sucks, igniting a trail of tingling sensations.

His phone buzzes incessantly. "Shit," he says, pulling away and leaving me breathless. "Hello?" he answers, his voice gruff. "There's no one else?" he asks, pausing to listen to whoever's on the other end. "Leo and I are planning to go celebrate tonight." Another pause. "He got his diploma today," Tony says, smiling.

He switches the phone to speaker mode and extends it towards me. "Congratulations," Owen's voice booms with excitement from the other end.

"Thank you. I can hardly believe it." I look at the paper I'm still holding and reread it to make sure the words don't magically change.

"You put in the hard work. You deserve every bit of it," Owen praises me before directing his attention back to Tony. "I hate to impose, especially on such an important evening, but I'm really in a bind."

"Just a moment," Tony says, muting the phone. "Star was supposed to manage the club tonight, but she's down with a terrible migraine. Owen asked me to step in since he's out of town, but I explained we have plans."

"It's okay. He needs your help," I answer.

"I'm more concerned with letting you down."

I hesitate, chewing my lower lip briefly before suggesting, "I could go with you."

"To Fire and Ice?" Tony asks, surprised.

I've been intrigued by the club since I was doing deliveries there. But other than casual comments, they never shared much about it with me. Despite living with Tony for over six months, he's not gone to Fire and Ice at all. I've done some reading and am eager to see for myself what this lifestyle he's a part of entails.

"Yes," I answer and nod slowly.

"Are you sure?"

"I'd like to learn more about what you like."

Tony's eyes linger on me with a mixture of admiration and affection before speaking softly, "You never cease to amaze me, Leopold." He unmutes the phone. "We'll be there."

Anthony

Leo catches me off guard as he expresses an interest in going to Fire and Ice and learning more about BDSM. For a moment, I'm at a loss for words. I can only take in the sight of this man I just fell more in love with. "You never cease to amaze me, Leopold." I finally say before taking the phone off mute. "We'll be there."

I haven't been this nervous to go to the club since my first days in the lifestyle.

Being raised in Manhattan meant that from a young age, I was surrounded by diverse cultures and communities. My parents, who I believe recognized my homosexuality before I did, celebrated my individuality and encouraged me to explore my interests and pursue my dreams—which included my passion for cooking.

During my time in culinary school, I became interested in one of my classmates, Oliver. He shared my passion for experimenting both in the kitchen and in life. Our chemistry was explosive. We'd barely made it out of school and into his apartment before we were ripping each other's clothes off and fucking all night long.

One night, he invited me to go to a new club he heard about through another friend. Intrigued by the promise of adventure, I accepted the invitation, unaware of the journey it would set me on.

Nestled discreetly in the heart of New York City's eclectic underground, The Velvet Sanctuary catered to those seeking an escape from the ordinary. A haven of indulgence and exploration, this exclusive BDSM club offered a refuge where fantasies came to life in a realm of opulent decadence.

Stepping through the unassuming entrance, I found myself transported into a world of sensuality and intrigue. The ambiance is rich with the scent of exotic incense and the soft murmur of whispered desires. Plush velvet drapes adorned the walls, giving the space an intimate, inviting glow.

In the main lounge area, guests gathered in clusters, their laughter and conversation mingling with the sultry strains of ambient music and the sensual moans of couples having sex. Plush couches and low tables offered comfortable seating, while discreet alcoves provided privacy for more intimate encounters.

Venturing further into The Velvet Sanctuary, I discovered a labyrinth of luxurious bondage chambers, dimly lit dungeons where leather-clad Dominants reigned supreme, and decadent sensory deprivation rooms. The club boasted diverse play spaces where guests were free to unleash their imagination and indulge their darkest desires. For me, it felt like I was home.

Oliver liked to take charge in the bedroom, and, at the time, I was open to trying almost anything, so I assumed the role of submissive. I surrendered to the exquisite agony of pleasure and pain. With each binding restraint and whispered command, I felt myself slipping deeper into the throes of ecstasy, my senses ablaze with the heady rush of adrenaline and desire.

However, as our relationship progressed, my dominant nature began to assert itself. Despite my initial attraction to submission, I found myself yearning for control and authority. At first, the transition was subtle. Small gestures and hints of dominance crept into our interactions, igniting a spark of excitement and anticipation between us. But as our connection deepened, so did my hunger for power and control. The more I thought about it, the more I realized that submission alone could never satisfy the depths of my cravings.

Oliver confessed his intrigue with the idea of witnessing my Dominance in action. It wasn't a request born out of jealousy or insecurity but rather a genuine curiosity and desire to explore the boundaries of our connection. With his encouragement, I embraced my Dominant nature. Knowing that Oliver was watching heightened the intensity of the experience.

But we were young and didn't have a clue how to manage a dynamic. We never vetted one another or adhered to any list of limits. Communication wasn't high on our list of strengths.

For Oliver, the thrill of watching soon gave way to a sense of unease and discomfort. What had once been an exciting exploration of our desires now felt like a constant reminder of his insecurities and vulnerabilities. As he struggled to reconcile his conflicting emotions, resentment and jealousy began to fester. What had once brought us together now served as a catalyst for our downfall. In the end, our shared exploration into my Dominant side proved to be our undoing.

My journey into submission left an indelible mark on my understanding of the BDSM lifestyle. Through the exploration of my desires, I discovered my true calling as a Dominant. I sought out a new club with a strict code of conduct that prioritized consent, communication, and respect.

That's how I found Fire and Ice. The club has become more than a simple venue to push the boundaries of pleasure and liberation. It's a community—a family where individuals from all walks of life come together to explore their sexuality, forge deep connections, and celebrate the beauty of human desire.

Could Leopold be exactly who I've been waiting for? With everything in me, I hope Leopold feels like this place could be his home, too. A place where we could explore our desires together.

***

"Are you sure you're okay that I came with you?" he asks nervously.

"Of course," I say, looking up from the computer screen. "I'm sorry if you think I'm ignoring you. I'm not. I don't want to screw anything up."

"Is there anything I can do to help?"

"Just be your charming self." I smile. "And maybe unlock the doors."

"I can do that." Leo steps out from behind the desk.

As he strides across the carpet, I can't help but notice the changes in Leo's physique. Thanks to regular visits to the gym in my apartment building, he's become more than just handsome—he's mouthwateringly gorgeous. The image of him, all rippling muscles and raw masculinity fills my mind, igniting a fire of primal longing. I've stroked myself to orgasm more times than I care to admit, thinking about him.

The taste of Leopold's lips lingers on mine, a potent reminder of the desire that simmers between us. Owen's call prevented us from crossing a line that I'm not sure we're ready to navigate. I want nothing more than to be with Leopold, to explore the depths of our connection, but I can't ignore that it's only been six months since his suicide attempt. He's just beginning to put his life back together—to learn who he is and what he wants. Starting a relationship now feels like tempting fate. I don't want to complicate his recovery by beginning a relationship that may or may not fit the person Leopold grows to be.

"Are you okay?" Leo asks, getting my attention.

"What do you mean?"

"You look a million miles away," he says as he perches on the stool beside me.

"I've just got a lot on my mind," I reply, turning toward him. "We need to talk about what almost happened at home."

"You regret it—"

"Tony, it's so good to see you," Lacey, one of the club's regulars, says as she walks in, and once again, we're interrupted.

"I haven't seen you in forever. How are you?"

"I'm doing well," she smiles and glances between Leo and me.

"Leopold, I'd like to introduce you to Lacey. She's one of our regular Domme's."

"It's very nice to meet you," Leo says politely.

"You as well." She looks at me. "It's nice to finally see you with a new sub."

"Leopold's not my sub," I clarify, hoping to nip any misunderstandings in the bud. "He's just curious about Fire and Ice."

"I see."

"How's the baby?" I ask while I finish checking her in.

"He's perfect." Lacey beams.

"Lacey and her husband just had their first child," I explain. "Where are Caleb and Shawn?"

"Shawn had to work late, and Caleb is waiting for the sitter to get to our house."

Leo's forehead is scrunched as he tries to figure out the dynamic. "Caleb and Shawn are Lacey's submissives." He nods in understanding.

"How did you end up at the desk?" she asks.

"Star's home sick, and Owen's out of town," I reply. "I'm filling in for them."

"How is Leopold going to experience the club from out here?" She taps her long red nails on the counter.

"I haven't worked out the details yet."

"If Leopold consents. I'll gladly escort him this evening so he gets a proper introduction," Lacey suggests.

"What do you think?"

Leo's gaze meets mine, his big blue eyes wide with concern. "Is that okay with you?" he asks, his voice carrying a hint of uncertainty.

"Excuse me for one second," Lacey says, holding up her phone. "It's Caleb."

After Lacey steps away, Leo says, "If you'd rather I stay with you, I will."

"You came to see what the club's like, and that can't happen if you're out here all night." Leo looks between Lacey and me, and I answer his unspoken question. "I've known her for many years. She's trustworthy," I say, trying to ease his nervousness. "If you'd like to join her inside, you're more than welcome."

"What about the conversation we need to have?" Leo's voice is tinged with apprehension.

"We'll continue it at home." I lower my voice. I assure him, my voice softening. "But know this, Leo—I have no regrets about what happened."

"Are you sure?" Leo's doubt is evident.

It pains me that Leo continues to question his worth. "I'm positive."

"Am I going to have a third man on my arm tonight?" Lacey asks.

"Yes, ma'am," Leo says politely.

"Such good manners." Lacey leans closer to me and whispers, "If you don't scoop him up, I just might." She winks at Leo, and he laughs softly.

Turning my attention back to Leopold, I begin to explain the rules. "We have a color-coded system to identify everyone in the club," I explain and point out the sign on the wall.

Listed are the colors of the rainbow and what each color signifies.

White- Vanilla, very new, wishes to take it slow.

White with polka dots- Looking to play with multiple partners.

Silver with Bells- Into pet play/ role-play bottom.

Grey- Bondage, top, rope play, latex fetish.

Blue- Mentor, safe person, willing to instruct.

Dark Purple- Likes spanking.

Light Purple- Likes Wax play.

Red- Do not approach directly. If interested, go directly to sponsoring Dominant only.

Red with stripe- Do not approach. Just watching and learning.

Pink- Females only.

Orange- Monogamous, Not likely to play.

Brown- Interested in role-play.

Yellow- Watersports. Likes urine-play.

Green- Wants to play. Open-minded.

"You'll get this one tonight." I secure a red with white stripe bracelet to his left wrist. "Other than Lacey and her subs, no one will approach you."

"Okay," Leo says, his grip tightening on my hand. His body is tense with apprehension.

Sensing his discomfort, I lower my voice. "If you're uncomfortable, you don't have to do this. We can come back another night."

"You said you trust her, right?" Leo's voice trembles slightly.

"I do," I respond, offering him a reassuring smile.

"And I can come back out any time I want?"

"Of course."

Leo takes a deep breath, visibly collecting himself. "Then, I'll be okay," he says, his voice steadier as he steps around the counter.

"Are you ready?" Lacey asks.

"I am," he states, his smile warm and reassuring as he shoots me a quick glance.

"Don't worry. I'll return you to Tony in one piece."

As Leopold steps into Fire and Ice, immersing himself in the world of BDSM, I can't help but feel a pang of jealousy that I'm not experiencing it with him.

My thoughts keep returning to Leopold, wondering what he's thinking and feeling. I can't shake the feeling that I should be in there with him—that we should be exploring this together, but the busy night keeps me tied to the desk.

Leopold

"Where would you like to explore first, Leo?" Lacey asks.

I look around the large space, already feeling overwhelmed and uncertain about where to go or what to ask about. Part of me wants to run back out to the safety of Tony. The other part knows that if I'm going to be a part of Tony's life, I need to stay and see what this BDSM stuff is all about.

Lacey's touch startles me, causing me to jump slightly. "I'm sorry," she says quickly, retracting her hand. "It can be a lot your first time here."

"Yeah, it is," I reply.

"Let's start at the beginning," she suggests. "What do you know about the lifestyle?"

"I know there's kink and stuff."

She watches me expectantly, waiting for a response. When I don't say anything more, she nods understandingly. "How about we go grab a table and sit and chat?" The petite woman moves gracefully across the concrete floor, exuding confidence with each step. I trail behind her, feeling a twinge of inadequacy in her presence. Lacey chooses a table in the café and gestures for me to sit opposite her. "Would you like something to eat?"

"No, thank you." I'm too nervous to eat.

With a soft clink, the server places two glasses of ice water in front of us, and I waste no time taking a refreshing sip, grateful for the relief it brings to my dry throat. Around us, the room slowly starts to come alive as people of all kinds filter in. Couples, both same-sex and opposite-sex, move through the crowd with ease.

There are those adorned in elaborate fetish gear, their outfits a testament to their commitment to the lifestyle. Others opt for a more casual look, blending seamlessly into the diverse crowd. It's a melting pot of desires and orientations. A place where everyone is free to express themselves authentically without fear of judgment.

"How did you and Tony meet?" Lacey asks.

"At work." I fidget my fingers on the table in front of me.

"You seem really nervous." She glances at my hands, and I still them. "There's no reason to be. I don't bite. Well, I do," Lacey chuckles. "But I won't bite you."

"I'm sorry. This is all very new to me," I confess.

"We were all new at one point." She smiles warmly. "What has Tony told you so far?"

"Nothing."

"Wait a minute," she says, surprised. "You two are together, but you haven't discussed the lifestyle at all?"

"Oh, we're not together," I say quickly. "We're just—"

Lacey holds up her hand, stopping me. "It's okay. You don't have to explain it. There's no judgment for whatever is or isn't going on. Let's go back to the very beginning," she says, then takes a sip of her water. "BDSM stands for bondage and discipline, dominance and submission, sadism and masochism."

"That's quite a mouthful."

"It is," she acknowledges, her tone gentle yet confident. "There are many different roles one may fit into. A Dominant, submissive, or switch are probably the three most common."

"What's Tony?" I ask quietly.

"Tony's a Dominant," Lacey says matter-of-factly. "He's also a master of body art with wax." Two men walk over to our table, Lacey smiles at them. "Leo, I'd like you to meet Shawn." She motions to the taller of two men. "And Caleb. This is Leo, he's a friend of Anthony." After we exchange greetings, they join us at the table. "Leo's not currently in the lifestyle," she explains. "But he's curious. We were going over some basics."

I remain quiet as I observe their interactions. The care they show for one another is evident, but what strikes me most is the respect Lacey affords each of the men. Despite her Dominant role, they still have a voice in their dynamic. It's not what I imagined a BDSM relationship to be or what I experienced in my toxic relationship with Krew. "I'm confused," I admit. "I thought they didn't get a say in anything."

"What do you mean?" Lacey asks.

"You're their Dominant, right?"

"I am," she confirms with a nod.

"But you ask their opinions, and you listen to them?"

"This lifestyle is built on three tenants. Safe, sane, and consensual. Nothing happens between us that we all haven't consented to," she explains. "Consent is the most important part of this lifestyle."

Consent has been something missing in my life. With my father, it was a silent decree— an unspoken rule. His wishes superseded my own. David abused his role by using manipulative tactics that coerced compliance and broke every sacred boundary between therapist and patient. Consent became a weapon Krew wielded against me in moments of vulnerability.

Their disregard for my boundaries left me feeling powerless and voiceless. As a result, I was robbed of healthy interactions and loving relationships. I withered away into near nothingness, a shell of the person I once was.

I was broken and alone.

"The bondage demonstration is beginning," Lacey announces, pulling me from my thoughts. "Let's go get some good seats."

Anthony

"You've been quiet since we left the club. Is everything okay?" I ask.

"Yeah. It was a long night, and I'm tired," Leo answers but doesn't look up. "I'm going to head to bed."

"Leo." I reach out and touch his arm, but he flinches away. "I was hoping we could talk about us."

"Us?" he asks, taken aback.

"I don't think it's just me that feels things shifting. At least, I hope it isn't just me."

Leo forces a smile on his face, but I know him too well and see through his façade. "Do you think we can talk about this tomorrow?"

"Are you okay?" I ask concerned.

"I'm just tired."

Something feels off, and I don't like it. "Leo," I call, and he stops. "The lifestyle, if it's not something you're interested in, that's okay. I'll walk away from it right now to be with you."

"Good night, Tony."

Leo disappears into his room closing his door with a soft thud, shutting me out. I ache to follow him, but I don't want to push. Too wired for sleep, I turn to my sketch pad and pencils, losing myself in the soothing rhythm of drawing until my eyes are heavy and my body's ready to settle in for the night. The tranquility of the night is abruptly shattered by a loud crash echoing from Leo's room.

Abandoning my art supplies, I rush down the hall and knock on his door. "Are you okay?" My question is met with silence. "Leopold, answer me," I demand, my worry mounting as I hear his muffled voice from inside. I try the handle, but it's locked. "Unlock the door," I plead, my fist hammering against the unforgiving wood.

A sense of déjà vu washes over me as I recall the frozen pizza incident from months ago. He's come so far since then. I never anticipated a setback like this.

Grabbing the key from my dresser drawer, I unlock his door and push it open.

"Get away from me," Leo yells, holding his bedside lamp in front of him like a weapon. His eyes are wide, and his pupils are dilated, but it's as if he's looking through me rather than at me.

"Leopold," I say softly, my hands held up in front of me. "What's going on?"

He waves the lamp around wildly. "Stay back," he yells and lunges forward.

I take a step back. "I'm not going to hurt you." I lower my voice. "But I need you to tell me what's happening."

"You know exactly what's happening," he snarls, his breaths coming fast and heavy. "This is all because of you." My heart sinks. Going to Fire and Ice was too much, and now he thinks I'm going to hurt him. "I liked you and wanted to be with you. You. Not all these other people." He looks around the room, and it's as if he's seeing people who aren't here.

"It's only me and you, Leopold," I say, taking a cautious step forward.

"Don't come near me." Leo lunges again, swinging the lamp like a bat. "They'll be here soon. They always come."

"Who's going to be here?" I ask, trying to understand. Trying to find any opening to bring Leopold back to the present.

"I don't know who they are. They're *your* friends." He gasps for air. "I don't like them."

"You know *our* friends. They—"

"No, I don't," he yells. "You bring them all in here, and you let them hurt me." He stabs his finger in my direction. "I've begged you to stop, but you don't. You don't help me." Leo's voice cracks. "You laugh and make them do more. Then, you hurt me, too," he says as tears pour down his face. "I didn't *consent* to any of this, Krew."

My breath catches. "Leopold, It's me. Tony." I manage to choke out, my heart racing.

"Get out," he screams and lunges at me again. "Or I'll hurt you."

"I'm leaving," I say and slowly back up.

I'm barely through the door when he slams it, the sound echoing in the hallway as the lock clicks into place. On the other side, Leo's voice rises in a frenzy, lost in his own world. My hands tremble violently as I dial the emergency number Sarah gave us at his first appointment.

"Hello?" The voice on the line is groggy as if roused from sleep.

"It's Tony Genovese," I say, managing to compose myself somewhat. "I'm sorry to call in the middle of the night, but I didn't know what else to do."

"Tell me what's happening?"

Describing the unsettling encounter, I struggle to articulate the details. "He thinks I'm Krew," I admit, a mixture of confusion and concern coloring my tone.

"It sounds like he's having a flashback," she says in a clinical tone.

"It's happened before, but not like this." I run my hands through my hair nervously. "He's yelling and breaking things. Leopold doesn't know who I am."

"You're going to have to call 911 and have him brought to the emergency room for a psychiatric evaluation," she states matter-of-factly.

"There's no other option?" I ask, desperation evident in my voice.

"I'm afraid not," she replies with a somber tone.

I pace back and forth, each step heavy with nervous energy as I struggle to decide what to do. Behind the door, Leo's voice wavers with fear, his pleas growing increasingly desperate. I don't know how much more of this I can take.

"Tony," Sarah says softly, her voice gentle and understanding. "I know this is hard, but you have to think about what's best for Leo right now."

"What the hell else do you think I'm doing?" I snap, my frustration bubbling over. "All I'm thinking of, all I ever do, is what's best for Leopold."

"I'm not the enemy here," Sarah replies calmly.

"I'm sorry," I apologize. "I didn't mean to yell at you."

"It's okay. I understand."

"I'll call for an ambulance," I concede, my resolve crumbling.

"You're doing the right thing, Tony," she reassures me.

"I hope you're right," I admit, uncertainty clouding my words.

As soon as we hang up, I dial 911. The dispatcher takes all the information and assures me an ambulance is coming.

My hand slides into my pocket, and my fingers run over the smooth metal of the boxcutter in its protective sheath. My irrational fear tells me I can't leave it in the house because Leopold could find it. What if seeing it triggers those thoughts and feelings to return? What if he uses it to hurt himself? And I don't think throwing it away is the right thing to do with it. So, I carry it with me. Letting go of the boxcutter, I take the key out.

"Leopold," I say with a hint of urgency as I unlock the door. He continues muttering to himself as I cautiously enter the room. He whirls around to face me, the lamp now broken at his feet. "How about you let me get you out of here? Let me take you away from Krew," I offer, taking a chance by using his delusion to help me.

"Where are you going to take me?" he asks, desperation evident in his voice.

I falter, unsure of how to respond. Fear grips me, knowing that the wrong words could trigger another outburst. "Where would you like to go?" I ask tentatively.

He stops to consider my question. "Will you bring me to Donnie and Lindsay? They'll keep me safe," he says, his voice small and scared.

"We can go there, yes. There are some people in uniform," I say cautiously, opting not to use the word *friend* so I don't trigger him. "They'll help us get to them safely, okay?"

"How are they going to do that?" he asks, suspicion evident in his voice.

"They have an ambulance. We'll go in that, so we trick him," I explain, trying to keep my voice steady while my heart silently breaks. "Does that sound okay to you?"

"Why should I trust you?"

"Because I love you, Leopold," I respond earnestly, hoping wherever he is that he recognizes the truth in my words. "I promised you I'd keep you safe."

"Do you know Ramiro?" he asks, his eyes narrowing.

"I do."

"You are a good guy, then," he concedes, a glimmer of trust returning.

"Yes, Leo. I am," I say, extending my hand to him. "Will you come with me and let me help you?"

He hesitates for a moment before tentatively threading his fingers through mine. "I think I like you," he murmurs softly.

"I'm glad to hear that," I respond with a warm smile, brushing a strand of hair away from his face. The doorbell rings, and I glance toward it. "That's them."

"I'm scared," Leo admits, his voice barely above a whisper. "Krew's going to try to find me."

"Keep holding onto me. I won't leave you. I promise," I assure him as we answer the door together, his hand clutching mine tightly.

"We got a call for an emergency," the female EMT says.

"Yes, please come in." Leo and I step aside, letting the pair in.

"Is this Mr. Wagner?" she asks.

"It is," I reply. "I explained that we're going to use your ambulance to keep us hidden so we can get Leopold to safety," I say, hoping the EMTs go alone with my narrative.

"Mr. Wagner, can you tell us what's going on?" the male EMT asks, disregarding me.

"I don't know you," Leo says, stepping behind me. "I'm not telling you anything."

"We're medical technicians—"

"I know them, Leopold," I interrupt, narrowing my eyes at the man.

"They're going to keep us safe while we go to Donnie and Lindsay." I turn my attention to the pair. "Isn't that right?"

"Yes, that's right," the female replies, finally catching on. "My name's Kate, and this is Vince. What's yours?"

"Leo."

"It's nice to meet you, Leo." She smiles brightly. "How about you come with me and my partner?"

"My friend needs to come too."

Kate's gaze shifts to me, her expression questioning.

"I promised I'd stay with him," I explain quietly, hoping she'll understand.

"Okay," she relents after a moment, her tone softening. "We can do that."

The EMTs follow us into the elevator, where Leo tucks himself into the corner shielded by my body. Everyone's silent as we ride to the lobby and walk out the front door to the waiting ambulance.

Kate opens the back of the vehicle, and we help Leo inside.

"Okay, Leo, how about you sit down right here," Kate suggests, pointing to the gurney. Leo hesitantly perches on the edge. "Can you slide back so we can buckle you in?"

Leo's eyes fly open. "You tricked me," he accuses, his voice trembling with betrayal.

"It's okay, Leopold," I reassure him, reaching out to touch his shoulder.

"No, it isn't," he retorts, pulling away from my touch. "Get away from me."

"You need to relax," Vince intervenes, attempting to guide Leo back with a gentle touch on his shoulder.

"Don't touch me." Leo pushes him away.

"Can't he just sit there?" I ask, hoping for some sort of a compromise.

"It's against policy. He needs to be buckled in," Kate explains. "Leo, can you please sit back so we can secure you safely?"

"No. I won't let you hurt me again," Leo shouts, his voice filled with anguish and fear.

"You're going to need to relax, Mr. Wagner, or we'll be forced to medicate you to make you calm down," Vince says sternly.

"You lied," Leo shouts, his voice cracking with emotion. "I need to get out of here." He shoves Kate aside. His movements are frantic as he tries to escape.

"Leopold, please," I implore, reaching out for his arm. He whirls around with alarming speed, his fist connecting with my face in a swift, unexpected blow. I reel backward, colliding with the hard metal bench.

"That's enough, Mr. Wagner," Vince states firmly, moving to restrain Leo. Despite his resistance, Vince manages to overpower him, securing him onto the gurney with tight buckles around his arms, legs, and chest.

My heart shatters as I witness the distressing scene playing out before me. Leo's face contorts with agony as he struggles against the restraints, lost in his delusion.

"Please help me," Leo begs desperately, tears streaming down his face. "You promised you'd keep me safe."

"You are safe, Leopold," I assure him, my voice trembling with sorrow and regret.

Movement catches my attention from the corner of my eye, and Leo's gaze follows suit. Kate finishes filling a syringe.

"I don't want that. Don't drug me." Leo's guttural cries fill the space as he fights against the restraints.

"Please, Leopold, listen to me," I beg. "You're only making it harder." I turn to Kate. My expression is desperate. "Please don't do this. He'll calm down. Won't you, Leopold?"

"No." He thrashes back and forth. "I won't let them do this."

Kate nods to Vince, who holds Leopold tight as she approaches with the syringe. "I'm sorry, Leo," she says a second before she pierces his arm with a needle. "This will help you relax."

"What is that? What did you give him?" I ask, panicked.

"It's a sedative. It'll help him relax," Kate explains, her tone compassionate.

"Why did you do that?" My voice wavers as tears blur my vision.

"He's too combative to transport safely," she responds matter-of-factly, handing me an ice pack. "Put this on. Your eye's already starting to bruise."

I accept the ice pack and set it next to me. "I don't care about me."

"Please don't hurt me," Leo sobs, his voice quivering. "I promise I'll be good," he repeats softly, his words a desperate plea.

"Everything's going to be okay," I whisper, tenderly caressing his tear-stained face. "I'm right here. I'm not leaving you."

"Don't let them hurt me," he murmurs as his eyes close.

Vince and Kate work in tandem, their movements focused and determined as they start an IV. Once it's in place, Vince takes his place behind the wheel, his demeanor calm yet urgent as he steers us through the maze of city streets toward the hospital.

Each moment feels like an eternity, my mind swirling with doubts and fears about the consequences of my actions. Silently, I question whether I've made the right decision, agonizing over the possibility that bringing Leopold to the hospital might exacerbate his distress. That instead of bringing us closer, I've driven him further away.

Anthony

Vince and Kate unload a drugged and sleeping Leo. I follow them through the ambulance bay doors into the New York Presbyterian Hospital Irving Medical Center, where we're placed in a small sterile room.

"Good luck with everything," Kate says before she and Vince leave us with a nurse.

"My name's Patty," the woman says. "We got most of Mr. Wagner's information from the EMTs. Can you tell me a little bit more about what happened tonight?"

My voice is shaky as I recount the events of the evening. The terror Leo relived and how he didn't recognize me. "His therapist suggested bringing him here to get him stabilized. Everything was going okay until they tried to strap him in," I explain.

"Is that when he became violent?" she asks, motioning to my swollen eye.

"He didn't mean to do this," I whisper, my voice strained with emotion as I glance at the man lying on the bed beside me, his face peaceful in slumber. Tears prick at the corners of my eyes, but I force myself to hold them back. "Leopold wouldn't intentionally hurt anyone."

"I'm sure that's true," she replies softly, her eyes reflecting understanding and compassion. "But sometimes, during a mental health crisis, people can behave in ways that are out of character."

The weight of her words hangs heavy in the air, a stark reminder of the unpredictable nature of mental illness. I feel a knot tighten in my chest as I grapple with the realization that, despite his gentle nature, Leopold's struggles have led us to this harrowing moment.

"He's not a violent person," I insist, the words a fervent plea for understanding. "He's just... lost right now, and I don't know how to help him."

Her expression softens with empathy as she meets my gaze, offering silent reassurance.

"What happens from here?" I ask.

"One of our crisis specialists will be in shortly to talk to you and eventually to Mr. Wagner when he wakes up," she explains, her voice professional and composed. "Then, they'll consult with one of our staff psychiatrists to determine the best course of treatment." Her words come out rehearsed and lacking any emotion. "Most likely, they're going to recommend a stay in our in-patient facility to get him stabilized and on medication."

"No. He doesn't need to be admitted," I insist.

"Let's leave that up to the professionals," she says, a tight smile on her face. "For now, just relax. I'll put in an order so someone can look at your eye, too."

When the nurse leaves the room, I dim the lights so Leo can rest peacefully. My hope is when he wakes, he'll be cognizant of his surroundings. Then, we can go home and try to forget this awful night ever happened.

Although it's the middle of the night, I pull out my phone to text Ramiro. He'll want to know what's going on.

Me: I'm at the emergency room with Leopold. He had a flashback and was completely disoriented. His therapist suggested I bring him in for an evaluation. I don't know anything yet, but I knew you'd want to be made aware.

Not expecting an immediate response from him, I carefully stow my phone away and press the ice pack against my swollen eye. The swelling feels like it's closing it shut, and the relentless pounding in my head isn't doing me any favors.

My phone suddenly starts ringing, shattering the silence of the hospital room. I quickly retrieve it from my pocket, swiping to answer before the noise disturbs Leo's rest.

"Hello?" I answer in a hushed tone, jumping to my feet. Dizziness washes over me, and I stagger, reaching out to grab onto Leo's bed for balance.

"What's happened?" Ramiro asks.

I check to be sure Leo's still asleep before walking out to the hallway and closing the door behind me. "I'm not positive on what triggered it," I hesitate. "Well, I have an idea."

"Go on."

"Leopold and I have been growing closer, romantically," I disclose, adding context to my statement. "We went to a club tonight."

"What kind of club?" Ramiro inquires, his curiosity piqued.

"A BDSM club."

"What the hell were you thinking?" Ramiro's voice explodes with anger. "I knew letting Leo stay with you was a mistake. I shouldn't have accepted no for an answer."

"You're not Leopold's father. He doesn't require your approval for his living arrangements," I state, my anger simmering beneath the surface.

"Leo's been drugged and raped. And you bring him to a seedy BDSM club? What kind of monster are you?" Ramiro's accusation slices through the air.

I clench my teeth, fighting the urge to lash out. "I'm not a monster. I don't know what you think the club is, but whatever you're assuming is wrong." I pause, taking a deep breath to regain composure. "We can pick up this conversation another time. The only thing I care about right now is ensuring Leopold's okay."

"Excuse me. Are you Mr. Genovese?" a woman in a white doctor's coat asks.

"Hold on." I drop the phone from my ear. "I am."

"I'm Dr. Thompson," she introduces herself. "I'd like to take a look at your eye."

"Sure. One second." Bringing the phone back to my ear, I say, "I'm going to have to call you back. The doctor's here to examine me."

"You? What for?"

He's going to lose his shit again. "Leo and I had an altercation on the way to the hospital."

"An altercation?"

"He hit me," I explain, my voice strained. "The doctor's waiting for me. I'll explain it to you later."

"Don't you hang—"

I disconnect without letting him finish.

"I apologize for making you wait."

"It's not a problem," she says kindly. "If you'll follow me, we'll go to an exam room."

"What about Leopold?"

"He'll be sleeping for a while still," she explains. "The staff will keep an eye on him while you're gone."

"Can I look in on him first?"

"Of course," she smiles kindly.

I crack the door and look into the darkened room. Leo's silhouette is visible, curled up on his side, sound asleep. Another wave of dizziness washes over me, and I instinctively reach out, grasping the doorframe for support.

"Are you dizzy?" Dr. Thompson asks, concern lacing her words.

"I'm fine," I say and close the door softly. "Is this going to take long? I don't want Leopold to wake up and find me not there."

"I understand. I'll be as brief as possible," Dr. Thompson reassures as she leads me through a maze of hallways before we come to an empty exam room. She opens the door, and the lights automatically turn on, illuminating the space. "Have a seat on the bed," she instructs.

Reluctantly, I rest my weight on the edge of the bed, understanding that the less I resist, the sooner we'll finish, and I can return to Leopold.

Leopold

STRANGE SOUNDS AND UNFAMILIAR SCENTS SWIRL AROUND me. My eyelids are heavy and remain stubbornly closed. Snippets of conversation filter through each one, tugging at the fringes of my awareness.

"His partner described a dissociative event at their apartment earlier this evening," a male voice says.

"I heard they were at some kind of sex club," a female voice says.

"Crazy, right?" another voice, deeper and gruffer, responds. "I can't believe someone would drag their mentally unstable partner into shit like that."

"What kind of freaks are they?" the female voice asks.

"Some people are into all kinds of kinky stuff," the male voice says.

"Should we be gossiping about this?" a quieter voice questions.

"We're not gossiping. We're just discussing," the first voice retorts defensively. "It's not like he can hear us."

"I know, right." They share a laugh. "Dr. Morgan already read the chart. He's recommending an inpatient stay. We have to wait for his partner to get back and sign the papers for an involuntary admission."

My heart pounds. Tony promised he'd never send me to an inpatient facility. He lied.

What did you expect? Lies. Everything is lies. He was waiting for his turn to control you.

"He's going to be a little while. Dr. Thompson ordered a CT," the female says, "I guess he got hit pretty hard on his way here."

"Come on," a deep voice says. "I have to message Dr. Morgan and let him know this guy's still out cold."

I wait until I hear the door click closed before forcing my eyes to open. Tony's hurt? He got hit. I try to force myself to remember what happened.

When we got home from the club, I felt off. Snippets of the evening replay in my mind. The cross. The ropes. The blindfold. The whips. While the submissive's skin turned red with welts and he cried in pain, memories of the atrocities I endured at Krew's hands paralyzed me with fear.

I assumed I'd be okay once we left the club, but then Tony wanted to talk about the kiss, and I couldn't focus. All I could think was that Tony would like to do those things with me—to me and that I couldn't do it. After that, there's nothing until I woke up here.

A heaviness settles in my chest as I confront the truth—Tony lied. He's going to admit me to a psychiatric hospital. How could he do this?

What did you expect? You're a screw-up. You'll never deserve someone good like him.

The last time I was inpatient—no, I can't go through that again. Grabbing the IV, I pull it from my arm and press the palm of my other hand over it until the bleeding stops. In my other pocket is my cellphone. It's my connection to everyone I know, but it's also a way to be traced.

Thankfully, I still have my shoes. It wouldn't be the first time I've gone without, but it's not a pleasant experience. Stuffing cash into my pocket, I toss my wallet onto the bed. Then, I pull my cellphone out of my pocket. I wrestle with conflicting emotions on what to do with it, finally settling on placing it beside my wallet. Walking out of this room means leaving Tony and the life we've started to build together behind. I'll be alone again, but I don't have another choice.

Turning the handle, I crack the door open and peek out into the quiet hallway. I take a tentative step out and scan my surroundings. To the left is a nurse's station, so I go to the right, hoping it will lead to an exit. With my hands stuffed into my pockets, I keep my gaze low, hoping to avoid attracting unwanted attention. But it's taking too long and feels like I'm walking in circles. I can't find a way out.

"Excuse me," I say to someone in scrubs walking my way. "I've got myself all turned around in here. Which way is the exit?"

"Down the hall, make a left and another left."

"Thanks," I mumble and hurry down the hall until I'm pushing the door open and stepping onto the unfamiliar side street.

For a brief moment, I have second thoughts and consider going back inside and running into Tony's arms. But then, a bitter realization crashes over me. It's his fault that I'm here. He always promised he'd never leave me, but when I woke up, I was alone.

Of course, you're alone. Nobody wants you. Nobody loves you. You're always going to be alone.

With tears dripping down my face, I start walking away from the hospital and into the anonymity of the city.

Anthony

"Your CT is clear," Dr. Thompson says. "You might still have a mild concussion, so I'd like you to take it easy for a few days." A knock on the door interrupts her instructions, and she calls, "Come in."

"I'm sorry for interrupting," Patty says as she enters the room. "Is Mr. Wagner with you?"

"No, he's in his room sleeping," Dr. Thompson answers.

"May I speak to you in the hall, doctor?"

"Whatever you have to say about Leopold, you'll say in front of me."

Patty looks between me and the doctor before explaining, "I went in to check his vitals, and he was gone."

"What do you mean he was gone?" My heart rate increases, exacerbating my headache. I jump up from the bed, my movements fueled by panic. Thankfully, the pill Dr. Thompson gave me for the dizziness appears to be working. "How could a patient just disappear?"

"Perhaps he got up to use the restroom?" the doctor suggests.

"He pulled his IV out," Patty explains, her brow furrowed. "And he left his cell phone and wallet on the bed."

"Excuse me, I have to go find him," I say, already hurrying toward the door.

"Mr. Genovese, I haven't discharged you yet," Dr. Thompson calls after me.

"I don't care. I have to find Leo." I look to the nurse. "Can you help me get back to his room?"

"Take him to Mr. Wagner's room. I'll alert security," Dr. Thompson directs.

"Please don't do that. He's going to be scared—" I protest, but the doctor cuts me off.

"It's protocol, Mr. Genovese," she states firmly.

"Do what you need to do," I concede, turning back to Patty. "We're wasting time here. I have to go find him."

Security felt it was better for me to wait in Leo's room if he wandered off and found his way back. Meanwhile, they're scouring the halls of the hospital. I'm going stir-crazy sitting in an empty room, knowing he's not coming back. He's not here. I can't feel him—he's gone.

An hour later, my concerns are validated as Nurse Patty enters the room, followed closely by a doctor.

"Mr. Genovese, I'm Dr. Morgan, one of the staff psychiatrists," he introduces himself, offering his hand. "I was assigned to Mr. Wagner's case when he arrived."

"Were you able to locate him?" I ask, although I already know what his answer will be.

"When we couldn't find him in the hospital, we had security pull the footage from the exits. Mr. Wagner was seen exiting onto 168th St. almost two hours ago," Dr. Morgan confirms."You're telling me you have cameras, and you just thought of checking them?" I'm livid. "How could he walk out of here without being noticed?"

"It was an oversight, and our staff will be educated on patient safety," Dr. Morgan replies calmly.

"Have the police been called?"

"They have not. Since Mr. Wagner hadn't been evaluated or admitted, he was within his rights to leave."

"You're kidding me, right?" I scoff, gripping my head in an attempt to soothe the throbbing headache assaulting my temples. "When we arrived, everyone was in a panic, insisting Leo was dangerous and needed to be admitted. And now that he's disappeared, suddenly his safety doesn't matter?"

"I understand your frustration, Mr. Genovese, but—"

"Enough," I cut in sharply, holding up a hand to silence the doctor. "I don't want to hear any more excuses. Bringing Leopold here was a mistake. I have to go find him." I brush past the doctor and nurse and hurry to the exit.

Outside, the sun's gentle rays are just beginning to peek over the horizon, painting the sky with hues of rose and gold and offering a glimmer of hope in the stillness of the morning. I find myself standing alone in the middle of the sidewalk, praying Leopold is out here waiting for me. But after I scan the area, my greatest fear is realized. He's not here.

Gripping his wallet and cell phone tightly—the only remnants of him I have left—I begin walking the maze of the city's streets, searching for any sign of him but finding nothing.

My head throbs and the vision in my right eye is blurry from the swelling. The doctor said I have a mild concussion and need to rest. But how can I rest when Leo's out here, alone and vulnerable? Is he lost in a world of delusions, running from shadows in his past? Or did he wake up thinking I not only betrayed him but also abandoned him?

"Leopold, where are you?" I ask quietly. "Please come back to me."

⚱

I walked the streets until exhaustion made my steps nearly impossible, and I returned to an empty apartment. I sink onto the couch and drop my head back. I'll only close my eyes for a minute, enough time to regroup and come up with a plan.

I don't know how long I've been asleep when my phone rings, startling me. "Hello?" I answer quickly, hoping it's news about Leopold.

"I've been waiting all night for an update," Ramiro says, frustration lacing his words.

I groan inwardly. "He's gone."

"What the hell does that mean?" Ramiro demands.

I explain the situation calmly. "I don't even know where to start looking," I confess. "He could be anywhere."

"I'm getting a plane ticket and coming out there," Ramiro says. "And when I find him, he's coming home with me."

"You're more than welcome to come out and help me search, but Leopold's not going anywhere. *This* is his home," I insist.

"We'll discuss that after we find him." Ramiro doesn't back down.

I soften my tone, knowing Ramiro cares about Leo too. "Let me know when you'll be arriving. You're welcome to stay at my place."

Anthony

⁂

"IT WAS A MISTAKE TO BRING HIM TO THE CLUB," I SAY AS I sink onto the couch in the office. "What the hell was I thinking?"

"You can't blame yourself," Sarah says calmly. "When someone's living with PTSD, triggers can appear from seemingly nowhere."

"Except this wasn't from nowhere. There was a bondage scene. Leo's terrified of being restrained. I should've known." I bring my hand to my chest. "It's my job to anticipate these things."

"No, Tony. It isn't your job." Sarah pins me with her stare. "Leo's lucky to have you as a support person, but that's where your role ends."

I can't believe what I'm hearing. What kind of therapist is this?

"I know what you're thinking. You feel responsible for Leo's well-being." Sarah shifts forward in her seat and places her hand on my arm. "It's not an uncommon belief, but it's also incorrect." I raise my eyes to meet her. "By providing Leo with the necessary resources, you've offered him a pathway to healing," Sarah explains, her voice steady. "But ultimately, Leo is the one who must take the steps forward. No matter how deeply you care for him, *you* can't fix him."

"Leopold's gotten his life together. He has a steady job, and he's earned his GED," I explain, even though Sarah is aware of his accom-

298

plishment. "He comes to therapy every week. He's putting in the work," I insist.

"Showing up for his appointments is one thing. But opening up and being honest with me is another."

"What are you implying?"

"I could lose my license for having this conversation with you." Sarah takes a deep breath. She's clearly at odds with how to proceed. "Leo's holding back. He's allowed me glimpses into his past, but when we get too close to the truth, he puts up walls to keep me out. Then, he tries to assure me he's coping and doing fine."

Fine. There's that word. The same one I used to keep those who cared about me at arm's length. I thought if I told them I was *fine*, they'd believe it and not worry about me. How could I be so blind to not see that Leo's been doing the same thing?

"I feared something like this might happen," Sarah adds, sitting back in her chair. "But Leo didn't want to hear it. Unfortunately, my hands were tied."

"So, what now?" I ask, my voice betraying my uncertainty.

"First, we have to find him. Then, we have to hope he's at a place where he's ready to actually accept the help we're offering," Sarah responds, her words laced with concern.

"I refuse to have him admitted anywhere," I state firmly, my resolve unyielding.

"Tony." Sarah begins to argue, but I cut her off.

"It's not up for discussion. If you're going to try to go down that path, we're done talking," I assert, unwilling to budge.

"For now, I'll go along with it. But, when we find him, if I think he's in danger, I'll sign the admission papers myself," Sarah concedes, her voice steady.

After leaving her office, I make my way to Fire and Ice. When Owen heard what happened, he cut his trip short and came straight back. He and Star are meeting me there so we can come up with a plan to find Leo.

Instead of taking the subway, like I usually would, I walk, my eyes scanning the streets, hoping to spot Leo. Before going into the club, I take a detour to Hudson River Park. Fate brought us together once before. Perhaps she'll be on my side, and I'll find him there again.

The park is alive with the buzz of summer. Families are enjoying picnics. Dogs chase frisbees with their owners, and children laugh and play. But there's no sign of Leopold. With a sense of defeat settling over me, I reluctantly turn back toward the club.

"Tony." Star rushes over to me and wraps me in a comforting hug. "How are you holding up?"

"I have to find him," I say, my voice hollow with numbness.

"We will," she assures me, pulling away slightly. "What happened to your eye?"

I skirt around the truth, unwilling to cast Leo in a negative light. "It's nothing," I try to brush it off.

"It's not nothing. Who did this to you?" Star presses, her worry evident.

"It was an accident. It happened in the ambulance on the way to the hospital," I fabricate, protecting Leo's dignity.

""Leo hit you?" Her question is barely audible, filled with shock.

"They were trying to buckle him in. He didn't know what was going on. He thought they were trying to restrain him and hurt him." Tears pool in my eyes, but I force them away. I can't fall apart right now. "Leopold was scared. He didn't mean to hurt me."

"We know that," Owen says, joining Star by my side. "I made some lunch. We'll discuss a plan while we eat."

Despite my lack of appetite, I force myself to join them at the table. For the next few hours, we pore over maps and schedules, dividing Manhattan into segments we'll scour daily. It feels like searching for a needle in a haystack, an immense challenge. But the thought of Leopold out there alone fuels my determination. I won't rest until Leo is safely back in my arms.

Leopold

THE HUNDRED DOLLARS I HAD WITH ME IS LONG GONE. I should've kept my phone and sold it at a pawn shop. If I took my ATM card, I could've emptied my account and destroyed the card. Why didn't I think this through a little more?

Because you're a stupid fool. A loser who never gets anything right.

"I did get it right," I say aloud, drawing the attention of passersby.

I stop in the middle of the sidewalk, and the person behind me slams into me.

"What the hell is wrong with you, freak?" the man says as he pushes me out of the way.

What am I doing out here? I duck into the next alleyway and crawl behind a row of dumpsters. Being out in the middle of the day is a recipe for disaster. Krew or one of his minions will find me and drag me back to his house. They'll torture me until they kill me. I have to stay hidden until it's safe—after dark.

The stench of rotting trash jerks me awake. What the hell am I doing here? I crawl out from behind a rusty blue dumpster and brush my hands over my clothes. I'm not exactly clean, but I don't want to be covered in garbage.

Why was I sleeping amongst trash? This isn't the first time something like this has happened. I suspect I'm losing gaps of time, but I don't know why.

I think I'm losing my mind.

A door swings open, and a man wearing a white chef's jacket steps out. The man doesn't see me standing there as he hoists two large bags into the dumpster before returning inside, the door slamming closed behind him.

My stomach growls, and not for the first time, I climb up the side of the dumpster and tear into a bag. It's disgusting, but I don't care. I'm desperate to put something in my belly.

Tonight's a good night. I find a half-eaten burger and some fries—they're still warm. I shove the fries into my mouth before taking a big bite of the meat.

After finishing the sandwich, I start walking around looking for money dropped by one of the many tourists in Times Square. The lie I tell myself is that it's not stealing if I find it on the ground. And like most nights, it doesn't take long before I spot a wadded-up bill lying by the curb.

Trying not to be obvious, I stoop down to tie my shoelace and quickly swipe the cash. I hit the jackpot tonight. It's a ten-dollar bill. After shoving it into my pocket, I hurry away. I don't stop for several blocks until I find a street vendor where I buy a bottle of water. Tonight's a good night. I won't go hungry or thirsty.

Anthony

In the wake of Leo's disappearance, time seems to have lost all meaning. Days bleed into nights and nights into days as I navigate a world consumed by uncertainty. Work has become a distant concern, and sleep is a luxury I barely afford myself. Instead, I wander the streets, my eyes scanning every face and corner for any trace of him. But despite the overwhelming sense of despair threatening to engulf me, I refuse to give up hope.

Ramiro wanted to be here sooner, but Jacinta's mother had a medical emergency, and he was unable to leave California immediately. His plane touched down about an hour ago. He's in an Uber on his way to my apartment. I expect him here any minute.

While I wait, I keep my mind occupied with making dinner. I've hardly been able to eat since Leo disappeared, but I assume Ramiro will be hungry after his flight.

The sound of the doorbell jerks me from my thoughts. The strained dynamic between us leaves me unsure what to expect. Frankly, I don't have the energy to fight.

I pull the door open to reveal Ramiro, clad in jeans and a dark blue T-shirt, a backpack slung over his shoulder. "Come on in," I murmur, stepping aside to let him enter my apartment. "I hope you're hungry. I

"

made dinner," I say, attempting to ease the palpable tension that hangs heavy in the air.

"Dinner sounds great. Thank you," he replies politely.

"Let me show you to your room first so you can put your stuff down," I offer, leading Ramiro down the hallway. "Here we are." I gesture, opening the door to reveal the cozy space. "There's an attached bathroom. Take your time. I'll be in the kitchen."

While Ramiro settles into his room, I ready the table and put the finishing touches on the food.

"Whatever you've made smells good," Ramiro says as he walks over to the table.

"It's eggplant parmesan," I reply. "What can I get you to drink?"

"I'll have whatever you're having."

"Red wine."

"Perfect," he says, sitting at the table while I pour the wine and serve the food.

Dinner unfolds in uncomfortable silence, punctuated only by the clinking of utensils against plates. Each attempt at conversation feels forced, as if we're both grasping at straws to fill the silence. I find myself counting down the minutes until the ordeal is over.

Relief washes over me when Ramiro finally excuses himself and goes to bed early. The quiet of the apartment settles around me, but I can't sleep yet. Instead, I quietly slip out to roam the city streets, praying for a miracle.

As the next afternoon unfolds, my apartment gradually fills with the presence of familiar faces. Owen and Astrid are the first to arrive. "When's the last time you slept?" Owen asks, concern lacing his voice.

"Last night."

"For how long?"

"I don't know." I shrug. "An hour or two, I guess."

"You have to start taking care of yourself. If you end up in the hospital, how will that help Leo?"

I sink onto the couch. "I'll sleep soundly after Leopold is home."

The doorbell rings again, and I go to stand, but Owen puts his hand on my arm, stopping me. "Astrid, please answer it." Owen directs his sub.

"Yes, Sir," she responds and dutifully goes to the door.

"Where's Ramiro?" Owen asks quietly.

"He's in his room. His wife called." I turn toward Star and Corbin, who are entering the room. "Thanks for coming."

"We brought coffee and donuts," Star says, holding up the donut shop bags.

"You didn't have to do that."

The sound of footsteps grows closer.

"You must be Ramiro," Owen says, stepping toward him and offering his hand. "I'm Owen."

"Good to meet you."

"This is my girlfriend, Astrid." The doorbell rings again.

"Excuse me, please," Astrid says as she goes to answer the door.

"This is Star and Corbin," Owen introduces the pair.

"It's a pleasure to meet you all," Ramiro says politely.

Astrid returns with Emmanuel, Pastor Andrea, and Kelly.

I push to my feet as Andrea and Kelly take turns giving me a hug. "Thank you both for coming."

"We're glad to be here."

"This is Ramiro, a friend of Leopold's from California." I motion to the ladies. "This is Pastor Andrea and her girlfriend, Kelly. They run the grief support group I attend."

"It's nice to meet you both."

After getting everyone acquainted, we gather at the table to brainstorm additional strategies to expand the search for Leo.

"Does he have anywhere he likes to hang out?" Ramiro asks.

"Outside of work? Not really." Ramiro raises his eyebrow in disapproval. "He spends a lot of time in the gym downstairs," I explain. "The doormen know to let him in and to call me right away if he happens to show up."

"Who are his friends?" he asks.

"He spends the majority of his time with me." Ramiro narrows his eyes but doesn't continue his line of questioning.

"Drea and I have connections at homeless shelters and soup kitchens. We've shared Leo's picture and your phone number," Kelly says.

"I can't thank you enough."

"We love Leo. Getting him home safe is all the thanks we need," Andrea adds.

"After Sept 11, people put posters up all over the city. Maybe we can do that too?" Astrid offers, her suggestion sincere.

All eyes turn to me.

The vivid memory of the city awash with missing person posters in the aftermath of that fateful day remains seared into my mind. Each one was a poignant reminder of the agony endured by those left behind, a testament to their unwavering hope and determination. At that time, I stood on the periphery. Kameron wasn't among the missing. He was already gone. But today, as I grapple with the agony of uncertainty, I understand the anguish of those desperate souls. Now, I'm among those who cling to hope, desperately searching for a missing loved one.

"That's a great idea, Astrid," I say, sincerity in my voice. "Thank you."

"We can use the church's printer," Andrea offers. "Kelly and I will start on those when we leave here."

"I'll stop by tomorrow if it's okay. I'll distribute them to our volunteers so we can cover the city faster."

"Corbin will call the hospitals again to see if anyone matching his description shows up," Star offers.

"I'm going out again tonight. Leopold has to be out there somewhere," I murmur, my tone filled with desperation.

"I'll go with you," Ramiro adds, and I offer a grateful smile.

After my guests leave, I get my shoes and two bottles of water. Handing one to Ramiro, I say, "Then, let's get moving." I turn and start to walk away.

"Wait," Ramiro says, grabbing my arm. "I want to apologize for how I reacted when you told me Leo was missing. I was out of line," he says, and I see the pain on his face. "I'm protective of Leo, especially after what he went through with Krew."

"He told me everything," I assure him.

"But you weren't there. You didn't see the condition Leo was in." A haunted look shadows his features. "Krew force-fed him drugs and allowed him to be raped repeatedly. We had to watch him go through withdrawal for weeks. There were some days I wasn't convinced he was going to make it," he adds, his voice trembling with emotion. "New York was his fresh start. He was doing so good here. I don't understand what happened?"

"What did he tell you about the night I found him?" I ask, my hand going to the metal in my pocket.

"You were there. You know what he said."

"He never told you anything else?" I ask.

"When I asked, Leo said things were better, and he didn't want to talk about it anymore."

Although I shouldn't be, I'm surprised by Ramiro's answer. I assumed that because they were close, Leo would've told him the whole story. There's no easy way to say it, so I take a direct approach. "When I found Leopold that night, he was in the process of committing suicide."

"Leo would never." Ramiro scoffs, his disbelief evident.

"Everyone has their breaking point, and Leopold was at his," I whisper.

The reality of my words begins to take root. Ramiro asks, "What did he do?"

"He tried slitting his wrist with this." I pull the boxcutter from my pocket. "I've carried it with me ever since that night to remind me just how close I came to losing him. If I was a minute later, it might've been too late."

"You should've taken him to a hospital. He needed the help of professionals with experience treating someone in his condition," Ramiro states.

"The last place Leopold needed to be was in a facility. That's how we ended up in this situation." I take a deep breath, trying to quell the anger threatening to spill over. "When I brought Leo home, I made him promise me thirty days. One month to prove to him why he needed to keep living."

Ramiro listens intently as I bring him up to speed on the events of the past six months. I detail all the progress Leo has made on his journey towards wellness, as well as all of the things Sarah pointed out. Things I'd stupidly been blind to.

"You care about him, don't you?" Ramiro asks.

"I love him," I admit, my voice trembling with emotion. "But I'm so scared."

"We're going to find him, Tony," Ramiro promises, his tone brimming with determination.

The thought of Leopold out there, lost and alone, is almost too much to bear.

Leopold has to be okay.

I'm clinging to the hope that he'll return home—to me, where he belongs.

Leopold

LEAVING THE HOSPITAL THAT DAY MAY BE THE BIGGEST mistake of my life. Hearing those hospital workers talk about having me admitted for treatment terrified me. The thought that Tony was willing to sign the papers to do that shook me to my core. But as I replay those conversations in my mind, I question what exactly I heard. Did Tony ever agree to sign the papers? Or was I jumping to conclusions?

Why was I at the hospital in the first place? They said Tony was getting a CAT scan. Did I do something to hurt him? Is that why Tony wasn't there when I woke up? I have so many questions that will forever remain unanswered because I walked away from him.

Living on the streets and often waking up in places I don't remember is a constant reminder that something terrible is happening to me. It reinforces the thought that Tony brought me to the hospital because he was concerned about me.

Don't be naïve. He was having you committed. He thinks you're crazy.

"Shut up." I grab the sides of my head and yell, trying to silence the repetitive thoughts in my head.

Deep down in my heart, I don't believe Tony would've betrayed me. If only I'd waited for him to come back, I could've asked him. He's never lied to me, and there was no reason to think he would've started then.

I've seen him—Tony. He was walking down the street, unknowingly heading straight toward me. He briefly glanced down at his phone, giving me a split-second to duck down an alley. I couldn't bring myself to face him, not after what I had done. But it didn't stop the ache in my chest as I watched him walk past where I hid in the shadows.

He'll eventually move on and forget about me. I'll be left to live with the knowledge that my mistakes cost me the only person who ever truly cared about me.

I'm lost. Torn between the desire to move forward and the fear of facing the consequences of my choices.

How do I find my way back from this?

More importantly, do I have the will to try?

Anthony

Ramiro stayed for two weeks. He woke early every day to comb through the streets, hang posters, and go from one homeless shelter to another, hoping to find him or at least get information about any sightings. At the end of each day, he returned home empty-handed. Eventually, he had to return to California. In the time he was here, we were able to come to a tentative truce. But without Leopold, none of that matters.

The thought of facing another day without my love often feels unbearable. It's only through the unwavering support of my friends that I have the strength to continue. While one group of people plastered the city with posters, Andrea and Kelly mobilized their contacts in the city's homeless community. I was sure it would only be a few days before we found him, but as each day came and went with nothing, a sense of futility crept in.

Six weeks have passed since Leopold slipped out of the hospital, leaving me to navigate life without him. My days blur together as I walk the streets chasing fleeting glimpses that might be him. Instead, each sighting turns out to be a cruel tease that feels like a fresh wound slicing through my heart. Truth be told, I don't even know if Leopold is still in New York City. He could be anywhere by now.

After enduring the heartache of losing Kameron, I begged the universe to bring me someone to love. Someone who would be my forever. That's when I met Leopold. The thought that he's gone forever is too agonizing for me to comprehend.

What began as casual conversations and shared meals with a man I knew was going hungry most days gradually blossomed into friendship. Somewhere along the way, I fell in love with him. If I'm honest, it was the very first time he walked into my restaurant, his blue eyes peeking out from behind his scarf. In that instant, my heart fell for him, and in the blink of an eye, he vanished, leaving behind an aching emptiness. Now, I'm left grappling with the sheer magnitude of his disappearance, unsure of how to navigate this new reality where he no longer exists by my side.

"The last table just cleared out, Chef," Raina says, popping her head into my office.

"Thanks," I mumble, my head in my hands as I struggle to comprehend the words on the paper I've been trying to read for the past twenty minutes.

"Please don't give up," she says as she steps further into the room.

My head jerks up. "What?"

"On finding Leo," she states, her voice laced with conviction. "I have a feeling he's closer than you think."

Her comment catches me off guard, and I'm unsure how to respond.

"I'm sorry if I overstepped," she adds, sensing my hesitation.

"Not at all," I respond, managing a faint smile. "I appreciate your support."

"The front is cleaned up and ready for tomorrow," she informs me, changing the subject. "Is it okay if I head out?"

"Absolutely," I reply. "Take care on your way home."

As the night wears on, my staff filters out, each confirming their tasks are completed and their areas ready for tomorrow's opening. It's well past 2 am when I finally conquer the stubborn order form I've been struggling with all night, faxing it to the supplier so they receive it first thing in the morning. Before I leave, I do a quick sweep of the restaurant, ensuring everything's in order before shutting the lights off and locking up.

With a heavy heart and exhaustion deep in my bones, I transition to the next part of my night. The city pulses with life around me as my footsteps echo against the pavement. My heart is heavy as I scour the shadows and peer down deserted alleyways with the hope of even the faintest glimpse of him.

My search comes to an abrupt halt as Owen appears in my path. "What are you doing here?" I question, surprised by his sudden appearance.

"Looking for you," Owen replies, his tone urgent. "Star's been trying to call you for the past two hours."

I pull my phone from my pocket and check the screen, my stomach dropping at the sight of forty missed calls. "I must've muted it accidentally."

"Leo's at the club," Owen states matter-of-factly.

"What?" The intensity of my reaction mirrors the rapid pounding of my heart as Owen's revelation sinks in.

"Star and I were both at the club tonight. She stepped out to get some fresh air," he explains, his voice steady. "She went over to the river walk, and he was there, sitting on a bench."

"Are you serious?" I ask, a surge of hope rising within me.

"I wouldn't joke about this."

"Leopold's with Star?" I ask, my voice trembling with emotion.

"He's not in great shape," Owen explains, concern etched in his voice. "He's dehydrated and thin, but he's there and safe."

I'm afraid to believe what Owen's saying. Terrified I'll find this is yet another dream where I wake up to an empty house.

"Why aren't you moving?" Owen asks, sensing my hesitation.

"I don't want to get there, and this not be real," I confess, my voice barely above a whisper.

"I was there when she brought him to the club," Owen adds.

"You saw him?" I ask, desperate for confirmation.

"When we couldn't get ahold of you, Leo got nervous. I told him I'd come get you," Owen explains, his grip firm on my arm. "Let's go. He's waiting for you."

For the first time since Leopold disappeared, a glimmer of hope pierces through the darkness. Leopold's at Fire and Ice.
He's safe.

Leopold

THE GENTLE RHYTHM OF THE WATER AGAINST THE CONCRETE wall lulls me into a trance-like state. I'm sitting on the bench, the same one I sat on with Tony the night he saved me. Exhaustion, both mental and physical, overwhelms my senses. Hunger gnaws at my stomach while loneliness threatens to consume me. Coming here was supposed to bring me closer to him, even if only for a few minutes. My eyelids are heavy. I pull my legs up tight against me and drop my head onto my knees. "I'll just close my eyes for a minute."

"Leo? Is that you?" a familiar woman's voice causes me to stir. I lift my head and blink a few times until her face comes into focus.

"Oh my God." She throws her arms around my neck, not caring about my grimy appearance. "It's really you." Pulling back slightly, she places her hands on my shoulders. "Let me get a good look at you."

I drop my head, ashamed of my disheveled state.

"Are you okay? Where have you been?" Star rapid-fires before pausing to take a breath. "I'm sorry," she slows down, lowering her voice. "I shouldn't be bombarding you with so many questions."

"It's fine," I say quietly.

"Let's start with one at a time." Star sits next to me. "Are you okay?"

"I don't know," I admit feeling lost.

"We've been searching everywhere for you. Where have you been?" Star's concern is palpable.

"You've been looking for me?" I ask, genuinely surprised.

"Of course we have," Star reassures me. "Tony's been beside himself since you disappeared. He's going to be so relieved to know you're safe."

"I doubt that."

"What do you mean?" Star's concern deepens, her eyes searching mine for answers.

"He brought me to the hospital," I explain, my voice wavering slightly. "They said he was going to have me admitted."

"Who told you that?"

"I overheard some people talking. They thought I was asleep," I admit, chancing a glance up. "I couldn't let them make me stay."

"Oh, honey," she murmurs, cupping my cheek. "Tony wasn't going to let them do that. He took you to the hospital because... We don't need to worry about that right now. All that matters is you're here now. Will you come back to the club with me so we can call Tony?"

"The club?" Uncertainty creeps over me.

"Yes," she says hesitantly. "If you'd like, we'll use the back entrance and go straight to my office."

"Are you sure Tony's going to want to see me?" I ask, my anxiety mounting.

"I'm positive," she assures me, rising to her feet and offering her hand. "Will you come with me?"

If I say yes and Tony refuses to see me, I'll be devastated. I don't know if I could survive that. But if I don't go with her, if I choose to walk away, this is it. I won't get another chance.

Tony's everything to me. I love him. My hand trembles as I consider reaching out to take hers, but at the last moment, I hesitate.

"Please, Leo," her voice cracks. "Come with me."

"I don't want to touch you. I'm filthy," I protest, feeling unworthy.

"That doesn't matter to me," she insists, her hand still outstretched.

Should I trust her?

Don't do it. You're dirty. Damaged. You're nothing.

I hate that voice—the one that always creeps up and makes me doubt everything.

She's using you. Tony doesn't want you. She'll make a fool out of you.

Deciding to ignore my negative thoughts, I push to my feet and place my hand in hers. She gives it a reassuring squeeze.

"Thank you for trusting me, Leo." Star keeps her word and brings me in through the back. "I'm going to text Owen and ask him to come back here, okay?"

"Are you sure he's going to want to see me?" Insecurity plagues me again, and I wonder if I've made the wrong choice by coming here.

"I guarantee he wants to see you."

"Okay," I say, even though I'm still uncertain.

Star texts back and forth. The longer the conversation goes on, the more I lose hope that he's coming. Suddenly, the door to her office swings open.

"Holy shit," Owen says, his hands flying to his mouth. "Where did he come from?"

"I found him on a bench by the river," Star explains, relief evident in her tone.

"We've been looking for you everywhere," Owen says as he takes me in from head to toe. "When's the last time you ate?" he asks, concerned, and I shrug. "Did you call Tony?" He turns to Star.

"I've been trying," she replies, frustrated. "But it keeps going to voicemail."

"I'm sure he'll call back soon," Owen says, turning his attention back to me. "Are you hungry? I'll get you something to eat. Is there anything special you want?"

"Whatever is fine," I reply, grateful for whatever he gets me.

"I'll be back in a few minutes."

Star checks her phone again before shaking her head.

"It's not like Tony to not answer his phone," I say, worry bubbling inside me. "Maybe he doesn't want to see me?" I ask as the negative voice gets louder.

He tried to get rid of you. He wants nothing to do with you.

"I assure you he wants to see you. He's searched day and night for you," she adds. Her phone buzzes, and she grabs it quickly. Her face falls. "Corbin needs me at the desk. Will you be okay alone here for a few minutes?"

"Yeah."

She walks over to the door and pauses with her hand on the knob. "Promise you won't leave?"

"I promise."

She studies me momentarily before nodding and leaving me alone in her office.

I look around, knowing the only way out is through the door. I'm certain Star has someone watching to be sure I don't disappear again. I don't like feeling trapped in small spaces. Standing up, I begin to pace back and forth.

A stack of papers on the filing cabinet catches my attention. Reaching out I take one off the top. "It's me," I mumble. The heading on the page reads: HAVE YOU SEEN THIS MAN? Underneath is a recent picture of me—one Tony took in the garden of his restaurant when we were having dinner together. The bottom of the page has Tony's contact information, asking anyone with any information on me to call him.

"I told you he was looking for you," Star says softly.

"I didn't hear the door," I say as I spin around to face her with the paper still in my hand.

"It's okay," she offers a reassuring smile.

"He was really looking for me?" I ask, swallowing over the lump in my throat.

"Since the day you disappeared," she replies. "He's never given up on finding you."

The door opens again. This time, it's Owen carrying a plate with a steaming burger and fries. Two bottles of water are tucked under his arm. "I'm assuming you haven't eaten in a while," Owen remarks as he sets the food on Star's desk.

"It's been a few days," I reply.

He motions for me to sit. "Go slow so you don't get sick, okay?"

"Mhm," I mumble with my mouth full. My eyes close instinctively, relishing the delicious taste of the freshly cooked food made just for me.

"Any luck reaching Tony?" Owen inquires, his voice filled with concern.

"No," Star replies, frustrated. "It keeps going to voicemail, and my texts are unread."

"I know he's working at the restaurant tonight. I'm sure he's busy," Owen remarks with a sigh. "Let's give him a little more time."

Over the course of the next hour, Owen pops in and out of the office, juggling the responsibilities of running the club and checking on me. "Anything?" Owen asks.

"Nothing," Star responds with a weary shake of her head, her disappointment evident.

"We've waited long enough. I'm going to the restaurant to get him," Owen states before disappearing a final time.

Leopold

Star's phone dings with an incoming alert. She looks at the screen, her face lighting up before she turns it to me.

Owen: We're on the way. Tell Leo Tony can't wait to see him.

I'm relieved he's coming, but another wave of nerves washes over me. "Tony's going to want to know what happened," I say, my voice tinged with apprehension.

"Yes, he'll probably have some questions," Star replies calmly.

"You weren't here, but I came to the club with Tony earlier that night," I explain.

"Did something happen while you were here?" she inquires gently.

"No. Lacey, Shawn, and Caleb were great. I really liked them, but..." My voice trails off.

"You're safe to tell me anything," Star encourages.

"There was a scene where the Dominant tied up his submissive. He was gagged and blindfolded." Squeezing my eyes shut, I try to block out the unwelcome memories. "It brought up a lot of memories. Things that were done to me."

"I'm deeply sorry that you were silenced by so many people. Their actions were cruel and unjust—they were wrong. You didn't deserve to be hurt like that," Star says softly, her voice laced with empathy.

"It was my fault," I whisper, unable to shake the shame and guilt from my past.

"No, Leo. It wasn't. Please look at me," Star says, her voice gentle yet firm. I lift my head, meeting her gaze. "You need to understand that being raped was not your fault," she insists.

"But—" I attempt to protest, my words catching in my throat.

"Let me make this clear," she says. "There's nothing you did or could ever do that would give anyone the right to touch you in any way without your consent." Her tone is unwavering. "But it's important to recognize the distinction between what happened to you and what you witnessed at the club," she says.

"That Dominant and submissive discussed their scene ahead of time. They established rules and boundaries. In addition, the protocol at Fire and Ice requires all public scenes to be written out and submitted to Owen or me as an added security measure," she explains patiently. "Chase, the submissive you saw that night, enjoys bondage. Everything that was done to him was consensual."

"Lacey talked to me about how important consent is in BDSM."

"It's arguably the most important part of this lifestyle," Star agrees. "Nothing happens in a responsible Dominant/submissive relationship —whether it's for one night at the club or a more permanent relationship, that isn't fully agreed to by both parties. There's no room for coercion or not respecting boundaries, and safewords are always respected."

"I like Tony," I confess, my voice barely above a whisper. "As more than a friend."

"I know," Star responds, her smile warm.

"But I can't be with him," I admit, my voice tinged with regret.

"Why not?" Star inquires gently.

"As much as I'm comforted by everything you explained," I say, my heart pounds just talking about it. "I can't get hit or be blindfolded."

"Oh, Leo honey," Star responds, her tone tender and reassuring. "None of that would stop Tony from being with you. If you and he were to be in a relationship and if BDSM was part of it, you'd discuss what things are acceptable and what are not. Tony would never ask you to do anything you were uncomfortable with or that would trigger you."

"Really?" I ask, surprised.

"Yes," Star replies, her tone filled with conviction. "Communication is a big part of this lifestyle. Don't ever be afraid to tell Tony what you're thinking or feeling," she continues, her voice gentle but firm. "He needs to know what you want or don't want. Tony will never force or hurt you."

There's a knock on the door a second before it opens. "Leopold," Tony says, his voice thick with desperation as he takes long strides across the room to reach me. I scramble to my feet, my heart pounding with anticipation, and meet him halfway. With a sense of urgency, he pulls me into his arms, enclosing me in his strong embrace.

"I didn't know how to find you," he murmurs, his voice trembling with relief as he presses a tender kiss to the side of my head, his touch a comforting reassurance. "I was so scared."

Star and Owen make a discrete exit, leaving Tony and me alone.

"I'm sorry," I sob, tears streaming down my face. "I'm so sorry."

His hold on me tightens. "You have nothing to apologize for, Leopold," Tony says, his voice cracking. "God, I'm so happy you're back." Taking me by the shoulders, he holds me away from him as he scans my body. "Are you okay? You're not hurt, are you?"

"No," I shake my head, meeting his tear-filled gaze. "You're crying?"

"I thought I'd lost you forever. I didn't know how I could go on without you," Tony confesses, his voice choked with emotion. "Why did you leave?"

"There were people in the room who said you were going to sign papers to have me admitted," I confess. "They didn't know I was awake."

"The doctor wanted me to sign the papers, but I refused. I made a promise to you, and I won't break that."

"They said I hit you?" I swallow over a lump in my throat.

"Do you remember what happened at home? Why we were at the hospital?" Tony asks cautiously.

"No." I shake my head slowly.

"You were having a flashback of some kind. You thought I was Krew and that I was going to hurt you. I couldn't get through to you. When I called Sarah, she directed me to bring you to the emergency room for an evaluation," he explains, his tone gentle but firm. "When we got in the ambulance, they tried to restrain you to the gurney. I begged them not to, but they didn't listen. You got scared. You didn't know what was happening, and you hit me."

"Oh my God," I utter as my legs give way, and I collapse to the floor. Tony sinks down beside me.

"It's okay, Leopold," he whispers, comforting me. "It's over now."

"It's not. I think I might have had more flashbacks while I was gone," I admit, fear tainting my voice.

"What do you mean?" he asks, his brow furrowing with concern.

"I kept waking up in alleys and behind dumpsters, but I didn't know how I got there," I explain and cling to him. "I'm scared, Tony. What's wrong with me?"

"I don't know, but we're going to figure this out," he murmurs as he kisses the top of my head. "Just promise you won't leave me again," he pleads, his voice filled with desperation.

"I won't leave you. I promise." Drawing a shaky breath, I say, "I want to be with you as your submissive."

Anthony

MY EYES OPEN WIDE. LEOPOLD WANTS TO BE MY SUBMISSIVE. "You don't have to say that because you're afraid."

"That's not why," he insists. "I knew it before this, but I got scared after seeing the scene at the club and I thought I had to let you do those things to me. But Star explained that's not how it works."

"No, it isn't. You never have to do anything you don't want to do," I reassure him, my heart swelling with affection.

"Will you let me submit to you?" he asks again, his gaze fixed on me.

Leo's blue eyes shimmer with unshed tears. I can't lie and say I've never thought about having him as my submissive. I've done more than think about it, but this isn't the right time. "No," I say with a heavy heart. "Not like this."

"You don't want me." Leo tries to pull away, his voice trembling with insecurity.

"Stop," I plead, gently holding his hands. "I want you, Leopold. I've wanted you for so long, but this isn't the right way. You need to learn more about the lifestyle, and we need to figure out why you're having flashbacks—how to help you heal."

"I need to tell Sarah the truth. I've been keeping so much from her," he admits, his voice laced with vulnerability. "I was afraid she'd say I was too damaged and needed to be in a hospital and that you wouldn't want me anymore."

"There's nothing that could change my mind about you," I murmur softly, my voice carrying the weight of my emotions. "I love you, Leopold."

"You love me?" he asks in disbelief.

"Yes." I lean in and brush my lips against his. "I love everything about you."

"No one's ever loved me," he whispers, his expression pained.

"You'll never have to feel that way again, Leopold," I promise, gently brushing his hair behind his ear.

"I love you, Tony," he confesses, his gaze searching mine with a mixture of longing and fear. "I don't want to screw this up like I do with everything. I'm so scared."

"Lean on me. Allow me to be strong for you. Let me love you." My words carry a depth of sincerity as I offer him the reassurance he seeks.

Leopold

AUGUST 15

My session with Sarah last week was one of the scariest things I've ever had to do. Even though I've been seeing her every week for months, I never really let my guard down. I kept her an arm's length away. In my attempt to skate by, I only allowed her limited access to my thoughts and fears.

I held back so much—the most important details, not realizing I was only hurting myself. It all came to the surface the night I had a flashback that dissociated me from the current reality.

Sarah allowed me to invite Tony into my sessions while I told them both everything. For real, this time. Then, when I was ready, Tony recounted the full story of what happened that night. I was horrified and embarrassed at my behavior—even though I couldn't remember it.

It was difficult for me to accept that although I did those things, it also wasn't me. Had I not been in a dissociative state, I would never have become violent with anyone.

Then, Sarah suggested something that almost made me quit therapy for good. She proposed seeing a psychiatrist and trying medication for my anxiety and PTSD. At first, I resisted. After being involuntarily addicted to whatever illicit substances Krew fed me, the last thing I wanted was to be drugged. In my mind, I envisioned becoming a groggy mess of a person whose life was once again ruled by the unwanted effects of medication.

Sarah made the case that a reputable doctor would give me the least amount of medication possible to control the symptoms. She challenged me to try approaching the medication discussion with an open mind. She assured me that Dr. Chen wouldn't force me to take something I wasn't comfortable with.

Tony came with me to my first appointment. It was a two-hour intensive, during which Dr. Chen started by taking my entire medical and psychological history. We had a very straightforward conversation about the forced drug use I experienced and subsequent addiction. He was sympathetic and understanding regarding my fear of becoming addicted to drugs again.

Dr. Chen took the time to educate me about the various classes of prescriptions and then proposed what he felt would be an appropriate medication plan for me. Even though Sarah assured me the doctor wouldn't try to coerce me into anything, I was still nervous. What if Dr. Chen insisted I give him an answer right then? But he didn't. When I asked if I could think about the proposed medication, he gave me not only the paper script but also several printouts full of information. And he told me to call him if I had any further questions.

After taking some time to talk more with Tony and think about it further, I decided to give the low-dose anti-anxiety medication a try. It's only been a few weeks, but I already feel some relief from the persistent negative thoughts and feelings of foreboding that have always dictated my life.

I wasn't sure what would happen between Tony and me after I asked to be his submissive, and he turned me down. At first, I was not only hurt but embarrassed. But once I was able to stop and not just listen to him but really hear him, his explanation made more sense. I was in no condition to make an important decision, and he would've been irresponsible in allowing it to happen. But that didn't stop the feelings we now know we share.

He loves me, and I love him.

We're more openly affectionate with one another. However, Tony will not allow our physical relationship to go any further than kissing, espe-

cially while we're still getting to know each other on a deeper level and while I'm learning more about the BDSM lifestyle.

Star has agreed to be my mentor. She's teaching me all the basics of the lifestyle. What it means to be a submissive in a healthy relationship. I'm learning important lessons about communication and how it's essential, especially in a Dom/sub relationship where one person is surrendering so much power to another and where the couple is often participating in activities that could be dangerous.

We talk about consent all the time. Something I didn't realize is that consent is equally essential for the Dominant as well as the submissive. Many people in the lifestyle debate who holds the power, the Dominant or the submissive. The way I understand it, neither role is able to be fulfilled without the other.

The Dominant must prove themself worthy of the trust the submissive is gifting them with. Likewise, the submissive has the responsibility of being open and honest with the Dominant about their experience, past traumas, limits—everything really. It reminds me of a circle. There's no beginning or end. There's no Dominant without submission and no submissive without domination. I don't think one is more powerful than the other.

I've been going to Fire and Ice with Tony more often. With the lessons Star's been teaching me, I'm better able to understand what I'm witnessing. Seeing a person on their knees willingly giving themselves to another brings tears to my eyes. The look of pure devotion on the Dominant's face, whether they're doing a one-time scene or in a committed dynamic, is incredible. Seeing two individuals wholly trusting one another is breathtaking. I want that so badly with Tony, but I don't want to push.

Thankfully, Sarah's a kink-friendly therapist, and I'm able to freely discuss this new part of my life with her as well. We've included Tony in many of my sessions because he wants to learn how best to support me. We're talking about known triggers and planning for the unknown ones that are certain to creep up when we're least expecting them. She's given him tools to help ground me and hopefully keep me from dissociating again.

I'm not without responsibility for this. Being open and communicating my thoughts and feelings is the first line of defense. When I keep *those things to myself under the guise that I'm 'fine,' is when I run into trouble. Part of my therapy goals are to be accountable for my internal thoughts and to be willing to reach out to someone I trust so they don't build up. It's not always easy, but it does work.*

Together, Tony, Sarah, and I have decided it would be safer and in my best interest to not make any decisions regarding a Dom/sub dynamic until I'm stable on my medication for longer and a bit farther into my therapy. It's not an answer I'm thrilled with—something I've openly communicated to both of them, but it's one I understand and accept.

Most importantly, I'm having good days—more good than bad. The negative thoughts that were so loud are still there. I've learned a lot of people have them. I'm also learning that I have power over them, not the other way around. Thoughts cannot harm me. It's okay to have them and then to let them float away.

I am not a loser.

I am not damaged beyond repair.

I am deserving of love.

Leopold

December 23

I've been seeing Dr. Chen for several months, and I think it's safe to say that his treatment plan is working. I haven't felt this good in well, ever. In the beginning, I'd leave my appointments feeling exhausted from information overload. Naps were almost non-negotiable.

Once I understood the quirky doctor better, that went away. He's a brilliant man who cares deeply for his patients. Now, I find myself looking forward to our conversations.

It's been one year since I hit rock bottom. One year since Tony stumbled on me attempting suicide. I want to say every day has been perfect, but that would be a lie. Some days, my path seemed effortless. Others, it felt like an unattainable uphill climb.

One of the hurdles I've dealt with was feeling like a coward for trying to end my life. What kind of person thinks it would be better to be dead than to confront their problems head-on? It's taken a lot of therapy to be able to not only say but also accept as truth that I was not a coward that night.

I was a man who was depressed and alone. I couldn't see a way out. Those thoughts and feelings were nothing to be ashamed of. The fact that I put the blade to my wrist and cut doesn't make me any less of a person—doesn't make me unworthy.

I've worked hard with Sarah on being completely honest and vulnerable, even when I would rather say I was fine and move on to something easier.

Sarah has proven herself to be trustworthy and has given me the tools I need to take ownership of my life and my story. I no longer allow others to choose my narrative. That's mine and mine alone. It feels good to finally take control over my life and to believe I am good enough.

Star and I have continued to meet, and I've learned so much about the BDSM lifestyle. Tony has assured me that he'd walk away from BDSM if it wasn't what I wanted. It's been a part of his life for so long, and I know how important it is to him. I would never ask him to give that up for me. I decided that if I couldn't see myself in the lifestyle, I'd walk away from Tony.

One of the most important things I've worked on with Star and Sarah is learning more about healthy submission and what it would mean to submit to a Dominant. They were both concerned with my mental and emotional health, not because they feared Tony would ever take advantage of me. It's more about being responsible and safe, ensuring I'm well and strong so I'm making the best decisions for me. I don't want to offer my submission to Tony if I'm going to crack under the pressure and end up hurting both him and me.

My biggest concern is still being strong enough within myself to recognize what my wants and especially needs are and not be afraid to voice them. Without that, it would have put Tony at a disadvantage, always trying to guess if my needs were being met. If what we were doing was hurting me. The results could be disastrous for us both.

Star has ensured I have a solid understanding of the lifestyle and what my role would be if I were a submissive. She's helped me develop a detailed list of what I'm okay with and what are limits—soft and hard. We've had very frank discussions after scenes at the club I was unfamiliar with or made me uncomfortable. She and I dissected every action and word in the scenes, trying to ensure my limit list was as accurate as possible.

Which brings me to today. I'm not entirely sure how Tony is going to respond. I hope he's going to accept what I offer him.

Anthony

I've been on edge all week, bracing myself for today. One year ago tonight, I found Leopold in the park, ready to end it all. In the year that followed, I witnessed his struggles and came dangerously close to losing him again. Since then, I've had the privilege of watching him flourish and soar. Despite that, the anticipation of tonight and the memories it holds still weighs heavily on me. I suggested we stay home tonight, but Leopold insisted he wanted to join me at the annual Christmas Eve Eve Party at Fire and Ice.

Our connection has only deepened as Leopold has healed. The love we confessed to one another that night in Star's office has blossomed with each new day. There have been countless nights when I've said goodnight to him outside his bedroom door, only to struggle with returning to my own room alone. It's been the ultimate test of my self-control and resolve.

We both want more, but I don't know when the right time is to take the next step. My biggest concern, the thing that holds me back, is the fear of causing Leopold any pain. Owen insists that I'll know when it's right. I'm trusting him on that.

"Are you ready?" Leo asks from my doorway.

As I turn around to respond, I'm momentarily rendered speechless by the sight before me. Leopold stands leaning against my doorway, his arms casually crossed over his chest. He's dressed in dark trousers paired with a navy blue dress shirt, the top buttons left undone, hinting at the sculpted chest and abdomen beneath.

It's evident that Leopold's been diligently hitting the gym downstairs daily. He's regained a few pounds and added substantial muscle. My hand instinctively moves to cover my mouth in awe. "You're... wow," I manage to utter, making my way across the room with determined steps, my eyes never leaving his mesmerizing form.

"You don't look so bad yourself." His lips quirk up in a smile.

The age gap between Leopold and me has been an ongoing source of insecurity. With nearly fifteen years between us, I couldn't help but question if he'd ever see me as anything more than a friend despite being attracted to him from the moment we met.

"You're positively edible," I say, licking my bottom lip.

His eyes roam up and down my body, pausing at the bulge in my pants. "It wouldn't hurt if we were fashionably late to the party," he murmurs, his voice low and deep.

It would be so easy to give in to the allure of his proposal. The thought of undressing him and worshipping his body like I've dreamt of so many times sends a shiver down my spine. "I'd love to," I confess softly, pressing my lips to his before reluctantly pulling back. "But they're expecting us. Let's go."

⚬

The club's already full. Holiday music plays through the speakers when Leo and I arrive.

"Glad you two could join us," Star says, hugging us both.

Astrid, who's talking with Shawn and Caleb, waves from across the room. "Do you mind if I go say hello?" Leo asks, glancing at me for approval.

"You don't need my permission," I reply, giving him a reassuring smile.

"I won't be long," Leo assures before heading off to greet his friends.

As I watch Leo gracefully weave through the crowd, my heart swells with pride. A sense of admiration washes over me, seeing him interact effortlessly with everyone around him.

"When are you going to do something about that?" Star's voice cuts through my thoughts, drawing my attention.

"What do you mean?" I ask, raising an eyebrow in confusion.

"If you don't ask that boy to submit to you, someone else might beat you to it." I whip my head around to look at her. "Ah, that got your attention," Star says, her voice laced with amusement.

"Why would you say something like that?" I ask, feeling a pang of unease. It's not just the thought of someone else vying for his attention, though that certainly nags at me. It's the fear of losing him again, of him slipping away from me once more.

"Just look at him." She gestures discreetly. "He's not only stunning to look at, but his personality shines brighter than any star. Everyone in this room adores him—and I mean everyone," she emphasizes.

My muscles tense from a surge of jealousy. "Who was asking about him?"

"Not answering that."

"You can't dangle that in front of me and then not tell me who," I argue, casting a glance around the club, trying to spot any telltale signs.

"I can, and I did." She touches my arm, pulling me back into the conversation. "He's strong and ready to take the next step."

"I don't know," I reply, feeling a familiar sense of uncertainty.

"Excuse me, Mistress," Corbin says, interrupting us. "Master Owen sent me to get you. He needs your assistance."

"Thank you," she responds, dismissing him. "Think about what I said." With that, she turns and walks away.

Choosing to remain on the periphery, I take a moment to quietly observe Leopold. Star's words ring true—there's an undeniable strength exuding from him, and it's apparent he's garnered quite the following within the club. Surrounded by a supportive network of friends, he's thrived, shedding his inhibitions and embracing his true self.

"Tony?" A familiar voice calls my name. I turn my head and am shocked to see Trevor. "It's been a while," he says with a hint of nostalgia.

After our scene, we kept in touch for a while, but it seemed like overnight, he disappeared. "It has," I reply, trying to process his unexpected appearance.

"I apologize for losing touch," Trevor says, a hint of remorse in his voice. "Paisley and I were moving around a lot, and my phone went missing. I lost all my contacts, including yours, and I didn't have your last name to try to find you."

"No worries," I assure him, offering a forgiving smile. "Life happens."

"But I want you to understand," he insists earnestly. "You've been on my mind since that night."

"It's really okay. You don't owe me any explanations," I insist.

"Paisley and I are living in Manhattan now."

"Permanently?" I ask, surprised by his revelation.

"Yes," Trevor confirms, nodding. "The company I work for offered me a management position. It meant no more traveling. With Paisley being old enough to enroll in school, it was time to settle down, so I took it."

"That sounds like a wonderful opportunity," I reply, offering him a warm smile.

"They gave me the choice of three locations, and I chose New York City," he confesses.

"It's a fantastic place for families," I remark, reflecting on my upbringing in the city.

"It is, but there's more," Trevor adds, his hand resting on my bicep. "You were a factor in my decision."

"Me?" I ask, taken aback by his admission.

"Before we lost touch, I felt like we were building on the connection we had that night," Trevor explains, his eyes searching mine for a reaction.

My mind drifts back. The atmosphere between us was undeniably charged with sensuality, catching me off guard with its intensity. Trevor and I kept in touch for quite a while, but my feelings toward him had always remained platonic. When we first crossed paths, it was too soon after I lost Kam, and I wasn't ready for anything beyond friendship. I didn't realize Trevor was experiencing something entirely different.

I don't want to cause him any pain, but my heart belongs to someone across the room—to Leopold, the man I'm in love with.

Leopold

Fire and Ice is so much more than just a BDSM club. It's a community of individuals from all walks of life who've come together not only to indulge in sensual delights but also to support each other. Within these walls, I've found my tribe. The people who accept me just as I am—faults and all. It's what I've been longing for my whole life. Finally, at almost twenty-three years old, I'm healthy and whole in a way I never imagined.

While conversation continues around me, I take a moment to center myself. I've known for some time now that I was ready. Not wanting to force anything, I didn't plan how or when to do it. But as I was getting dressed earlier, I knew this was it. If all goes well, tonight will mark a significant milestone in my relationship with Tony. Despite the butterflies in my stomach, everything feels perfectly aligned. It's time.

"If you guys will excuse me, there's something I have to do," I state, excitement beginning to build.

"Does it have anything to do with your handsome man?" Astrid teases.

"Possibly," I tease back, unable to hide my grin.

"When are you and Tony going to stop dancing around each other and finally become a couple?" Shawn asks.

"Hopefully tonight," I reply, my gaze darting around the room until I find Tony in the corner, engaged in conversation with a stranger. Our eyes meet briefly, sending a jolt of electricity through me before he returns to his discussion.

"Good luck," Shawn says. "We're all rooting for you."

My gaze remains fixed on Tony and the handsome stranger, whose hand rests casually on Tony's arm. They seem comfortable with each other, a familiarity that sends a pang of jealousy and hurt simmering just beneath the surface. "Who's that?" I finally manage to voice my question, unable to mask the hint of concern.

The trio exchanges worried glances before Caleb answers cautiously, "That's Trevor."

"Trevor?" I repeat, glancing back at them over my shoulder. "Is he another Dominant?" I ask, puzzled by the lack of mention of Trevor in my conversations with Tony, yet they clearly share a connection.

"He's a submissive. Trevor and Tony have a history together," Astrid says casually. "Trevor has a *thing* for Tony."

"Oh," I reply quietly, processing the new information.

"Really, Astrid?" Caleb shoots her an annoyed look before turning to me. "It was a long time ago," Caleb assures me, though his attempt to help falls somewhat flat in the face of my growing discomfort. "I'm sure it's nothing," he adds.

"Yeah. I'm sure you're right. I have to go," I say quietly, my voice fading as I move away.

Watching Trevor lean into Tony twists my emotions painfully. My heart begins to fracture as I hurry toward the heavy wood doors that mark the exit to the club.

"Is everything okay, Leo?" Corbin, who's sitting at the desk, asks.

"I'm not feeling well," I reply, not bothering to stop as I push open the doors and step outside into the biting cold of the winter air.

Anthony

"THIS IS SOMETHING I'VE THOUGHT ABOUT, HECK DREAMED about for so long now. Wow. I can't believe I'm finally doing this," Trevor admits, his words rushing out in a jumble. "I know you weren't ready for anything more when we first met, but I'm hoping that maybe now... you might consider exploring what's between us."

"Trevor," I say softly, trying to process his sudden confession.

"I probably just broke all kinds of protocol," he continues, his hand anxiously reaching for the back of his neck. "I really screwed this up."

"It's okay, really," I reassure him, trying to ease his nerves. "You're a great guy—"

"I read things between us wrong, didn't I?" he interrupts.

"The scene we did together was an important night for me. One I'll always remember. It was the first time I scened with anyone after losing my partner," I explain. "I enjoyed getting to know you after, but as a friend."

"Oh no," Trevor murmurs softly, his expression falling. "I must look like a complete idiot."

"Not at all," I try to reassure him, hoping to ease the weight of his embarrassment.

"I asked around and was told you were still single. A part of me hoped that you were as affected as I was that night and that you were waiting for me to come back," he confesses, shaking his head in disbelief. "Now that I say that out loud, it sounds ridiculous."

"I don't think it's ridiculous," I offer, feeling compelled to provide an explanation. "I met someone a year ago. It was complicated for a long time, but we're finally ready to make a more serious commitment." Trevor's disappointment is palpable. ""You're a great guy, Trevor. Any Dominant here would be lucky to earn your submission," I add, hoping to comfort him.

"Whoever he is... He's a very lucky man," Trevor says sadly before walking away.

I feel guilty for hurting him, but I genuinely didn't realize he felt that way, especially after he stopped contacting me. I assumed he understood I wasn't interested in pursuing anything further and had moved on. Fortunately, there are plenty of experienced Dominants in the club who I'm sure will be more than interested in Trevor.

But right now, I have something else I need to do. I glance around, searching for Leo, but he's nowhere to be seen. I'm sure someone in the group will be able to point me in the right direction, though.

"Do you know which way Leopold went?" I inquire asking the group of his friends.

"I'm not sure," Shawn responds cautiously, uncertainty lacing his words. "He seemed a bit upset, and then he just left."

"What was he was upset about?" I probe further.

"He saw you talking with Trevor," Astrid adds.

"Sir Genovese," Corbin calls as he rushes across the room toward me.

"What is it?" I ask sensing the urgency in his voice.

"It's Leo," he says, catching his breath.

"What about Leopold?" I demand, a knot forming in my stomach.

"He left about a half hour ago," he confesses, and a wave of dread rushes over me.

"Left?" I repeat, my heart sinking.

"Yes, sir. He seemed in a hurry," Corbin explains, his voice filled with regret. "I didn't know. Didn't think to come get you."

"Did he say where he was going?" I press, trying to mask the panic rising within me.

"He just said he wasn't feeling well," Corbin replies, his expression apologetic.

"No. Oh God, please, no," I whisper frantically as I push the glass door open and rush outside. Memories of last year surge back with brutal force.

Snow falls softly around me as I sprint down the sidewalk toward the river park, my breaths coming in ragged gasps. This cannot happen. I will not lose him.

Leopold

Snow gently blankets the park bench where I sit, overlooking the Hudson River. I ran out so fast that I forgot my coat at the club, but even though I was shivering, I couldn't bring myself back for it.

Confusion clouds my thoughts as I replay the scene with Tony and Trevor in my mind. Our conversations about what I was learning with Star about the dynamics of dominance and submission had seemed to draw us closer, but seeing the way Trevor touched Tony shattered that illusion. Finding out they had a past together was more than I could bear.

Perhaps it's my own boundaries that are the problem. It's the only thing that makes any sense right now. I know Kameron enjoyed bondage. Maybe being free to restrain or blindfold his submissive are things Tony needs in a future dynamic.

Could I compromise on that? Change me to be what Tony needs? The thought twists my stomach with uncertainty because deep down, I know it's not possible. If this is what's going to stand between Tony and me being together, it hurts. It hurts so bad, but it's the painful truth I'll have to accept. Maybe in another life—

"Leopold," Tony's voice breaks through my thoughts as he hurries toward me. "What are you doing out here?"

"I needed some air," I reply, my voice barely audible.

"You're not even wearing a coat. You'll catch a cold," he scolds gently, worry etched on his face.

I don't feel the cold. Perhaps I'm too numb from the hurt and disappointment. "I'm okay. You should go back and enjoy the party," I insist, trying to push him away.

"Why did you leave?" Tony asks as he sits next to me.

This is the moment of truth where all the self-work I've done over the past year is put to the test. It would be so easy to revert to old habits —deflect and shut down. I know that path always leads to isolation. So, I choose to do something terrifying, hoping it will lead to a different result.

"I saw you talking with Trevor," I admit quietly, bracing myself for his reaction. "Astrid told me about you two."

"And what exactly did she tell you?" His tone is edged with frustration.

"That you have a history together," I confess, my voice barely above a whisper. "And that Trevor's interested in you."

"It's true, we have scened before—once," Tony acknowledges, his tone calm but resolute. "And yes, he expressed an interest in me. I made it clear to him that there could be nothing between us. What you saw was me respectfully declining his advances."

"Oh," I murmur, feeling a knot form in my stomach as I wring my hands in my lap.

"Do you really think I would betray you like that?" Tony's voice carries a hint of hurt.

I shrug, unable to meet his gaze. "We aren't anything official. You don't owe anything to me."

"I came looking for you to change that. Look at me, Leopold," Tony's voice holds a quiet intensity, urging me to meet his gaze. With a hesitant breath, I lift my eyes to his, seeing a depth of emotion I hadn't expected. "You've breathed life back into me. Made me feel things I never thought I would again. It's been my own fear holding me back for too long."

Tony rises to his feet, his movements deliberate as he retrieves something from his pocket. With a solemn expression, he extends his hand, revealing an object that sends a shiver down my spine. "The boxcutter," I whisper, my voice barely audible. "Why?"

"It's been with me for the past year," Tony admits, his voice thick with emotion. "Initially, it was a precaution, a fear that you might stumble upon it and use it to hurt yourself. But over time, it became a symbol of the fragility of life. How close I came to losing you." His voice wavers with emotion. "Then they told me you rushed out," he continues, anguish washing over his features, "I feared the worst. I couldn't get here fast enough."

"I'm sorry," I murmur, my heart heavy with guilt. "Seeing him touch you, and then Astrid's words..."

"She crossed a line," Tony says firmly. "I'll address it with Owen."

"No, please don't—" I begin, but Tony holds up his hand.

"Astrid insinuated there was more to my history with Trevor than there ever was," he explains, his tone resolute. "She was wrong, and Owen will ensure she understands that in whatever way he sees fit."

I nod in understanding.

"This boxcutter has become a crutch for me," Tony continues, his voice softer now. "As long as it's in my pocket, a part of me remains tethered to that night—to the past. It's time for me to return it to you."

With gentle reverence, he passes the shielded blade to me. It's the first time I've seen it and held it in a year. My hand trembles as memories flood back, overwhelming me like a tidal wave. "I remember that night so vividly," I say, looking up at him. "The voices of my past were deafening, but now they're nothing more than a distant memory. This little object seemed to hold so much power over me, but it doesn't anymore. It's nothing because I'm strong."

"Yes, Leopold. You are incredibly strong," Tony affirms quietly.

I walk to the edge of the railing, watching the dark water below. With a steady hand, I release the boxcutter, watching it sink into the depths with a soft splash.

Silently, I turn to face Tony, who's still sitting on the bench, and drop to my knees. The gesture is one of both reverence and vulnerability. Tony's sharp inhale punctuates the quiet air as I place my open palms on my thighs, head bowed in submission. "The day I walked into *Italiano Desiderio* and looked into your eyes, all I saw was kindness," I confess, my words gentle but weighted with emotion.

"I fell for you then, though I never dared to hope that a man like you would ever notice me. Night after night, I dreamt of you, longing to understand what it would mean to be loved by you. Before you, I never truly understood what it meant to be cherished," I admit, my voice trembling with vulnerability.

"You took me in without knowing me, showering me with kindness and equipping me to become a better man—a stronger man," I express, my voice filled with gratitude and sincerity. "Each day, my love for you deepens." Lifting my head, I meet his gaze and know I've found my home. "Last year, in this very spot, you saved me. Now, I kneel before you, flawed but deeply in love. I offer you all that I am—my life and my heart. My submission."

In the heart of the bustling city, where chaos usually reigns, a profound silence descends. No honking horns, no blaring sirens—just the tranquil hush of a world blanketed in snow. It's a silence so complete it's almost tangible.

"Leopold," he breathes my name like a prayer. "I've never felt fear like I did last year when I found you here. The thought of losing you nearly destroyed me. Witnessing your healing and growth has been a profound privilege. "And now, seeing you kneel before me, offering yourself," his voice softens. "Your submission is a precious gift I cherish. I promise to honor and protect it as we navigate this lifestyle together."

"You're accepting?" I ask, a glimmer of hope in my voice.

"I never planned to let another moment pass without binding myself to you," he answers, leaning down to cup my face in his hand. "From now on, I'll be your guide, your mentor—your Dominant. I'll introduce you to pleasures beyond your wildest dreams."

Our lips crash together in a passionate embrace as Tony pulls me closer. I eagerly climb onto his lap, straddling him as our kiss deepens. His fingers tangle in my hair as we lose ourselves in the moment. A low moan escapes my lips as I grind against his erection.

Tony breaks the kiss, his breath coming in ragged gasps. "If we keep this up, we'll end up getting arrested for public indecency," he murmurs, a hint of amusement in his voice. "Do you want to head back to the party?" he asks.

"No." I shake my head slowly. "Will you take me home?" I ask as I crawl off him and then stop. "Wait, what should I call you?"

"How about we stick with Tony for now," he suggests, standing up. "We can figure the rest out later." He takes my hand. "Come on. We'll stop at the club to get your coat, and then we're going straight home."

As we step back into Fire and Ice, Tony leads me straight to the coat room. I'm sliding my arms into the sleeves when Owen appears.

"I've been looking for you everywhere," Owen says, looking between us. "Are you two leaving already?"

"We are," Tony replies firmly.

"It's early even for you," Owen observes, his smile fading. "Is everything alright?"

"It is," Tony reassures him, squeezing my hand.

Owen looks between us. "I wanted to ask you about—"

"Whatever it is will have to wait," Tony says, his grip firm on my hand. "We'll talk tomorrow."

"Goodnight," I call with a grin and give a final wave as I turn to leave. "Happy Christmas Eve Eve."

🕯

The subway ride back to our apartment feels agonizingly long. Tony's posture is tense, his silence unsettling. I'm starting to worry that he's having second thoughts, but I don't voice my concerns in public. When we're finally in the safety of the apartment, I finally speak up. "Is everything okay?"

"What do you mean?" Tony's response is guarded.

I crack my knuckles, trying to summon the courage to continue. "You seemed distant on the way home."

"If I didn't," Tony replies in a low, gravelly tone. "I wouldn't have been able to control myself. I've wanted you for so long, Leopold."

Hearing Tony say he wants me is a dream come true, but at the same time, I'm scared. "I don't know how to do this," I admit.

"Our situation is somewhat unique, considering our discussions about your limits for the past few months, even though we weren't officially vetting," he explains. "But if you prefer, we can take a step back and formally vet each other."

"You know everything about me, and I trust you to respect my limits. That's not what I mean," I admit, taking a deep breath. "It's... sex. I've never willingly experienced it before. I'm scared, and I don't know what to do..." I pause, feeling the weight of my fear pressing down on me.

"Thank you for telling me. I know it wasn't easy," Tony replies, his voice gentle as he presses a tender kiss to my lips. "We'll take things at your pace, and we can stop whenever you need to. Let's establish safewords now. Yellow means you're nearing your limit, and red means stop immediately. Your voice will always be heard in everything we do together."

Tears well up in my eyes as Tony's words wash over me. We'd discussed safewords extensively before tonight, and he understands my fear, my past trauma of having my voice silenced. Knowing that's one of his top priorities quiets my fears.

"Are you ready?" he asks softly.

For most of my life, I felt unworthy of love. A failure in every sense of the word. A hopeless screw-up. Last year, Tony found me at my lowest. He could've turned a blind eye and left me to fend for myself. Passed me off as someone else's problem. But he didn't.

Instead of abandoning me, Tony brought me home. He didn't just lend a helping hand. He empowered me with the means to chase my dreams, including ones I hadn't dared to envision. He celebrated my victories with me and held me close when I stumbled and fell. Through it all, Tony has demonstrated what it truly means to love someone unconditionally. Submitting to him feels like the most natural thing in the world.

Nerves still flutter in my belly, but I take comfort in his gentle reassurance. With Tony as my Dominant, I have faith that everything will be okay.

Leopold

The only times I've been in Tony's bedroom are when I put his clean laundry on the bed. But tonight, it's different. Tonight, I'm here with him—as a couple.

"You're trembling," Tony observes, taking my hands in his. "What's your color?"

"Can there be a color before we even start?" I inquire hesitantly.

"Yes, absolutely. Where are you at? Talk to me," he encourages.

"I'm nervous, but I think I'm green," I stammer, unsure of myself. "I don't know what to do. How to touch you," I admit. "Could you teach me how to please you?"

"There'll be plenty of time for that," Tony murmurs, his hand tender against my cheek. I lean into his touch, feeling a sense of comfort. "Tonight is about making this moment special for you." His lips meet mine.

The kiss is gentle, filled with a sense of wonder and excitement. We explore each other's mouths slowly, as if savoring every moment. When we finally pull away, I find myself breathless. "I can't believe this is happening."

"Believe it, Leo," Tony says with a reassuring smile, his eyes reflecting sincerity. "Tonight is real, and it's just the beginning." He runs his fingers through my hair, his touch calming my nerves. " This moment, this connection between us—it's the start of something beautiful," he says as he trails kisses down my neck.

My hand hesitates in mid-air, unsure whether to reach out or withdraw. Tony's slight step back makes me second-guess myself, fearing I've already crossed a boundary. "You're free to touch me," he reassures me, undoing the buttons of his shirt and letting it fall to the floor. " Just as much as you belong to me, I belong to you."

Taking a deep breath to steady my nerves, I run my trembling hands over his chest, marveling at the firmness of his muscles beneath my fingertips. Feeling the warmth of his skin beneath my touch. It's smooth and inviting, and I'm filled with a sudden desire to explore every inch of him. Leaning in, I press a soft kiss to his chest. A quiet moan escapes Tony's lips, and his fingers find their way into my hair, urging me on.

I continue to trail kisses down his torso, tracing the contours of his abs with tender reverence. As I near the waistband of his pants, my fingers instinctively move to undo the button, but Tony's hand stops me before I can proceed. "You don't have to," he whispers, his voice filled with understanding.

"You don't want me to—" I start to say, my fingers hovering over the button of his pants.

"Leopold," he says, his voice breathy. "It's not that I don't want you to. I can't wait to feel your mouth wrapped around my cock, but not tonight," he says with a pained groan. "But I want to make love to you tonight," he says, his gaze meeting mine.

His hands move to my shirt, his touch deliberate as he undoes each button. "We'll take it slow," he murmurs, his voice filled with reassurance. With each button released, he adds, "I'll ensure your body is ready to accept me," he promises, his voice low and intimate as he opens the last button. He slides my shirt off my arms and tosses it to the side.

With practiced ease, he undoes the button of my pants, his touch gentle yet purposeful. "You'll feel every inch of me as I enter you," he repeats softly, his fingers sliding down the zipper as he slowly lowers my pants. "But I won't hurt you." Stepping out of them, I kick them aside, feeling exposed yet liberated in his presence. His touch remains tender as he removes my boxer briefs, leaving me bare before him.

He steps back, studying every curve and contour of my body with a mixture of desire and reverence. At this moment, I realize this isn't just about physical intimacy—it's about trust, connection, and the promise of something deeper.

"You're beautiful," Tony murmurs, his words causing a warmth to spread across my cheeks. I glance away shyly, unable to meet his gaze.

"I hope I don't disappoint," he adds, his tone tinged with vulnerability as he removes his pants and boxers.

Despite the age gap between us, Tony's physique is nothing short of impressive. His dedication to his fitness routine is evident in the way his body is toned and muscular, with a well-defined six-pack drawing my eyes lower to his cock that hangs long and thick.

"You could never," I breathe, my voice barely above a whisper as I take him in. This is the first time I've seen him completely undressed, and I can't help but feel a rush of desire at the sight of him. He's more than perfect—he's everything I've ever wanted.

"Lie down," he says and then opens one of his drawers, taking out lube that he tosses next to me.

Tony climbs onto the bed, straddling my legs. Leaning down, he kisses me tenderly, his tongue exploring my mouth. I reach up and caress his back, noting the muscles contracting in response to my gentle pressure. Pulling him to me, his erection presses against my stomach, and I moan into his mouth.

Breaking the kiss, Tony explores my body with his lips, leaving a trail of kisses along my chest. He gently takes one of my nipples into his mouth, sending waves of pleasure coursing through me. My anticipation grows as Tony moves to the other nipple, grazing it with his teeth and causing me to gasp in delight. "Do you like that?" he asks, his voice husky with desire. "Yes," I reply breathlessly.

A pleased smile graces his lips as he moves lower, leaving a trail of kisses in his wake. "You are going to look amazing with my wax covering you."

Every touch sends a jolt of sensation through me, and I can't help but wiggle slightly as his tongue dances over my navel. When he reaches my thighs, a sense of anticipation fills the air. "Are you ready?" he asks, his gaze fixed on mine.

I've never had a man touch me there. Never had anyone offered me pleasure that didn't come from coercion. Consensual wasn't a part of the narrative—until now. I nod, my voice caught in my throat. I'm aching for Tony to touch me again.

I feel his warm breath on me as his tongue caresses my slit, teasing the head until he slowly takes my length into his mouth. He licks the underside from root to tip before he takes me deeper into his mouth. My back arches off the bed. "Fuck, that feels so good," I moan.

He pulls off and looks at me, "I'm glad you like it." Then he moves his attention to my balls, licking and sucking them before sitting back on his heels.

Lifting my head, I watch him open the lube and squirt some onto his fingers. "What's your color?"

Pausing briefly, I assess my current emotional state. I've never felt pleasure like what Tony's giving me, but at the same time, knowing he's about to touch me triggers a wave of fear through my body. Gritting my teeth and squeezing my eyes shut, I attempt to force the memories of searing pain from unwanted invasions from my mind.

"Leopold, look at me," Tony's voice is firm. I blink, meeting his gaze, and I find nothing but love and concern. "Stay with me," he implores softly. I nod in response. "What's your color?"

"Yellow," I whisper, my voice barely audible. "I want you to keep going even though I'm scared."

"Remember to stay calm and breathe. I'm right here with you," Tony says soothingly as his finger presses against my entrance. The sensation is overwhelming, but his steady presence grounds me. "You're doing so good, *cuore mio.*" When he's fully inside, he stills and asks, "Color?"

"Green," I say quietly.

"Good boy." Tony's voice carries a note of approval, sending a shiver of excitement through me. "I'm going to start moving."

As his finger moves in and out of me, it banishes the memories of pain and replaces them with pure, unadulterated pleasure. Pre-cum beads at the tip of my cock. With his spare hand, Tony traces a finger along my slit, then brings it to his lips. "You taste divine."

"I'm going to add another finger," Tony says, his touch deliberate and controlled. I feel the pressure as a second finger joins the first, stretching me in a way that's pleasurable but not painful. Once fully inserted, he pauses, allowing me to accommodate the sensation before adding a third.

Then, he begins to move, starting off with slow, deliberate motions as he leans down to tease the tip of my cock with his tongue. Tony gradually increases the rhythm, finger fucking me while he works my body, taking me deeper, sucking harder, and using his tongue with skill.

"Tony," I whimper, my voice barely audible amidst the heat of the moment.

Tony withdraws his fingers, shifting up the bed to kiss me tenderly. His erection presses insistently against my stomach as I taste my essence on his lips. Maintaining our connection, he rolls onto his back, drawing me on top of him.

I press against his chest and sit up, taking his throbbing cock in my trembling hand and stroking it slowly. Leaning down, I lick the tip, swirling my tongue around the head before taking him eagerly into my mouth. He groans appreciatively as I suck, guiding him deeper.

Tony's hand weaves through my hair, but he doesn't force my movements. Meeting his gaze, the satisfaction on his face bolsters my confidence. Shifting my focus, I massage his balls with my free hand, intensifying his pleasure as I continue to suck him.

"Leopold," he whispers, tilting my head back tenderly. "I need to be inside you."

"I don't know what to do," I confess, feeling uncertain.

"Take the lube and rub it on me," he instructs. Squeezing a generous amount onto my palm, I coat his rigid length with the slick substance, my movements hesitant. "Remember, you're the one in control," Tony reassures me.

With his arousal in my grasp, I align it with my entrance. Tony places his hands on my hips, supporting me as I slowly descend onto him. Despite his preparation, the initial penetration burns, and I inhale sharply in discomfort.

"Don't force it," he advises, his touch steadying me.

I take a deep breath, steeling myself for the sensation as I lower myself onto him. The pain is sharp, but I push through it, determined to feel him inside me.

"That's it," he murmurs, his voice laced with encouragement. "Take your time." I proceed cautiously, feeling every inch of him stretching me.

"Fuck, you're so tight," he groans, his words sending a thrill through me.

I pause, allowing my body to adjust to the intrusion. Gradually, the pain gives way to a pleasurable sense of fullness. I begin to move, rocking my hips back and forth, savoring the sensations of every vein and ridge of him rubbing against me. It's a feeling of intense pleasure I've never known.

Leaning forward, I capture his lips in a passionate kiss, our bodies melding together in perfect harmony. Pleasure builds with each thrust, and I feel myself nearing the edge.

Tony senses it, too. "Sit up. I want you to come with me," he urges, his voice hoarse with desire. I comply, resting my hands on his muscular thighs as his hands begin to roam my body.

He reaches up, teasing my nipples before pinching them gently, sending jolts of electricity through my body. I ride him harder, craving deeper penetration with each thrust.

"Yes, just like that," he encourages, stroking me in time with my movements. Gripping me firmly, he thrusts up into me, his movements becoming more urgent. "You've never looked more beautiful—more powerful than you do right now. Come for me," he commands, and I obey, surrendering to the pleasure as I reach the peak of ecstasy.

As I convulse around him, Tony finds his own release. "Leopold," he whispers my name as he fills me with his cum. My body trembles as another wave of pleasure crashes over me.

He pulls me close, his cock still buried inside me, whispering words of love and reassurance as we bask in the afterglow. "You're perfect, Leopold," he murmurs.

Tears stream down my cheeks, overwhelmed by the intensity of our connection. "I've never felt like this before," I confess. "I love you, Tony."

His touch soothes me as he kisses away my tears. "I love you too, Leopold."

Anthony

I'VE BEEN FORTUNATE THAT MY PAST SEXUAL ENCOUNTERS have always been positive experiences. But the connection Leopold and I shared tonight transcended everything. It was as though our bodies had been waiting for this moment, and our souls found their missing piece.

Leo lays in my arms, his shoulder shaking as he sobs, hopefully purging himself of everything negative from his past. Never again will sex be used as a weapon to hurt him. I brush the hair off his face, whispering words of love and reassurance, promising him a future free from fear. "You're safe." I kiss his forehead.

As he drifts into a peaceful sleep, his breathing steadies against my chest. In the still of the night, I vow to be his rock, his constant companion in a world that once felt so lonely.

Leo's lips brush against mine. "Happy Christmas Eve," he says between kisses.

I blink awake, relief flooding me as I realize last night wasn't just a

"

figment of my imagination. "Happy Christmas Eve," I reply, meeting his gaze.

His innocent blue eyes, so full of wonder, search mine. "What's on the agenda for today?" he asks, his voice filled with anticipation.

Tracing circles on his bare chest, I murmur, "As much as I'd love to stay in bed with you all day, we've got a houseful of guests coming tomorrow. That means food prep today."

Leo groans dramatically. "Can't we just skip the whole Christmas thing?"

I laugh, sitting up and pulling him with me. "Nice try, but no. We've got work to do."

His playful expression shifts, a hint of sincerity in his eyes. "Yes, Master," he says, the words slipping out without thought.

I pause, a pang of concern flickering through me. "You don't have to call me that."

He meets my gaze, his expression serious. "I know. But that's why I want to. If you're okay with it."

I nod slowly, needing to understand his reasoning. "Can you explain why 'Master' and not 'Sir' or something else?"

"I understand your concern, given everything with Krew." I nod in acknowledgment. "But to me, that title holds no power when it's forced. With you, it's a choice—a symbol of my trust and love. You are the Master of my heart and soul."

His vulnerability touches me deeply, leaving me in awe of the man beside me. "You never cease to inspire me," I confess, my voice filled with reverence.

"Why?" he asks, genuinely confused.

Taking his hand in mine, I speak from the depths of my heart. "You've been to hell and back, yet you're willingly offering me everything." Pressing a gentle kiss to his forehead, I vow, "I treasure you and will spend every moment proving that to you."

Leo's response is a soft affirmation. "There's nothing left for you to prove. I already know."

With a loving kiss, we solidify our commitment to each other.

"Let's go shower," I suggest, a smile gracing my lips.

Leo trails behind me as we enter the bathroom. While I busy myself gathering towels, he takes charge of adjusting the water to just the right temperature. With everything ready, we step into the spacious walk-in shower together. My body ignites as our tongues explore each other in a passionate kiss.

Leopold's movements catch me off guard as he pulls back and drops to his knees, his lips parting to envelop me. As he takes me into his mouth, his gaze meets mine through the mist of water droplets, intensifying the sensation. Watching him with his lips wrapped around my dick is incredibly erotic, sending shivers of pleasure down my spine. I'm so aroused it's almost painful. I feel every movement as he swallows, his throat working to accommodate more of me.

His technique is exquisite, alternating between sucking and lightly grazing his teeth along my shaft. With a firm grasp at the base of my cock, he licks the bead of pre-cum from the tip, sending a jolt of pleasure through me. "God, you feel incredible," I groan, my voice strained with lust. "Touch yourself. I want to watch you pleasure yourself while you suck me."

With one hand steadying himself on my leg, Leo's other hand finds its way to his own arousal. He strokes himself in time with the movements of his mouth, each stroke pushing us both closer to the edge of pleasure.

"Leo, damn, this is incredible." My fingers tangle in his hair as I thrust into his mouth, gauging his limits. He nods eagerly, and I guide him deeper until I'm hitting the back of his throat. He relaxes, surrendering control to me as I dictate the pace. His hand moves faster around his own cock. His eyes never leave mine, adding to the intensity of the moment.

"I'm close," I warn, feeling the familiar tightness in my groin. "If you want me to stop, raise your hand." His grip on my thigh tightens, a clear signal to continue. As my thrusts grow more urgent, my release approaches with unstoppable force. He moans around my cock, and I reach the peak of ecstasy, my body trembling as I release into his waiting mouth. He swallows eagerly, his hand working furiously on his own arousal until he's coming at my feet.

As the last waves of his orgasm subside, Leo leans back, breathless. "Holy shit," he gasps.

After helping him to his feet, I kiss him deeply, tasting myself on his tongue. "That was—amazing."

"One by one, you're erasing every bad memory," he whispers, his eyes filled with gratitude. "Soon, you'll be all I know."

"That's my goal," I reply, my voice thick with emotion.

Turning him around, I reach for the shower gel, eager to care for him as tenderly as he has for me. After washing each other clean, we wrap towels around ourselves and return to the bedroom to get dressed.

"We should move your clothes in here," I suggest.

Leo's eyes widen in surprise. "You want me to share your room?"

I smile, the warmth of his presence filling me with joy. "I want us to share everything, including this space. I want you in my arms every night as we sleep."

"If this is a dream, I don't ever want to wake up," Leo murmurs.

But this isn't a dream—it's the beginning of something far greater. It's the start of forever.

***

It's as if Leopold and I have completed a journey back to where it all began. Last Christmas, I clung to the fragile promise he made not to harm himself for thirty days—my opportunity to show him his value. Terrified doesn't begin to capture the depth of my emotions. Leopold's life rested in my hands, and I was grossly underqualified for that responsibility.

Watching him tonight, you'd never believe he's the same man whose life hung in the balance just last year. He's radiant, effortlessly working the room, engaging in lively conversation with our Fire and Ice friends. I can't take my eyes off him.

"It's about time," Owen says, a grin spreading across his face.

"What are you talking about?" I ask, pretending I don't know what he's referring to.

"You and Leo." He nods toward Leo across the room. "You two

have been dancing around each other since the first day he walked into the club making his delivery."

"He wasn't ready to commit to anything, then. It would've been irresponsible," I explain.

"Maybe not," Owen muses.

"We're together now. That's all that matters."

Leo joins us, looking curious. "What's going on?"

"Just discussing you," I reply with a smile.

Leo looks concerned. "I hope it's nothing bad."

"All good things," Owen reassures him. "I was just telling Tony that it's about time the two of you made things official."

Leopold's face lights up. "I've never been happier."

"I can't wait to see you two scene at the club. It's been too long since we've gotten to experience one of your wax masterpieces," Owen adds.

"It's going to be a while before we do that," I interject.

Leo speaks up, his gaze determined. "I've been thinking. I'd like our first scene to be at the club."

"Are you sure?" I ask, surprised. "I don't want it to be too much for you."

Leo nods, his gaze steady. "I've thought about it. It might be tough, but it'll also mark my progress—that I'm no longer controlled by fear."

Once again, this man has rendered me speechless. The things that were done to him would make most of us cower in fear, yet Leopold is suggesting our first scene as a Dominant and submissive be done at Fire and Ice. What have I done to deserve the trust and love of this man?

"Unless you don't think it's a good idea?" he asks, his eyes searching mine for validation.

"If you feel it will be a positive experience and will continue your healing, then I support it," I reassure him.

"Thank you, Master," Leopold says quietly.

For the rest of the evening, my attention is only half on the conversations around me. The rest is focused entirely on Leopold. Images of him, naked and covered with my wax, dance through my mind. The urge to dismiss our guests so I can fuck him senseless grows with each passing moment.

Leopold

As I chat with Shawn and Caleb, I feel the weight of Tony's stare on me from across the room. His gaze is a palpable force, undressing me with an intensity that leaves me breathless. Despite my attempts to maintain composure, a smile tugs at the corners of my lips, unable to resist the magnetic pull of his attention.

The hours stretch on before the party slowly winds down, each moment feeling like an eternity as we bid farewell to the last of our guests.

As I'm finishing loading the dishwasher, I feel Tony's presence behind me before his lips make contact with my neck, igniting a wave of desire that courses through my body. "I want you to fuck me," he whispers, his voice deep with longing.

"What?" I spin around, shocked, and ask, "Why?"

"I've had the exquisite pleasure of being inside you," Tony murmurs, his breath hot against my ear. "Tonight, I want to feel you inside me."

"I'm not sure I can do that," I confess, my heart racing with uncertainty. "I've never done that before."

"I know," Tony reassures me, pressing a gentle kiss to my lips. "I'll guide you through it."

I've never experienced the sensation of being inside another man, of being the one to bring pleasure in that way.

"If you're uncomfortable, we don't have to," he offers.

"I want to," I reply, the intensity of my desire matching him. "I want us to explore everything together."

Taking my hand, Tony leads me to our bedroom.

"Undress me," he commands, firm yet tender.

"Yes, Master," I respond, eager to fulfill his wishes.

His intense gaze never wavers as I slowly peel off his deep red shirt, revealing the chiseled contours of his chest. My fingertips dance over the taut muscles before I discard it, captivated by the sight before me. Leaning in, I capture his lips as my hands move to the button of his pants. As I push them down, his thick cock springs free.

Tracing a path of kisses down his torso, I revel in the taste of his skin, each caress igniting a spark of desire. Finally reaching his throbbing erection, I take it in my hand, relishing the sensation of his arousal against my skin. Meeting his gaze, I find a hunger burning in his eyes as I take him into my mouth, eliciting a low growl of pleasure.

Tony's hands find their way to my hair, guiding me with gentle pressure as I continue to pleasure him. "Fuck, your mouth feels so good," he says, his voice deep. "You have to stop, or I won't last." His eyes are full of desire as I stand up and remove my clothes. "Lie down," he says softly.

I comply eagerly, my heart racing as Tony crawls on top of me, his body over mine. Pressing his lips to mine, we grind against each other, igniting a firestorm of desire. I lose myself in the intoxicating rhythm of our passion, surrendering to the ecstasy of our shared intimacy.

Without breaking the kiss, Tony rolls us over so I'm poised on top. He reaches into the nightstand drawer, retrieves the lube, and hands it to me with a silent understanding.

"Do you need me to prepare you like you did for me?" I ask, my voice laced with uncertainty.

"Yes," he replies, his tone leaving no room for doubt.

With trembling hands, I apply the slick gel to my fingers before slowly inserting them into his waiting entrance. Tony's soft moans of pleasure urge me on, my own excitement mounting with each move-ment until I can barely contain myself.

"I want you inside me, now," Tony whispers, his legs parting to welcome me in.

"Fuck," I whisper, taking in the sight of him spread and waiting for me.

I position myself at his entrance, gently pushing inside as I watch his reaction, his eyes fluttering closed in rapture. Tenderly brushing his cheek, I ask, "Are you okay?"

"Yes," he breathes, his voice filled with need. "Feels so good."

With a slow, deliberate motion, I push further, feeling his muscles stretch to accommodate me as I sink all the way in, and a wave of plea-sure washes over me. "I've never felt anything... Oh my God," I murmur, my voice breathy. After taking a second to compose myself, I begin to move, the rhythm slow and deliberate.

I reach out to touch him, but he stops me, his voice filled with deter-mination. "No, this is for you. Only you," he insists.

I nod, my desire fueling each thrust as I continue to penetrate him deeply. "You feel incredible." My voice is hoarse from desire. Despite the building pressure of my impending release, I'm determined to make this moment last.

"Fuck me harder, Leopold," Tony demands, his voice laced with a hunger that mirrors my own.

"Yes, Master," I respond eagerly, seizing his hips and increasing the intensity of my movements. "I'm so close," I admit, the tension coiling tightly within me.

"Come inside me," he urges, and I do, releasing myself completely as my climax crashes over me in waves.

Collapsing against him, I struggle to catch my breath as he strokes my back soothingly, grounding me in the aftermath of our passion. "That was incredible," I say, my voice filled with awe.

He smiles, his eyes alight with satisfaction. "Now, it's your turn to please me," he says, his voice a promise of what's to come. "Get on your knees and look back at me."

I watch, transfixed, as he retrieves my cum from between his legs, using it to slick his own cock before positioning himself behind me.

With a sharp intake of breath, I feel him enter me, his size stretching me in the most delicious way.

He grabs my hips and starts to move. "You're so big, Master. I feel you everywhere," I moan, the sensation overwhelming yet exhilarating. I'm already growing hard again.

"Fuck your hand while I fuck your ass," he commands, his words sending a thrill through me.

Following his directive, I reach between my legs, stroking myself eagerly.

"Your ass belongs to me," Tony growls, his thrusts growing more urgent with each passing moment.

"Only you, Master," I gasp, my hand moving faster as I feel my climax approaching.

"I'm almost there," he grunts, his movements becoming more frenzied. "Now, Leopold, come with me."

With a final, desperate thrust, he plunges into me, his release flooding me as my own orgasm consumes me, painting the bed in ribbons of cum.

As we collapse together, spent and sated, he whispers, "I love you so much, *cuore mio*."

"I love you, too, Master."

Leopold

DECEMBER 31

Tony was surprised, to say the least, when I suggested I'd like our first scene to be public. Of course, we discussed it at great length after we had the most mind-blowing sex of my life. When Tony asked me to fuck him, I was completely thrown off. In my head, I thought a Dominant always did the penetrating. Looking at that now, I realize how naïve and foolish that assumption was. Regardless of who was physically on top, Tony was every bit in charge.

Being given the privilege to be inside of him is something I'll never forget or take for granted.

It's been over a year since I was at my lowest point imaginable. At times, I still struggle when I look back and realize how desperate I was for the pain to stop and the awful voices in my head to be silenced. That night, as I stood alone in the park, I felt so alone and unworthy. I honestly believed I had no business being alive.

Tony will never know how grateful I am that he happened to walk that way. I genuinely believe something greater was at play that night. Since then, he's not only given me the tools to succeed, but he's also shown me love like I've never experienced.

He knew I wanted to get a tattoo, so for Christmas, one of his presents was a gift certificate to Infinite Ink. I now have two meaningful pieces of art on my body. The first is a semi-colon that's over the scar on my wrist.

Although it seems plain in design, it's a statement that's become widely recognized for its deep meaning. The semi-colon symbolizes the continuation of a story. It's a reminder that I've overcome hardship, abuse, and severe depression, and even though I attempted suicide, I didn't succeed. Instead of trying again, I made a choice to keep living. To say that my life matters and my story isn't over.

The second design I got was a surprise for Tony. When he saw it, he was moved to tears. On my chest, above my heart, is a scene of a tumultuous sea, the ink deep indigo. Waves crash with unrestrained fury. Amid the chaos, an anchor emerges—a symbol of strength and stability. The anchor, intricately detailed with weathered textures and rugged contours, has the name 'Tony' subtly etched in it. It's a reminder that even in the darkest of storms, there's always hope.

For the rest of the week, Tony and I spent countless hours planning every detail of our scene for tonight. I know he's still worried that it'll be too much for me and I can't say that I'm not nervous, but I'm also very much looking forward to it.

My history is filled with being forced to be naked in front of people who wished to use me. To make me feel less than human—a toy for their sick pleasure. Everything we're going to do has been discussed and agreed upon. The only thing I don't know and asked Tony not to tell me are the specifics of the design he'll make on my body.

Tonight is my choice. Tonight, I will reclaim everything that was taken from me.

Leopold

Fire and Ice is busier than I've ever seen it. The energy in here is electric. It's a fitting backdrop for what promises to be a night of empowerment and liberation. Trying to avoid the gnawing anxiety clawing at my insides, I focus on my task at hand, arranging his candles on the table like I practiced all week.

"Are you holding up okay," Tony asks, his voice familiar and reassuring as he approaches from behind.

I lean back into his chest, and he wraps his arms around me. "I'm scared out of my mind."

"We don't have to do this," he reminds me, concern evident in his voice. "It's not too late. We can put this all away and do it at home."

"Is that what you'd prefer?" I ask.

"No matter the setting, you are the only thing that matters to me," Tony replies, his voice deep and velvety. "But if doing our first scene at Fire and Ice is important to you, then our journey begins here. The decision lies with you, *cuore mio*."

The temptation to call it off and retreat to the safety of our apartment is there, but I refuse to take it. "No, I want—need to do this here," I say, looking out at the crowd. "This is about reclaiming my body and sexuality—my power. Showing the world that I refuse to be a victim defined by my past."

Tony's expression softens, a mixture of pride and tenderness in his eyes. "What did I ever do to deserve you," he murmurs, his fingers tracing patterns against my skin.

"You saved me," I whisper back.

Dressed in a black one-piece accentuating her voluptuous curves, Star's heels click as she steps to center stage, and a hush falls over the crowd. The nerves I felt earlier calmed and gave way to a serene calm. Nothing has ever felt more right to me.

After the PTSD episode that shattered the fragile semblance of control I was clinging to and sent me spiraling out of control. I found myself at a crossroads. I could continue on as I was, barely hanging on and hurting those around me, or I could allow myself to be vulnerable and honest in my therapy sessions.

With Tony by my side, I bared my soul and recounted every harrowing detail of the abuse inflicted on me by David and Krew. It was the scariest thing I've ever had to do. I feared Tony would turn his back and walk away when he learned of all the depraved things that were done to me. How could a man as good as him love someone as dirty as me?

The most difficult lesson I had to embrace was to stop judging myself and accept my worth as a person is not defined by the abuse I lived through. I am more than the sum of my traumas. I'm a whole and worthy individual—a proud gay man deserving of love and happiness. Accepting those truths was more challenging than it sounds. It was a revelation that eluded me for far too long, buried beneath layers of guilt and shame. But tonight, as I step out onto the stage alongside my Master, I embrace my truth with unwavering conviction.

"Ladies and gentlemen," Star addresses the audience, her voice carrying across the room with a commanding presence. "Tonight, we have a very special presentation for you. Anthony and Leopold have finally entered into a Dom/sub relationship." Star glances our way with a knowing smile as the room erupts in cheers.

When they quiet, Star continues, "They've chosen to mark the occasion by allowing us to witness their first scene together," she says, followed by more applause. "Many of you are long-standing members of Fire and Ice and know the amazing work Tony does with wax. For those of you who are newer, you're in for a special treat. I'm as excited as all of you, so I'm going to make my exit and allow these two men to take the stage."

Star stops in front of me and takes my hand in hers. "I'm so very proud of you," she says, her voice tinged with emotion. "The strength you're demonstrating tonight is something I don't ever want you to forget."

"Thank you, Mistress," I respond respectfully.

"And you," she says, turning to Tony, her eyes brimming with tears. "I'm so happy that you've found love once again. No one deserves happiness more than you—both of you," she adds, casting a warm glance between us.

Tony leans in to embrace her, his lips brushing against her cheek as he whispers something I can't quite catch in her ear. With a nod of gratitude, she gracefully exits the stage.

The lights dim, and sensual music begins to play.

Tony turns to me. "Take off your robe."

With his words, everything else fades away. This intimate moment is reserved for only Tony and me. Our eyes lock, and in that silent exchange, I feel a surge of connection that transcends words. My eyes are locked with his. Those deep brown eyes and the kindness they've always held when he looked at me. His deep brown eyes, always a source of comfort, now hold a newfound tenderness that fills me with warmth. It's a love born from mutual respect and unwavering support, a love that has carried us through the darkest of times.

"Yes, Master," I whisper as I open my robe, letting the silky fabric flutter to my feet.

"You're perfect," Tony says as his gaze travels down my body. "There's no one else I'd rather share this moment with."

"Are you ready?" he asks, his voice filled with anticipation.

"I've been waiting for this moment my whole life."

Anthony

Star stops in front of Leo and reaches for his hand. "I'm so very proud of you," she says, her voice steady yet laced with emotion. "The strength you're demonstrating tonight is something I don't ever want you to forget."

"Thank you, Mistress," he replies, bowing his head slightly.

Even though he's new to the lifestyle, submissive behaviors come naturally to him. His abusive past plays a role in that, something I remain vigilant about. I never want him to silence himself or allow his wants and needs to go unmet because of carryovers from his past trauma. Through his submission, I want him to find freedom.

"And you," she says, turning to me, tears shimmering in her eyes. "I'm so happy that you've found love once again. No one deserves happiness more than you—both of you," she adds, looking between us.

I lean in, placing a kiss on her cheek. "Your friendship was a lifeline for me when my life fell apart. I'll always be grateful for it," I whisper, my words meant only for her. "But what you've done for Leopold. You found him when he was lost and brought him back to me." My voice wavers with emotion. "Your unwavering support and role as a mentor in his life. I can never repay you, my friend."

Star brushes away a tear that escapes down her cheek as she exits the stage.

Motioning toward Owen, who waits at the back of the club, I signal for him to lower the lights and start my chosen playlist. Then, I turn to Leopold and command, "Take off your robe."

"Yes, Master," he whispers, allowing the robe to fall open, exposing his nude frame.

Stepping back, I fix my gaze upon the man standing before me. Leopold's captivating blue eyes shimmer with an undeniable intelligence, their depths hinting at the wisdom he carries within. Set against his fair complexion, they gleam like sapphires against porcelain. Each glance he casts exudes a quiet strength, a silent reminder of the challenges he's faced and conquered. Through the beauty and harshness of life, Leopold's emerged stronger than ever before.

Society often perceives submissive men as weak, but Leopold challenges that notion. Inside, he's a warrior who's battled demons that would break the spirit of most. Yet, in his demeanor, there's a tranquility that speaks to the inner peace he's found despite the storms he's weathered. It's a rare quality that draws others to him like moths to a flame, eager to bask in the warmth of his aura.

On the outside, his body is a masterpiece. Broad shoulders taper to a narrow waist, every sinew meticulously sculpted. The swell of his biceps and the tautness of his abdomen hint at hours dedicated to physical fitness. A tattoo adorns his chest, weaving the narrative of his triumph over adversity and the role he feels I played in it. It steals my breath when I look at it.

Despite the strength evident in his muscular frame, there's a softness in his mannerisms, a compassionate aura that defies conventional notions of masculinity. This contradiction adds depth to his character, portraying him as a man of both power and empathy. He's journeyed through the labyrinth of his own soul and emerged finally at ease with himself and the world around him.

"You're perfect," I say in amazement. "There's no one else I'd rather share this moment with."

Extending my hand, Leo willingly intertwines his fingers with mine as we walk to the bed that awaits him. With a gentle ease, he reclines onto the soft surface, his eyes fixed on me with a mixture of trust and anticipation. Leaning closer, I murmur words meant for him alone, our connection deepening in the quiet intimacy of our exchange. "*Sei la vita mia. Sei il mio cuore.* You are my life. You are my heart."

His sapphire eyes shimmer with unshed tears as our lips meld in a passionate kiss. I step back, breathless. "Are you ready?"

"I've been waiting for this moment my whole life."

This past week, I've spent every free minute sketching the design I intend to create on my canvas tonight. It's important that I capture not only Leopold's unbreakable spirit but also the significance of this moment.

Grabbing the bottle of body oil, I pour a generous amount into my palm. This step is crucial to ensure the wax lifts cleanly from Leo's skin once the design is complete. Taking my time, I massage the oil onto his body, starting at his shoulders and moving downward to cover his chest in a smooth, even layer.

"Your body was made to be worshipped," I murmur, my hands trailing down his abdomen to his waist. His eyelids flutter closed, his breath hitching as I follow the defined V leading to his erection. With a firm grip, I wrap my hand around his cock, eliciting a guttural groan. "Do you like that?" I ask.

"Very much, Master," he responds, his tone laden with longing.

"So do I," I say, feeling the urgent pulse of my own desire pressing against the constraint of my zipper.

I glide my hands over his well-defined thighs, causing a ripple of sensation to cascade through his body. Although doing this scene in public was Leopold's idea, a part of me remained concerned with how he'd cope once we were under the spotlight. However, seeing his responsiveness and hearing his moans of pleasure assures me that he relishes this exhibition as much as I do.

Once I'm sure his skin is fully coated, I briefly pause to cleanse my hands before turning my attention to the candles. Selecting several, I ignite their wicks, giving them a minute to burn.

With precision, I tilt the candle over Leopold's calf, watching the warm liquid pool against his fair skin, painting it a rich crimson. "Considering this is your first foray into my world," I note, a sense of anticipation coloring my words. "I'm eager to hear your initial thoughts."

"It's silky and warm," he responds.

As I guide the liquid higher, allowing it to trickle over his thighs and onto his groin, a sharp gasp escapes Leo's lips. "Is it too much?" I ask, mindful of our ongoing exploration of his boundaries.

"No, Master," he assures me. His gaze is filled with a profound devotion that nearly overwhelms me. "It feels different in each place—different in a good way."

"Let yourself surrender to the sensations," I encourage, my voice laced with seduction. "Imagine the wax as my touch, my lips caressing every inch of you."

Leo inhales deeply as he shuts his eyes, immersing himself in the scene. Silently, I blend shades of red, orange, and yellow, their fusion swirling into a raging fire that engulfs his lower body.

Across his chest, I carefully dribble streams of blue and purple, setting the stage for the centerpiece of the design—a phoenix, fierce and majestic, emerging triumphantly from the fiery inferno below. Every drop of liquid wax must be placed with precision as I coax the avian form into existence. Gradually, its contours begin to take shape.

This design is undoubtedly the most intricate I've ever embarked upon. From the moment the concept ignited within me, I knew I had to bring it to fruition. It symbolizes my Leopold perfectly—he's the phoenix, rising unscathed from the ashes. The life he now possesses, forged amidst the hottest flames, is a testament to his unwavering resilience. Each day, he continues to astound me.

With a soft breath, I extinguish the candles, casting the stage into shadow. Stepping back, I take a moment to appreciate what I consider my greatest artistic achievement. Then, turning to face the audience, I extend an invitation. "For those interested, please join me on stage to appreciate my canvas up close."

Excited murmurs fill the room as club members eagerly approach to inspect Leopold and the intricate artwork gracing his skin.

"Your talent with wax knows no bounds," Owen remarks, his tone filled with awe. "But this surpasses anything you've done before. It's truly magnificent."

"Thank you," I reply, gratitude swelling at his heartfelt praise.

"I need to say something, and please understand, it's not meant to undermine your bond with Kameron," Owen says carefully. "But in all the years I've known you, I've never seen you as content and fulfilled as you are with Leo. There's a connection between you two that transcends anything I've seen. He completes you in a way Kam never could."

My love for Kameron will always endure. Even after his passing, a piece of my heart will forever belong to him. But the dynamic with Kameron was distinct from what I share with Leo. When I met Kam, he was already established in his career and accustomed to being the one in control.

Throughout our vetting process, Kameron and I navigated discussions surrounding the roles in our dynamic. It was challenging for him to accept nurturing from another. Kameron's submission will always hold a special place in my heart because I knew he didn't need me to care for him, but he allowed it nonetheless. It's different with Leo. He craves the nurturing I freely give.

"I genuinely believe Kameron guided Leo to me. The day he walked into my restaurant was the first time I felt alive since Kam's passing," I confess, my gaze unwavering from Leo, who lies peacefully on the bed. "He's everything to me, Owen. He's the forever I've been waiting for."

Leopold

FIVE YEARS LATER

While Star was mentoring me, I suggested that Fire and Ice should do classes for people looking to get involved in the lifestyle. Star liked the idea so much that she and Owen developed a curriculum for a six-week intro session and began offering them. Over the years, they've been an overwhelming success both with bringing new members into the club as well as providing general information and hopefully diminishing the stigma about the BDSM lifestyle.

Last year, Star approached me with a proposal of her own. She and Owen wanted to add a mentor portion to the classes. Starting in week four, they planned to pair the prospective Dominants and submissives with someone living the lifestyle. Star asked me to be one of the mentors. At the time, I was taking extra credits to finish my hospitality management degree and had to decline. Now that I've graduated, I have more free time and can get involved.

"Do you know who I'm going to be mentoring?" I ask Tony as I walk down the street.

"I do," he chuckles, the warmth in his voice palpable.

"Will you tell me?"

"No."

"Not even a little hint?"

His laughter rings through the phone. "I think we need to work on delayed gratification," he teases.

"You're cruel." I can't help but laugh in return.

"But you love me."

"Yes, I do," I reply tenderly.

"I have to go, *cuore mio*. It's a mad house here tonight."

The restaurant's popularity continues to soar, establishing it as one of the most sought-after venues in New York City.

"I'm about to walk in anyway. I love you, Master."

"And I love you."

I toss the phone into my bag and pull the door open.

"Good evening, Leo," Star greets me as I enter. "Are you all ready for tonight?"

"I could be more ready if you tell me who I'm going to mentor," I say, leaning against the counter.

"And ruin all the fun? No way."

I pout playfully. "You're as bad as Tony."

"And you love every second of it." She smiles. "You're going to be in room seven."

"Yes, Mistress."

"Leo," she calls after me. I pause and turn back. "The name of your mentee is in there."

I quickly return to her side, planting a kiss on her cheek. "Thank you, Mistress."

Room seven, the boudoir chamber, greets me with a vibrant red envelope resting on the bed's center. With anticipation coursing through me, I tear it open. "Natalie Clark," I read aloud. Why does that name sound familiar? Then, I have a flicker of recognition. She's Svetlana Solonik's roommate. I met her a few weeks ago at the club. She was with Alex Montgomery.

After evaluating the room's arrangement, I decide to make a slight adjustment. With purposeful movements, I reposition the chic, black armchairs to the room's center, flanking them with a delicate table. "Perfect," I remark. "Much cozier." I retrieve a notebook and pen from my bag and place them on the table before stowing the bag away. Now, all that remains is to await her arrival.

A short time later, the door opens, and Natalie hesitantly walks in. When she sees me, she squeals, "Leopold."

"The one and only," I say, pulling her in for a big hug. "I hope you're not upset you got paired with me."

"I'm thrilled to be with you." A smile lights up her face.

"Me too. Come on and sit down so we can get started." I say warmly, indicating the seating area I've prepared. Trying to be professional, I take the pen and notebook from the table and turn to Natalie. "The first thing we need to do is list any questions you have. That'll give us a starting point."

She bites her lip. "I can't think of anything off the top of my head."

I wasn't prepared for that, but I can still work with it. "That's okay." I set the items back down and opt for a more natural approach. "Tell me about yourself, and we'll go from there."

"There isn't much to tell," she says. "I'm originally from Northmeadow. It's a very small town in Missouri."

"How did you end up here?"

"Much to my parents' dismay, I came here for school," she remarks, her tone tinged with a hint of amusement. She then shifts her gaze to me. "Have you always lived here?"

I shake my head. "No. I'm originally from California."

She raises an eyebrow. "Wow. You're a long way from home. Do you miss it there?" she asks, genuine curiosity evident in her tone.

"I haven't thought about that in a long time. I used to consider California my home, but that seems like a lifetime ago," I muse, feeling a twinge of wistfulness. "Nope. There's nowhere else in the world I'd rather be than right here," I assure Natalie, offering her a warm smile. Natalie plays with her hands in her lap, a nervous habit I recognize immediately. "Do you have any siblings?" I ask, and her smile fades, making me instantly regret bringing up the topic.

"I had an older brother, Michael. He passed away a few years ago," she shares, her voice trembling slightly. "My parents didn't accept him when he came out as gay. He and his boyfriend took their lives within a few weeks of each other."

"Oh my God. I'm so sorry," I offer quietly, my heart aching for her. "I know a bit about that. My family didn't accept me either. They sent me to a conversion therapy center to try to cure me of my gay ways. Clearly, they failed," I add with a soft chuckle, which elicits a smile from Natalie.

"Do you have any brothers or sisters?" she asks.

"I have two younger sisters, but I haven't spoken to them in years," I confess, feeling a pang of regret and sadness. "I used to be close with London, my youngest sister. I miss her a lot."

"Are they still in California?"

"I really don't know," I admit with a shrug. "London would be twenty-four now, so she could be just about anywhere."

"She's the same age as me," Natalie remarks and then offers, "I can volunteer as a stand-in."

"I'd love that," I respond warmly. Despite our brief conversation, it feels like we've known each other for ages.

Natalie tells me more about her small town and her parents. They sound just as marvelous as my own. Every pun intended.

"So, what brings you to the BDSM lifestyle?" I probe.

"That's a bit of an embarrassing story," she admits, her cheeks flushing a vibrant shade of pink.

"Don't hold out on me. Spill it," I urge, a playful grin tugging at my lips.

"You already know that Svetlana and I are roommates," she states, her tone slightly resigned. I nod in understanding. "I was supposed to be home visiting my family and my now ex-boyfriend. That's a story for another time," she explains with a roll of her eyes. "Anyway, I cut my trip home very short, but I didn't tell Lana. Oh God, I can't believe I'm telling anyone about this," she groans.

"It was the middle of the night when I got home. I just wanted to crawl into bed and forget everything that happened. On the way to my room, I heard something. Lana was begging for help. I thought she was being attacked," she recounts, her eyes meeting mine. "So, I called 911 and then went to stop whatever was happening."

I pull my feet up under me and settle in, eager to hear the rest of her story.

"I threw open her door and flipped the light on while I yelled at the person to stop. I figured I'd startle whoever it was, and boy, was I right," she admits, shaking her head in disbelief. "Except Lana wasn't being attacked. Brandon was there, and they were doing what I've since learned is a consensual/non-consensual scene."

"Are you making this up?" I inquire, my eyebrows raised in disbelief.

"I wish," Natalie replies with a resigned sigh.

"Wait. You said you called 911. Did the police show up?" I ask, leaning forward in anticipation. Natalie nods slowly. "I wish I could've been a fly on the wall. What happened next?"

"The cops had Brandon at gunpoint while Svetlana did her best to explain that it was all a horrible misunderstanding," Natalie recounts, her voice tinged with disbelief. "It took some doing, but she finally convinced them of Brandon's innocence. After he left, she told me about BDSM and her involvement in it."

"And you wanted to know more?" I ask, my interest growing with each revelation.

"Not exactly. It took months before I brought it up to her again," Natalie admits. "Lana asked me to come to the club to see her first scene with Brandon. I agreed, not knowing that she and Brandon had gone behind my back to set me up."

"This story keeps getting juicier," I remark with a grin.

Natalie laughs softly, her eyes sparkling with amusement. "They arranged it so Alex and I would have to spend the evening together." She then shifts the conversation. "What about you? How did you get involved in the lifestyle?"

The jovial atmosphere dissipates as I delve into the darker chapters of my past. "Life hasn't always been good to me," I confess, the weight of my words evident in my somber tone. "I met Anthony at one of the lowest points." Briefly, I touch upon the trauma of the therapy center, glossing over the painful memories and choosing to focus on the pivotal moment when Tony entered my life. "I was in a bad place, ready to end it all when Tony found me. He saved me. He taught me it was okay to trust again."

Before I realize it, the hour has slipped away, and our session draws to a close. Natalie kindly assists me in rearranging the furniture, a gesture of camaraderie that warms my heart. As she reaches the door, she hesitates, a glimmer of uncertainty in her eyes. "Would you like to grab a bite to eat with me?" she asks tentatively.

"I'd love that," I respond with genuine warmth, touched by her invitation.

Leopold

DECEMBER 9

I don't know by what stroke of luck Star paired me with Natalie, but I'm so thankful. When she volunteered to be my sister, I melted. We've become very close in a short amount of time. We text every day and have made dinner and drinks after class—a new tradition. The only negative is that I've thought about London more in the past few weeks than I have in years. That's a boundary that cannot be broken.

Last night was the last training class. Natalie and I went out for margaritas and discussed Alexander Montgomery. She's head over heels for the guy—who wouldn't be. He's tall and fit with dark hair, and the most beautiful blue eyes. His alpha male energy is everything. I'm pretty sure everyone at Fire and Ice would gladly submit to that man. But I digress...

Natalie told me Alex asked her to consider a Dom/sub dynamic with him. She's hesitant because she has to return to Northmeadow, her hometown, in a few months. Natalie came to New York for school on a full-ride scholarship with one caveat—in exchange for the scholarship, she had to agree to return to Northmeadow and work for the school district for five years.

Alex has offered to buy out her scholarship so she can stay in Manhat-

tan. I'm fully in support of that, by the way. Natalie, on the other hand, is not. She feels a sense of responsibility to the youth in her hometown and is insisting she go back and see it through.

As an alternative, I suggested asking Alex to put a time limit on their contract to help manage expectations. The problem is that she's falling for him as more than just a potential Dominant. Distance complicates things when the heart is involved.

I really hope fate intervenes and they find a way to be together.

Anthony

LEO'S SITTING IN THE KITCHEN WITH HIS LAPTOP OPEN WHEN I walk in. "Who's that?" I ask, looking over Leo's shoulder.

He slams his laptop closed. "It's no one," he says, a bit too hastily. "I didn't hear you come in."

I raise an eyebrow at his abruptness. It's not like Leo to be secretive. "I see," I say, walking over to the fridge to grab a bottle of water.

"How long have you been home?"

I crack the seal and take a drink. "I just walked in."

"You're home early," he says as he fidgets his hands nervously.

"I thought I'd surprise you. Seems I did just that," I say, taking a seat at the kitchen table behind him.

Leo drops his head into his hands and admits, "I was looking at my sister's profile."

I knew if I didn't push, he'd eventually tell me what he was looking at, but his sister wasn't any of the answers I would've ever guessed. "London?"

"Yes," he says, opening his computer and turning the screen to face me. Looking back at me is a petite young woman with honey-gold hair and eyes that match Leopold's. "She's studying to be a doctor," he adds with a hint of pride.

"Are you thinking about contacting her?" I probe.

"No," he says firmly. "That can't happen."

"London's an adult now, Leopold. She's free to decide who she wants in her life."

"I can't risk my father hurting her," he admits, his voice strained. "It was just a stupid search. How was the restaurant?"

"Busy," I answer and move to sit beside him at the island. "As usual. How was your night?"

"Ramiro called. He wants me to visit him," he murmurs. "To celebrate my graduation."

Leopold had been a busser at *Italiano Desiderio* for several years when my floor manager, Ryan, approached me about promoting him to host. He pointed out how natural Leo was on the restaurant floor. In addition to clearing tables, Leo was engaging with the patrons—who often sought him out to chat. When I approached Leopold with the idea of promoting him, he revealed his aspiration to pursue a college degree in Hospitality Management.

He threw himself into his studies, taking on extra courses each semester, and finally graduated magna cum laude earlier this year. Despite my suggestion of throwing a big graduation party for him, he begged me not to. "I think a trip to California would be the perfect way to celebrate," I suggest.

His lower lip is caught between his teeth for a moment before he finally asks, "Would you come with me?"

"Of course," I answer without hesitation. Despite the fact that Leopold and I have been together for a little over five years, Ramiro's acceptance of me remains uncertain. This trip could offer me the opportunity to gain an understanding of why he still distrusts me.

"Maybe we can arrange to see Donnie and Lindsay, too?" he asks excitedly. "You can finally meet them in person. They'll love you."

"Talk to Ramiro and let me know when he wants you to visit, and we'll make it happen." Leo watches me, his expression filled with questions. "What is it, *cuore mio*?"

Silently, he moves and lowers himself to his knees, resting his head on my lap. I run my fingers through his hair, comforting him.

"How is it that even though you know Ramiro isn't your biggest fan, you didn't even think about it before agreeing to go with me?"

"Ramiro's important to you, so I'll continue to do everything I can to extend friendship to him," I reply. I'm hopeful he'll give in and accept me as part of Leopold's life. Not for my sake, but for Leo's.

"Have I ever told you what initially attracted me to you?" he asks curiously.

"Not that I recall," I admit.

Leo raises his head, a soft smile forming. "It was your eyes and the kindness they held. It was as if you could see straight into my soul and understand my every need without a word.""From the instant I saw you all bundled up in your hat and scarf," I reflect with amusement. "My heart felt an instant connection. I knew then that I had to take care of you however I could."

Memories of a younger and more vulnerable Leo play in my mind. There was something about him that day, a silent plea that resonated with my soul. Despite knowing little about him, I felt an innate desire to nurture and shield him from the world. With each encounter, that urge grew stronger. But I never dared to hope he'd return my affection.

"I spent so much time fearing you'd never feel the same way," I confess.

"Why would you ever think that?" Leo's voice carries genuine confusion.

"Our age gap. I couldn't shake the feeling that you, being much younger, wouldn't be interested in someone older," I admit with a soft laugh.

"When I look at you, age is the last thing on my mind," Leo insists, rising higher on his knees.

I spread my thighs, making room for him. "What do you see, Leopold?" I ask, lowering my voice.

"I see a man who's capable and sure," he whispers, deftly unfastening my leather belt and letting it drop to the floor. "A man who isn't afraid to show tenderness," he continues, undoing the button and easing down the zipper. "I see a man who gives of himself so freely," Leo says, slipping his hands beneath my shirt to trace the contours of my abdomen before gripping the waistband of my pants and boxers. "A man who rescued me when I was drowning." Lifting my hips, he gently pulls my pants off my legs. "A man whose body I plan on worshipping so he never doubts my desire for him."

Leo takes hold of my throbbing erection, his touch deliberate and enticing. I release a low groan as he teases the tip. He then trails his tongue along the length of my shaft, his movements sending waves of pleasure through me. I tilt my head back, surrendering to the intoxicating sensations. Finally, he lowers himself until my cock hits the back of his throat. He gags slightly but doesn't pull away.

Understanding that, at times, oral can still be a challenge for him, I lift my head and offer, "You don't have to do this."

"I want to," he mumbles around my cock, his lips continuing their diligent work. His head bobs up and down my length, his tongue skillfully teasing and licking. He takes me deep into his throat once more.

"That feels incredible," I manage to utter, overwhelmed by the sensations. Leopold guides my hand to his head, silently signaling his readiness to relinquish control. "Are you absolutely sure?" I ask, concerned about pushing him beyond his limits. He nods, his eyes determined. "Tap my leg if you need to stop. Understand?" Once more, he nods in agreement.

I begin to gently thrust my hips upward, watching as my erection slides in and out of his throat. He gags with each movement. "Are you alright?" I ask, concerned about pushing him beyond his limits. Once again, he nods, lowering himself until his face meets my groin.

Firmly grasping his hair, I intensify the rhythm and force of my thrusts, penetrating deeper with each motion. He emits a soft hum around my cock, his efforts unwavering. Saliva cascades from his mouth, coating me, while tears trickle down his face. "You look absolutely stunning——powerful, with my cock in your mouth."

Leopold meets my gaze with his captivating blue eyes, and at that moment, I'm overwhelmed. Unable to restrain myself any longer, I release with a final thrust. He swallows every drop before diligently cleaning my cock. "You taste exquisite. Thank you, Master."

"You never stop amazing me, *cuore mio.*"

Leopold

Me: I'm going to miss you, girlfriend.

Natalie: I'm going to miss you too, but we'll keep in touch.

Me: Did you get on the plane yet?

Natalie: No. We're still waiting to board.

Me: It's not too late, then. Change your mind and come back to me.

Alex hasn't stopped begging her to allow him to buy out her scholarship. Lord knows he has the money to do that, but she refuses to give in. I'm convinced they're soulmates. Except right now, she's sitting at JFK, ready to return to Missouri instead of being with Alex, where she belongs.

"You're supposed to be packing. Who are you texting?" Tony asks, a hint of frustration in his tone.

"Natalie," I sigh, a hint of sadness coloring my words. "She's at the airport with her parents. I wish she would've let Alex buy out her contract so she could stay here."

"I'm sure she has her reasons," Tony remarks calmly while folding a shirt.

"She does, but she belongs here—with Alex."

"Alex is a big boy. He'll handle it," Tony replies firmly.

"But—" I begin to protest.

"Leopold," Tony interrupts with a warning tone.

"I know. I know. Don't butt into their relationship." My shoulders fall in defeat. "It's partially selfish. I don't want her to leave because I'm going to miss her," I confess, feeling a pang of guilt as I admit my true feelings.

"There's video chats and airplanes. We can go visit," Tony suggests, tossing a shirt at me. "Right now, you need to pack your suitcase, or we won't make our flight tonight."

Tony and I are flying to California to spend time with Ramiro and his family. Surprisingly, he didn't give me grief when I told him Tony was coming with me. I'm hopeful that means he's finally ready, after all these years, to accept that Tony's a permanent part of my life.

While we're there, we'll also get to spend time with Donnie and Lindsay—something I'm very much looking forward to. We've kept in touch over the years, but I haven't seen them since I came to New York. It's not for lack of trying. Whatever Donnie's job is, and it's something he refuses to answer questions about, he can't be away for long.

Initially, I was concerned about the safety of visiting, given the issues with Krew. I don't know how long people like him might hold a grudge. Donnie reassured me that Krew's been taken care of, and there's no need for me to worry. He brushed it off when I pushed for more details, telling me to trust that he handled everything.

"Seriously though," Tony adds, his tone thoughtful. "Natalie's commitment to the school district is something she values deeply. Her reasons for not letting Alex intervene with money are significant to her. If she and Alex are meant to be, they'll find a way."

"I know," I acknowledge while I fold the last of my clothes and place them inside my suitcase.

"You and Natalie will always be friends, regardless," Tony reassures, leaning in to plant a kiss on my forehead.

"I truly hope so. I cherish her friendship," I admit, a fond smile gracing my lips.

Natalie's presence highlighted a longing I tried to keep buried deep inside. The closer we became, the more I wondered about my sister. Natalie's presence highlighted a longing I tried to keep buried deep inside. The closer we became, the more I wondered about my sister. Eventually, curiosity got the best of me, and I caved. I promised myself it would be a one-time thing, but it quickly turned into a weekly occurrence.

Thankfully, London isn't particularly cautious with her privacy settings, granting me access to her posts and photos. It fills my heart with happiness to see that she's grown into a confident young woman who's currently in med school.

There are many pictures of her surrounded by friends. One thing I don't see is any photos of London and the rest of our family. There's not a single picture of them. I don't know what to make of that. In each image, London's smile is radiant. It appears she's surrounded by friends and is happy. In the end, that's all that matters.

Anthony

Opting for a short-term beachfront rental house instead of a hotel was a decision I don't regret. We've only been here for two days, and I've already grown accustomed to the calm, serenity beachfront living offers. For the first time in my life the allure of Manhattan begins to fade, and I question the possibility of living somewhere other than the city. But today isn't the day for such contemplation. We're expecting a visitor — one Leopold remains unaware of.

Ever since seeing Leopold's sister's social media profile, I haven't stopped thinking about it. I know he misses her, but his fear of their father prevented him from reaching out. Taking a leap of faith, I contacted her, introducing myself and providing Leo's profile, where he goes by my last name. It was the only way I could think of to prove my identity since she never would've found Leo on her own. I gave her my phone number and asked if she was open to seeing her brother that she would please call me. Two days later, my phone rang.

Thankfully, Leo was out with Natalie when she called. We spent over an hour talking. She's as sweet as he described her. She was eager to learn everything about Leo's life and where he'd been all these years. I shared that he's been living in Manhattan for seven years but added anything else she'd have to ask him.

I did mention his reluctance to reach out because of their father but that he and I would be making a trip to California. She expressed the desire to see him while we were on the West Coast. London knows Leopold is unaware we've spoken.

Glancing at my phone, I anticipate her arrival any minute.

Leo and I are sitting on the deck, watching the waves roll in.

"Is everything okay, Master?" he asks, concern evident in his voice.

"Yes," I reply, though the truth lingers unspoken. The closer this reunion gets, the more I question if I did the right thing.

"How about we go for a walk on the beach?" he suggests, trying to ease my tension.

"Maybe later. I'm enjoying just watching the water from here."

"Okay," he sighs, sensing my unease. "Are you sure you're okay?"

I don't have a chance to respond because the doorbell rings. "Can you get that?"

"Sure," Leo responds, standing up. "It's probably just the wrong address for a delivery."

I allow him to enter before quietly trailing in his wake, my phone ready to capture the scene. I'm concerned at first that he's going to be angry at me for going behind his back. But I hold onto the hope that he'll eventually appreciate having this moment preserved on video.

Leopold

Tony's behavior today is bizarre. He claims to be enjoying the opportunity to unwind before we meet up with Ramiro later this week. But instead of relaxing, he's noticeably tense and kind of cranky.

I was trying to convince him to go down to the beach when the doorbell interrupted us. He's not getting off the hook. As soon as I send this person away, I intend to make Tony tell me what's going on.

I pull the door open and squint in the sunlight. "I'm sorry, I think you have the wrong address."

"Leo," a familiar voice says my name and launches into my arms.

Instinctively, I close them around the girl who's sobbing. "London? How—" I look up and see Tony holding his camera with tears pouring down his face. "You knew about this?"

"I reached out to her," Tony admits.

"London." I take her by the shoulders and hold her back to get a good look at her. "Is it really you?" She nods, unable to speak from crying. I pull her back against me, afraid if I let her go, she'll disappear. "I can't believe you arranged this. Why didn't you tell me?" I ask.

"I was afraid if I did that, you wouldn't come." Tony slides his phone into his pocket.

"Please don't be mad at him." London pulls away from me. "I've looked for you for so long. I'm so glad he messaged me."

"I could never be mad at him," I say, focusing on my Master.

"I'm going to go upstairs and make a few calls," Tony offers.

"Wait." I hurry over to him and wrap my arms around him. "Thank you for doing this."

"You don't have to thank me."

"I know. I want to." I press a kiss on his lips. "I love you."

"I love you too, *cuore mio*." He glances over my shoulder. "Go spend some time with your sister. She's a pretty incredible young lady." With that, Tony walks up the steps and disappears down the hall.

London comes up next to me. "That man is crazy about you," she whispers conspiratorially.

"I feel the same about him," I say, putting my arm around my sister. "Are you hungry or thirsty?"

"I'd love some water," she responds.

"Go on outside. I'll get you a drink, and then we can sit and talk," I suggest, motioning toward the door.

"Can we go down to the beach?" London asks, her eyes bright with anticipation. "Do you remember when we were younger, and Mom and Dad would take us on vacation to the shore? We'd sit on the sand for hours planning out our lives."

Even though I tried not to dwell on those memories, they were always there, lurking in the recesses of my mind. "Of course, I remember."

London and I walk down the weathered wood steps to the private beach. We settle onto the soft, sun-warmed sand, the rhythmic pulse of the waves providing a soothing soundtrack to our impending discussion.

"Tell me about you," I prompt, hoping to steer the conversation away from my past for as long as possible. "I saw on your social media that you're studying to be a doctor."

"I'm currently in my third year of med school at the University of California San Diego," she replies confidently.

"What's that like?"

"This year is crazy. We started our rotations. I'm in pediatrics right now," London explains, excitement lacing her voice. "It's great because I intend to do my residency in pediatrics."

"I can't believe my baby sister is all grown up and is going to be a doctor," I say, my chest swelling with pride.

"What about you? What happened to you after you left Walking in the Light?" she asks, curiosity evident in her tone.

There's no way I can tell her the things I went through. My hand scoops up sand, letting it run through my fingers as I contemplate what to reveal.

Sensing my discomfort, she asks, "Do you want to know how I ended up at UCSD?"

"Yes," I reply quietly.

"My senior year of high school, I did dual enrollment at Rolling Hills Community College. I applied to a bunch of schools and got accepted at all of them. I was also awarded scholarships at most of them," she adds, a smile tugging at her lips. "But Dad insisted I stay close to home my first year. Since I was still seventeen when I graduated high school, I had no choice but to do what he wanted."

She pauses, gazing out over the water for a brief moment.

"Once I turned eighteen, I secretly applied to UCSD and made all the arrangements to live on campus," she grins mischievously. "Dad was furious when he found out."

"Did he hurt you?" I ask, panic creeping into my voice.

"Not anything I couldn't handle," she responds calmly.

My face snaps to look at her. "What do you mean not anything you couldn't handle? Did he touch you?"

"He hit me," she says softly, her words barely audible.

"How many times?"

"What do you mean?"

"How many times did he hurt you?"

"It happened a lot," she admits, her voice tinged with sorrow.

"I'm going to kill him," I declare, my anger rising.

"No, you're not." She puts her hand over my fist. "It was a long time ago." When I don't relax, she persists. "Please, Leo. It's over. I haven't seen him since that night. I walked out and never looked back."

Maybe I was wrong for not going back for her? If I had, I could've spared her from being hurt by our father. I can't go there, though. I was barely surviving myself. I would never have been able to take care of London, too. "Out of everywhere, why did you choose San Diego?"

"I wanted to find you," she says softly, then continues, "I was so happy when David called Dad to tell him you got kicked out of the facility."

"He told them I got kicked out? What exactly did he say?" I inquire, curiosity tinged with a hint of anger coloring my tone.

"David said they found you and another boy having sex—rough sex, to be exact and that because you forced the other person. So, they expelled you from their program."

"David's a damn liar," I mutter, my frustration evident in my tone.

"What really happened?" London persists, her voice soft yet insistent.

I deflect her question with one of my own. "Did Mom and Dad try looking for me?"

"Mom wanted him to," she responds, her voice tinged with sadness. "She cried for weeks, but Dad refused. Said you were beyond saving, and he needed to protect Arianna and me by never letting you near our family again."

Hearing it confirmed hurts more than I anticipated.

"What really happened?" she presses further.

"Nothing. I just left," I lie, the words tasting bitter on my tongue.

"That's not true. There was a reason David emphasized the *rough* part of his story. What did he do to you?" London's voice is gentle, yet there's a firm resolve behind her words. I pull my knees up to my chest and wrap my arms around them. I can't do this. "Leo, please don't shut down on me," she pleads. "I'm not a kid anymore. You don't have to protect me now." She tugs at my arms until I drop them.

"David raped me," I admit, the words heavy on my tongue.

London sucks in a breath, her eyes widening with concern.

"Just once?" Her voice is barely a whisper. I shake my head. "How many times?"

"I don't know for sure," I confess, feeling the weight of uncertainty pressing down on me.

"Everything I read about that place was true," she mumbles, her tone filled with sadness. "Why didn't you go to the police?"

"I did," I reply. "But David lied to them, too."

"And they believed him over you." Her words hang in the air like a heavy cloud of injustice, and I can only nod in silent agreement, feeling the sting of betrayal all over again. "I had a bag packed so I'd be ready to run away," she continues, her voice soft but resolute. "I fell asleep every night with my phone in my hand, waiting for you to call me."

Her words cut me to my core. "I'm so sorry, Lulu," I say softly, wrapping my arm around her as she rests her head on my shoulder. "I didn't want to risk Dad finding out and doing something to hurt you. I'm so sorry he did. I'll never forgive myself for what he did to you, but you were safer there than with me."

"You would've made sure I was safe."

"I wish that were true, but it isn't," I admit, my voice heavy with regret.

London turns to me, her eyes searching mine. "How did you end up in New York?" She isn't going to let me get away with not telling her. I owe her the truth, especially knowing she waited for me to rescue her, and I never came. She was hurt because of me.

"When I got away from Walking in the Light, I stayed at a center for homeless LGBTQ youth. It was a nice place with people who were helping me get on my feet. Things were good until I met a guy, Krew. He was dangerous," I explain but leave out details she can never know. "I went to New York for safety."

London's eyes grow wide. "Why are you back here then? Are you still in danger?"

"No, I'm not."

"Tell me about New York and about Tony. I'm jealous, by the way," she giggles. "He's stunning."

I glance back at the house. "He is," I admit, a smile tugging at my lips. "Tony saved me—literally and figuratively."

"What do you mean?"

"I was in a bad place, Lulu. I didn't deal with everything that happened with David and then Krew. Then, I found myself in an unfamiliar city. Things were okay. I had an apartment and a job. That's how I met Tony," I explain, recalling those difficult times. "I was delivering groceries to local restaurants. One of them was the restaurant he owned. He always made something for me to eat on delivery days."

"Didn't you have enough food?" she asks, concern lacing her words.

"No," I admit, a hint of vulnerability in my tone. "Until Tony, I often went hungry."

"Is that how he saved you?" Her question is gentle, probing for deeper understanding.

I shake my head solemnly. "My boss died suddenly. I lost my job and my apartment on the same day. I gave up. I tried to kill myself." London gasps, her eyes welling with tears. "Tony found me and brought me to his home. He cared for me."

She wipes her cheeks with the backs of her hands, visibly moved. "How long have you been together?"

"Six years," I reply, my voice tinged with gratitude. "We fell for each other long before we took the next steps. He wanted to make sure I was healthy emotionally before we got involved with each other. Tony's the kindest person I've ever met. I love him more than I have words to describe."

"I'll forever be indebted to him," London says, emotion thick in her voice. "He brought you back to me." She throws her arms around me.

Out of the corner of my eye, I spot a shadow. Looking up, I see Tony walking our way.

"I don't mean to interrupt," he says, his tone gentle. "I thought you two might be getting hungry."

"What time is it?"

"It's going on six." I had no idea several hours had passed since we came outside. "Are you hungry, Lulu?"

"I could definitely eat," she says, getting to her feet and wiping off the sand. "But first, I have to hug you." She wraps herself around Tony. "I don't know how to thank you for loving Leopold."

"You don't need to thank me. Loving him is easy," Tony says, his eyes never leaving mine.

Leopold

Tony cooks dinner while London and I sit at the expansive island. The three of us talk and catch up on years of missed time. She updates me on our sister, Arianna. Not surprisingly, Arianna remains closely tied to our parents. She married a man of my father's choosing, and they now have two children—a boy and a girl. London hasn't seen or spoken to her since she left our parents' home.

"Tell me more about you," I encourage. "Are you seeing anyone?"

Her cheeks turn pink. "Not really." She shrugs.

"Something tells me there's more to that answer." I elbow her playfully. "Keep talking, Lulu."

"He's my professor," she confesses, her voice muffled as she buries her face in her hands.

"Sweetheart," Anthony says, a spatula in his hand. "There's nothing you can say that would bother us."

"Is it consensual?" I ask.

"Yes," she says and lifts her head. "It's completely mutual. He's a good man, and he treats me well." She glances between Tony and me. "We have to be careful, though. He could lose his job if he's caught with a student."

"Can we meet him before we go back to New York?" I ask.

"If you want, you can meet him tonight. He brought me here. He'll be back to pick me up."

"Why don't you call him to see if he wants to come for dinner?" Anthony suggests.

"Are you sure?"

"I'm positive. We'd love to meet him."

"Okay," she agrees and pulls out her phone.

"If you want privacy—"

"I don't need privacy from you," London reassures, squeezing my hand. "Hey, baby," she says into the phone, her smile evident in her voice. "Everything's great. They want to know if you'd like to join us for dinner." She nods. "Great. We'll see you soon." Setting the phone down on the counter, she turns back to us. "He'll be here in a few minutes."

"How far away do you live?" I inquire.

"About ten minutes," London responds with a grin.

The evening sky paints a vibrant sunset backdrop as we gather around the deck table for dinner. Patrick, London's boyfriend, effortlessly blends into our conversation, fielding every question Tony and I toss his way.

"London, can you give me a hand in the house?" Tony's request momentarily breaks the flow of our conversation.

"Sure." She gives Patrick a quick peck on the cheek. "I'll be right back."

"Take your time," Patrick says, his eyes following her as she disappears indoors.

I'll thank Tony later for giving me this time to talk to Patrick alone. With no time to waste, I dive straight into the heart of the matter. "How many other students have you dated?"

"None," he responds without hesitation.

"Have you ever been married?"

"I have," he admits. "We met towards the end of my residency. It was a whirlwind romance. We got married after only knowing each other for six months," he explains. "After my residency, I started working in an emergency room. We found out we were having a baby. I thought things were great until I came home and found her in our bed with another man." His shoulders sag. "Lisa, my ex-wife, had been having an affair with him for nearly a year. I was devastated."

"So, you have a child, too?"

"No." He shakes his head. "The baby wasn't mine. Apparently, Lisa had taken a paternity test without me knowing."

"That's rough. I'm sorry."

"It was hard. I lost my wife and my baby all at once. I don't blame her, though. I had responsibility there, too. I was so focused on work—too focused. I didn't pay enough attention to my wife, and I lost everything. It's a mistake I won't make again."

"Fair enough."

"I love your sister," Patrick admits, leaning forward. "I tried not to. She didn't need to get involved with her professor. There's too much for her to lose."

"What do you mean?"

"She could get kicked out of school if anyone finds out," he explains. "Your sister is a force to be reckoned with." He laughs softly.

"What are you two talking about?" London asks as she steps back outside.

"You," I say, fixing her with my gaze.

Tony joins us on the deck, his eyes shifting between London and me. "What's going on?"

"Patrick is just telling me that London could get kicked out of school for being with him," I say, focusing on my sister.

"Get over it, Leo. I have." She places her hand on Patrick's shoulder.

"Forgive me if I'm worried about you."

"Were you aware of the consequences of getting involved with your professor?" Tony inquires.

"Of course I was." London crosses her arms. "He did everything he could to get me to stay away. He didn't want me to jeopardize my residency. But I told him, and I'll tell you both, I love him." Her expression softens. "I have one more year, and then we'll be free to go public."

"You could lose everything you've worked so hard for," I argue.

"Being together is worth any risk," she insists, taking Patrick's hand. "Patrick finally accepted that, and I hope you both will, too."

"Love has no boundaries and doesn't follow rules," Tony adds.

"You're happy?"

"More than happy."

"And you're going to make sure London doesn't get kicked out of school?" I ask, pinning Patrick with my stare.

"London agreed—"

"Grudgingly," she interjects.

"Grudgingly," Patrick confirms. "If our relationship were to be exposed, she'll let me take the blame. I'll tell them I forced her. Whatever I need to do to protect London." She rolls her eyes. "And you're not going to break your promise to me, are you?"

"As much as I hate it. No, I won't," she agrees. "But we aren't going to get caught, are we?"

"I'll do everything in my power to ensure we don't."

"Doesn't living together increase the risk?" Tony asks.

"Yes and no," Patrick explains. "On the record, London rents a small apartment close to campus. We live more than a half hour from the school."

"We don't go out together, and I Uber back and forth to campus," she adds.

"It bothers me that I can't take her on dates and do things she deserves in a relationship."

"I've told him I don't care about that stuff. I only want him."

"It sounds risky," I say, looking between the two. "But I can see how much you love each other. As long as you're happy, then I'm happy."

"Thank you, Leo." She beams.

We spend the next few hours talking. I have to stop several times and pinch myself. I can't believe I'm sitting here with my sister. This is more than I could've ever imagined, and Tony's responsible for making it happen.

"I don't want tonight to end," London says, grabbing my hand, her voice tinged with regret. "But I have to be at the office for seven in the morning."

"I understand," I respond, sympathizing with her busy schedule.

"I know you're only in town for a few more days, and London's schedule is crazy, but we'd both like to see you again before you leave," Patrick suggests warmly. "Would you be willing to come to our house for dinner?"

Glancing to Tony, he replies, "We'd love that."

After a final emotional embrace with my sister, we confirm our plans to visit their home later in the week. Tony and I stand together in the doorway, silently watching London and Patrick head toward his car. Patrick opens the door for her, and she gives him a tender smile before getting in.

"Thank you, Tony," I express, squeezing his hand gratefully.

"You aren't mad at me?" he asks, seeking reassurance.

"Having my sister in my life is something I never dreamed possible," I confess, overcome with emotion from the evening's events. "You gave her back to me. I don't deserve you."

"*Cuore mio*, I'd pull the stars from the sky and lay them at your feet. You're deserving of every good thing, and I plan to be the one to give them all to you."

"The only thing I want is you."

"I'm yours. I'll always be yours," Tony pledges.

Anthony

Our driver pulls up in front of a single-story stucco home at the end of a cul de sac. Before we get out of the car, the front door opens, and an older version of the Ramiro I met years ago in New York steps out and meets us on the sidewalk.

"I can't believe you're actually here," he says before hugging Leopold.

"It's been far too long," Leo responds.

"Yes, it has," he agrees.

"Good to see you again, Tony." He offers his hand.

I accept his gesture of friendship. "You as well."

"Come on. Jacinta can't wait to finally meet you in person." Entering the house, we're greeted by an unexpectedly spacious interior, bathed in natural light pouring through large windows. The rooms feel airy and expansive, inviting us to explore further.

"Everyone's out back," Ramiro says as he opens a set of glass doors.

We step out onto a concrete patio situated under a stunning pergola. Encircled by flourishing trees, the backyard exudes a sense of tranquility and privacy. On one side, a well-appointed outdoor kitchen beckons, while across the yard, an inviting inground pool and bubbling hot tub tempt us with promises of relaxation. The sound of children's laughter fills the air as they splash around, adding to the lively ambiance. Beyond the pool, a sprawling deck extends into the distance, offering ample space to unwind and enjoy the outdoors.

"This place is stunning," I comment, admiring the picturesque surroundings.

"The backyard is what drew us to this property. With the canyon, we'll never have neighbors overlooking us," Ramiro explains. "Come on, there are some people here who are eager to see you."

"Leo!" a young woman calls out excitedly, dashing across the yard.

"I had no idea you guys were coming!" he exclaims as he lifts the girl from the ground.

"We wanted to surprise you," she replies with a grin as he sets her down.

"You clean up well, Leo," a man in a black T-shirt remarks. "It's great to see you."

"You too," Leo responds before introducing us. "Tony, this is Lindsay and Donnie."

"It's a pleasure to finally meet you face-to-face," I say warmly.

"The pleasure's ours," Donnie replies.

"Leo, Tony," Ramiro interrupts, drawing our attention. "Meet my wife, Jacinta." We exchange greetings, and Ramiro continues, "And these are our children: Camila, Marisol, and Dante."

"I can't believe we're all here," Leo says as he looks around at everyone who's gathered to see him and presses the heels of his palms against his eyes. "I promised myself I wouldn't cry anymore, but I just can't help it," Leo admits, his voice choked with emotion. He reaches for my hand, and I draw him close, wrapping my arm around him for comfort.

Seeing the questioning look on Ramiro's face, I explain, "We've had an emotional week. Unbeknownst to Leopold, his sister London came to see him two days ago."

"How did she find out you were here?" Ramiro questions.

"I've been curious about her," Leo interjects. "I showed Tony her social media a few weeks ago."

"After that, I reached out to her and introduced myself," Tony adds. "Once our travel plans were finalized, I arranged for her to surprise Leo."

While the adults engage in conversation, the children splash and laugh joyfully in the pool. Leopold's face radiates with joy as he recounts his time spent with his sister.

While I've communicated with everyone through video calls over the years, today marks the first occasion I'm meeting all but Ramiro in person. They form the chosen family who provided care and support for Leopold before he entered my life.

Donnie and Lindsay played a pivotal role in rescuing him from Krew's grasp. I'm confident they all experienced worry for his safety when he ventured to New York. Yet, it was that brave decision that paved the way for him to find his way to me. Each person present holds a piece of my gratitude.

"You should start cooking," Jacinta prompts her husband gently. "The children will be getting hungry."

"I didn't realize what time it was," Ramiro admits with a sheepish grin. He turns to Donnie, an invitation in his eyes. "Care to help cook?"

Donnie tilts his beer up in response, a smirk on his face. I don't know much about their story, only that Ramiro and Donnie share a somewhat tenuous past.

"Fine. I'll do it myself," Ramiro concedes, his tone tinged with annoyance as he trudges across the yard towards the grill.

Sensing an opportunity to assist, I wait a few minutes before excusing myself from the group and approaching Ramiro.

"I can give you a hand if you'd like," I offer, extending my assistance with a friendly smile.

Initially, I expect him to decline, but his response catches me off guard. "That would be great." We work silently for a few prolonged minutes before he speaks up again. "I owe you an apology for the way I've treated you. When Leopold came to Safe Haven, I knew there was something different about him—something special," he explains. "I don't typically get personally involved with the residents we have with us, but Leo's profile caught my attention. He never had anyone in his corner."

Ramiro deftly flips the sizzling burgers before continuing, "When he came in that day and was with Krew, my stomach sank. I knew Krew and that Leo was in trouble, but my hands were tied." His shoulders slump. "I offered to open my home to him, but Krew had his attention. I couldn't get through to him."

Knowing the hell Leopold lived through after this, I can't imagine how helpless Ramiro felt recognizing the danger he was in.

"I have so many regrets for letting him walk away that day," he confesses, the pain evident in his voice.

"You did the best you could," I offer, trying to reassure him.

"When Donnie called and said Leo was with them, I was so relieved. He didn't tell me his condition," Ramiro adds, his voice trembling. "Tony, if you saw him. He was so thin and strung out. I was afraid he wouldn't make it through the night."

"Why didn't you bring him to a hospital?" I ask.

"They would've asked too many questions. Ones we wouldn't have been able to answer. Donnie had experience getting guys through withdrawal, and Lindsay's a nurse. He was safer with just us."

"I understand."

"Once we knew he would be okay, the next problem I needed to address was where Leo would live. He couldn't stay in San Diego; even California was a risk. Sending him to New York killed me," Ramiro explains, his voice pained. "I knew the amount of help and support I could give him from here would be limited." He looks at me. "Then he called that night, and you were with him, I'll admit," he says regret lacing his tone. "I saw another Krew situation. I was scared."

Ramiro glances over to where Leo's laughing and talking with the small group. "I know I've not been the most accepting of you, and for that, I'm sorry. You've beyond proven that you only have Leo's best interest at heart," he says, softening his tone. "I know you love him."

I'm not sure what sparked this change of heart in Ramiro, but I'm not complaining. Up until now, he's merely tolerated me. Whether or not our relationship will evolve into friendship remains to be seen. Still, his newfound acceptance of me as part of Leopold's life is reassuring. "I do love him very much. Leopold is everything to me, and I intend to spend the rest of my life showing him that."

The hours melt away as I find myself enveloped in the warmth of togetherness, seamlessly blending into the fabric of what now feels like *our* extended family. Admittedly, I was nervous about this trip to the

West Coast. I wasn't sure how receptive this group would be to me. With each shared laugh and exchanged story, any lingering misgivings between us are swiftly dispelled, replaced by a sense of unity and understanding. It's a heartwarming reminder of the power of human connection to bridge differences and foster deep bonds, reaffirming that we're united in our affection for Leopold.

Leopold

DECEMBER 1

I can't describe the enormity of my emotions over the past few months. Having London back in my life has been remarkable. Despite being on opposite coasts, we text daily and try to have a video call at least once a week. Her schedule at school and now at the emergency room, where her current rotation is, is absolutely crazy. I don't know how she does it.

Natalie and I also talk every day. I wish I could go fly to Northmeadow and bring her back here. She's been positively miserable. Her parents are the most close-minded, judgemental, and just plain awful people I've ever heard of.

From the second she arrived back in Northmeadow, they were trying to set her up with her ex-boyfriend, Tommy—the same one who cheated on her with her best friend. Natalie, being the sweetheart she is, didn't have the heart to rat him or the girl out to anyone. I'm not as nice as her. I was ready to take out an ad in The New York Times. I still think she should make it public, by the way.

Anyway, everything came to a head on Thanksgiving. That crazy ass ex of hers proposed to her at dinner. Obviously, she said no. Her parents freaked out. It sounds like it was complete chaos. The one good thing that came out of the mess was that Natalie finally found the courage to stand up for herself to her parents. She told them Tommy cheated on her but still kept the secret of with whom.

She tried to get them to understand that she's in love with Alex, but that didn't happen. The bad thing is that her father blew a gasket and gave her an ultimatum. Either follow their rules or leave their house. They must've read the same parenting manual my parents did.

I was so proud of her when she called and told me she packed up and left. She couldn't find an apartment, so she's staying at a motel. It's not ideal, but I was hoping it would be a positive step forward.

But things can never be easy, can they? After the Thanksgiving dinner debacle, she went off the radar for a while, which freaked Alex out. He nearly lost his shit. Alex is still in Russia doing some top-secret work with Maxim Solonik. Since he couldn't get to Missouri, he sent Viktor, his scary Ukranian bodyguard, to stay with her. The good thing is I don't have to worry about her safety.

I hate knowing she's going through so much. I miss my best friend. I wish she'd give in and come back to New York, where she belongs.

Anthony

"THE SHOW WAS AMAZING," LEO SAYS, STILL WIDE-EYED after tonight's performance of *Wicked*.

"It's one of my favorites," I reply.

"*What's next on the list?*" he asks, curious.

"The Lion King," I respond with a grin. Pulling my cell phone from my pocket, I pretend to check my messages. "We need to stop at the club. Owen asked if I could check something in the café."

"Okay," Leo agrees.

Me: Is everyone at the park?

Owen: Yes. We're waiting for you to get here.

Me: We're on our way. Be there in a few minutes.

The Dominant/submissive dynamic Leopold and I share has grown and evolved over the past five years. In the beginning, I was cautious, probably overly so. Leopold was in the beginning stages of healing from his traumatic past. I didn't want the power shift between us to hinder that in any way. Since the beginning of our relationship, we've discussed the significance of being collared. Leo's expressed that he desires to wear my collar—to be owned by me.

I'm not and never have been a Dominant who makes a lot of demands of their submissive. I don't get off on cruelty or power trips.

I'm fulfilled knowing my submissive is provided and cared for. That he allows me to nurture him. Some might say our dynamic is unconventional, and perhaps they're right, but it's perfect for us.

With each passing day, Leopold's grown stronger and more sure of himself. Watching this metamorphosis and seeing him develop into the outgoing and capable man he is today has been an honor. He's the perfect example of a self-confident submissive.

Tonight holds the promise of a transformative moment in our dynamic. I'll present Leopold with my collar—an elegant piece crafted from a thick silver chain and embellished with a symbolic O ring. Its locking mechanism at the back signifies a permanent bond.

I've been planning this ceremony for the past several weeks. Knowing how close Leopold is to Natalie, I reached out to Alexander to see if they'd be back in town soon. Turns out he's planning to surprise Natalie by flying into Northmeadow for Christmas. He expressed his regrets that they would have to miss the ceremony.

"How about we take a walk along the river before we go to the club?" I suggest, intertwining my fingers with Leo's.

"Sounds perfect," Leo replies, a smile playing on his lips as our hands meet.

Leo and I often walk this path. I think we both have our reasons for being drawn here. For me, it serves as a gentle nudge to heed the soft whispers of intuition and a reminder of the fragileness of life. Of how blessed I am to have this remarkable man beside me.

Unlike our usual walks, I lead Leo from the riverwalk onto the pier.

"Is there an event tonight?" he asks, his eyes scanning the surroundings with curiosity.

"Not sure," I respond.

As we approach the gathering, Leo furrows his brow. "Tony?" he asks softly. "What's everyone doing here?"

"They're here for us," I reveal, a rush of excitement coursing through me.

Upon reaching the gathering, we pause. Leo's gaze is fixated on Owen as he ignites his candle, its flame a beacon of light in the gathering dusk. Astrid's candle meets his, the flickering flames intertwining. Slowly, the light is passed from one candle to the next, the circle around us glowing brighter until every candle flickers in unison, their glow harmonizing with the soft whisper of the breeze.

"We're truly grateful to have you all here with us despite the chill in the air," I express warmly. "Each one of you has been with us through thick and thin, and we're honored you're here to share this special night with us," I add, feeling a swell of emotion.

"This park is more than just a location," Anthony says, his voice soft yet resonant. "It holds the echoes of our past from the darkest depths of despair to the moment you offered me your submission. It's witnessed our laughter, tears, and everything in between. And tonight," he continues, a hint of anticipation in his tone, "it becomes the backdrop for another significant moment in our lives."

"I'm not going to have you kneel. The ground is too cold."

"Thank you, Master," he replies respectfully.

"Leopold, we stand here tonight surrounded by the warmth of our friends, others who share in the lifestyle. I find myself humbled by the strength and solidarity of our community—our family," I breathe, my voice filled with emotion. "Together, we'll celebrate not only the love you and I have found but also a commitment that is unique to our lifestyle. The offering and wearing of a collar."

Turning my attention to my submissive, I continue, "For the submissive, wearing a collar is more than wearing a piece of jewelry. This collar," I say, reaching into my pocket to retrieve the silver chain. "Represents a deep commitment between us. It's an outward sign of your willingness to submit to my authority and guidance. Do you understand what agreeing to wear my collar means?"

"Yes, Master. It's a symbol of my trust and devotion to you," Leopold answers, his voice resonating with devotion.

"At the same time," I say softly, the weight of the words heavy in the air, "the collar serves as a constant reminder of the power dynamic within our relationship—a reminder of the roles each of us has chosen to fulfill and the responsibilities that come with them. It's a symbol of ownership and possession, not in a controlling sense, but rather a mutual acknowledgment of our bond."

"I understand, Master," Leopold murmurs, his tone laced with sincerity. "It's a constant reminder of our dynamic, of the roles we've chosen to embrace."

"As your Dominant," I explain tenderly, my voice carrying the weight of my commitment, "when I see my collar on you, it's a daily reminder of the sacred trust you've placed in me. I hold the responsibility of cherishing, protecting, and caring for you. Your well-being is in my hands, and I do not take that lightly."

Leopold's eyes soften, a silent acknowledgment of the depth of my words as he responds, his voice barely above a whisper, "I know you'll always have my best interests at heart," he murmurs, his gaze never leaving mine. "I trust you completely, Master,"

"This collar," I assert gently, my fingers tracing the silver chain as I speak, "is a symbol of the deep connection and mutual respect between us. It's a tangible expression of our dynamic and the love that binds us together. It's a symbol of strength, vulnerability, and profound intimacy —a reminder of the beauty found in surrendering to love and trust." Leopold's eyes glisten with emotion as he listens to my words, his expression reflecting the gravity of the moment. "And I promise to always honor that trust," I continue, my voice steady with sincerity, "to guide you with love and respect. Will you accept my collar?"

"Yes, Master," Leopold declares, his words ringing with conviction. "I'm yours, now and always."

Moving closer to Leopold, I am acutely aware of the significance of this moment—the culmination of a journey that has led us here. Leopold has captured my heart in a way no other ever could. With trembling hands, I place the collar around his neck. It's as if time stands still, and in that moment, our souls intertwine. The ends come together and lock, sealing our bond in a moment that feels both surreal and inevitable.

I know with absolute certainty that Leopold is the one who I've been waiting for. He completes me in ways I never thought possible. He's the man who brings light to the darkest parts of my soul.

Leopold is my forever.

Leopold

As the ceremony concludes, I'm overcome by a flood of emotions swirling within me. The weight of the collar around my neck is both grounding and liberating, a tangible symbol of the commitment I've made to Anthony, my Dominant, and the journey we've chosen to take together.

I meet Anthony's gaze and am filled with overwhelming gratitude and love, my heart overflowing with emotion. Everything has fallen into place, and I'm exactly where I'm meant to be—wrapped in Anthony's embrace and bound by the unbreakable bond we share.

With a sense of profound contentment, I intertwine my fingers with Anthony's as we walk back to Fire and Ice, surrounded by the people who witnessed our ceremony. Their presence is a comforting reminder of the love and support that surrounds us.

"Natalie's going to be so upset she missed this," Svetlana says, coming up next to me.

Svetlana Solonik has undergone a remarkable transformation from when I first met her—when she wore Alex's collar of protection. She was infamous for her stubbornness and strong-willed nature. I wasn't sure anyone could ever tame her or if she really even wanted to submit. That all changed when she met Alex's best friend, Brandon.

"I wish she was here, too," I say, my voice tinged with longing.

"Hopefully, Alex will be able to convince her to let him buy out the remainder of her contract so she can finally come home," Lana says wistfully.

"I hope so," I say, though deep down, I know the likelihood is slim. It's not just a matter of fulfilling the terms of her scholarship. It's about Natalie's deep-seated obligation to advocate for the youth in North-meadow. She experienced firsthand the repercussions of inadequate services, particularly for LGBTQ+ teenagers, in the wake of her brother and his boyfriend's tragic deaths. Natalie's determined to ensure nothing like that ever happens again. As much as I miss her, I was once one of those kids without a voice or support. I know they need her there more than I need her here.

"Are you two staying for a while?" Star asks Tony.

"Just for a little bit," Anthony replies, a mischievous glint dancing in his eyes. He inches closer, the warmth of his breath sending shivers down my spine as he whispers, "I have plans for us tonight."

Throughout the evening, Tony keeps me on edge with his teasing touches and lingering caresses, heightening my arousal with each passing moment.

"Let's go home," he says, his voice carrying a potent mix of authority and desire.

"I've been waiting for you to say that all night, Master," I confess, my voice trembling with need.

* * *

The subway ride home is a test of restraint that only serves to heighten the anticipation. But the moment we step into the apartment, Tony's desire ignites. He spins me around and pins me against the door.

As we stand there, pressed against the door, the heat between us explodes into a fiery passion. Tony's hands roam eagerly over my body, igniting sparks of pleasure with every touch. He captures my lips in a fervent kiss, and his tongue moves with mine in a sensual dance.

I moan softly against his mouth, my hands tangling in his hair as I pull him closer, desperate for more. Our bodies meld together, fitting perfectly as if they were made for each other. My erection presses against him as our bodies move together, seeking the friction we crave.

With practiced skill, Tony begins to divest me of my clothing, each piece falling away to reveal the eager flesh beneath. His touch is electric, sending jolts of pleasure coursing through me. When I'm finally bare before him, he steps back to admire the sight, his eyes dark with desire.

"My collar around your neck is the most erotic thing I've ever seen," he murmurs. "Do you see what you do to me?" My eyes drop down to the bulge in his pants.

"Yes, Master. I do," I gasp, my voice thick with desire.

"I'm going to fuck you so hard," he whispers in a low growl that sends shivers down my spine. "Get in the bedroom, now," he commands.

Before I realize it, my feet are already in motion, carrying me to the bedroom. Tony's gaze pierces mine as he sheds his clothes with a sense of urgency.

Stepping closer, his hands explore my body, setting my skin ablaze with anticipation. Our lips meet in a passionate kiss, causing both of us to moan with longing. Reluctantly, he pulls away, leaving me breathless. "Get on all fours on the bed," he orders, his tone commanding yet filled with desire before he turns to his dresser.

Tony returns to the bed and settles behind me, placing nipple clamps, a slender rod, a ring, and lube within reach. Then, I feel his hands on my ass. Spreading it open, he leans in to tease my entrance with his tongue. A low moan escapes my lips as I push back against his tongue as he fucks me.

"That feels incredible. Please, don't stop," I plead, the sensation driving me wild.

With a swift motion, he withdraws his tongue and slaps my ass hard, eliciting a surprised yelp. Another stinging slap follows, even harder this time, sending a jolt of pleasure through me.

"Do you enjoy that?" he asks, his voice filled with authority.

Tony and I have experimented with spanking. At first, I was tentative yet curious. He started with light taps that gradually heated and got stronger until any hesitation was gone, and in its place was only undeniable pleasure. It was a profound awakening that transcended the purely physical sensation but was, more importantly, a testament to the trust and intimacy of our relationship.

"Yes, Master. Please, I want more," I reply eagerly.

Tony obliges, his hand meeting my skin repeatedly in a rhythmic pattern. He suddenly stops and reaches for the bottle of lube, coating his fingers before sliding one into my waiting heat. With expert precision, he adds a second finger, plunging them into me, igniting a fire of desire within me.

"Are you up for trying something new?" Tony's voice is filled with anticipation, his eyes locked on mine.

"Anything," I respond, breathless.

"Lie on your back," he instructs, his tone firm yet gentle.

"You're absolutely breathtaking," he murmurs as his gaze traces my body with admiration. He reaches for the nipple clamps. "I need you to remember your safewords tonight," he reminds me. "Don't be afraid to use them."

"Yes, Master."

With practiced skill, he attaches the clamps, each sensation sending waves of pleasure through me. Linking them with a chain, he pulls lightly, eliciting a gasp of delight.

"Are you ready for more, *cuore mio*?" Tony's voice is filled with desire, his gaze smoldering.

"I want to do everything with you," I whisper, surrendering to the allure of our shared journey.

Tony lifts the thin metal rod. It glistens in the dim light. I watch intently as he traces it along my skin, each touch sending shivers of pleasure down my spine. "This is a sound rod. I'm going to insert it slowly, he explains, guiding me further into the realm of ecstasy and trust.

Excitement had bubbled within me during our discussions, but as Tony readies it with a generous amount of lube, a sudden wave of apprehension washes over me.

"Color?" Tony checks in.

"Nervous but green," I reply.

With a firm yet gentle touch, he cradles my erection as he guides the rod toward me. As it begins to slide inside, I can't help but gasp at the unfamiliar sensation.

"It's... it's bigger than I expected," I admit the blend of discomfort and pleasure, creating a heady mix of sensations.

"Do you want me to keep going?" he asks, seeking my consent.

"Yes," I reply, my voice betraying my desire, a needy edge to its tone.

Tony proceeds to insert the rod further until it's fully inside me. "Are you prepared?" he teases, a playful glint dancing in his eyes. I nod, rendered speechless by the anticipation. He begins to move the rod in and out, starting slowly before increasing the pace.

"Oh, it feels incredible," I breathe, overwhelmed by the sensation.

Once again, he comes to an abrupt stop, and I groan.

"We're far from done, Leopold," his voice oozing with desire as he retrieves the cock ring and slides it down my rigid length. Securing the chain from the clamps to the end of the sounding rod, he adds, "I'm eager to witness you unravel beneath me."

Tony dispenses more lube onto his hand and begins to stroke his own erection while teasing my entrance with his other hand. A whirlwind of sensations overwhelms me, yet I stay fixated on the sight of his self-pleasure.

"Is this what you want?" he asks, and I respond with eager nods.

"I ache for you," I plead, my voice trembling with desire. Tony positions himself at my entrance. I gasp at the sensation of his thick, hard length pushing past my tight muscles. "More, please," I whimper, yearning for a deeper connection.

Tony chuckles softly as he drives all the way in. "Like this?" he asks, his tone playful yet commanding.

"Yes, Master."

He withdraws, and I groan at the loss. "What's the matter, Leopold?" he teases, playfulness evident in his voice.

"I need..." My plea is cut short as he switches on the cock ring, sending intense vibrations through me, leaving me panting and desperate for more.

Tony thrusts inside until our bodies are pressed together, then pulls back slowly before plunging in again. "You're so responsive tonight," he moans, increasing his pace.

"I'm close," I rasp, the urgency evident in my voice.

"There is no coming without permission," he commands firmly. "Do you understand?"

"Yes, Master," I reply, biting my lip to suppress the rising tide of pleasure.

With renewed determination, Tony increases the force of his thrusts, the sound of our bodies colliding filling the room as he drives me closer to the edge.

"Please, may I come?" I plead, desire consuming me.

"Not yet," he murmurs, withdrawing momentarily. He reaches for the lube, coating his cock once more before plunging back into me with force. "You feel incredible, Leopold," he growls, eliciting a moan from me in response.

As he thrusts into my ass, Tony simultaneously moves the sounding rod in and out of my dick. "Oh, fuck," I gasp, overwhelmed by the intense sensation, my breaths coming in ragged pants.

"This is unbelievable," he moans, his voice filled with ecstasy. "I've never experienced anything like this."

"Please, Master, let me come," I plead, on the brink of release without permission.

He pauses, his cock buried deeply inside me. "I'll count down from ten," he says, his gaze piercing into mine. "You must wait until I reach zero to come. Do you understand?" I whimper in frustration as he begins the countdown.

"Ten," he starts. "Nine, eight..." With each number, he withdraws and thrusts back in, the anticipation driving me wild.

"Please," I beg, tears welling in my eyes as my climax nears. "I'm not going to make it."

"You can do this. Focus on my words," Tony encourages as he continues the countdown. "Seven, six, five."

Tears cascade down my cheeks, each breath a struggle as I teeter on the brink of oblivion, the promise of release tantalizingly close yet agonizingly out of reach.

"Four, three," he counts, his movements becoming more urgent.

"I'm so close," I whimper, my voice barely above a breathless murmur. My entire being pulses with raw, visceral need. The ache in my core is almost unbearable, a delicious torment that twists and coils with every movement. Every fiber of my being screams for release, pulling me closer to the edge of oblivion.

"Two," he says, pulling almost entirely out. "One. Come for me, now," he commands, pulling on the chain and sending me spiraling into ecstasy.

As the nipple clamps release, a wave of intense sensation floods my senses, the simultaneous removal of the sounding rod from my cock pushing me over the edge. "Oh fuck... Tony... Master," I cry out as ecstasy consumes me, experiencing a climax more intense than anything I've ever felt before.

Observing my reactions, Tony remarks, "You've never looked more beautiful," his voice husky with desire as he maintains his steady rhythm. "Your ass is clenching so tight around my dick."

"Please fill me, Master," I implore.

With a final, powerful thrust, he drives into me. With a primal growl, he stills as his release fills me completely. Tony's body trembles with the force of his climax. His touch is tender yet possessive, a silent declaration of ownership and devotion.

He slams into me one last time and stills as his cock twitches deep inside me. Tony collapses on top of me. "You were magnificent," Tony murmurs softly, his words carrying a depth of emotion that resonates within me.

"That was..." I search for the right words.

"Perfect," he whispers, his words a soothing balm to my soul. "You were meant to be mine, *cuore mio*."

"Everything I am belongs to you, Master," I pledge, my commitment unwavering.

Leopold

I had my last session with Sarah yesterday. To say it was bittersweet is an understatement. My treatment lasted far longer than it does for most people. Sorting through my messy, complex trauma wasn't a walk in the park. But Sarah and I tackled each issue head-on. Some things were difficult to process and took extra time. I had some rough panic attacks in her office, but Sarah was there every step of the way, helping me push through.

From the beginning, the goal was clear—to attain a state of wellness where therapy is no longer needed. And yes, that's copied straight from my treatment plan.

My plan was to be completely off anxiety medication before being discharged. But Sarah explained complete independence from medication may not always be feasible and that taking medication isn't wrong, nor does it mean I'm a failure. It took a lot of exploration of that topic to get to the bottom of why I felt that way.

Not surprisingly, it went back to when I was an inpatient at Walking in the Light. They drilled it into my head that if a man was on medication to control his anxiety, then he wasn't a 'real' man. I didn't realize it then, but that was their answer to anything they didn't want me to do. Why? Because even though I'm a gay man, I still identify as a man. I *want to be looked at as a man. If they wanted to control me, all they had to do was play on my insecurities—and they did.*

Sarah helped me reframe what I believe a 'man' is. It isn't something defined by sexual orientation or the medications a person takes but rather by the strength of his character, the depth of his compassion, and the courage to live authentically. For the first time ever, I didn't feel shame for who I loved. I felt worthy of being called a man.

With each day that passed, I shed the shackles of society's expectations and forged a new path for myself. One that was paved with self-love, acceptance, and unyielding pride.

Still, goodbyes are never easy. Although Sarah's my therapist, she's been a part of my life for the past five years. It's hard to say farewell to someone who's played such a pivotal role in my life. But I'm no longer a broken man. I'm walking away with my head held high. I have a newfound confidence and the knowledge that no words, no matter how cruel, could ever dim my light.

Still, it's going to feel odd when next Wednesday comes, and I don't have an appointment.

If you'd asked me a few years ago what my life would be like, I would never have guessed I'd be involved in BDSM, let alone be a willingly collared submissive to the kindest Master. Tony's surpassed everything I could've ever asked for in a partner. He's been patient and so unbelievably kind. Tony's taught me what it's like to be loved unconditionally—something I'd never experienced before.

Tony's impact on my life goes beyond what he and I share together. He's been the driving force behind some of the most significant changes in my life. It's because of him that I not only have London in my life but also a new family. A family of choice.

These are the people who have welcomed me with open arms, embracing me as one of their own without question. They've stood by me through thick and thin, offering me their unwavering support and love. They've supported me through my darkest moments and celebrated with me in times of joy. Tony's the thread that binds us all together, and for that, I'll always be grateful.

The past few months have been a rollercoaster of emotions. Tony and I were still riding the high from my collaring when I got a text from

Natalie with a picture of her and Alex. She was holding up her hand. On her ring finger was a stunning diamond engagement ring.

It's kind of a crazy 'Gift of the Magi-esq' story. Natalie talked Viktor into helping her surprise Alex by flying back to New York City without telling him. Meanwhile, Alex was planning to surprise Natalie by coming back from Russia early and flying to Northmeadow. But when he got there, she wasn't there. So, he flew back and planned an even bigger surprise—he proposed to her in Central Park.

Unfortunately, their happiness was short-lived. Natalie got a phone call in the early morning hours of Christmas morning that her father had been shot in a robbery gone wrong at his pharmacy. Her crazy ex-boyfriend, Tommy, who apparently has an addiction, was trying to steal some pills when her father showed up. Stanley was shot in the lung. It was touch and go for a while, but thankfully, he survived. He's been in the hospital for months, but he's still in the hospital with a long road to recovery.

In the middle of all that, Alex went CRAZY. Without telling Natalie, he bought out her contract. I don't blame him. If Tony would've let me, I would've done the same thing. Except Natalie didn't see it the same way. She was furious and broke up with him.

They were miserable. For months. There was nothing I could say or do to help cheer her up. I offered to go stay with her, but she refused. Natalie said it would be too much with her traveling back and forth between the hospital in Branson and Northmeadow while she tried to keep her parents' store.

Fortunately, Brandon and Lana staged an intervention to get Natalie and Alex in the same room together. They were able to talk about their issues with communication and re-negotiate a contract. Thankfully, they're back together.

The other good thing to come out of this near tragedy is her parents apologized for their behavior and now accept Alex with open arms.

I was hopeful that, with her contract bought out, they'd be coming back to the city. But they're not. They've decided to stay in Missouri until further notice to help her parents.

Once again, I'm struggling with the selfish wish that Natalie would just come home.

Anthony

"Natalie's father's finally been discharged," Alex explains, relief evident in his voice. "So now we can move forward with our wedding plans."

"I know it was touch and go for a while there. I'm so glad to hear the good news. Leo will be, too," I remark, my tone filled with genuine happiness.

"I have a special request," Alex adds hesitantly.

Alex is never one to ask for frivolous things, so now I'm paying attention.

"We had the chance to discuss the bridal shower with Natalie's parents. Charlotte's insisting that we have the bridal shower in Northmeadow," he says, a note of exasperation evident in his voice.

I'm catering the shower, so I understand his concern. "That's fine. We don't mind traveling," I reply, hoping to alleviate some of his stress.

"That's not everything," he adds cautiously.

"Okay," I reply, noting the change in his tone.

"This is our wedding. It's supposed to be a time of fun and anticipation," Alex laments. "I wanted Natalie to enjoy planning this, but Charlotte's giving her a hard time with everything. I thought if we gave in and agreed to have the shower in Northmeadow, she'd calm down. But nope," he sighs loudly.

"She disapproves of us getting married in Manhattan. Forget about the fact that we're having it at your restaurant and not a church. Charlotte was carrying on because she doesn't know what your food tastes like—"

"How about Leo and I take a trip out there and do a tasting?" I offer, trying to be helpful.

"You wouldn't mind?" he asks tentatively, seeking reassurance.

"Not at all. Natalie deserves the wedding of her dreams. And so do you, of course," I add, chuckling softly. "If I can help make that happen by coming out there to cook for her parents, then I'm all in."

"Do you and Leo have plans for the Fourth of July?" he asks with genuine curiosity.

"We don't," I reply.

"Would you like to come out for the holiday? My father and Luna, as well as Brandon and Lana, will be here. We can make a party out of it," Alex suggests, his tone much lighter now.

"That sounds like a lot of fun. We'll be there," I confirm.

"Natalie's going to be so excited," Alex says.

His excitement is contagious, which gives me an idea. "How about we do a scene when we get there?"

"What do you have in mind?"

"Something for both our subs." Leo enters the room and casts a curious glance my way. "I'm going to have to text you the details. My sub just walked in." Alex laughs. "I'll be in touch soon." We hang up, and I turn to Leo, who's practically bouncing with excitement. "Go ahead and ask."

"Where are we going, Master?" Leo asks eagerly.

"Northmeadow," I reveal, watching as Leo's eyes widen in excitement. "Alex invited us for the Fourth. Sam and Luna will be there. So will Brandon and Svetlana."

"Really?" Leo's excitement is palpable.

"We'll be doing a tasting for Charlotte and Stanley. She's giving Natalie a bit of a hard time about the shower and the wedding," I explain.

"Shocking," Leo responds dramatically, placing a hand over his chest.

"Leopold," I caution, sensing where his thoughts are going.

"I know. Natalie does everything she can to please them, but Charlotte's always giving her a hard time. It's not right."

"Right or wrong, it isn't any of our business," I assert firmly.

"But—"

"There are no buts. If you can't promise to behave, you won't go," I state, setting the boundary.

"I'll be on my best behavior," Leo assures me, flashing a charming smile.

"You better be. For Natalie's sake."

Me: We're signing the papers for the rental car.

Alex: Excellent. It's only about twenty minutes to get to the lake.

Me: We'll see you soon.

Our flight landed at a small airport just outside Northmeadow not long ago. After sorting out the paperwork, we locate our rental car, a white Volkswagen Jetta, in the parking lot. Leo and I stow our bags in the trunk, and he heads towards the passenger seat.

"Here." I toss the keys to him. "You're driving."

"I am?" he questions, eyebrows raised in surprise.

"You're the one who loves to drive," I jest, a playful smirk tugging at my lips.

Living in the city, driving isn't something we often do, but when we do, Leopold always jumps at the chance to drive. I don't mind at all. I've had plenty of driving experience and am more than happy to relax in the passenger seat.

"It'll help keep my mind occupied," Leo answers enthusiastically. "I can't wait to see her."

"Soon enough," I reply, a soft smile gracing my lips.

As we make our way from what was already a fairly remote location to a lake nestled in the Ozark Mountains, the breathtaking beauty of the surroundings captivates me.

"Now I understand why Alex and Natalie have a cottage here," I observe, marveling at the picturesque scenery.

"But it's so far away from everything," Leo muses quietly.

"It's a bit secluded," I concur, nodding thoughtfully. "But I'm certain you'll find a variety of local businesses that offer everything you might require."

"I've never lived in a small town. Rolling Hills, where I grew up, was a pretty big area, and then I lived in San Diego. This—" He motions around us as we drive. "—is not like anything I've ever experienced."

Guided by the GPS, we make a turn onto a gravel road that leads us straight to Alex and Natalie's charming cottage. Leo's anticipation is evident as he quickly brings the car to a stop, practically bounding out of the driver's seat.

The front door of the cottage swings open, and Alex steps out onto the porch, with Natalie following closely behind. With a bright smile, Natalie rushes towards the car, presumably eager to greet Leo, but I quickly step forward, intercepting her path.

"Pixie," I say affectionately, pulling her into a tight hug. She's so tiny that lifting her off the ground is effortless.

"I can't believe you guys are here," she squeals in delight.

"You can put my sub down any time now," Alex teases, his laughter filling the air.

"She's cute," I comment, gently setting her down. "But I brought my own sub with me." Leo steps forward, holding our bags.

Natalie throws her arms around him, exclaiming, "Leo! I can't believe you're here." "I can't believe we're here either," Leo responds, leaning in to plant a kiss on her cheek. He then takes a look around. "You really live in the middle of nowhere."

"Wait until nighttime," she suggests, her gaze drifting upwards. "It gets so dark you can see all the stars."

"And risk getting eaten by a wild animal," Leo scoffs, shaking his head. "I'll take a pass," he quips, eliciting a giggle from Natalie.

"Let's go inside," Alex suggests. "Natalie will show you to your room so you can get settled in."

As we make our way into the house, I lean in and whisper, "I'd like to ask you to keep an open mind while we're here."

"I'll try my best, Master," Leo replies in a hushed tone.

Leopold

"It's this way." Natalie hooks her arm through mine, and I let her lead me through the contemporary yet inviting interior. Sunlight streams in through the skylights, creating an open and expansive atmosphere.

"This place is gorgeous. Your pictures don't do it justice, girl."

"Alex has a great eye for design," she says as she opens the door to what I assume is our room. "I'll miss this place when we go back to the city."

Stepping inside, I release the bags and immediately gravitate towards the windows, captivated by the panoramic scenery. "Look at that view," I marvel as I look out the expansive windows that showcase the lake.

Natalie joins me at the window, and together, we soak in the warm breeze drifting through the open window.

"I've missed you," I confess, pulling her close. "But I can see why you've been holed up here. Even I might be able to get used to this."

"You guys are welcome here anytime," she says softly, resting her head against my chest.

We share a moment of silence, gazing out over the tranquil water. Two boats glide past, their wake creating gentle ripples along the rocky shore. It's a scene straight out of a storybook.

"Natalie. Leopold. We need you both out here," Alex's voice interrupts the moment.

"Coming," she replies.

"That sounds suspicious," I remark with a playful grin.

"It sure does. I wonder what's going on?"

"Let's go find out," I suggest, taking her hand.

As we step into the living room, we're met with a sight that hints at something more. The furniture has been moved aside, creating an open area in the center of the room. A black blanket lies on the floor. Tony's candles have been arranged next to it. Alex and Tony stand poised and confident, exuding dominance as they take control of the space.

"Go change," Alex instructs, handing Natalie some clothes.

"Yes, Sir," she responds with a smile before making her way past me.

"You, too," Tony directs, offering me a pair of spandex shorts.

"Yes, Master," I reply, hurrying to join Natalie. "Looks like we're about to have some fun."

Somehow, Natalie changed and made it back to the living room before me. When I get there, she's already on her knees. I join her, spreading my legs slightly and resting my hands with my palms up on my thighs.

"Anthony has graciously offered to give us an early wedding present," Alex says as he steps in front of Natalie. "Are you willing to allow him to create a wax design on you?"

Engaging in public scenes has become a thrilling aspect of my dynamic with Tony. Each one has been exhilarating. The idea of sharing a wax scene with another couple, especially that it's Alex and Natalie, is a tantalizing new adventure, one that promises to be both intense and exhilarating.

"Yes, Sir. I'd love that," Natalie responds eagerly.

"You and Leo will lie next to one another, and you will remain clothed," he continues, and I bite my lip to keep from laughing. Alex and Natalie don't do public scenes—ever. He's extremely territorial where she's concerned.

"Leo, I want you on your stomach," Tony directs. "Pixie, lie on your back with your arm and leg against Leo's." While Tony lights the candles, he carries on speaking. "Alex tells me you two have played with wax."

"Yes," she replies respectfully.

"My wax is similar in burn temperature to what you've used. However, if you're uncomfortable in any way, you are to use your safewords. What are they?" he asks.

"Yellow and red."

"First, we're going to prepare your skin. It'll help with removing the wax later," Tony explains, kneeling beside me.

Drizzling warm oil down my spine, Tony's fingers work the liquid into my skin, his fingers dipping beneath the waistband of my shorts. Leaning towards me, his voice soft against my ear, he whispers, "Are you hard for me?"

"Yes, Master," I reply, licking my lower lip. "Very."

"Ready?" Anthony asks.

"I'm ready," Natalie answers.

"Let's have some fun," Anthony announces with a grin as he reaches over me. The scent of bergamot and cedar fills my nose, and I close my eyes, savoring it. "Your Dominant is going to be my assistant. I'm going to teach him how to be an artist," he adds, sharing a laugh with Alex.

Tony patiently guides Alex's hand, showing him where to drip the wax. Together, they work in harmony, covering us in the warm, cascading liquid. With closed eyes, I surrender to the sensation, letting myself drift into a state of deep relaxation.

"Head down," Alex admonishes sternly. "You'll see it when it's time."

"May I have a hint?"

"No," they echo in unison.

I chuckle, well aware of Natalie's impatience with surprises.

"Patience, little pixie," Anthony reassures with a gentle tone. "Relax and enjoy this."

Tony steps in, focusing on the delicate nuances of the design he's creating, while Alex assists with the broader strokes. Soft strains of music filter through the room, enveloping us in a cocoon of calmness. With a contented sigh, I shut my eyes and surrender to a blissful drowsiness, letting myself drift into a peaceful slumber.

"It's done," Tony announces, bringing me back to awareness. Natalie turns her head to look at me and gives me a sleepy smile. "Alex, can you grab the black light from my bag?"

Tony dims the lights and closes the curtains, casting the room in darkness. Then, he activates the black light, casting an ethereal glow across the space. Beside me, Natalie lets out a soft gasp of awe at the magical display.

"Shh," Anthony corrects her gently.

The air is charged with anticipation as I lie motionless, eagerly awaiting the reveal of Tony's handiwork. Meanwhile, Alex diligently photographs the scene from various angles, each click of the camera capturing the essence of the moment. Despite the meticulous preparation, a sense of apprehension lingers, knowing that the fragility of the wax designs leaves them vulnerable to breakage upon removal.

"I think I got enough," Alex states, satisfied with his photography.

"It's time to lift the wax. Hopefully, we can get it off in one piece."

He and Tony take their positions on each side of us. Alex whispers to Natalie, "You look gorgeous covered in so many colors, baby girl."

Side by side, they methodically remove the wax from our skin, handling it with utmost care. It appears mostly intact, but I continue to watch with bated breath until they set it safely on the dining table.

Alex returns to Natalie, helping her get to her feet. "Ready to see it?" he asks.

"I'm so ready." Something tells me there's a double meaning to Natalie's words, suggesting an underlying truth about the transformative power of hot wax. It's impossible to experience the sensuality of hot wax without being affected.

Alex leads Natalie to the table while I linger behind with Tony.

"As usual, you looked beautiful as your skin turned pink," Tony croons softly, his voice carrying a hint of desire. "The things I want to do to you. I can't wait—."

"Is that glitter?" Natalie's voice breaks through the moment.

"It is," Tony replies, moving away from me. "Do you like it?"

With my erection straining against the spandex shorts, I inch away, my thoughts turning to the predators lurking outside. A definite mood killer.

"Like it? It's the most beautiful thing I've ever seen," Natalie exclaims. "Thank you so much. I'll treasure this always."

"I have a custom frame for it in the car," Tony explains. "Leo and I will arrange it in the frame for you before we leave."

Alex clasps Tony's shoulder. "Thank you. This means a lot to both Natalie and me."

"It's my pleasure," Tony replies warmly before turning to me. "You two go get cleaned up so we can eat."

"Come on in," Natalie invites, her voice welcoming. "I'll wash your back off."

I follow Natalie into her room.

"I don't know how Tony does that," Natalie muses.

"It's something that comes naturally to him," I explain. "And I'm glad. I love being on the receiving end."

"I can see why."

"Thank you, sweetheart." I kiss her forehead. "I'm going to go get dressed or hopefully undressed."

"Go get 'em, tiger," she giggles.

Entering our room, Tony's sitting on the edge of the bed waiting for me. "Lock the door."

I follow his command. When I turn to go back, Tony's behind me. His hands gently frame my face as he kisses me softly, the tenderness gradually giving way to passion. "Take your shorts off," he instructs between kisses, his voice husky with desire.

With fluid grace, I slide the spandex down my legs, letting it drop to the floor without a sound. Stepping out of it, I kick the garment aside before focusing on his belt. "May I, Master?" I request permission as I reach for it.

With a subtle nod, he consents, and I swiftly unbuckle it, letting his pants fall away. Tony sheds his shirt and discards it. He stands before me, his boxer briefs straining against the evidence of his arousal.

Gliding my hands down his torso, I feel the defined contours of his abdomen beneath my fingertips, trailing lower until I reach the waistband of his underwear. With deliberate slowness, I ease them down, freeing his pulsing erection.

Dropping to my knees, I wrap my fingers around his thick shaft, applying gentle pressure as I stroke him. With my other hand, I cradle his balls, relishing the weight of them in my palm.

With a gentle yet firm grip on the back of my head, he guides me closer. "Suck my cock, Leopold," he instructs, his tone laced with urgency.

I part my lips and ease him into my mouth, gradually sliding his length deeper. He lets out a low groan, holding me still for a moment before granting me air. "Damn," he breathes out. "You're incredible at that."

When we first met, this scenario, willingly giving a blow job, seemed impossible. But I'm not the same man I was back then. I've reclaimed everything stolen from me. I have complete trust in the Master I've chosen to submit to.

I maintain my rhythm, gradually intensifying my efforts until he signals for me to stop. "Get on the bed," he instructs.

Tony drops to his knees behind me, spreading my cheeks to expose my waiting entrance. His tongue dances around the rim before pushing inside, evoking unrestrained moans of pleasure from me. With each sensual caress, I'm reminded of just how much I love it when Tony pleasures me this way, his every movement driving me wild with desire.

With his hand wrapped firmly around my throbbing cock, Tony continues to expertly tongue-fuck me, sending waves of pleasure coursing through my body. "Master, I'm so close," I pant desperately, the need for him overwhelming me. "I need you inside me, please."

"You want this?" he asks as he rubs his cock against my hole.

"Yes," I plead, my voice trembling.

With a slow, deliberate motion, he eases the head of his cock into me, gradually sinking deeper until I'm completely filled. The sensation elicits a mutual groan of ecstasy. Tony's hand snakes around my waist, finding my throbbing cock and wrapping around it, adding an extra layer of pleasure as he jerks me off. His other hand finds purchase on my waist, anchoring himself as he increases the speed and intensity of his thrusts.

"Feels so good," I say through gritted teeth.

"Come for me, Leopold," Tony commands as he ruts into me with furious abandon.

Waves of ecstasy crash over me, my body trembling as I release onto the bed. Tony's unwavering rhythm only intensifies the pleasure, sending tremors of delight coursing through me. With one last, powerful thrust, he fills me completely, his cock pulsing with warmth inside me.

Breathless, we sink onto the bed, our bodies spent from the intensity of our passion.

"Do you think they heard us?" I ask, and Tony chuckles heartily. "What?"

"Alexander had these rooms soundproofed when he remodeled," Tony explains with a grin.

"Phew," I exclaim, dropping my arm over my forehead. "I wouldn't want them to think we're bad guests."

"Come on," Tony says, still chuckling. "Let's go get cleaned up."

After a quick shower, we rejoin Alex and Natalie in the living room, where they're already tidying up.

"Here, let me help," I offer, bending down to collect the leftover bits of wax from the floor.

"Thank you," Natalie responds appreciatively as she carefully folds the blanket and picks it up. "Shall I put this in the washer, Tony?"

"That would be great," Tony confirms, nodding his head.

While Natalie starts the laundry, Alex, Tony, and I quickly restore the furniture to its original position. With the house back in order, Alex suggests ordering takeout for dinner, and we all agree. Outside, we enjoy our meal together, captivated by the beauty of the night.

When Tony asked me to try to keep an open mind, I anticipated a struggle, yet here, beneath this vast expanse of stars, I'm spellbound. The stars shimmer with an intensity I've never witnessed before, casting a radiant glow upon the earth. Fireflies dance in the meadow, adding to the enchantment. All around, the night is alive with the harmonious chorus of bullfrogs, crickets, and the occasional bird. Amidst the symphony of nature's nocturnal chorus, I feel a profound sense of peace and connection.

This place exudes magic.

Leopold

As the new day dawns, a flurry of anticipation and apprehension fills the air. Alex's bodyguard, Viktor, appears particularly tense, his usually composed demeanor slightly strained as he keeps a watchful eye on the surroundings. Despite Viktor's unease, the other guests seem unaware. They're immersing themselves in the joyful atmosphere and eagerly anticipating the festivities ahead.

Tony and I spend most of the day prepping for this evening's dinner.

"Go on outside," Tony urges, wiping his hands on a kitchen towel. "I'm just about done."

"I'm fine here," I reply, enjoying the familiarity of the kitchen and the comforting routine of helping Tony.

"I want you to go outside and enjoy yourself," he insists, his tone gentle but firm.

"Are you sure, Master?" I ask, torn between staying and going.

"Yes," he replies, pressing a quick kiss to my lips before nudging me towards the door.

As I step outside, I notice the only empty seat is next to Natalie's mom, Charlotte. With a deep breath, I approach her. "Is this seat taken?" I ask politely.

"No, it isn't," she replies, gesturing for me to sit.

"Perfect," I say with a smile, settling into the seat beside her. Leaning closer, I whisper, "I never thought I'd say this, but I think I'm starting to love it here."

"You are?" she asks, clearly surprised.

"Trust me. It shocks me more than you. I've never been to a lake," I reply with a chuckle."Never?" Charlotte repeats, sounding incredulous.

"Nope," I shake my head, a hint of nostalgia creeping in. "My parents would only take us to the shore when we were young."

"Where did you grow up?" she asks, curiosity piqued.

"California," I answer.

"Whatever made you move to New York City?"

"That's a long story," I reply, glancing around. "But I think we have time. Would you care to join me for a walk?"

"A walk?" she asks tentatively, then surprises me when she says, "Sure."

I rise and extend my arm, offering it to her. She hesitates before sliding hers into mine. Natalie shoots me a questioning glance, and I respond with a reassuring wink before leading Charlotte away.

What am I doing? This woman rejected her own son for being gay. Yet, something inside me urges me to talk to her, and I've learned from Tony's experiences not to ignore such impulses. Everything happens for a reason.

"How I ended up in Manhattan isn't a happy topic. I don't want to bring all that negative energy to the table," I explain.

"That's very thoughtful," she says softly, patting my arm.

I wait until we're out of earshot from the group before continuing.

"When I came out to my parents, they had me pack my bags and sent me to live at a conversion therapy center," I begin my tale. Charlotte keeps her eyes forward as I speak. "I was there for two years until I escaped."

"Escaped?" she questions. "Do you mean until you were discharged?"

"No, I mean escaped," I repeat before continuing, "My therapist regularly abused me," I explain. "It wasn't until he drugged me and raped me for several days that I couldn't take it anymore," I explain.

"Even though I was eighteen, they had no plan to discharge me. So, in the middle of the night, when no one was watching, I made my move. I had to threaten the woman at the front desk to let me out. Then, I ran."

"I'm very sorry the people who were supposed to help you hurt you," she says, her tone laced with sorrow. "Did you go back home when you escaped?" The word sounds almost foreign this time.

"No. I've not seen or spoken to my parents in nearly ten years."

"Oh," she says, her voice barely above a whisper. I continue my story. "I went to the police to report the rape. They took my statement and set me up in a program for homeless LGBTQ+ youth."

"Was that in New York?"

"It was in San Diego. It was a good place with good people, except I was so desperate to be loved that I messed up. I met someone and even though I was warned he was trouble, I didn't listen." We stop walking when we get to the water's edge. "His name was Krew. He pretended to care about me enough that I let my guard down. He drugged me, got me hooked on heroin and other drugs all so he could invite people in to rape me," I admit. "More people than I can count. I looked forward to the next time he'd drug me so I could stay numb."

"Please, Leo. I can't hear any more," Charlotte says, her voice quivering and tears streaming down her face. "I had a son, Michael. I'm sure Natalie told you about him."

"She did."

"You remind me so much of him. Your blonde hair and blue eyes and your gentle soul." She pauses to catch her breath, her words laden with guilt. "It's my fault he's not here. When he told us he was gay and was in a same-sex relationship, we rejected him—I rejected him. I was his mother, the person who was supposed to love him unconditionally, but I failed him."

"If we didn't kick him out. If we tried to understand him, he'd still be here," she says, her voice trembling with regret. "If I could go back and do things differently, I would." She looks up at me, and I see a familiar brokenness reflected in her eyes. "I'd give anything to have my boy back. I want to tell him that even though I don't like the lifestyle he chose, I love him."

"I'm sure he knows." I offer what comfort I can.

"I'm a Christian woman, Leopold. I believe God works in mysterious ways—ways we often don't understand," she says, attempting to regain her composure.

"Admittedly, I haven't gone to church in many years."

"That's okay. God still loves you," Charlotte says tenderly. "And I believe he sent you to me so I can love you, too." Her unexpected words catch me off guard, and she notices. "I'm the last person you thought you'd ever hear that from, right?"

"To be honest, yes," I admit.

"Ever since Natalie and Alex told us about you and Tony, I couldn't get you, in particular, off my mind," she explains, her voice filled with sincerity. "I've prayed for you for months, and I've asked God why He's bringing you into my life. The answer I kept getting is love heals." Tears trickle down my cheeks as her words sink in. "I'm not your mom, and I wouldn't try to replace her, but I will do my best to show you the kind of unconditional love I should've shown to my son and the kind your mother should've shown to you."

"I don't know what to say, and I'm rarely ever speechless," I admit, my voice thick with emotion.

"I'm not perfect, and I'm going to make mistakes. But I ask that you give me a chance."

Inviting Charlotte for a stroll had seemed like a simple gesture. But as we walked and I began to bear my soul to her, I realized the profound impact it was having on both of us. Setting aside her long-held convictions, she embraced me with a mother's love, filling a void that had long haunted me. It was a moment of catharsis, a healing journey shared between two souls unexpectedly brought together by circumstance.

Wordlessly, I wrap Charlotte in a gentle embrace, feeling a rush of gratitude and emotion surge through me. She responds immediately with a silent promise of understanding and compassion. "Thank you, Charlotte," I murmur, my voice trembling with emotion. "This... this means everything to me."

After regaining our composure, we make our way back to the table just as Tony begins to serve the food. It's no surprise that everyone thoroughly enjoys the meal.

"Anthony, dear," Charlotte gushes, her eyes sparkling with delight. "Your food is exquisite."

Tony, seated next to me, beams with pride. "Thank you, ma'am."

"Our wedding guests will be getting a real treat."

Sam stands, raising his glass. "I'd like to propose a toast to the future, Mr. and Mrs. Montgomery."

Glasses clink together as everyone raises a toast to the soon-to-be-wedded couple.

The awareness of being gay dawned on me from a young age. It was accompanied by the knowledge that legal marriage in America was reserved solely for heterosexual couples. It was a bitter pill to swallow, a reminder of the systemic barriers that stood in the way of LGBTQ+ individuals. Unless I somehow magically turned straight, marriage was a privilege that wouldn't be afforded to me.

Until now.

With the recent legislative changes, the tide has turned. Gay couples are now afforded the legal right to marry in every corner of the U.S. While it's a milestone worth celebrating, the fight for acceptance and equality is far from over. Yet, the mere fact that we have the right to marry—to be seen as equal in the eyes of the law—fills me with hope for what lies ahead.

Except for one small or rather large detail. I don't know if Tony would want to get married.

Anthony

Leopold pulls our car into a mundane parking lot, the crunching of the gravel beneath the tires echoing softly. I can't help but envision the potential lying in this unassuming space. The picture in my mind is so clear—smooth pavement accented by lush greenery. A flagstone path lined by bursts of colorful blooms invites guests to wander toward the three-story log cabin.

"Wow," Leo marvels, his eyes sweeping across the scene. "This place is gorgeous."

"It is," I agree, still lost in my daydream of how much better Water's Edge could look with a little TLC.

We retrieve our bags from the trunk, and my eyes are drawn to the shimmering lake that's only steps away. As we approach the front porch, the gentle marks of age become more apparent in the building's weathered exterior. Yet, it doesn't detract from the allure. Together, we walk up the natural stone steps. I'm delighted to discover raised flower beds lining the space, their blossoms adding bursts of color to the weathered wood.

Rocking chairs line the porch, their well-worn surfaces inviting us to rest awhile, while ceiling fans, some of which no longer seem to work, continue their slow rotation. A few strategic improvements could evolve this area into a true gem. An elderly woman appears from around the corner, a watering can in her hand.

"Good afternoon, you must be the guests I was waiting for," she greets us warmly, a smile spreading across her face. "Anthony and Leopold, right?"

"Yes, ma'am. Can I help you with that?" I offer, stepping forward to lend a hand.

"That would be wonderful," she says, passing me the metal can with a grateful nod. "It seems to get heavier each day."

"Your flowers are breathtaking," I comment, pouring water into the closest container filled with geraniums and evening primrose before tending to the hibiscus.

"When my husband Carl was alive, gardening was his passion. Having them helps me feel close to him," she shares, her voice tinged with nostalgia.

"That's a beautiful way to honor his memory," Leo adds, his tone empathetic.

"Come on inside," Mrs. Wilson says. "Let's get you checked in."

As we follow the woman into the foyer of the home, she takes her place behind the desk, slipping on wire-rimmed glasses before reaching for a notebook. That's when I notice the absence of a computer or any other modern technology to check us in. "Anthony and Leopold Genovese. You're Italian," she remarks, glancing up at me.

I offer a nod in response, attempting to maintain my usual calm demeanor. "Yes, that's correct," I confirm and notice a flicker of surprise dance across Leo's features.

The contrast between the commitment of our D/s relationship and the possibility of legal marriage weighs heavily on my mind, leaving me to wonder if Leopold would ever desire such a conventional bond.

I catch his gaze for a moment before quickly returning my attention to the woman at the desk.

"You'll be my guests for the next six nights. Until Sunday," she confirms, her tone conveying a sense of hospitality as she reads from the page before her. "I've arranged for you to stay in my largest room on the third floor. You'll have a view of the water from your balcony.""That's perfect. I'm just glad you had vacancies," I say with a grateful smile.

"You boys are my only guests this week," she states, her tone carrying a sense of resignation. "Unfortunately, business gets slower each year."

"How is that possible in such a beautiful place?" I wonder aloud.

My gaze sweeps across the space, taking in the meticulous craftsmanship of the natural woodwork that graces every corner, from the polished floorboards to the intricately carved beams overhead. My gaze then drifts toward the expansive windows that dominate the walls, offering uninterrupted views of the tranquil lake just a stone's throw away.

"I don't keep up with all the fancy on-the-line things those big hotel chains have," she comments, and I suppress a chuckle at her charming term for the internet. "No one knows this place is here."

"That's a shame," I sympathize, and she offers a casual shrug in response.

"Here's the key to your room," she says, presenting a physical key with a slight flourish. "You just missed lunch, but if you're hungry, I can throw something together for you."

"We actually ate before we arrived, but thank you for the offer," I decline politely.

"Dinner's at five thirty," she adds, her tone hospitable.

"What's on the menu?" Leo asks.

"Stuffed haddock," she replies.

"That sounds delicious. I'll definitely come hungry," Leo responds eagerly.

Mrs. Wilson's face lights up with genuine delight. "I look forward to seeing you boys later," she says warmly, her eyes twinkling.

Looking around, I inquire, "Is there an elevator?"

"There isn't. Are you okay with the steps? If not, I can move you down to the ground floor," she offers, her voice filled with concern.

"The steps are just fine," I assure her.

Making our way up the grand oak staircase, I'm struck by the craftsmanship of the hand-carved railing, each curve and twist a testament to the artistry of its maker. The details are exquisite, something you don't often find in modern fixtures. Along the walls, picture montages depict scenes from years past, each labeled with the corresponding year—a poignant reminder of this place's vibrant history. It's disheartening to witness the emptiness that now pervades, especially during the peak of the summer tourist season.

After settling into our room, Leopold and I are eager to take advantage of the sun-soaked day. We venture down to the lake, where the bed and breakfast boasts a picturesque sandy beach. There, a young family with three playful children catches our eye, their laughter mingling with the gentle lapping of the waves. Nearby, a dock extends into the water, its sign tempting us with the promise of boat rentals, but there's no attendant.

"Would you care for a walk?" I suggest.

"That would be great," Leo agrees.

As we set off, the gentle lapping of the water against the shore accompanies our steps, a soothing rhythm that guides us forward. Sunlight filters through the canopy overhead, dappling the ground with patches of golden warmth. With each twist and turn of the path, we uncover new vistas and hidden nooks, each one a testament to the beauty of this tranquil oasis.

"This place is a hidden gem," I remark, casting a thoughtful glance around. "She just needs the right tools to get it seen."

"Something tells me it's all a bit too much for her," Leo adds, his expression reflecting a mix of sympathy and concern.

"You might be right." We continue our stroll in contemplative silence for a while. "I wonder when the last time was that someone cooked for Mrs. Wilson?"

"What are you thinking, Master?" Leo's voice carries a note of curiosity.

"I'd like to find her before she starts cooking and see if she'll let me make tonight's meal," I suggest, my voice laced with determination.

"This is one of the many reasons I love you," Leo replies, admiration shining in his eyes. "Your kindness knows no bounds."

The late afternoon sun filters through the windows as I seek out Mrs. Wilson. I find her in the kitchen peeling potatoes. She stops every few minutes to rub her hands, which appear sore from a lifetime of work.

"May I take over for you?" I ask, extending a helping hand.

"Don't be silly," she chuckles, waving off my offer. "This is just part of the job."

"When's the last time someone cooked for you?" I inquire gently.

She takes a moment to reflect before replying, "It's been quite a while, I reckon."

"Did I mention I'm a chef?" I interject, hoping to sway her decision.

"His food is absolutely divine," Leo chimes in with a smile. "You should come visit us in New York."

"I've never been out of Missouri," Mrs. Wilson admits wistfully.

"I'd be honored if you'd allow me to cook for you this evening," I press once more, my determination unwavering.

"Okay. I'd like that very much," she concedes, passing the potato peeler over to me. "Would you care to join me on the porch?" Leo suggests, offering a change of scenery. "We can relax for a while."

"I'll pour us some sweet tea," Mrs. Wilson announces, her voice carrying a hint of Southern hospitality as she retrieves three glasses from the cupboard. "The fish is in the fridge. So is the broccoli." With practiced efficiency, she pours the drinks. "The spice cabinet is the one on the end. The utensils are all in the big drawer." She offers a thorough rundown of the kitchen before excusing herself and disappearing with Leopold.

I set my phone on the counter and cue up my favorite playlist, the familiar tunes serving as a comforting backdrop as I dive into preparations for tonight's meal.

An hour later, the three of us gather around the table, plates filled with the fruits of my labor.

"This isn't my stuffing recipe," Mrs. Wilson remarks, taking another bite with evident curiosity.

"It isn't. I hope you don't mind," I reply, my tone tinged with a touch of uncertainty.

"Mind? It's scrumptious. Would you be willing to give me the recipe," she insists, a warm smile gracing her lips.

"I can do that," I agree, relief flooding through me.

We continue to eat in companionable silence, the clink of cutlery against plates the only sound filling the room until Mrs. Wilson breaks the quiet. "What brings you two boys to Finn Lake?"

"Friends of ours have a cottage here. We came to join them for the holiday," I explain, hoping to satisfy her curiosity.

"Oh, who are they?" Mrs. Wilson asks, her interest clearly piqued.

"Alex Montgomery and Natalie Clarke."

"Yes, Natalie Clarke. I heard she was getting married," Mrs. Wilson remarks, taking a sip of water. "I remember when she and that handsome fiancé of hers stayed here."

"I've known Alex for a long time. He's a good guy," I assure her.

"How do you two know each other?" Mrs. Wilson asks innocently, her curiosity catching me off guard.

"Leopold and I are a couple," I confess, gauging her reaction carefully. "We've been together six years."

"No one around here knows," Mrs. Wilson confesses quietly, her voice tinged with a hint of sadness. "My grandson, Lance, is gay, and I love him unconditionally." Despite her candidness, her words hold a sense of grace, reflecting her deep-seated acceptance. "People around here might not understand," she confides further, her tone gentle yet resolute. "But for me, it's simple. He's my grandson, and that's all that matters. Love knows no bounds."

"I hope Lance knows how lucky he is," Leo remarks sincerely.

"I'm sure he does," Mrs. Wilson replies with a warm smile.

"How many children do you have?" I ask.

"Just one. A son."

"Does he live close?" Leo inquires.

"No. He and his family live in Florida. He's a marine biologist," Mrs. Wilson explains, a hint of pride in her voice. "He wants me to retire and move in with them," she adds.

"I'm sure they miss you. Why don't you do that?" Leo presses gently.

"I'd love to," she says wistfully.

"But?" I prompt, sensing there's more to her hesitation.

"I'd have to close this place," she confesses.

"Have you considered selling it?" I ask.

"Not seriously. Who'd want to buy a bed and breakfast that has no boarders?" she asks, gesturing around with a resigned expression. "And I don't have the heart to see it shut down," she adds, rising from the table to gather the dishes. "You cooked, so I'll wash."

"I didn't cook," Leo says, jumping up from his seat. "I'll help you."

⁂

Leopold and I lose ourselves in the rhythm of lazy days spent by the lake and leisurely strolls through quaint streets lined with colorful storefronts. But beneath the surface of our carefree exploration, Mrs. Wilson's words weigh heavily on my mind. *No one would want to buy a bed and breakfast that has no boarders, and I don't have the heart to see it shut down.* Her heartfelt sentiments tug at my conscience.

On the eve of our departure, a wave of reluctance washes over me, and I find myself not wanting to leave.

"We've had a truly wonderful time this week," I say to Mrs. Wilson, who's dabbing at the tears in her eyes.

"I have too. I'm going to miss you boys," she replies, her voice tinged with genuine affection.

"We'll be back in a few weeks for Natalie's bridal shower. Can we make reservations to stay here now?" I inquire eagerly, already anticipating our return to this beloved retreat.

"Oh yes, that'll be wonderful," she exclaims, a smile brightening her tear-streaked face as she hurries to retrieve her notebook. After providing her with the necessary information, she embraces us both warmly. "Have a safe trip back to New York."

"Thank you," I respond, returning her hug and planting a gentle kiss on her cheek. "We'll see you soon."

Leopold

RECLINING ON THE SOFA NEXT TO TONY, MY MIND DRIFTS back to our recent stay in Northmeadow. Memories of lazy mornings by the lake, leisurely walks through the quaint downtown, and heartfelt conversations with Mrs. Wilson flood my thoughts. It's hard to believe that when we first got there, I was ready to turn around and come back to the city, but by the time we had to say goodbye, I didn't want to leave.

I'd intended to bring up the topic of marriage to Tony while we were there. The romantic atmosphere and picturesque surroundings seemed like the perfect backdrop for such a conversation. But as each day passed, I found myself hesitating. Now that we're back in the city, it feels like I missed my chance.

A text from an unknown number interrupts my lamenting.

Unknown: It's Lana. Natalie's postponing her bridal shower. We'll be in touch.

The cryptic nature leaves me feeling uneasy. I attempt to text back, but my message fails to send.

"What do you think this means?" I show Tony the peculiar message.

"It sounds as though they're extending their Russian vacation," Tony muses, glancing up from his book to examine the text on my phone.

"Natalie wouldn't postpone her bridal shower for a trip to Russia," I reply, a note of concern lacing my words. "I've tried calling Natalie a million times, but my calls go straight to voicemail, and my texts are all unread."

"They don't have cell service where they're staying," Tony responds, his gaze returning to the book in his hands.

"Then how did Lana text me, and why was it from an unknown number?" I press, a sense of unease settling in the pit of my stomach.

"Why does Svetlana do anything?" Tony suggests with a nonchalant shrug. "She probably lost her phone. I'm sure it's nothing."

"I have a bad feeling," I confess, my apprehension growing with each passing moment.

"Viktor's with them, and they're at Maxim's, so all of his security is there too. I'm sure they're fine," Tony reassures, though his words do little to ease my concern.

Scanning through my social media feeds, I hope to find an update from either Natalie or Lana, but there have been no recent posts. I toy with the idea of reaching out to Charlotte but decide against it. She was upset enough when Alex and Natalie left in a hurry. I don't want to cause her any more distress. I'm sure Tony's right. Given Maxim's affiliations with the Russian Bratva and his extensive security, they're probably safer in Russia than they are in New York City.

Anthony

A QUICK GLANCE AT MY CELL CONFIRMS THAT MY UBER HAS just pulled up.Leo and I have to be at the airport in three hours. But I'm stuck at the restaurant meeting with the architect. We're ironing out the intricate details for the installation of wrought iron gates that will mark the entrance to our highly anticipated garden wedding venue.

However, our permits hit a snag. There were some bureaucratic hurdles dealing with logistical issues impeding our progress. My architect worked diligently to make the necessary adjustments to obtain the permits. He's here now reviewing the changes with me.

"Is there anything else you need from me?" I ask, my irritation thinly veiled.

"Your signature on the proposal," the architect replies, tapping a few screens on his tablet. "Here's the final design."

"And this will meet the city's requirements for the permit?" I seek confirmation.

"Yes, Mr. Genovese."

With a swift motion of my finger, I sign the screen. "I apologize for any abruptness. I have a flight to catch and am on a tight schedule."

"That's all I need from you at the moment," he acknowledges.

"Excellent. I'll be reachable via text if any issues arise."

"Safe travels," he bids farewell.

Me: I'm getting into the car now. We'll be there shortly.

Leopold: Perfect. I'll grab the bags and head down to the lobby.

The sluggish progress through Manhattan's bustling streets affords me plenty of time to peruse the detailed spreadsheet crafted by Emersyn, our newly hired wedding consultant. She's meticulous with her details, listing all the couples who are looking to celebrate their special day at the new venue.

It was Leopold's suggestion to hire someone to oversee this part of our business. It seems he was correct. Emersyn has appointments every two hours all weekend to show the space to interested couples. Our venue is in high demand, with bookings likely extending well into the upcoming year.

Italiano Desiderio is the culmination of years' worth of dreams and hard work. After Kam died, I almost walked away from it. Let it die with him. But as I healed, I rediscovered my purpose and passion. The restaurant served as my sanctuary, the place where I could still feel close to Kam on the days the pain of his loss seemed too much to bear.

Leopold has thrived here, as well. In those early days, bussing tables, although a menial job, was a means for him to find direction—something to help give him a purpose in life when he didn't have one. But as time went on, and he found healing, his charm and charisma captivated diners. Promoting him to a full-time host was a natural progression. From there, he earned a college degree, and now he helps me run the business.

Today, this restaurant embodies not just my dream but Leopold's as well. So, why do I feel so unsettled lately?

It all stems from my recent discussion with Mrs. Wilson about her wish to move to Florida to be with her son and his family and her resignation from being unable to sell the bed and breakfast. I haven't been able to stop thinking about Northmeadow, the serenity of the lake, or the quaint yet failing inn. I'm hoping this second trip is what's needed to dispel these nagging thoughts. After all, our life is here, not in Northmeadow.

When the car is a block away, I text Leo.

Me: We're about to turn onto our street.

Leopold: I'll be outside.

Several hours later, we find ourselves back at the bed and breakfast. This time, the lot is not as empty as before. Two other cars are already parked there, hinting at the presence of other guests.

"It looks like there's some other people here," Leo points out, nodding towards the other cars in the parking lot. "Mrs. Wilson must be thrilled."

"I'm sure she is," I reply, noting the increased activity with a smile.

With our bags in hand, we make our way to the entrance, where Mrs. Wilson greets us warmly.

"Good afternoon, boys," Mrs. Wilson beams as she rounds the desk to greet us.

"How are you?" I ask, giving her a friendly kiss on the cheek.

"No use complaining," she says with a grin. "How was your flight?"

"Uneventful," Leo responds.

"I'm told those are the best kinds, she replies and turns to me. "Tony, dear, I have a favor to ask."

"What is it?"

"Would you be willing to make that haddock dish for dinner tonight? There are two other couples here this weekend, and I hate to admit this," she confesses, casting a cautious glance around. "I haven't been able to get the stuffing to taste the same as when you made it.""I'd be delighted to," I assure Mrs. Wilson.

"Do you mind if I stayed and watched? Maybe I can figure out what I'm doing wrong," she inquires, her eyes reflecting a mix of curiosity and determination.

"Of course. I can walk you through it if you'd like," I offer, eager to assist.

"That would be wonderful." She retreats behind her desk. "Let's get you checked in so you can get yourselves settled. I put you boys in the same room. Is that okay?"

"That's perfect," I reply with a smile.

After we get the key, Leo and I start the walk upstairs.

"I'm jealous, Master," Leo remarks with a soft laugh.

"Jealous?" I echo, raising an eyebrow.

"I'm pretty certain Mrs. Wilson was flirting with you," Leo pouts playfully.

"I know the perfect cure for jealousy," I tease, turning the key in the lock to our room. "Take your clothes off and get on the bed, ass in the air, so I can remind you why there's no need for such feelings."

Leo wastes no time, dropping his bag to the floor and kicking off his shoes with casual ease. Then, he indulges in a tantalizing striptease, shedding his clothes with deliberate sensuality, piece by piece.

As Leo gradually reveals more of his skin, I find myself mesmerized by the canvas of his body. Over the past few years, he's gotten several more tattoos. But none hold the same significance to me as the phoenix rising from the flames gracing his back.

He used my sketches for the wax art I created on him from our first scene and had it recreated into something permanent. To know he chose to immortalize that memory upon his skin still leaves me breathless and fills me with a profound sense of connection.

He saunters by me, and his fingers dance lightly over the bulge in my pants. I'm transfixed as he seductively crawls onto the bed, lowering his face to the mattress and baring himself to me. I waste no time grabbing the lube from my bag and opening my pants to free my erection.

"There will never be anyone else for me," I breathe, my voice laden with desire as I enter him. "Every damn breath I take is for you," I gasp as I thrust into him.

"I love being yours, Master," he whispers, his voice laced with devotion.

"Say it again," I demand.

"You own every piece of me, Master," he exhales, his words heavy with desire. "Take me. Use my body for your pleasure," he pleads, his tone submissive yet eager.

His words ignite a primal need within me, a desire I hadn't realized was there. I grab his hips firmly, knowing my fingers will leave a mark—my mark, a testament to my ownership. I pound into him relentlessly, ensuring he feels every inch of me. I crave the sensation of claiming every part of him as my own. Leo's moans turn into screams, his fingers clawing at the sheets as he eagerly pushes back against me.

"That's right, Leopold. Let me hear how much you love your Master's cock in your ass," I growl.

"Yes, Master. I do," he moans, his voice a mix of pleasure and desperation.

I slam into him, the force causing our bodies to collide, our skin slapping together. My orgasm builds as he begs for more, his words fueling my desire. Reaching around, I grab his hard length, pumping fast. "You're going to come for me while I fill your ass."

Leo tenses as he climaxes, his ass clenching around my cock, driving me over the edge. "Fuck," I roar, the intensity of the moment over-whelming.

I pull out and collapse on the bed next to him, my chest heaving with exertion.

"Is it always like this?" Leo asks, his voice laced with awe.

I know what he's asking but not saying.

"No," I reply without hesitation. "It's never felt like this with anyone." I prop myself up on my arm, meeting Leopold's gaze. "I want to spend forever with you. Make me the happiest man ever, and marry me."

Leo's eyes widen in disbelief. "What did you say?"

"I want you to share my life. My last name. I want you to marry me."

"Oh my God, yes." He pulls me close, his legs straddling my waist as he leans down, his lips meeting mine. "Yes," he says between kisses. "A million times, yes."

After a refreshing shower where we both have another mind-blowing orgasm, Leo and I make our way downstairs, eager to find Mrs. Wilson and start the dinner preparations.

Leopold

Lost in a whirlwind of emotions, I find myself grappling with the reality of the moment. Tony asked me to marry him, and I said yes. For so long, I doubted whether Tony truly wanted marriage, whether he saw a future with me beyond our Dom/sub dynamic. Now, as I bask in the glow of his proposal, those doubts feel like distant echoes. I have a fiancé. I'm engaged. It's a surreal realization, one that fills me with a mixture of joy, disbelief, and excitement. How did I get here? How is this my life? Every dream I never dared to entertain is suddenly within reach, coming true in ways I never imagined possible.

As I drift through the haze of my daydream, I'm vaguely aware of Tony's presence nearby, his voice mingling with the sound of Mrs. Wilson's laughter as he guides her through the process of making his famous crab meat stuffing. Their conversation drifts in and out of my consciousness, overshadowed by the magnitude of the moment. Yet, even as I revel in the euphoria of our engagement, a part of me remains grounded in the simple beauty of this ordinary moment – the clinking of utensils, the aroma of spices in the air, and the warmth of companionship shared in a cozy kitchen.

"Did you say you were coming in for Natalie's bridal shower this weekend?" Mrs. Wilson asks.

"Some of Alex's family lives in Russia," Tony explains, his tone tinged with understanding. "They wanted to celebrate with both families, so they're currently there with them, and they're going to reschedule the shower here."

"Oh, that's very nice," Mrs. Wilson replies, her expression softening.

"Yes, it is," Tony agrees, with a hint of warmth in his voice.

It's been over a month since I last spoke with Natalie. My mind swirls with all sorts of unsettling scenarios about what could be happening, but I choose to keep those thoughts to myself. I can only hope that Maxim is as powerful as Svetlana claims and that whatever's going on, he's keeping them safe.

"How serious were you when you said you've considered selling so you could move to be with your family?" Tony inquires, steering the conversation in a new direction.

"Why do you ask?" She sets her knife down, her expression curious.

"If you're serious about selling, I'm serious about buying and keeping Water's Edge open," Tony declares.

My head snaps up in surprise. I had no idea he was considering purchasing this place.

"Are you joking with me?" she asks, her tone incredulous.

"No, ma'am. The last time I was here, I fell in love with this place. I haven't been able to stop thinking about it," Tony responds earnestly.

"And how do you feel about this, Leo?" she asks, turning to me.

"Leo and—"

"Being here and operating a bed and breakfast together is a dream we share," I reply, my gaze shifting between Tony and Mrs. Wilson.

"We understand this is a lot to process at all once," Tony adds diplomatically.

"Like you, I, too, haven't stopped thinking about our conversation the past few weeks," she says, smiling. "If you didn't bring this up, I was going to."

"Really?" Tony asks, visibly surprised.

"I spoke to my son, and he thinks it's a great idea," she confirms.

"Don't feel you have to make any decision today," Tony reassures.

"Right now," she says, pointing at the clock on the wall. "We need to get this food made, or our guests will start getting rowdy. Before you leave, we'll discuss numbers."

"It's a date," Tony agrees, nodding.

The dining room is alive with chatter and laughter as Mrs. Wilson's guests relish the delicious meal. Tony reclines in his seat, a grin of satisfaction tugging at his lips as he observes her enjoying the praise.

As we linger over coffee and dessert, my phone vibrates on the table, signaling an incoming text.

Natalie: We're back in New York.

Me: Where in the world have you been?

Natalie: It's a long story, one that I can't get into on a text.

Me: I've been so worried about you. Are you okay?

Natalie: I am.

The following notification brings with it a picture. My breath catches as I open it.

"Is everything okay?" Tony inquires, and I turn the screen toward him. He leans in closer before asking, "Whose ultrasound is that?"

"Natalie's," I reply, barely containing my excitement. "She just texted me that they're back in New York."

"I'm glad they're home," he says, relief evident in his tone. "Send my congratulations."

Me: OMG, I'm going to be an uncle! Congratulations!

Natalie: Thank you.

Me: I have news for you, too.

Natalie: Spill it. 😊

Me: Tony and I are engaged.

Natalie: Oh, Leo, I'm so happy for you!

Me: When can I see you?

Natalie: In a few weeks. I had some complications and am on bed rest.

Me: I'm just so glad you're safe and home.

Natalie: Me too. We'll talk soon. Love ya. <3

Putting away my phone, a sense of relief washes over me, knowing Natalie's safe, allowing me to fully engage in the conversation at the table.

As I reflect on my response to Mrs. Wilson's question from earlier in the kitchen, I realize I hadn't given it much thought. All I knew was that if running this place was Tony's dream, then it would be something I would support. However, at this moment, as I sit here sharing a meal with individuals who were strangers mere hours ago, I come to the profound realization that this dream belongs to me just as much as it does to Tony.

Perhaps this is why I felt drawn to earn my degree in Hospitality Management. I thoroughly enjoy my role as host at *Italiano Desiderio* and working alongside Tony in the restaurant. I also know I'm not fully utilizing the skills and knowledge I've acquired.

The idea of us owning a bed and breakfast, both of us putting all of our skills to use, excites me to no end.The prospect of managing both a restaurant in New York City and a bed and breakfast in Northmeadow, Missouri, seems daunting. But I have every confidence that we'll navigate the challenges together and make it work.

Leopold

The past several months have been a rollercoaster of emotions. After we returned from our trip to Northmeadow, I learned the truth about what Alex does with Maxim Solonik—a revelation that shook me to my core.

Svetlana revealed she had an older sister, Jelena. Years ago, when Svetlana was a little girl, Jelena was kidnapped and sold to traffickers. Despite Maxim's connections in the Bratva, he wasn't able to save his daughter. Since then, he's assembled a network of individuals around the world who work on busting trafficking rings. Alex uses his marketing firm as a cover, helping relay covert messages for Maxim.

A data breach in Alex's company sent them to Maxim's safe house in Russia. While they were there, Natalie found out she was pregnant, but she needed to leave the safety of Maxim's compound to see a doctor. Even though Maxim took every precaution, she and Alex were taken by a trafficker. They were brought to Mexico, where they were tortured for weeks. Thankfully, Viktor was able to find them and get them back safely. The trafficker—I'm told he's no longer breathing.

After nearly losing each other, Alex's perspective on life seemed to shift. He didn't want to wait any longer to get married. He, along with everyone's help, planned a surprise wedding at their cottage. Seeing my bestie get her happily ever after with the love of her life was nothing short of breathtaking.

They exchanged their vows with the backdrop of the sun setting behind the lake. The love radiating between them was palpable, filling the air with a sense of hope and promise for the future.

While we were there, Tony and I took a leap of faith. With only Charlotte privy to our secret, we signed papers taking ownership of Water's Edge Bed and Breakfast. Mrs. Wilson agreed to stay on for one more summer, giving us the breathing room needed to plan our next steps. There are a lot of logistical decisions we have to make. Managing businesses in both Manhattan and Missouri will undoubtedly pose challenges, but we're prepared to tackle them together.

For the next few weeks, we're putting all of those concerns aside so we can celebrate the holidays with our friends and loved ones.

Anthony

From childhood, we're taught to believe in the myth of 'happily ever after,' a fictional construct woven into the fabric of fairy tales. It's a beguiling fantasy that whispers sweet promises, enticing us to chase after an unattainable ideal.

It makes us wish for—believe in something that isn't possible.

The reality is that life is unforgiving and unpredictable. The childhood dream of "happily ever after' is an elusive dream that will forever be out of reach.

This past week brought with it the heavy burden of hosting another memorial service at *Italiano Desiderio*. I'm tired of saying goodbye to loved ones who were taken from us too soon, their untimely departures leaving behind a trail of shattered hearts.

The restaurant that was once a place of joy has become a haunting reminder of loss and sorrow. Stepping into the restaurant, I am met with an oppressive weight that threatens to suffocate me.

"I can't do this anymore," I confess, my voice heavy with resignation, as I pull up Charlie, my realtor's contact.

The phone rings several times before he answers.

"This is Charlie. How can I help you?" he answers professionally.

"Charlie, this is Tony Genovese," I identify myself.

"Mr. Genovese, how are you?" Charlie greets me warmly.

"I'm well," I respond mechanically.

"What can I do for you?" Charlie prompts, sensing the seriousness in my tone.

"I want to put my restaurant on the market," I state firmly.

A long pause follows, hanging in the air like a weight.

"That wasn't what I was expecting to hear," Charlie admits, his surprise evident.

"It's time for a change," I reply, trying to maintain composure. "When can we meet to get the process started?

After arranging to meet next week, I end the call, knowing I have to face the daunting task of telling Leo when I get home.

"You're home early," Leo says, peering over his laptop screen.

"We need to talk," I announce.

"I can't take any more bad news," he groans as he closes his computer and sets it aside.

"I want to get married. Right away," I announce. "As soon as we can."

"I'd like that too," Leo agrees.

"You don't care if we skip the big wedding?"

"Where's all this coming from?" Leo asks, concern lacing his voice.

"If the past few weeks have taught me anything, it's that we're not guaranteed a tomorrow. If there's something we want to do, we can't wait," I explain.

Leo searches my face, and I know he sees I'm not done. "What else?"

I take a deep breath. "I called Charlie, my realtor. I'm putting the restaurant on the market. I want to focus our attention on running the B&B." Leo's quiet for too long. "Say something, please."

"Wow. That's a lot," Leo responds, swiping a hand over his mouth. "Where are we going to live?"

"Northmeadow."

"I need a minute to process all this," he says, standing up and walking over to the window. "I figured that's where we'd eventually end up. But I didn't think it would happen so soon."

"I didn't either," I admit, going to him and wrapping my arms around his waist. Leo leans against my chest. "After everything that's happened, I just can't do it anymore. I can't breathe when I'm in the restaurant. There are too many sad memories here," I explain, my voice cracking with emotion. "I want a fresh start for us as a married couple. I want a home that only holds memories of you and me." Leo turns in my arms. "Unless you don't want that."

"I want you, Master," Leo says, enveloping me in his arms. "Wherever you are is my home." He leans in, pressing his lips against mine. "And we'll fill that home with nothing but love."

"Yes," I murmur, gently resting my forehead against his. "With nothing but love and happiness."

Leopold

✦

THE PAST FEW DAYS STRETCHED ON ENDLESSLY AS I anxiously awaited the moment when Tony and I would make our way to the city clerk's office for our civil ceremony. Now, at last, we're stepping through the doors with Star and Owen, our accomplices in this clandestine affair.

We're guided to a modest room and informed that the clerk will join us momentarily.

"Can you believe we're about to get married?" Tony's voice carries a mix of excitement and disbelief.

I don't get a chance to answer because there's a knock on the door a second before it opens. "Mr. Genovese and Mr. Wagner?"

"That's us," Tony responds, rising from his seat.

"I'm Mr. Lewis," he introduces himself and shakes our hands. "I'll be conducting your ceremony today. Are you ready to get started?" he asks, his gaze shifting between us.

"We are," we both answer in unison, our voices filled with nervous anticipation.

"We're gathered together to celebrate the marriage of Anthony Genovese and Leopold Wagner. If there's anyone who knows of any reason this couple can't be legally married, please speak now." He looks between Star and Owen, giving them a chance to object before continuing, "Perfect. I was told you've written your own vows."

"Yes, we have," Tony confirms.

"Mr. Genovese, would you like to go first."

"From the moment we first met," Tony begins, his voice filled with warmth and affection. "I knew there was something special about you. Something that called to the deepest recesses of my heart and soul. Together, we've weathered storms that would've shattered lesser souls," he continues, his eyes never leaving mine. "We've laughed, we've cried, we've celebrated, and we've mourned, but through it all, one thing has remained constant—our love for each other."

"Leopold, you're my greatest blessing," Tony says, his voice soft and tender. "In you, I've found my soul's true counterpart, my perfect match in every way. With you, I've discovered a love that transcends time and space, a love that knows no bounds and only grows stronger with each passing day. I promise to nurture and cultivate this love," Tony pledges, his gaze filled with adoration. "To water its roots with patience and understanding as it continues to blossom in the years to come."

"I vow to cherish and honor you. I promise to be your unwavering support, your constant companion, and your greatest ally. I vow to be your confidant, your shoulder to lean on, and your safe harbor in the storm. I'll celebrate your victories and share in your sorrows as though they were mine own. I pledge to listen to you with an open heart," Tony promises, his words filled with sincerity. "To communicate with honesty and kindness, and to always treat you with the utmost respect and tenderness."

"Together, we'll build a life filled with laughter, adventure, and unwavering devotion. We'll create a home," Tony says, his eyes shining with love. "That's a sanctuary for our souls, a place where we can always find solace and comfort in each other's arms."

"Leopold," Tony whispers, his voice filled with love and longing. "You're my heart, my soul, and my everything. I'm grateful beyond words for the love we share and for the opportunity to spend the rest of my days loving and being loved by you. Today, I give you not only my vows but also my heart, my hand, and my eternal devotion. I give you not only my love but also my commitment to always strive to be the best husband I can be."

"I promise to learn and grow alongside you, to support your dreams and aspirations, and to stand by you as we navigate the highs and lows of life's journey. I'll treasure every moment we share together," Tony promises, his voice filled with emotion. "Knowing that our love is a precious gift that must be cherished and nurtured each and every day. With you, I've found my home and my happiness. I love you now and always."

With a steadying breath, I center myself before reciting my vows.

"Tony," I say, my voice trembling with emotion. "As I stand here on the threshold of forever with you, my heart overflows with gratitude and love. In your eyes, I see the reflection of a love that has transformed my life in ways I never thought possible."

"In your presence," I continue, my gaze locking with his. "I feel a sense of peace and contentment that I've never known before. It's as if the chaos of the world fades away. You're my refuge, my anchor in the storm. You're a warm embrace, wrapping around me and filling me with a sense of security and belonging. It's in your eyes that I find home, in your smile that I find hope, and in your touch that I find healing."

"In your love, I find a strength that empowers me to face life's challenges with courage and grace. With you, I feel empowered to embrace my true self," I murmur, feeling my heart swell with emotion. "To embrace my flaws and imperfections, knowing that you love me all the more for them. Your love gives me the courage to be vulnerable, to let down my walls and share my deepest fears and insecurities, knowing that you'll always be there to catch me when I fall."

"You've taught me the true meaning of love," I reflect, my words carrying a depth of understanding. "It's a love that's patient, allowing us to grow and evolve at our own pace, never rushing or demanding, but always understanding and accepting. It's a love that's kind, showing compassion and empathy even in the face of adversity, always choosing understanding over judgment, forgiveness over resentment. And it's a love that's selfless, putting the needs and desires of the other before our own, sacrificing without hesitation, and giving without expecting anything in return."

"Tony," I say, my voice filled with love and reverence. "You're my rock, my confidant, and my greatest love. You are my heart's desire. My true north. The love of my life and my partner in all things. Today, I give you my heart, my soul, and my unwavering devotion."

Finally, I whisper, "I promise to love you fiercely. To honor you deeply and to cherish every moment we share together. To support you in all that you do and to walk hand in hand with you through the journey of life. I am blessed beyond measure to call you my husband."

"As a symbol of your promise, please place your ring on Leopold's finger," Mr. Lewis instructs, his voice steady and solemn.

Tony gently slides the platinum band over my ring finger, his touch warm and reassuring.

Mr. Lewis then turns to me. "As a symbol of your promise, please place your ring on Anthony's finger."

My hand trembles slightly as I carefully slide Tony's matching platinum band onto his finger, our eyes locked in a moment of profound connection.

"In as much as you both have consented, by the power vested in me by the State of New York, I now pronounce you married. You may kiss."

Tony takes a step closer to me, anticipation evident in his gaze. Our lips meet in a tender yet passionate kiss as Owen and Star erupt into applause and cheers.

"I love you, Leopold Genovese," Tony whispers against my lips.

"And I love you, my husband," I reply, my heart overflowing with joy and love.

Anthony

If you asked me ten years ago if I'd ever be a married man, I probably would've told you that you were crazy. Yet, here I am walking out of the City Clerk's office holding Leopold's—my husband's hand, I've never been happier.

"There's something I didn't tell you," I admit.

"Oh?" Leo raises an eyebrow inquisitively.

"I rented a cozy cottage on Lake Ontario for our honeymoon," I reveal, hoping he'll share my excitement.

"That sounds wonderful," Leo's smile widens. "When do we leave?"

"Tonight," I reply, a sense of anticipation tingling in the air between us.

Following our wedding ceremony, we celebrate by having a leisurely lunch with Star and Owen. Their unwavering friendship and support have been a constant in our relationship. It only feels fitting to have them share in the joy of our special day.

Now that the vows have been exchanged and we're officially married, we take the opportunity to spread the news by sending out text messages to our friends and family with pictures from the ceremony.

Me: Surprise! Leopold and I are overjoyed to announce that we're now officially married!

The soft hum of the small plane's engines fades as we touch down in Rochester, signaling the beginning of our honeymoon. As we step onto the tarmac, the late afternoon sun envelops us in its warm embrace. With the rental car ready and waiting, we set out on the winding roads that lead us further from the populated town and closer to our secluded haven. Finally, we arrive at our destination—a cozy cabin perched on the shores of Lake Ontario.

"How did you find this place?" Leo asks as we gather our bags from the trunk.

"Keirnan, a friend of mine from Fire and Ice Hamptons, owns it," I explain. "They only rent it to club members." With a cautionary tone, I add, "Fair warning. There's a lot of bondage equipment in here that we won't be using."

Leo's unexpected question catches me off guard. "What would you say if I wanted to try it?"

"Bondage?" I ask, taken aback.

"Yes."

I swipe the key card, and the front door unlocks. "Let's see what you think when we go inside."

Leo's gaze sweeps across the main room of the cabin, taking in every detail of the seductive décor with a mix of intrigue and fascination. His fingers trace the intricate stitching of the red leather tantra chaise.

A smile plays on my lips as I imagine Leo reclining on it, bathed in the soft glow of candlelight, his body relaxed and inviting. We're lost in a world of sensual pleasures, our bodies entwined in a dance of desire. I can almost feel the weight of Leo's touch, his hands trailing along my skin with a gentle yet insistent caress. I can taste the sweetness of Leo's lips as they meet mine, the heat of our passion building with each breathless sigh. The idea ignites a flicker of longing deep within me, but I quickly push it aside, focusing instead on giving Leo the freedom to explore at his own pace.

"How does this work?" he asks, his attention captured by a sleek black pole nestled in one corner of the room.

Wanting to give him space, I don't approach when I answer, "It's a restraining pole. There are countless positions to put a sub in," I explain. "The dildo, well, that's self-explanatory."

"I think I'd like to try that," Leo remarks before striding towards the bedroom door and disappearing inside. "Tony?"

"Yes, *cuore mio*?" I reply, closing the distance and positioning myself in the doorway.

"Why is there a cage under the bed?"

"Some Dominants use it for their submissive who craves bondage. Others use it for their human pets. We will not be using it," I state matter-of-factly.

He runs his hand over the spreader bar lying on the foot of the bed. On one side of the room, a black leather sex swing hangs from hooks in the ceiling. Across the room, leaning against the wall is a St. Andrews Cross. "That." Leo points. "Is a hard limit. I've seen Brandon do impact scenes with Lana. No. Just no."

"Fair," I reply, crossing my arms as I lean against the doorway.

A large oak armoire sits adjacent to the cross. Leo opens the doors, revealing a vast array of impact tools, sensory toys, travel containers of lube, and condoms. "Wow. This is a lot of stuff," he remarks before closing the doors.

"Yes, it is," I say as I advance towards Leo, each step deliberate. Reaching in, I pull out a silicone sleeve and a remote. "Are you up for trying something different?" I whisper.

"What are you suggesting, Master?"

Leopold

"Kiernan owns over a hundred acres. We can do what we want where we want, and no one will bother us," Tony explains, watching me closely. "I have a fantasy of knowing you're out there, exposed and being hunted by me."

A thrill shoots through me. "I like the sound of that."

"Tell me to stop, and I will," he reassures.

"Don't stop, Master," I reply, my heart racing at the promise of what's to come.

"Strip for me," Tony commands.

There's something in the tone of his voice and the hungry look in his eyes that awakens a part of me that seeks to be his prey. My hands tremble as I slowly remove my clothes. The cool air of the cabin caresses my skin as I stand before my Master, naked and vulnerable.

"Good boy," Tony purrs, his eyes drinking in every inch of my exposed body. He wraps the black silicone around my cock. It's a snug fit that sends a delicious shiver down my spine. "I can control this from anywhere," he explains. My cock twitches in response. "I'm going to give you a head start to find a hiding spot in the forest," he explains, his voice low and filled with lust. "Then I'm coming for you. Go now, Leopold. Run."

Without hesitation, I dart into the trees, the thrill of the hunt fueling my every step as I seek out the perfect hiding spot. My heart pounds at the thought of being chased through the forest by Tony. It doesn't take long for me to find a place that conceals me.

Now, I wait for Tony to find me.

Anthony

As I wait for Leo to get his head start, I can't help but feel a surge of excitement coursing through me. The anticipation of the chase, the thrill of the hunt, it all stirred something primal within him that I couldn't ignore.

With each passing moment, my anticipation grows, my senses tingling with the promise of adventure. Outside, the sun dips below the horizon, casting a warm orange glow in the sky. The air is heavy with the scents of pine and earth. As I stand here, poised and ready to give chase, a surge of adrenaline courses through my veins, knowing this is unlike anything I've ever experienced before.

I move at a leisurely pace, my senses on high alert, attuned to every sound and movement around me. Each step I take brings me closer to my elusive prey, and I can't help but feel a surge of excitement at the prospect of finally catching him.

The forest is alive with activity, the air thick with the scents of pine and earth. I move with purpose through the dense foliage, my eyes scanning the shadows for any sign of movement. Every rustle of leaves, every snap of a twig, sets my heart racing with anticipation.

After what feels like an eternity, I finally catch sight of Leo's naked form pressed against a tree, but he doesn't see me yet. Reaching into my pocket, I press a button turning on the vibrations around his cock. He gasps from the sensation as he looks around. When he spots me, his eyes widen in anticipation. A predatory smile curves my lips as I close in on him, a primal energy coursing through my veins as I close the distance between us.

Without a word, I grab Leo's wrists and pin them above his head, holding him in place as I capture his lips in a heated kiss. Leo moans against my mouth, his body arching into my touch as our tongues tangle in a fierce dance of desire.

My free hand roams over Leopold's body, taking in every contour as I explore his form with reverence. Leo's breaths come in ragged gasps as my mouth trails down his neck, leaving a trail of heat in its wake. My teeth nip at his sensitive skin, causing him to cry out in pleasure.

"Turn around and bend over. Keep your hands on the tree," I order as desire surges through me.

Leopold's body quivers with anticipation as I open my pants, allowing my erection to spring free. Leaning in close, I ask. "Are you ready to be fucked by your husband?"

"Yes. Oh god, yes," he says through panting breaths.

Positioned behind him, I take my time, relishing the moment as I tease his entrance with feather-light touches. With a flick of my fingers, I turn up the intensity of the vibration as I ease inside him, sending a jolt of desire through both of us. The raw intensity of our connection takes over, and I begin thrusting into him.

"Fuck, Leo. I'm not going to last," I pant.

"Don't hold back, Master," Leo rasps, glancing over his shoulder. "Fill me. Use me."

My movements grow more forceful and possessive. With each thrust, I fall deeper into our shared desire. "You're mine in every way, Leopold," I grunt as I thrust into him. "Your collar bound your soul to me, and now our marriage seals that union."

"I'm yours," Leo repeats, his voice filled with conviction. "Only yours. Forever yours."

Our connection reaches a fevered pitch, and I feel an urge I've never experienced before—a need to mark Leopold as mine. Leaning over his back, I press my hot breath against his skin before sinking my teeth into his shoulder in a display of desire and ownership.

"Fuck," Leopold gasps at the sharp sensation, his pleasure mingling with pain. My fingers find the remote, and I turn the vibrations higher, adding another layer of stimulation.

Leo's gasp of desire and need fills the air, and my control falters. I release my raw, unbridled passion as I rut into him with a fierce urgency, igniting a fire that brings us closer to the brink.

As my climax approaches, Leopold's body tightens around mine. With a final thrust, I let go with a roar, succumbing to the overwhelming pleasure coursing through my body. Leo follows soon after, his cries of ecstasy mingling with mine and echoing through the trees.

I withdraw from Leo and remove the vibrator, slipping it into my pocket as we sink to the ground. Leopold's body is slick with sweat as I cradle him against me.

"I know this stretched your boundaries," I whisper, tracing my fingers along his spine. "You're so fucking brave."

"There was no fear because I knew it was you coming for me," Leo confesses. "I'm yours, Master. In whatever way you want me."

The stars above us shimmer with a radiant brilliance as we lie together, spent and breathless. The beauty of the night sky serves as a silent reminder of the bond that binds Leopold and I together. It's stronger and more powerful than anything I have ever known.

Leopold

THE SUN IS BEGINNING TO CAST ITS GOLDEN HUES OVER THE horizon, painting the sky with hues of pink and orange. Our week here is coming to an end. I can't help but feel a pang of regret that it's passed by so quickly, and I find myself cherishing the final moments of our honeymoon.

Beside me, Tony is still sleeping, his expression peaceful. Running my fingers through his now salt and pepper-colored locks, I'm struck by how age has only added to his allure, leaving me marveling at the passage of time.

"Good morning, *cuore mio*," he greets before even opening his eyes.

"Good morning, my husband," I reply with a smile, the endearment bringing a flutter to my heart.

"Did you sleep well?" he inquires, his fingers already finding their way through my hair as I rest my head on his chest.

"I had the most vivid dreams," I share, feeling the warmth of his embrace comforting me.

"About what?" he asks, his touch gentle and reassuring.

"A child. Our child—a son," I admit, the concept of having children together quietly taking root in my heart.

"Do you want to start a family, Leopold?" he asks, his voice filled with sincerity and longing.

"I'd love for us to have a child. Maybe more than one," I respond without hesitation, the thought bringing a sense of excitement and anticipation. "What about you?"

"Yes. I want to have children with you," he affirms, his gaze meeting mine with unwavering determination.

"How do we do it?" I inquire, curious about the practicalities of starting a family together.

"If we want a biological child, we can look for a surrogate," he suggests, his tone thoughtful and considerate.

"What about adoption? It's just an idea, but... do you think it's something we could explore?" I propose hesitantly, aware of the complexities involved but curious to see if he shares my willingness to explore non-traditional routes to parenthood.

"I think adoption would be a wonderful avenue to explore," he replies warmly, his words filling me with a sense of reassurance and possibility. "There are many children waiting for a family to love them, and we have a lot of love to give."

"Yes, Master. We do," I agree softly, my heart filled with love and determination.

"When we get back to the city, we'll look up an agency and get the process started," he promises, his words infused with a sense of purpose and determination as we embark on this new chapter together.

This week surpassed all of my expectations. Each moment has been an exploration of my soft limits. Tony approached each new experience with careful consideration. The bondage pole quickly became a favorite of mine. The sensation of being bound and helpless while knowing I could stop it at any second was an exhilarating experience. Tony already ordered one for our apartment.

At my urging, we tried using a blindfold, a seemingly innocuous piece of fabric that promised to heighten my senses and intensify the experience. However, as Tony gently secured it over my eyes, I found myself engulfed in a suffocating darkness that sent panic coursing through my veins. As soon as I uttered my safeword, Tony removed it and gathered me in his arms until my senses returned to normal.

I didn't think I could feel closer to him than when we arrived, but as the cabin door closes behind us, our bond is inexplicably stronger—unbreakable.

Leopold

MARCH 13

I've lost count of how many times we've flown back and forth between New York City and Missouri. Trying to juggle the responsibilities of running Italiano Desiderio and planning for a complete remodel of the bed and breakfast is exhausting.

One positive about spending time in Northmeadow is getting to spend more time with Charlotte. Currently, she's the only person in our circle who knows we've purchased Water's Edge. Her unwavering support has been invaluable as we navigate the complexities of our new endeavor.

I've had to stay behind in Northmeadow on several trips. Instead of allowing me to stay at the bed and breakfast alone, Charlotte insisted I stay with her and Stanley. They welcomed me into their home with open arms, immersing me in the rhythm of family life, from sharing meals around the kitchen table to watching movies together in the evening with a bowl of popcorn. It healed a part of the little boy Leopold, who desperately needed to feel the love of a Mom and Dad.

For Charlotte, my presence offers a chance at redemption, an opportunity to rewrite the narrative of motherhood. Despite her initial discomfort with my sexuality, she's embraced the journey of acceptance and understanding. She's found peace by willingly offering unconditional *love and acceptance to a 'son' who has embraced his identity as a gay man and who has chosen to love someone outside of her deeply ingrained beliefs.*

Our conversations about God, spirituality, and the meaning of love have been both challenging and enlightening, allowing us to navigate the complexities of our relationship with honesty and respect.

I even attended church with her as I tried to understand where her beliefs came from. It wasn't a particularly wonderful experience, as I was clearly unwelcome, but Charlotte didn't flinch. She proudly stood by my side in support and love. Through all of these experiences, we've found common ground and a deeper appreciation for each other's perspectives.

One particularly poignant moment etched itself into my heart when Charlotte brought me to Michael's grave, her eyes heavy with the weight of grief and loss as she introduced me to her son. As we sat in the cemetery, Charlotte shared stories of her beloved son. Through her words, she painted a vivid picture of his laughter, his quirks, and his dreams.

With each memory shared, I found myself feeling an unexpected connection to Michael, as if his spirit hovered nearby, reaching out to touch my own. It was a profound sensation, one that stirred a mixture of emotions within me—a sense of longing mingled with sadness for a life lost too soon.

Charlotte and I have formed a bond that goes beyond mere biology. We've discovered kindred spirits willing to extend unconditional love and support in a world that is often unkind and anything but predictable.

Things here in the city are also moving along. Several weeks ago, Tony received a call from Charlie, letting him know a full-price offer for Italiano Desiderio came in. Of course, Tony accepted it right away. If all goes well, the closing could be in as soon as two months.

In between the whirlwind of planning a move and navigating the intricacies of selling the restaurant, there's another crucial aspect of our lives that demands attention—the adoption process. From filling out mountains of paperwork to undergoing thorough home studies, it's been a painstakingly slow process, completing the necessary steps, but we're finally making progress.

Cora, our adoption worker, called several days ago to let us know she has information on waiting children for us. We'll be back in Manhattan tomorrow and plan to stop by her office on the way home from the airport. Everything suddenly feels so much more real.

Looking from the outside, one might think our lives, at the current moment, are in complete chaos. But do you want to know something? Despite the uncertainties and challenges that I'm certain await us, I'm not afraid.

I'm exceedingly happy and eager to embrace this next chapter in our lives.

Anthony

Due to tornado-producing storms sweeping across the country, our flight from Missouri faced delays, pushing our arrival time to an unfathomable four am. Despite the exhaustion, I managed to reach out to Cora, explaining our predicament and apologizing for missing our appointment. Thankfully, she understood our situation and kindly dropped off the sealed envelope containing information about waiting children at our building, ensuring we could review it at our convenience.

Despite our bubbling excitement, we made the mutual decision to prioritize a few hours of sleep before delving into the contents of the envelope. Recognizing the gravity of the moment, we wanted to approach it with clear minds and open hearts.

While Leo finishes making our coffee, I settle at the kitchen table, eyeing the envelope containing the children's pictures and information.

"Can you believe our future child is in that envelope?" Leo's voice is filled with a mix of wonder and disbelief.

"Yes and no," I admit as I carefully pull the stack of papers out of the manilla envelope. "It still feels surreal."

"How are we supposed to choose just one?" Leo's brows furrow in concern, and as he passes me my coffee mug, it slips from his grasp.

Reacting quickly, I shove the papers away, preventing them from being drenched in coffee.

"Are you okay?" Leo's immediate reaction is to ensure my well-being.

"I am," I reassure him, grabbing paper towels to help clean up.

"I didn't ruin any of the children's profiles, did I?" Leo's remorse is evident in his tone.

"Only the edge of the top one, but it's okay," I reply, offering him a reassuring smile.

Leo crouches down to pick up a fallen paper. "We dropped one," he remarks, lifting it from the floor and pausing to read it. "This is him." With a solemn expression, he hands it to me.

On the paper is a photo of a baby boy with dark hair and striking blue eyes.

Leo moves closer. "It says he was born at twenty-nine weeks to a drug-addicted mother," he murmurs, his voice tinged with sorrow. "He's too young to tell, but they suspect he'll have neurological problems because of it. He's the one, Tony."

My heart races as I fixate on the picture. "How do you know?" I manage to ask, my voice barely above a whisper.

"The same way I knew when I looked into your eyes the first time. My heart recognized yours," he murmurs, his voice gentle and sure.

Feeling overwhelmed, I choke out, "His birthday... September eleventh." A tear trails down my cheek, my voice thick with emotion. "I don't need to look through the other profiles, do you?"

"No, Master. This is our son," Leo declares, his voice steady and sure.

As soon as the clock strikes nine, we dial Cora with the phone on speaker. "We found him," I announce eagerly.

"That was fast," she remarks.

"Perhaps, but we knew the second we saw him," Leo adds confidently.

"What's the name and his number?" She asks, her tone almost callous, as if these aren't living, breathing children.

"It's baby boy September," I respond, noting the lack of a given name. "Number 36125."

"He's brand new on the waiting child list," she elaborates, her voice tinged with clinical detachment. "He was born preterm and went through withdrawal. There's no way to know the extent of any neurological disabilities he may have. Are you sure you want to take that risk?" she questions.

"Leopold and I are certain," I answer firmly. "What happens next?"

"I'll send your dossier to my contact in Columbia. It could take quite some time," she says matter-of-factly. "I'll be in touch when I have more information."

Anthony

I've been a bundle of nerves waiting to hear from Cora about the status of our potential adoption. Yesterday, I couldn't hold back any longer and called her. She informed me there's a backlog on the Colombian end, and it could be upwards of six to eight months before we hear anything.

Leopold and I will be leaving New York to relocate permanently to the lake in two weeks. While the idea of raising a child in the city holds its own appeal, we're both eager for the slower pace of life that awaits us at the lake, a setting we believe will be more conducive to raising a child. Knowing our apartment will always be here provides comfort, allowing us the flexibility to return and stay whenever we feel the need.

While we were in Northmeadow a few months ago, we consulted with an architect regarding some major renovations for the building. Since we'll be living there full-time, we need to have a private living space. The architect proposed an extension to the current structure. Alongside modernizing all the plumbing and wiring, we're also installing an elevator to ensure the entire property is accessible to guests with varying abilities.

We're completely overhauling the third floor, which currently consists of six smaller rooms and two shared bathrooms. Our vision is to transform this space into two spacious, soundproof suites, each equipped with its own private bathroom. Additionally, we're customizing these rooms with BDSM furniture, catering to guests seeking a kinkier vacation.

We have an extensive list of renovations planned, including paving the parking lot and planting flowering dogwood trees to line the edges. The building, with its current log cabin appearance, is a bit misleading —I've discovered that the logs are actually manufactured and serve as a façade. We're opting for a more authentic look by replacing them with cedar siding.

Our wraparound porch, already a striking feature, will undergo enhancements. We're installing large, southern-style fans to amplify its charm, and custom-made rockers will offer the perfect spot for guests to relax. The built-in stone planters, a nod to Mr. Wilson's memory, will continue to grace the porch, overflowing with vibrant flowers to add a touch of natural beauty.

Leopold and I approached Charlotte with the idea of her joining us in this venture. Her enthusiastic acceptance was a welcomed relief. Since then, she's been an indispensable asset, helping to oversee the ongoing renovations while we're in New York and assisting us in selecting new linens and décor for the rooms. When we're ready to re-open, she plans to continue her involvement, transitioning to a part-time role to ensure the smooth operation of our establishment.

As I look ahead to the future, I'm filled with excitement at every-thing that lies ahead. However, before I can fully embrace it, I must navigate the emotional hurdle of informing my staff that I'll be stepping down as the owner of *Italiano Desiderio* by the end of the month.

While I try to reassure myself that this announcement will be straightforward, deep down, I know it will stir up a mix of emotions. Yet, amidst the uncertainty, I'm filled with an overwhelming sense of peace that accompanies the decisions Leopold and I have made together.

Tonight has been unusually busy for a weeknight. We had patrons lingering until half an hour past our usual closing time. The staff is well aware that we'll be holding a brief team meeting as soon as the last of our guests clear out. Additionally, I've asked the off-duty staff to join us for this important announcement.

"Master," Leo announces as he strides into the office. "We're ready for you." Seeing my hesitation, he gently closes the door and approaches me. "Are you having second thoughts?"

"No," I admit, my gaze fixed on the distant horizon outside. "But leaving behind the memories that led me to sell... it's harder than I anticipated."

"Memories don't get left behind. They journey with us wherever we go," Leo murmurs softly, his hand resting over my heart. "Kameron will always be with you. Right here."

"How is it that my love for Kameron has never bothered you?" I ask, turning to face him.

Leaning against the desk, Leo meets my gaze. "I could never be jealous of the relationship and bond you shared with Kameron. Your love for him is why you can love me so deeply."

Drawing him closer, I embrace him, feeling his heartbeat against mine. "Do you know how much I love you, *cuore mio*?"

"I do," Leo replies, his lips meeting mine in a tender kiss.

"Let's go share the news," I suggest, intertwining our fingers as we leave the office to address the staff.

Anthony

Leo's disappointment at missing the restaurant closing today is palpable as we said goodbye earlier. Before we had the closing date, Star asked him to speak at today's submissive training class, a responsibility he's grown fond of. He was going to back out, but I encouraged him to go ahead, knowing how much he values these opportunities to share his knowledge and experience. It's moments like these that make leaving Manhattan bittersweet.

As I pull open the door to my attorney's office, my stomach churns with nerves. Today marks the moment I'll sign the papers and hand over the keys to the new owner of *Italiano Desiderio.*

"Tony, wait," Leo's voice calls out, and I turn to see him running down the street.

"What are you doing here?" I ask, surprised.

"Something told me I needed to be here," he explains breathlessly. "I apologized to Star, but I couldn't miss this."

"Thank you, *cuore mio,*" I say, thankful to have my husband by my side.

"Good afternoon," William, the receptionist, greets us as we enter the office. "Can I get you both something to drink?"

"Coffees would be wonderful," I reply.

"If you want to come with me, I'll take you to the conference room," he offers.

"Thank you."

"Tony. Leo." our attorney says, joining us in the hallway. We exchange handshakes. "This is a big day. Are you ready?"

I glance at Leopold, who offers me a reassuring smile. "We are."

"Let's do it, then," he says, opening the door to reveal Charlie and three other men seated at the table. "Thank you for your patience, gentlemen," he adds as we take our seats. "This is Brett Neilson, counsel for the buyer, Cassius Williams, and this is Christopher Young, the young man who's about to be a new restaurateur."

"Good to meet you all," I reply.

"We have a lot of paperwork to get through. Let's get started," our attorney suggests as William hands me my coffee.

For the past hour, I've observed Christopher Young, racking my brain to figure out why he looks so familiar, yet I'm drawing a blank. Finally, I interject, breaking the silence. "I have to ask," I address Christopher directly. "What inspired you to buy my restaurant?"

"You don't recognize me, do you?" the young man inquires.

"I feel like I should," I respond, my mind racing to place him.

"We first formally met about ten years ago in a courtroom," he reveals, and suddenly, the memories come flooding back.

"Levi Young?" I whisper, the realization dawning on me.

"Yes, Sir," he confirms with a nod. "Although since then, I've legally changed my name to Christopher Young. It was my middle name."

"Tell me about you," I inquire, genuinely curious to learn more about him and what has transpired in his life since our last encounter in the courtroom.

"You didn't come back after recess," he begins, his voice laced with emotion. "That day changed my life. The judge explained that, given the nature of the crime, she was prepared to sentence me to jail time. But after hearing you speak, she had a change of heart." He pauses, his eyes reflecting the weight of his words. "I was sentenced to five hundred hours of community service. That's where I met Cass." Christopher motions to the man beside him, his gesture filled with gratitude. "Cass is a chef who also volunteers at the kitchen."

"The director of the kitchen knows my history," Cass begins, his voice heavy with the weight of his past. "So when he found out that Christopher was being court-appointed to our kitchen, he asked me to keep an eye on him." His gaze flickers to Christopher, a mixture of empathy and gratitude in his eyes.

"I was raised in Chicago by a single mom who was too busy whoring herself out for her next fix," he explains, his words raw with pain. "My older brother was involved with a gang, and I wanted to be just like him. By the time I was thirteen, I was a regular in juvie. When I was sixteen, I found myself on trial for involuntary manslaughter."

Christopher places a supportive hand on Cass's shoulder, silently urging him to continue.

"I got myself in way over my head," Cass continues, his tone somber, laden with remorse. "My girlfriend had just had our baby. She was killed in a drive-by." His words hang in the air, weighted with grief. "Being young and stupid, I didn't think when the guys asked me to drive. We stopped at a house. They went in and shot the place up and used me as the getaway driver."

"How did you end up in New York?" Leopold inquires, his tone gentle yet probing.

"The judge had some connections and had me transferred to a maximum-security juvenile center here in the city rather than sending me to an adult facility," Cass explains, a sense of gratitude evident in his voice. "That action, I'm certain, is what saved me. While I was there, I received counseling and an education. That's how I got involved in culinary arts."

"What happened to your baby?" I inquire, eager to understand more about Cass's journey.

"After I got out, I was on probation for two years. I got a job and a place to live and fought to get visitation with Zuri, my little girl," he shares, pride evident in his voice. "CPS helped me get parenting classes, and eventually, I earned full custody of her. "A few years later, I met Tasmin, the love of my life. We married, and she legally adopted Zuri.""

"That's an incredible story," I respond, moved by his resilience and determination.

"Cass is eternally patient," Christopher reflects, his voice filled with gratitude, his eyes shimmering with emotion. "I wasn't the easiest to deal with at first, but Cass came back day in and day out. He waited patiently until I stopped acting like an ass," he chuckles softly. "Then, he and Tasmin petitioned the court to allow me to move into their home rather than stay in the youth shelter. He and Tamsin went above and beyond, stepping in as the parents I never had. They made sure I went to school every day and graduated from high school," he continues, his tone reverent. "That's when I decided to go to the Culinary Institute of America."

"Mr. Genovese," Christopher says, his gaze meeting mine with sincerity. "I never forgot what you said that day." His words hit me like a tidal wave, causing a lump to form in my throat and tears to well in my own eyes. "I'm not perfect, but each day I've tried to make a positive difference, no matter how small, in the world around me. It's what Zuri and I have taught our little girls to do as well."

"Zuri?" I falter, my voice betraying a mix of shock and disbelief as I look between the men.

"I fell in love with his daughter and married her," Christopher reveals, his tone filled with emotion. "We have two little girls. Isla just turned three, and Seraphina is ten months old." With a gentle motion, he lifts his phone and extends it to me.

I blink back tears as I study the image of Christopher, his wife, and their daughters. "You have a beautiful family."

"Thank you," Christopher responds, his voice cracking with emotion. "I was worried about how you'd react when you found out it was me buying your restaurant. I hoped you wouldn't reconsider the sale."

"Backing out hasn't even crossed my mind," I declare, my voice steady despite the emotional weight of the moment. "I firmly believe that what we often perceive as chaos and confusion is just a part of a larger, unfolding story. When it feels like I'm stumbling in the dark, I've learned to be still," I say, intertwining my fingers with Leo's. "To wait for the unseen force that guides my next steps." I cast a meaningful glance between Leopold, Cassius, and Christopher. "Every joyous moment, heartache, and twist serves a purpose. As long as we allow it, fate will ensure we reach our perfect destination."

The room falls into a momentary silence as I gather my thoughts. "I don't know by what stroke of fate you learned that my restaurant was for sale," I begin, my voice carrying a mix of awe and respect. "But I do know that you are the one who's been raised up for this time. I'm proud to know that you're the man who's destined to carry on the legacy of *Italiano Desiderio*," I say, feeling a swell of gratitude and admiration for the determined young man seated across from me.

Christopher pushes his chair back and circles the table until he stands before me. I rise, and he reaches out, pulling me into a tight embrace. "Thank you, Mr. Genovese," he says, his voice trembling with gratitude. "Thank you for seeing something in me—for believing in me when no one else did."

"It's been an honor, Christopher Young," I reply, my voice thick with emotion.

As I hand over the key, a sense of bittersweet emotion washes over me, mingling with the tears that threaten to spill. In our tearful exchange, there's a sense of comfort in the promises we make to stay present in each other's lives.

As Leopold and I stepped into the conference room earlier today, I never anticipated that the buyer would hold any particular importance. It never occurred to me that it might be someone from my past, especially not the boy who left a lasting impression on me all those years ago.

Over the years, I revisited the image of that boy from years ago, hoping he had found his way in the world. To now stand face-to-face with the man Christopher Young has become fills me with profound awe. Knowing that I played even a small part in shaping his journey touches me deeply.

Leopold

Tony and I have been living in Northmeadow permanently for a little over a month. The renovations to the bed and breakfast are finally complete. With Charlotte's help, we've managed to decorate and furnish the guest rooms and central areas of the bed and breakfast. Our private living area is still a work in progress.

Despite all the unscheduled trips to Missouri, we managed to keep our ownership of Water's Edge a secret from Natalie and Alex, one that will be revealed this weekend.

Charlotte extended invitations to everyone under the guise of celebrating Natalie's birthday, which we will do. However, nestled within the festivities, we've prepared a couple of surprises of our own to share with our guests.

Tonight, we have dinner plans with Star and her new submissive, Jackson, as well as Owen and Astrid, who've been enjoying their stay in our newly renovated third-floor rooms—the very first guests to experience them.

"Would you care to have dinner with us before you leave, Charlotte?" Tony offers, extending the invitation.

"Are you sure that wouldn't be an imposition?" Charlotte responds, her tone hesitant.

"We'd love to have you," I interject, wrapping my arm around her in a reassuring gesture.

Over the past few years, our bond has grown remarkably close. Charlotte has become like a mother to me, and I cherish her dearly.

"I already set you a place," Tony adds with a warm smile, indicating his readiness for her company.

"This pasta is delicious," Owen compliments, breaking the silence. "Astrid and I worked up an appetite with my rope and flogger this afternoon."

Charlotte's fork slips from her hand, clattering against her plate, freezing everyone in place.

"Anthony," she addresses Tony quietly, her tone laced with curiosity. "How do you all know each other?"

Tony takes a deep breath, steeling himself for the explanation. "We all frequent the same BDSM club in New York," he admits bluntly.

"Fire and Ice?" she asks quietly.

"Yes, ma'am," he confirms.

"The same Fire and Ice where Natalie met Alex?" Charlotte's questions come in quick succession.

"Yes, ma'am. That's the one."

"It's not a dance club or bar?" Her disbelief is evident.

"No, ma'am, it isn't," Tony affirms.

"And you go there, too?" Charlotte turns her attention to me.

"I do," I confirm with a slow nod. "It's really not what you think—"

She holds her hand up, halting my words. "I love you, Leopold, like a son. And Natalie is my daughter," she says before lifting her wine glass for a long sip. "But I don't want to know any more about what any of you do—" Charlotte surveys the table, her gaze steady on each of us. "Behind the closed doors of your bedrooms." Then, as if brushing off the moment, she resumes eating, her fork returning to her plate.

"I love you, Mama Charlotte," I say with a smile, planting a kiss on her cheek before laughing softly.

"I love you too, my dear," Charlotte responds warmly with a gentle pat on my hand.

As the tension dissipates, a wave of relief washes over the table, and we all resume eating, the atmosphere lightening with each passing moment.

Anthony

As the afternoon sun bathes the scene in warmth, a sense of anticipation fills the air. Maxim, Irina, and Svetlana's late-night arrival adds an element of intrigue to the gathering, especially with Brandon's unexpected presence after a year-long separation from Svetlana.

Dimitri, one of Maxim's guards, is here with Jessica. They were in town to visit Maxim and Irina's adopted daughter, Amelia, who is just pulling in with Viktor. Amelia recently wrapped up a cross-country tour with her rock band and is in town for a few days. Their playful puppy, Nadiya, adds a touch of joy as she frolics around, relishing the attention.

"They're coming," Stanley whispers urgently. "Quiet everyone."

The group gathers beneath the gazebo, anticipation palpable in the air as they await the arrival of Alex, Natalie, and their children. As the family rounds the building, a chorus of "Happy Birthday" erupts, breaking the silence with joyful exuberance.

Rose's laughter rings out as she rushes to Viktor, her favorite, who scoops her up in his arms and showers her with kisses.

Tears well in Natalie's eyes as she takes in the surprise celebration.

"I don't know what to say," Natalie admits, her voice wavering with emotion as she gazes around at the gathering.

Leo pulls Natalie into a tight hug. "Your mom made this happen," he says, nodding towards Charlotte.

Charlotte stands beside me, beaming.

"Thank you both," Natalie expresses her gratitude, her voice choked with tears. "I can't believe everyone's here."

There's no time like the present to continue with the surprises.

"Leo and I have an announcement to make," I say, moving to stand beside Leopold and intertwining our hands. "We'd like to tell everyone that we're now the proud owners of Water's Edge Bed and Breakfast." Our guests break into cheers and applause. "We thought it very fitting for our first event to be a birthday party for Natalie. Especially since we would've never found this place without her."

"You guys bought it?" Natalie's jaw drops in disbelief.

"We did," I confirm, a proud grin spreading across my face.

"We fell in love with the area when we were here for Natalie's wedding," Leo adds, his eyes alight with excitement. "Mrs. Wilson let us know she was looking to sell the place so she could retire, and we were looking at getting out of the city and slowing down. So, we took the leap and purchased it."

"Charlotte has been instrumental in helping us make some changes," I mention, giving Natalie's mom a grateful smile.

"How long have you been keeping this from me?" Natalie turns to Charlotte, a hint of amusement in her voice.

"For a very long time," she says and laughs.

"And you all knew and didn't tell me?" Charlotte admits with a laugh.

"Guilty," Owen confirms with a laugh, earning nods of agreement.

"We're going to be neighbors," Leo remarks with a grin, his excitement contagious.

"There's more," I announce, my voice trembling with emotion. "Over the past year, Leopold and I have been going through the steps to adopt. we've found our son—a little boy from Colombia who stole our hearts the second we saw his picture." Gasps of surprise ripple through our friends as they absorb the news. "It's been a rollercoaster of a journey, waiting for all the pieces to come together, but they finally have." I attempt to speak further, but the overwhelming emotions leave me speechless.

"We're flying to Columbia next week," Leo announces, his voice tinged with excitement. "There's a mandatory one-week cohabitation period before we go to the Columbian family court to formally adopt him. And since Nana Charlotte will be looking after him while we're running the B&B, she's coming with us."

"Oh, Mom," Natalie exclaims, her hands flying to her face.

"I'm so honored to be a part of this journey with you two boys," Charlotte responds, her voice filled with emotion.

"How old is he?" Alex inquires, his curiosity evident.

"He'll be one next month," Leo answers with a smile.

"Leopold and I are so grateful for the love and support you've all always shown to us," I express with heartfelt gratitude. "We can't wait until you all meet our son."

Many cultures lay claim to the legend of red thread. It's said that two people who are destined to meet are connected by a single red thread. This thread may stretch or become tangled for a time, but eventually, the thread of fate will bring you to the person connected to the other end.

That's why you'll find a drawing in each room of our bed and breakfast—a simple sketch of two hands clasped together by a single red thread.

Our journey, intertwined by these red threads, has led us to this moment—a gathering of the most unlikely family members bound together by fate.

No matter the time or distance that separates us, the thread that binds us to one another will never be broken.

Epilogue

ANTHONY

Charlotte opted to stay back at the hotel. At the orphanage, they requested only Leopold and me to attend. We find ourselves in a modest room with bare walls and a sparse collection of chairs. Leopold's legs fidget restlessly, anticipation mounting with each passing moment, knowing that at any instant, the door will swing open, and we'll lay eyes on our son for the very first time.Several months prior, we received a request from the orphanage to send photographs and personal items of clothing. Their aim was to acclimatize our son to our presence and scent, thus easing the inevitable uncertainty he'd face upon meeting us.

The doorknob squeaks as it slowly turns, and with bated breath, we watch as it cracks open. Yessenia, the adoption coordinator, steps into the room, cradling a little boy in her arms. He has long brown curls and big blue eyes.

I reach over and grip Leopold's hand tightly. We were instructed to remain seated and silent until Yessenia introduces the child to us. Right now, that feels like an impossible feat.She smiles brightly as she settles into the chair opposite us, the little boy nestled against her. "I explained to him that we were coming to meet the men from his pictures," she says softly, attempting to turn him to face us, but he resists. Instead, she adjusts her position so he's oriented towards us. "He just woke from a nap."

While we wait for him to adjust, we take the opportunity to learn more from Yessenia about his usual routine, his favorite foods, and anything else that might help us understand him and make his adjustment smoother.

As we converse, the child's eyes connect with Leopold's. In a poignant whisper, he utters, "Dada," evoking a surge of emotions that words cannot fully express.

Yessenia's voice is gentle as she praises him. "Very good," she says, her tone filled with warmth. "And who's that?"

His gaze, so innocent and pure, meets mine, and I'm consumed by a tumult of emotions, each one a testament to the depth of love I already feel for this precious child. "Papa," he says, his voice soft but clear.

"That's right, your Dada and Papa," she says tenderly, turning him to us. My gaze shifts to the toy he clutches tightly against his chest—a little red fire truck. "He refused to leave without this. It's his favorite toy."

"Kameron, do you like firetrucks?" Leo asks softly.

He nods shyly in response, his blue eyes meeting Leo's with a mixture of curiosity and timidity.

Leo looks to Yessenia for confirmation before sliding off his chair and settling onto the floor, offering his arms to Kameron. "Would you like to play down here?" he asks softly, a hopeful smile on his face.

Kameron, who hasn't yet taken his first steps, snuggles into Leopold's welcoming arms.

In a tender moment, Leopold holds Kameron close, his gaze filled with adoration. "I'm so happy to finally meet you, Kameron," he whispers lovingly.

Tears cascade down my cheeks as I witness our son, Kameron Matthew Genovese, play with his Daddy.

Adoption, poignant in its beauty, emanates from profound loss. Amidst my tears of joy are tears of sorrow and gratitude for the courageous young woman who gave our son life.

"Play," Kameron states with determination, squirming in Leo's arms.

Leo laughs softly. "Yes, Kameron. We can play." He steals a glance at me, tears pooling in his eyes.

I pull out my phone, capturing the precious moments of their first interactions as father and son. I watch with tears of joy in my eyes, recording every smile, every laugh, every touch. After a few minutes, I set the phone aside and join them on the floor, enveloped in the warmth of our new family.

Yessenia's voice breaks the tender moment, bringing our attention back to reality. "It's time," she says softly, handing Leo a small cloth bag containing all of Kameron's belongings. With a gentle kiss on the baby's head, she leaves us alone, allowing us to savor this precious time as a new family.

As we walk out of the building with Kameron's head on my shoulder and his firetruck cradled against him, I feel a surge of overwhelming emotion. Beside me, Leopold's hand finds mine, our fingers intertwining naturally.

Outside, the setting sun casts a warm, golden glow over the city streets, illuminating our path forward. A gentle breeze whispers through the trees, carrying with it the promise of a fresh start.

I turn to Leopold, pressing a tender kiss to his temple, my heart overflowing with so much emotion. "I love you, *cuore mio*," I whisper, my voice barely above a murmur yet carrying the weight of a lifetime's worth of moments shared between us.

Leopold's gaze finds mine, shimmering with unshed tears. "And I love you," he replies, his voice soft and filled with emotion. "And Dada loves you, too, Kameron." Leopold leans in to place a tender kiss on our sleepy little boy's cheek, sealing the moment with love and warmth.

Together, we take our first steps into the next chapter, knowing that as long as we have each other and our precious son, we have everything we need to build a life filled with love, laughter, and endless possibilities.

The End

Thank you for joining Anthony and Leopold on their journey in *Love Heals*.

If you're ready for another dark and emotional romance, don't miss *Beneath the Shadows*. This dark mafia standalone, an Edgar Allan Poe retelling of *The Cask of Amontillado*, will take you on a thrilling ride filled with passion, betrayal, and redemption. Start reading today and uncover the secrets waiting in the shadows.

Become one of Tara's VIP readers. Sign up for her newsletter today! https://subscribepage.io/FireandIceBooks

Acknowledgments

George- Without you—your support, your encouragement when I was ready to quit, your celebrating my victories, and most of all, your Love. There's no one I'd rather be on this journey with. I love you forever and a day.

To my children- Thank you for all of your Love and support. Each of you has played such a big role in bringing this series to life and helping me realize my dreams. I love you all bunches!

To Baby E- Thank you for being Nana's helper. This past year has been one of the best in my life. I can't wait to have many more adventures together.

Simon Dornet- Thank you for taking a chance on a new author and a new series. You brought my characters to life and for that, I'm eternally grateful.

To the 'real' Sarah- We met at one of the worst periods in my life and have become friends in quite an unconventional way, but I wouldn't trade it for anything. I'm glad I was able to honor you and what you do for others in some small way.

To my readers: I don't know where to start. Two years ago, each of you took a chance on a brand-new author and the cast of characters she created. I'm humbled that you've fallen in Love with the Fire and Ice World and everyone in it. There were some laughs and plenty of tears. There were bumps in the road and twists you didn't see coming. And in the end, there was healing.

The end—two words that are bittersweet. These characters have been such a big part of my life for so long now. I'm not quite sure how to say goodbye to them. I hold on to the knowledge that they each found their happily ever after.

So, as we close the book on Fire and Ice, I hope that you'll come back for the new worlds I have planned.

You can keep up to date by signing up for my newsletter: https://subscribepage.io/FireandIceBooks

And also, by joining my readers' group on Facebook: https://www.facebook.com/groups/571538573826855

Much love,

Tara

Also by Tara Conrad

Find Tara's Books Here

About Tara

Tara Conrad is the author behind sizzling and passionate love stories that ignite the senses. Her novels celebrate the fiery intensity of desire. They're known for having a blend of deep emotional connections, relatable characters, and captivating plots that ensnare readers from the very first page to the last.

Tara's married to her soulmate and Dominant, George. They are about to celebrate their 30th anniversary and are more in love today than yesterday. George encouraged Tara to start writing, and with each passing day, she's more thankful for his insistence that she tell her stories and his partnership on this journey. There's no one else in this world she'd ever want by her side. He is her happily ever after.